ABOUT THE BOOK

In the remote Australian outback, powerlessness drives desperation and all are powerless beneath the ancient landscape. The discovery of a horde of gold inspires self-appointed rebel leader Nelson. High aspirations are disfigured by lust and cruelty. News of the gold travels fast and soon everyone wants a share. Guns trump tradition, destroying love, alliances and friendships. Deception, lies and wrong-side love build to an explosive climax. All are committed to protecting country, but the ancient land is an unbridgeable gulf delivering a pyrrhic resolution.

GULF

DARYL GUPPY

I ACKNOWLEDGE THE MANY YEARS I worked with Yanyuwa, Garawa, Waanyi and Alyawarre people, and the ringers, road construction crews, water bore contractors, mining outfits and others in very remote regions of Gulf of Carpentaria and Barkly Tablelands of Northern Australia. And in particular Neville Andrews for his constant example of bush generosity and hospitality. The language used, habits and attitudes displayed by some of the characters in this novel, although offensive today, are an accurate record of the period in which the book is set and are retained for that reason.

Many massacres and murders of Aboriginal people occurred in the Northern Territory Gulf region and are well documented. Many more undocumented events are rumoured to have taken place, including up until the 1930s and beyond. Many are recorded in *Frontier Justice: A History of the Gulf Country to 1900* by Tony Roberts.

Stealing cattle – poddy dodging, cattle duffing, sweating calves; call it what you will – was not unusual and although now less common, continues to this day in the Northern Territory.

The wreck of a Liberator bomber lost on a 1945 flight between Darwin and Townsville, Queensland, was eventually discovered in 1994, 50 kilometres from a town of 5,000 people.

This is a work of fiction. Only the rugged Gulf country is real.

This story is set in the Gulf country of the Northern Territory of Australia. I acknowledge the traditional owners of this region and pay my respects to elders past and present. The geography of this area has been modified to suit the needs of the story.

Contents

Chapter 1

1985, MAY, START OF DRY SEASON.

"HE A CHEEKY ONE THAT BASTARD," Charlie Roscoe observed. The dark brown wrinkles and rough salt and pepper stubble of his face rippled in amused anticipation. He had ridden on enough musters to understand what was required and what might happen. He looked forward to more years of mustering, although each year it was harder to recover from the aches and bruises.

The brumby stallion stood his ground, watching the cut-down Toyota Landcruiser pick-up roaring in low gear along the other side of the steep gully. Behind the wheel, Nelson Shortjack searched desperately for a good crossing point.

He tipped his sandy-coloured broad-brimmed hat against the sunlight, dark eyes dancing along a possible track. The sun continued to bleach his already faded blue-checked shirt, sleeves ripped off to allow easier movement. Naturally thin and wiry, he was made more so by the physical work demanded in the bush. He glowered, his lean, deep brown face tense with concentration, as he leaned over the steering wheel and peered across the bonnet littered with twigs accumulated during the chase.

The large roan brumby stallion had evaded bullets and musters for many years past. Wise in the ways of men with their snarling machines, he led Nelson in a wild chase through the roughest country he could find. The stallion looked at the sandstone escarpment rising in front of him, the sandy ground covered with dense thickets of turpentine wattle. The burnt country, with its forest of fire sharpened stakes was tough on horses, but even tougher on tyres.

Nelson scratched the coarse black stubble bristle on his cheek with one hand and grunted an acknowledgement to Charlie as he peered at the faint cattle pad leading down the sides of the gully.

The brumby had taken them to the remote and rarely visited sharp and steep rocky escarpments in this part of the Gulf country. The wild bush stallion had stolen the station mares during the recently ended north Australia Wet season. Seventy kilometres from the station – ranch – homestead and another hundred to the nearest neighbour, meant Nelson was pushing through trackless scrub in areas not visited for decades. With nearly four thousand square kilometres to cover, it was no surprise wild cattle in these areas were rarely rounded up – mustered – in a cattle drive.

It was the first time he was in charge of the stock camp with its assortment of riders, horses and camp hands. All the white ringers – cowboys as the Americans called them – had pulled out, and the Missus, still new to the bush, had given him the job. Do this job right and, young as he was, he could challenge the leadership of Old Harry who still ruled the Aboriginal camp back at the station.

The brumby twitched his ears as he watched the grey open-roofed vehicle nudge its way down a washaway into the gully. He wheeled, coat glistening, and headed his mob back towards the burnt country near the end of one of the long winding open gorges flowing with heavy sand. He knew he could walk his harem through the picket stakes of the burnt black ground while the vehicle behind him would be forced to slow and stop if its tyres were punctured. He nipped the trailing grey mare on the rump and closed the mob up, trotting away from the vehicle across the gully.

Nelson had to separate the wild brumby stallion from the mares before he could walk them back to the camp at Buffalo Yard. When they caught them, Charlie would saddle a mare and take the lead while Nelson tailed behind the mob with the Toyota. He turned the pickup and edging forward, looked down into the gully. It was possible. He nosed down, nothing but empty space in front of him as he eased one wheel onto the cattle pad and the other over the high spots to one side. The Toyota tipped precariously and Charlie clutched at the grab bar on the dashboard. The lower part of the steel bulbar hit the sandy bottom, ploughed through, then cleared it.

"You watch the mongrel," Nelson shouted as he gunned the engine and charged at the opposite steep bank. The bullbar dozed through the base of the bank until the front wheels lifted high enough for clearance. Charlie's head sank deep into his shoulders as the vehicle leapt into the air. Power on, all four wheels feeling the whip of the motor, they scrabbled up the side of the gully. Nelson saw blue sky above the radiator and he waited for the front wheels to drop. The front wheels spun as the back wheels struggled for a grip and then in one convulsive heave, they were on level ground and ready to go.

"Where is he?" Nelson demanded.

"There, mate. To the left. Go!"

Nelson spun the wheel hard over and Charlie grabbed desperately at the heavy side rails to stop himself falling out. The pickup was cut down specially for mustering cattle in the wild rough country on the upper reaches of Punkatoy station. The doors had been taken off and the upper part of the cab removed. The windscreen was replaced with a low wire mesh grill leaving the men splattered with leaves and insects as they crashed through the light timber. Side rails of heavy steel stretched from the solid bull bar to the anchor points on the sides of the flat top tray. Two old tyres were lashed with wire to the front of the bullbar. When the cattle were mustered the wild bulls were rolled over with the crudely padded bar. Charlie's job was to leap out and hobble the beast before it got back on its feet. It was a young ringer's job but Charlie's experience gave him an edge in skill despite his age.

None of the instruments worked and only the bare remnants of the vehicle were still attached to the frequently welded chassis. Anything not of vital importance was stripped out, thrown away or had fallen off. The powerful petrol motor gulped air asthmatically as Nelson wheeled to the left, straightened, let the power drop off, straightened again and then turned right as sharp-tipped quinine bush scraped the side panels.

The roan brumby stallion worked his harem of station mares, cantering easily back and forth behind them as he herded them together and kept them moving towards the towering bluff. His favourite lead mare harried their flanks.

"Gotta cut the bastard out!" Nelson yelled.

Charlie nodded excitedly in silent agreement above the engine noise as the air intake snarled, tearing the air from the wind. He gripped the bar on the dashboard tightly with one hand and clamped his high-crown dusty broad-brimmed hat on his head with the other. He darted his eyes between the brumby stallion, the grey tree trunks flashing by and the gut-high brick-hard termite mounds rearing without warning from the tall spear grass sliding sibilantly against the bullbar and chassis.

He loved it and hated it, even knowing this would have to be his last year. Perhaps he would work as stock camp cook for a season or two before the station pensioned him off and let him live for all time at the Aboriginal camp near the Big House where the station owner lived.

No more bull catching next year, he decided, and hoped he could keep his promise better than he had in the past. A horse, you ride him down when he stumbles. A horse sees ahead while you look at the mob of cattle you be chasing, he thought wryly to himself. He flinched as a shoulder-high red spire of a termite mound flashed narrowly past the front wheel.

"Go, mate. Go!" Charlie whooped, dispelling his fears in the wind.

Nelson risked a glance at him and grinned happily, his face alive with the excitement of the chase. He returned his attention to the bush ahead and broadsided past a fallen tree. He let the drift continue, then straightened, fishtailing past a solid white ghost gum. They both ducked to avoid the stinging whip of low branches.

"Get right up him," Charlie demanded.

"Hang on!"

A small patch of open country loomed in front. Driving straight for the brumby, Nelson jammed the gears down, following close on the stallion's heels, accelerator hard to the floor. He watched the flashing hooves for any clue to which way the horse would break.

"I'll kill the bastard!" he snarled.

"Go! Go! Go!" Charlie urged.

"Come on, you buckjumping mongrel. Break!"

"Faster, faster! We catch him!" Charlie shouted wildly.

The brumby feinted to the left then broke desperately to the right. His flashing hooves nearly clipping the old tyres on the front of the bull bar, Nelson swung hard to the right intent on rolling the panicked horse. Rank sweat whipped back from the stallion's lathered flanks.

Wheels spun, gripped, then spun again as the loose sand built up against the tyres. The engine roared to a crescendo as the Toyota stopped and the stallion suddenly leapt ahead, long tail streaming straight out behind.

"Hey! What's wrong?" Charlie demanded.

Nelson kept his foot to the floor and yelped as the thrashing gear stick smashed his bony hand. He lifted his foot and gradually the motor idled back. Nelson tried to grab the dancing gearstick with both hands. "Bastard jumped out of gear. Hang on." Engine screaming, the gear stick refused to engage.

"You stuffed this one proper, hey?" Charlie admonished.

"Argh, shut up. Get out and have a look at him."

Charlie leapt over the smooth side rail, adrenalin still pumping and bent down to inspect the underside of the vehicle.

"Him broken real proper," he muttered.

"What?" Nelson snapped.

"You look at him," Charlie suggested as stood back, easing the hat on his head.

Nelson glared at the roan stallion not a hundred metres away, standing feet apart and head held high. Behind him the station horses milled in a tight circle. Their flanks heaved and sweat foamed around their muzzles. Tossing his head, the stallion turned and led his harem at a gentle trot into the clump of silver and grey leafed wattle.

Their escape would delay the muster for a few more days until they were recaptured. The Missus wouldn't be pleased. Nelson spat and then leant down beside the Toyota to have a closer look at the damage.

A black pool of oil seeped slowly into the sand beneath the split gear box.

"I reckoned something wrong this morning, boss," Charlie dryly commented.

"Yairs," Nelson muttered, reaching for his tobacco tin.

Charlie moved his thin cigarette to the corner of his mouth. "Well, boss?"

Nelson didn't answer as he rolled his smoke. Lighting his cigarette and taking a deep draw, he cast a long glance around. Ahead of them the Gulf country rose into steep escarpments, vertical slabs of stone topped with ragged gap-toothed battlements. The chase had twisted and turned, taking them many winding kilometres from the dusty stock camp at Buffalo Yards. He sighed, looked at the sun and breathed in the country.

My country, he thought with pride. He looked down and saw the battered riding boots, sand-blasted by two seasons of dust and hard work in the saddle. Pungkuthuyi country, he corrected. This is my singing. Carefully he scanned the ground nearby and picked out the slow moving sinew of a large goanna. He watched the reptile twist its dignified way across the churned sand where the horses had been racing a few minutes before. It paused for a moment, darting its long tongue towards the stink of petrol and oil. The reptile stalked off, unconcerned and unafraid.

Goanna dreaming, Pungkuthuyi country. Come on Old People, I'm listening, he reflected. He looked around at the distant ranges which were unfamiliar to him.

It had been a long slow drive this morning before we picked up the horses, he mused. We saw them just on dinner camp. He recollected the lay of the land, building a mental picture of the hills, the dry creeks, the distinctive vegetation and other landmarks he had subconsciously noted while they searched for the station horses. He created a pattern of unseen ridges and valleys between himself and Buffalo Yards.

He searched briefly for the goanna again, and not finding it, looked up at Charlie who, with one finger against the side of his nostril, blew snot onto the ground.

"We walk back this way," Nelson asserted confidently, lifting his chin and twitching his lips to indicate the scrub to the left. "We take a shortcut. It's rough country we always avoid in the muster. Quicker to go up and over than all the way back around him."

He didn't mention how long it might take them. In this, his country, it would take as long as it took because the country made those decisions, not men. They slurped water from the cooler strapped to the tray and confident of their ability to survive in the bush, they left the awkward water cooler behind. They set off through the blistering hot sandy scrub towards the first of the broken rocky rises in the distance. Neither of them knew that the trek would decide who would live and who would die.

Chapter 2

THREE STEEP SANDSTONE RIDGES LAY BEHIND them, Nelson noticed, as he stood on a tall vertical slab of rock and looked through the clearing. Each near-vertical rise sloped gently back to the base of the next. The pink and grey sandstone blocks were as jumbled as when they were created. The slabs made climbing relatively easy, but forced the two men to look carefully for snakes which used the shattered strata as a home. Lithe wallabies drummed their tails and flashed across the escarpments, pausing every now and then to peek back over nervous shoulders as the men disturbed their day.

Nelson turned and let his eyes scale the rise in front of him. He stood on a false crest which had been obscured from the ground below. Charlie sat easily against the rough yellow-brown bark of a green-leafed bloodwood tree. The ledge formed a natural basin trapping the water from a spring hidden somewhere above them. The sand-filled soak was an unexpected patch of green moisture on the arid hike. Charlie eased his feet from his battered riding boots. The sandy ground felt good under his broad calloused feet. He scratched the back of his shirt with a stick, attempting to free the sweat soaked fabric from his bony shoulder blades. Stooping, he scooped another handful of weedy-tasting clear water into his mouth and watched the hot world around him with languid unconcern.

He wondered what his wife, Ina, and the kids were doing. She was still at the ringers' camp near the station. She would not be worried until the end of the week if the men did not return from the camp at Buffalo Yards.

No use in worrying, he decided. I been sit about the bush for days last year with a busted arm. This time we only walking back. He smiled and relaxed.

"What you sitting down for? Let's go," Nelson snapped impatiently. Charlie didn't reply as Nelson searched the rock face for a path. In time, Charlie smiled contentedly. It was a pointless question. He was sitting down because he was not moving. Nelson roused on him, his strong voice battering against Charlie's recumbent form.

"Come on, you lazy boy. Get moving. We have longest way to go before dark." Nelson kicked at Charlie's boots discarded in the sand. "You gunna wear him?"

"No, boss."

"Well carry him, or leave him, but let's get moving." Charlie stood slowly, reluctant to leave the shade.

"We ain't got all day. Let's go," Nelson said over his shoulder, striding away from the soak.

He skirted the escarpment looking for the best way to the top. Spinifex grew on the upper reaches of the smashed rock and tumbled boulders. Nelson forged ahead and, barefooted, Charlie followed unconcerned by the sharp rocks and pricking spinifex spikes. Quinine bush grew in the sand between the rocks. Nelson pushed them aside and darted up the beginnings of a path.

"You as bad as them whitefellas," Charlie complained as he leaned forward to climb the steep slope behind Nelson.

"Say that again," Nelson demanded, wheeling around.

"You like that whitefella boss we had before you took over. Like that George. Him always rush about," Charlie explained easily as he rested on the broken rock.

"You just a lazy bastard. You and the rest of the mob. Whitefella takes this country away from me – from us – and you're too lazy to care about it. You're just shit," Nelson sneered.

"You right, boss. Me and the boys, we just shit. You been hedgjumuckated so you treat us like shit, and whitefella treat us the same way."

"See what I mean!" Nelson shouted with frustration. "You just sit back and take it. Come here," he commanded. He reached down and grabbed Charlie by the shoulder. "Come here. Come and look at this."

He hauled Charlie up and pushed the bewildered ringer ahead of him. Charlie fell forward on the steep slope, scrabbling on his hands and knees as Nelson hounded him from behind.

"Get up there. Move!"

Together they reached the top of the ridge. Nelson lunged forward and took Charlie by the shoulder before he could recover from the climb. Heaving Charlie to his feet, Nelson dragged him to the edge of the escarpment which dropped away until the jumble of cascading screes joined the base a hundred metres below.

"Look, you bastard. Look around you. This is our country. This is my country." Nelson jerked Charlie roughly as he pointed to the country-side slumbering under the rising heat.

The chain of ridges they had surmounted stretched away, tier after tier in front of them. The bald treeless rocky ridge tops slewed out of the drab green bands of scrub like shattered knives, some flat and others turned on their edge. Heat fell from the copper blue sky, sulking amongst the drab grey woollybutts and white ghost gums. The rock beneath their feet was grey and white with tiny grains of silica glittering in the unrelenting sun. On either side of their pedestal of rock, the escarpment ridge snaked an angular course, its broken buttresses sharp despite their age.

The country was as familiar as a childhood memory, even though this particular area was totally new to him. It was all part of his ancestral singing and he subconsciously knew of it, even if he had not been aware of this precise stanza until this moment. It was a dim memory re-kindled by each of his brief returns when he escaped from the Mission school in Darwin.

His infrequent childhood returns to the dusty camp on the station kept the spark of his belief alive. The years of enforced absence had glorified his vision of his country and the bonds of commitment had been forged in bitterness. In many ways he felt they were stronger than those binding the men who have lived in pungkuthuyi country all their lives. They took it for granted, but he could not.

At their backs, the ground sloped gently away as far as the eye could see. The nearby scrub was heavy tangled growth bursting from between broken rocks, some the size of fuel drums, others the size of sharp edged watermelons and beneath all, a scree of shattered gravel. Further out it gave way to more open country dotted with stringybarks and tall termite mounds. Beyond it, Nelson felt with strange certainty, lay rivers and creeks, dry now apart from the occasional pandanus palms and paperbark-lined waterholes.

Downstream would be the stock camp, and Nelson knew the ringers would be lounging under the deep shade of the bauhinia trees until he returned. He shrugged. It's a hunters camp, and the hunters have earned a rest after a long day in the saddle. The Old People rested at the end of their day's hunt. Nelson imagined the air full of the smoke tang of cooking fires and the rank furriness of a wallaby cooking on the coals.

"This is our country," he pronounced, proudly surveying the country surrounding him. "I know this country better than I ever knew my mother."

Charlie nodded dumbly. The land below was a natural part of his life, but he did not understand how Nelson could lay such a strong claim to it. He kept his disbelief to himself. Old Harry, back at the homestead camp, was the real custodian of this country.

"The invaders stole this country from us," Nelson spoke with sudden vehemence. "They came when my father was a boy. They shot and poisoned our people. They mustered up some of our mob and pushed them over one of those cliffs over there.' He pointed towards the towering pale escarpment shimmering in the distance.

"They forced our people away from the dreaming and separated us from our singing. They put their cattle in our sacred places and the bastards are still doing it."

"But we still live here," Charlie protested. "I been here all my life. No one ever tell me to leave. I be here and I sit down here. It my country too. I belong him."

"You only live here because they let you. We need their permission." Nelson spat. "You're grateful because they let you use what is rightfully yours in the first place. It's wrong way round. The Old People speared these whitefellas. We should do the same again. This time we should shoot and blow the bastards out. They have to ask us for permission to live here," Nelson snarled.

"Hey! Look out!" Charlie muttered defensively.

"Hey! Look out for what? Look out for that new whitefella owner?" Nelson spat out the words. "They don't even know this patch of country is on the station. They're so bloody stupid. They think they know everything. They know nothing. They think they own the land but the land owns us!"

With a wide sweep of his arm, he indicated the bush around them. "They call this place Punkatoy. It's the only way they can say pungkuthuyi. You know that language word?" he quizzed Charlie.

Charlie stepped back, a look of frightened bewilderment on his face. "Hey! You be wild man!"

Nelson stepped across to him and roughly grabbed his shoulders. "Don't run away, Charlie. You can't run away from this country. We belong this country. It is all part of sand goanna dreaming."

Charlie looked at him uncomprehendingly. Of course this was his country and he chose to stay in the station camp so he could look after it. There was no need to explain the obvious. Nelson shook him in his rage.

"You see what I mean? You don't know. No-one ever tell you and now you don't even care," he lamented, mistaking Charlie's bewilderment for ignorance.

Nelson flung Charlie to one side disgustedly, not caring if the ringer slipped from the rock.

"Land rights is not enough. We have to run the mongrels off. Shoot the bastards if we have to. We lost the first war but now we're strong enough to win this war. This is my land." He stabbed his finger at his chest. Turning, he stabbed his finger at Charlie, crouching where he had fallen. "This is your country too, you ignorant bastard!"

Nelson stared defiantly at the distant ridges while Charlie stood up and moved away from the edge of the rock.

"They teach you this when you go away down South?" he asked in disbelief.

"No. They only teach me whitefella garbage but I read my own books. I learned history is always history of the oppressor. That's why they kicked me out." He mimicked an educated man and his deliberate reversion to ringer's language jarred discordantly. "I'm hedgjumuckated. I been go to university. They teach me to speak proper good and accept their ways," he mocked.

"It was even worse than school. Twelve months of university and I puked it all up. They didn't want me and I didn't want them," he continued, stressing his Aboriginal accent in defiance.

"This country is what I want, and one day I'm going to get it. Until then they think I'm just an ignorant head stockman on a station that occupies my country," he finished bitterly.

"I never leave this country either, boss," Charlie agreed.

"Nor do I ever again. Let's walk."

Nelson turned on his heel and strode past Charlie, uncaring whether he followed. Charlie fell in beside him, deep in thought as he carefully absorbed the details of the bush they walked through.

Those city kooris could talk, Nelson recalled and shook his head slowly. By God, those city blackfellas could talk. That's all they ever did. Talked about how bad things were and how the coppers were always down on them. They were too long out of the bush to ever be able to come back, he decided. The thought brought to him, as if newly discovered, the delicate scent of the first wattle blossoms. He breathed in the heavy, superheated air and felt the tiny silver wattle leaves whip him as he walked. He breathed deeply, driving away the memory of the stench of the city, the leaden deadness of its air, and the clutter of poverty, unrelieved even by the cleanliness of the bush. The scent of wattle and the hot nothingness of the white dry grass goaded his dissatisfaction.

"Freedom grows out the barrel of a gun," he growled harshly, dredging up the slogan from long-past debates in overcrowded city hovels.

Charlie rolled his pale eyes with fright, startled by Nelson's conviction. He looked resolutely ahead and kept walking, head down, not wanting to hear. His ears would not plug up and he listened with mounting horror and fascination to the man who was suddenly a stranger after the years working together on the station.

"The only way to meet the violence of the oppressors is with violence of our own. The invaders are so secure in their victory that they can only respond with violence when we threaten them."

Nelson paused in thought for a few steps, building a patchwork quilt from the incomplete fragments he remembered of the revolutionary writers he encountered at university. Frantz Fannon's slim volume *The Wretched of the Earth* remained a powerful memory.

"The stronger their repression, the stronger we become. We hit them, and they try to destroy us. When enough of us are hurt by their cruelty, then we'll all rise up and smash the white oppressors. Only their violence can unite us again. Then we can drive the invaders out of our country."

"We must fight like our black brothers did in Zimbabwe. Robert Mugabe, he had the right idea. Kill the white bastards and drive them from our land. Treat the traitors in our camps with contempt. Burn them out like a cancer and let their death be an example to our own people," Nelson said savagely. "Mugabe won and I say we can win if we fight." He clenched his fists, swinging them by his side as he strode on.

"This Robert Mugabe. What station he be on?" Charlie asked.

Nelson stopped short and swung on the ball of his foot to hit him. Charlie's thin brow was puckered with the search to place the unfamiliar name. Deep in thought, he ignored Nelson, who dropped his fists to his side. Oh, my friend, Nelson thought in despair. We have so far to go.

Charlie looked at him, still striving to remember the Mugabe name on any of the local stations and put a face to it. His narrow features were screwed up in intense concentration. Nelson laughed cruelly at the sheer ridiculousness of it all. His people needed action, not revolutionary theory. After a moment, Charlie joined in, his laughter low and uneasy.

The country changed quickly as they passed through the band of silver-leafed wattle around the crest of the ridge. The grey sandy covered ground gave way to broken blocks of tumbled white sandstone and quartz strewn between the scattered trees and spindly quinine scrub. They picked and twisted their way carefully over the rough surface. Nelson swore as his boots slipped on the jumbled rocks.

"Don't know why I wear these bloody things," he complained. "The leather soles are good for nothing except riding mongrel horses."

"You hardly ever ride a horse now," Charlie observed non-committedly.

"I can't stand bastard horses. I never could," Nelson confessed, his despair with Charlie replaced with bitterness.

"But it's the first job they give a blackfella in the bush, so I had to take it on and I can't ride barefoot. Once I came back from down South it was the only way I could earn a living if you call garbage rations, tobacco and a few dollars a week a living," he snorted. "If I didn't learn to ride I would never be here."

"How that, boss?"

"It take me a long time to work my way back to here, back to my country. The only way I could do it was by working as a ringer, so I had to learn to ride a horse. But I'm here now, and the only way I'll leave is if they take me away after I am dead."

They scrambled over the hot jagged surfaces in silence. Nelson breathed lightly as they clambered and Charlie was relieved to let the tirade finish.

There was a wild fella like Nelson out at Fryers Creek years ago, Charlie remembered with a shudder. He had the same ideas as Nelson, but he didn't say them as strong. They shot him. I was just a boy, but I remember. They chased him like a mongrel dog through the scrub and shot him. The boss gave a flogging to a few of his mates as well. Came right down to the camp and did it in front of everybody. It shame us all.

He sneaked a look at Nelson who had slipped again and was cursing his boots, the station and the people who ran it. I don't want to run with him. He just like that brumby horse we chase. If we be part of his mob we'll all get into proper trouble. Better to do cattle work with sit-down time in the Wet and the opportunity to remain close to country.

"This plenty rough country," he observed as Nelson straightened up after a tumble amongst the boulders. "You get along better without your boots."

Nelson glared at him and shook his head vigorously. He knew Charlie guessed his feet were too soft and he admitted to himself with loathing that he had lived too long in his boots to be able to go barefooted through the scrub.

"Whitefella feet," he explained.

Charlie regretted the shame he had caused Nelson.

"This country too rough for mustering," he offered by way of diversion and apology.

"You're right there. We can never get vehicle in here and this busted rock is too rough for a horse to work. Probably only find a few scrub bulls in here anyway. Look at those white snappy gums. Even they're too thick and high for those chopper cowboys to see through."

The prehistoric upheaval of the earth had fissured and spring water found its way to near the surface through the twisted rocks. Low thick wattles had given way to bloodwood and stringybark. Several ghost gums dotted the thick bush, their trunks white against the monotony of rocks.

They walked on, sweltering beneath the trapped heat and cowered by the unexpected thick scrub. At their approach some birds flapped leadenly into the solid air. Charlie, following the ringer's habit, was casting around for tracks as he walked.

"Hey, boss. Somebody been here before us."

Chapter 3

CHARLIE STOOPED AND PICKED UP A piece of faded dull metal. Nelson took it from his hands and looked at the light twisted length curiously.

"This looks like a bit off a Landrover. You know those Landrovers. They had a couple over at Coolibah Downs a few years ago."

Charlie shook his head, never having been on the neighbouring station two hundred kilometres away.

"They made them out of aluminium, not steel like the Toyota. Useless machines. When they broke you couldn't weld them back together. And slow – too slow to catch a hobbled horse," Nelson laughed.

The metal strip was white with age and corrosion from many humid Wet seasons. Two circular holes punched in the twisted metal were too small for any instruments, but too large for bolts. Nelson shrugged, and threw it away, walking onwards to where the scrub thinned slightly ahead of them.

Within twenty paces Charlie pointed excitedly to the smashed skeleton of a tailplane elevator. The thin metal had long disintegrated in the succession of Wet seasons. Only the twisted framework of spars remained crumpled against a scree of rocks.

"What the hell!" Nelson muttered as he ran over to the framework and peered at the pale grey metal, dulled by exposure to the sun. "This is an old crash. I reckon all the whitefellas who ever owned this station didn't even know it was here. See how the sand has half-buried the metal? Look at the metal, it's old, just like the piece you find back there."

They both foraged around, Nelson more vigorously than Charlie. The sections of the aircraft gradually emerged from the cloak of bushes and trees.

The remains of a complete tailplane lay under a dense cluster of quinine bushes. The thin metal skin peeled back, the skeletal inside bearers peeping through the jagged holes.

Further to the right the rudder leaned against a stringybark tree. A Wet season creeper bound the tree and rudder together, the vine twisting like coils of rope. The tree had grown up alongside the wrecked tailpiece and the bend in its trunk accommodated the drunken tilt of the dull metal.

The faded camouflage colours still did their job. From more than a few metres away the plane was indistinguishable from the growth around it. Once they stood beside it they were able to clearly see the crumpled fuselage, its nose sticking up in the air, clawing to become airborne. The two powerful radial engines were melted hunks of scrap metal.

The port engine and wing had ploughed on when the wing root snapped. The now-twisted propellers had swung the unit in a semicircle so it lay at an angle to the main body of the crash. The outer section of the starboard wing lay flat on the ground, snapped from the engine nacelle. It was mostly covered with sand and several good sized saplings grew through the holes torn in the metal. It was clear the landing gear had never been lowered.

The body of the aircraft was a dull white where fire had turned the metal to talc. The port side was slashed open, the wide cargo door exposing the burnt interior. Inside the fragile structure, steel boxes peeped through the collapsed floor. No metal gleamed and the dullness of the burnt shell matched the faded shades of the green and brown camouflage pattern on the unburnt starboard wing. Decades of sun and rain had washed all into the same mottled olive grey of the scrub which twisted through the wreckage.

"It's an old plane from the war," Nelson concluded, recognising the twisted airframe and camouflage, so similar to the crashed American Liberator bomber he had played in as a child out on the Cox Peninsula near Darwin. He pulled his tobacco tin from his top pocket and began to knead the makings into a cigarette as he gazed over the crash site.

Charlie hung behind him and felt the long dead spirits of the crew rustle in the quiet bush. A willy wagtail, harbinger of trouble and lies, chittered angrily in one of the quinine bushes. Charlie was not afraid of death, but he kept well clear of all burial grounds.

"Let's go, boss. We can tell the Missus when we get back," he pleaded.

"What's wrong?" Nelson asked, not surprised at Charlie's lack of enthusiasm.

"This place kumanjayi." He used the language word to describe the dread he felt and to cover his unwillingness to use the name of those who had died, whoever they may have been. "This is a bad place," he quavered.

"That rubbish talk. That old time talk. We don't even know if anybody die here or not."

"I sure they did."

"Well, let's go have a look."

"No, boss. That place kumanjayi," Charlie lamented, unable to move.

"Bullshit. Gammon. But if you believe it, then you stay here. I'm going to take a look and then we can go on."

Nelson didn't bother to wait for confirmation, but walked towards the plane, cigarette in the corner of his mouth. Charlie's too superstitious, he sneered to himself. White fellas can't be kumanjayi. That's only for us. He walked all round the plane and then peered into the open interior through the ripped rear cargo door.

"No seats in this one," he muttered. "They must have taken them out for cargo. Not much cargo though, only those steel boxes." He inspected them more closely, peering into the gloom at the jumbled green metal boxes. They were similar to the old ammunition boxes many stations used as tool boxes, but flatter and more rectangular. Each was secured with two heavy locks. He looked beyond the boxes. The sand and dust had blown inside the plane and he clearly saw the fresh tail drag marks and claw prints of a large goanna.

Must be a good place to live, he thought as he looked carefully. He had no desire to frighten the big old reptile. They were dangerous when they were old and cornered. As the goanna was part of his skin he was forbidden by traditional law from killing them, so he did not want to disturb the lizard.

He shifted his attention to the cabin tilted up in front of him. He put one foot on the flimsy metal to climb forward for a better look. He stopped as the burnt metal crumbled. He grunted, and narrowed his eyes against the strength of the sun filtering through the smashed front cabin windows. Slowly they adjusted to the gloom. He saw the yellow spots first, and then the shape of the old goanna.

The big reptile flicked his tongue lazily but made no move to shift from his lair behind the pilot's bulkhead. Nelson watched the big fellow for a moment as the scattered white bones around his lair came into focus. The thigh bone had been too big for the reptile to swallow. You waited until they were rotten, then you tore their insides out, Nelson gloated silently. The reptile flicked his long thin tongue once more and then settled back to rest, secure in the knowledge of his supremacy of his country.

Nelson looked behind to where Charlie was standing uneasily beside the rudder. His thin companion had one hand behind his back and holding his elbow as he looked at the ground, carefully avoiding the place of death.

"Hey Charlie, come here."

Charlie resolutely shook his head.

"Come on," Nelson shouted. "I just want you to give me a hand. Then we can go."

Charlie shook his head desperately and pushed the plane and Nelson away with his outstretched hands.

"Come and give me a hand or I'll give you a flogging," Nelson snarled.

Charlie hesitated and weighed Nelson's anger. He wandered reluctantly across to where Nelson stood with hands on his hips.

"Grab this." Nelson indicated the top box.

Together they worked the box free of the broken floorplate and heaved it onto the ground.

"Bloody heavy," Nelson remarked. Charlie agreed morosely, sulkily standing as far away from the plane as he could.

"Give us that bar," Nelson commanded, pointing to a fragment in the sand.

Charlie reluctantly picked it up and dangled it from his hand. Nelson snatched the bar of perished metal and tried to lever the locks open. The heat-stressed metal twisted and bent in his hands.

"Find a rock," he grumbled disgustedly.

Charlie didn't move. Nelson stormed away and came back with a good sized rock. Charlie watched uneasily as he smashed the locks free, the old metal hasps giving way to the battering. The lid flew back as Nelson smashed at it with the lump of sandstone.

Both men gazed silently, stunned at the neatly stacked small ingots of gold, three rampart lions and the letters N.E.I stamped on each. Beside them, separated by a metal divide, was a stack of bank notes neatly bound with now perished rubber bands.

Nelson glimpsed all his ill-formed dreams. Jumping up, he brandished the rock at Charlie.

"You breathe one word of this to anybody and I'll fucking shoot you!"

Charlie nodded dumbly, amazement and fear frozen on his thin features. Nelson stared at the dull gold, and then greedily at the other six boxes.

Caught napping, the silent escarpment of fissured rocks basked silently under the sun.

Chapter 4

1985, JUNE, MID-DRY SEASON.

THE TWO EMPTY BRASS SHELL CASES from a Chinese copy of a Russian Kalashnikov assault rifle glinted in the sun as Ray Morgan drove towards Punkatoy station.

They were nestled securely between the dashboard and the windscreen of the Landcruiser pickup. The dull gleam caught his sun-narrowed eyes each time he turned east on the winding bush track. Steering with one strong hand he picked up one of the stubby tapered cases and read the numbers written on the headstamp again. He recognised it as Chinese manufacture. He put it back and, turning to more immediate problems, wondered if the station Missus would let him borrow one of the ringers for the afternoon so he could get his bulldozer mobile again.

He drove towards the station which was dominated by a massive tamarind tree standing in its carpet of tiny fallen leaves. He searched for its dark green crown above the grey straggling scrub, spotting it as he drove past the small rapidly drying waterhole, ignoring four grey brolgas as they tumbled on long legs beside him before launching themselves clumsily into the hot air. High above the station the kite hawks circled, always on the lookout for a feed from the scraps from the station kitchen and the Aboriginal ringers' camp nearby.

He drove towards the big open workshop standing well-used at the end of a forlorn line of equipment. The old red Toyota truck was parked beside the loading ramp, the portable stock crate still sitting on the ramp where it had been ten days before. Wendy, the new station owner, had excitedly predicted it would be on the truck and they would be carting cattle by the time he returned, he remembered with benign amusement. This country forced everyone to work at its far slower pace.

The old front-end loader had one perished flat tyre. The sagging oil drum still carried the weight of the trailer, waiting for wheel bearings to arrive. At least the cut-down bull catcher Toyota had moved so it is probably mobile, Ray thought as he slowed along the red gravel road to let the dust settle before moving into the homestead yard.

The station had been allowed to run down by the previous owners before it was sold, and the new owners had been hit by disaster soon after taking over. Wendy, her husband recently killed in a car crash, was left by herself with only the ringers and a station manager to help. She was determined, but struggling to keep the station going.

The ringers were busy under the high iron roof of the workshop and Ray saw the head stockman, Nelson Shortjack, look up as he drove in.

The white ringers' quarters, functional plain rooms with swishing fans, were attached to the workshop. There were no strange vehicles parked by them, so Ray assumed Wendy was still unable to get any white ringers. Beyond the workshop, almost out of sight by the station lagoon, were the huts used by Aboriginal ringers and their families.

The Big House, home to the station owner and family, hunkered behind a haze of water from a portable sprinkler that had been rooted to the one spot for weeks. The low, fibro house was shaded by well-established trees and white ghost tree gums. The kitchen and other rooms were strung together on one side. The wide enclosed lean-to veranda acted as an open lounge room. The house was deserted, apart from the Missus who was now the sole resident and owner of Punkatoy station.

Ray caught the satisfying smell of woodsmoke from the small camp fire at the back of the workshop where the corned beef was boiling in an old flour drum. Sleepy dogs stirred and then barked in a frenzy as his dust-caked pickup rattled to a stop. Before the dust had time to settle the dogs had quieted down.

Ray clambered out and the dogs wagged their tails in recognition. He leant his lean frame on the bull bar and waited. Dusty long khaki trousers matched the faded army-style khaki shirt with twin pockets but no longer with epaulets. His wrinkled clothes, bleached by weeks in strong sunlight, were bush clean, washed in cold water, hung to dry over a low hanging branch and never ironed. Well-worn, gravel scuffed high-set work boots were permanently stained with diesel and oil and from long disciplined field habit, parallel-laced so they could be cut off easily if need be. The same past habits had him shave every day.

He reached inside the cab and retrieved his tobacco tin and the two shell cases from the dashboard, stuffing them into his top pocket. He rolled a slow smoke as he watched the station come to life from under the bent brim of his dusty low crown stetson, stained dark with sweat around the plaited hat band. His face crinkled in a smile and the lines around his eyes deepened as a tall Aboriginal walked from the workshop as if he owned the station.

"Here's trouble," Nelson shouted jovially.

"Gooday there. Yair, I got trouble. Again," Ray answered laconically.

"You should go back to riding those horses, hey, old man," Nelson chuckled as he sauntered over. Nelson also leant on the bull bar, his bony elbows resting on the top rail. His liquid brown eyes, the whites discoloured from childhood bouts of hepatitis, smiled with enjoyment.

"Ever since you been doing contract station dozer work with your machine you had nothing but trouble, my friend," he chuckled.

Nelson reached into the top pocket of his faded blue checked shirt and started to pull out a tin of tobacco. Changing his mind, he slid it back again.

"You got cigarette for poor fella me?" he whined.

Ray snorted at Nelson's impersonation of a cadging beggar. Nelson laughed happily at his own joke as he pulled out his tobacco tin and started with the makings of a cigarette.

"Where's George?" Ray asked as he looked around for the white station manager.

"He pulled the pin weeks ago. Said he couldn't work for a mad woman. Reckoned he would be better off on the dole. Let the Government pay me, he said. The Missus made me head stockman. I moved into the quarters by the workshop," he answered proudly.

"Good for you. How's that mad Missus going?"

"She get by." Nelson rolled his eyes. "Someday she madder than a tree full of galahs but she's got guts, I'll give her that."

"I thought she would've pulled the pin by now. Not her sort of country this, nor her style of living. I gave her a few weeks at the most. Never thought she would have enough courage to come back after her husband's funeral."

"It was proper sorry camp here for a while. Hey. Look out," Nelson murmured calmly. "Here she come."

Ray rolled away from where he was leaning on the bull bar and watched the Missus of the station walk towards them. Her short hair was dusty brown. Her attractive face was getting fuller as she aged. She still carried a sense of command born from her brief days as a student counsellor and her later tasks as a hostess for her husband's business dinners.

Ray watched her move confidently across the yard, her figure accentuated by her tight fitting city jeans. How much confidence was real and how much an act to cover grief he couldn't decide. Her breasts moved freely in the spotlessly clean T-shirt and she knew every man was following her progress across the station yard. The ringers in the workshop shuffled and moved to get a clearer view. She knew what she, and they, were doing, and ignored them.

"Cheeky woman, that one," Nelson observed quietly while she was still out of earshot.

"Morning, Wendy," Ray said as she stopped a few paces away, head cocked to one side and fingers in her jeans pockets.

"Oh! It's so lovely to see you again!" she gushed, a dam of loneliness breached. Her voice was unnaturally warm and gay. "I was just thinking about you earlier this morning. Do come over and have a cup of tea. You'll stay a while, won't you?" she asked, the decision already made.

"Can't stay, sorry. Just called in to see if I can borrow one of your blokes for a few hours. Got a bit of a problem," he explained without apology.

"Oh gosh no!" She clapped her hands to her cheeks, the rush of over-played emotion not out of place in a suburban conversation. "Nothing serious, I hope. If it is you're welcome to stay at the station for a couple of days until it's fixed. Now it's only me there is plenty of room." She giggled at her grim humour and touched Ray's strong tanned arm.

"Thanks for the offer," he replied, uncomfortable beneath her touch, "but I'll just grab one of the blokes and get going."

"I just threw a track," he shrugged in explanation. "I couldn't jump it back on, so now it's a two-man job to split and re-join it."

Wendy was concerned, although she didn't understand the problem. "I hope it won't take too long. I've got to get the track bull dozed and cleared so I can truck cattle out by the end of the month." She was full of unrealistic optimism as yet untested by the reality of the unyielding land.

"It'll be done," Ray reassured her.

"I've got the choppers booked for the last week in July," she babbled on, heedless of the interruption. "I was out that way the other day. I counted twenty head of cattle," she boasted. "Andrew," faltering at the name of her recently dead husband, "reckoned we could get nearly a thousand head out of that paddock."

Nelson rolled his eyes and pretended to look at the kite hawks wheeling high above the station dump. Ray slowly took his cigarette butt from his mouth and pinched the end. Carefully he put it back into his tobacco tin. She looked expectantly at both men, ready for praise.

"Could be a fair number there," Ray volunteered cautiously, not wanting to totally extinguish her spark of hope.

Her enthusiasm was not dampened. "I've been out there, Ray and I've seen them. I know I only counted twenty head, but all the time I was driving I could see fresh cattle tracks," she insisted.

They always followed cleared tracks, you foolish woman, he thought. From the suppressed smile at the corners of Nelson's lips Ray knew he was thinking the same thing. You need money, and you need it fast, but enthusiasm and wishing doesn't add up to cattle in the yards, he decided, feeling sorry for her.

"Yair, I've seen a few tracks too, but not only cattle track though."

He delved into his top pocket and pulled out one of the expended cartridge cases.

He had first seen a Chinese 7.62mm bullet case more than twenty years before in an almost forgotten weapons lecture at the Canungra jungle warfare barracks.

"This," the dumpy aggressive warrant officer lectured, "is the standard Soviet small arms round. Notice the shorter and more tapered cartridge case." The warrant officer had casually abused them in the familiar military way which always crawled under Morgan's skin and itched.

"This round is the same calibre as the standard NATO round, but it is not interchangeable. It will not fire from your SLR. Remember these numbered headstamps. Report these if you find them because it's evidence the Chinese are supplying North Vietnam."

For us poor sods who went to Vietnam it was useful information, Ray reflected because it meant enemy ammunition couldn't be used in our weapons. Who would have thought I would be dredging up this information again on a run-down cattle station in far northern Australia? He shook his head slightly at the memory.

"Ever seen one of these?" he asked. He already guessed Wendy's answer, so he gave her a brief glance and tossed the empty case to Nelson. In his consternation, Nelson missed the catch. The few seconds needed to bend down and retrieve it gave him time to frame an answer.

"New one to me, chilpu," he answered formally, scratching the dark stubble on his chin to cover his concern. Ray noted the language word for 'old man' and was quite pleased at the implied respect. "Probably some tourist," Nelson continued boldly. "They always like to shoot at those old bull buffaloes. Where you find him?" he asked casually.

"Up towards the end of Cow Creek. Seems a long way out of the way for tourists," Ray answered easily as if the shell was only of passing interest.

"Those tourists seem to go anywhere here," Wendy complained. "They have no respect for private property and I don't like guns. It is so unfair to shoot animals just because they are there. They have a right to live and those old bulls look so majestic when you see them. They are just like the Old People who lived here before the pioneers came."

She touched Ray's arm again and let her fingers linger near his wrist. "Have you ever seen any of the Old People? I would love to see them. They must have a wonderful life," she sighed, "just living in harmony with nature like they did in the old times. They didn't have to worry about bills," she concluded bitterly.

Ray stepped back to avoid her touch, uncomfortable with the unnecessary physical contact. He held out his hand for Nelson to return the empty shell case.

"My people, the Old People, they all been killed. Only Old Harry left," Nelson answered matter-of-factly as he flicked the case into Morgan's outstretched hand. "No-one is left who can look after this country, but it is still our country – blackfella country," he added.

"There must be some of the Old People left, but I know what you mean, Nelson. Even though I hold the legal title I don't really own this country. I'm just a visitor here from the city. Already I sometimes feel as if this country owns me." She wrapped her arms around herself.

"Melbourne or the Bush?" Ray interrupted mockingly with the old derisive jest.

Wendy glared at him angrily.

"Well, I've been knocking around this country for quite a while, but it took me years to understand this country owns me," Ray persisted. "You wait until you have done a Wet season here and see if it changes your mind."

"You got to be born here, Missus," Nelson said. "I was born here," and he left the implicit reproach unfinished.

Wendy, stung by their apparent rejection, felt tears prick the corners of her eyes. Angrily she pushed them to one side with a toss of her head. It's a mongrel country, she stormed inwardly, inhabited by hard, insensitive men who either don't want to work or who tear it apart in their search for profit. She knew both men were watching her so she closed her eyes against the building tears, guessing they would despise her weakness. She retreated before the loneliness and strangeness of her new life.

She wanted to go back to the house, and further back yet to cool Melbourne, to the pleasures of daily shopping and expensive meals in good restaurants. To be away from the dust and dirt, the cockroaches, the dirty, sweat-stinking white contractors and the throat-grabbing stench of bush blacks. She shivered and opened her eyes. They were still there, lounging across the front of the filthy Landcruiser pickup.

She wanted to leave the station and its suffocating paint-peeling walls. It was sparsely populated with memories because the fatal crash which had killed her husband had come too soon after her arrival. I can't go back to Melbourne, she despaired, because the house has to be sold. The sale would provide the liquidity needed to pay off the never-ending bills that every day dogged the heels of station existence and the deceitful debts she discovered he had left behind. Only money could stave off the spectre of a return to poverty and that was a return journey she was determined not to make.

But if I can sell these cattle then Punkatoy is mine, she told herself with optimistic defiance and took a deep calming breath. To do it I need these two men and their co-operation.

"Nelson. You tell the boys here to keep working until we come back. You can give Ray a hand," she commanded briskly. "Oh gosh! I've got to get away," she added on a whim. "Do you mind if I come?" she added as a polite afterthought, still unsure of her new authority as the boss.

"Please yourself. Be a couple of hours before we get back," Ray warned.

"That's alright. Just give me a minute and I'll get some snacks to take as well."

Before Ray had time to answer she strode off towards the house. Ray pushed his annoyance to one side and climbed into the Landcruiser. Both men sat silently until Wendy came across the yard carrying a glinting new billy can and two bright new plastic containers.

"Bloody hell. A picnic lunch," Ray intoned and, indulgently agreeing, Nelson smiled happily.

"Might be some fresh fruit cake," he suggested.

"That would be bloody good for a change. At least she is learning," Ray acknowledged.

Carefully Wendy put the containers on the floor and sat in the passenger seat beside Nelson, forcing him to twist his lanky frame sideways so Ray could use the gearstick. Wendy slipped her arm around his shoulders to brace herself as they bumped along the dusty track. Nelson stared rigidly ahead and went without a smoke. He refused to ride in the open tray as tradition demanded, but as the pickup bumped along he wondered if he was taking his pride too far.

After twenty rough kilometres Nelson was jammed firmly and uncomfortably beside Ray in his attempt to avoid contact with the white Missus who was now his boss.

"Move over for God's sake, will you? I can't drive on this bloody track with you smashing into my arm all the time." Ray gave Nelson a shove with his elbow, laughing inwardly at his discomfort. Nelson moved over. Wendy relaxed and enjoyed the warm contact.

"Where did you find that shell?" Nelson asked.

"Just back from where I'm working."

Nelson tried to relax as Ray continued. Any distraction was worthwhile. As he listened, he concentrated on avoiding a return of the insistent accidental pressure on his leg, or responding to the message Wendy's fingers were inadvertently drumming on his shirt collar and neck.

"I wouldn't have found them if I hadn't thrown the track. The Toyota was back at my start point, so I had to walk about three kilometres. I got distracted by a big old goanna. His tracks were as clear as daylight across the freshly dozed cut, but I lost them about fifty metres into the bush. He was walking as if he owned the country. I was looking for his track when I spotted the shells."

The paperbark flats and the low grassed ridges stretched ahead. The track, really no more than two well-worn wheel marks twisting through the timber, was rough and covered with fine white powdery bulldust. In the deep holes it billowed in blinding clouds as Ray rammed the Landcruiser through.

It seemed to Nelson he was either thrown against Wendy or she was thrown against him. He was aware of her unfettered bouncing breasts rubbing against his arm. He shifted, but she was constantly thrown against him. He glanced away at Ray who, still amused at his discomfort, gave him a wry smile.

"Hey you mongrel, what's so special about those shells anyway?" Nelson demanded.

In an attempt to escape from Wendy he leaned closer to Ray so he could hear his answer.

"They're Chinese bullets. Means they won't fit your average .308 rifle which is the civilian version of the 7.62mm NATO round." He glanced at Nelson who looked uncomfortable and confused.

"Basically it's not the sort of ammo you expect to find in Australia. You can only use it with Chinese weapons like their copy of the AK47." He concentrated on the rough track and missed Nelson's sudden look of alarm. "And these shell cases have Chinese numbering on the back of the case. It's just a bit unusual."

Nelson tried to wriggle his way clear of Wendy as he fumed to himself. Thirty bloody rounds. One thirty round burst just for the fun of it, kilometres from anywhere. And what happens? I lose two bloody shells and this bastard has to find them. He remembered the thrill of the Chinese assault rifle bucking in his hands and the distinctive relentless mechanical hammering it made, the thirty rounds from the banana shaped magazine disappearing in a few seconds. It had been an extravagance, but it had felt good.

"What do you reckon it means?" he asked, keeping his voice calm but wondering frantically how much Ray knew or guessed.

"Blowed if I know. Why? You interested?"

"No. No, not really," Nelson protested mildly, covering his concern. "I just don't like whitefellas shooting on this country. Too many shoot just for fun and not for tucker. When I shoot, I only shoot to keep the camp in food."

"I agree. These tourists shoot at anything that moves with any sort of rifle. I've seen buffalo with old wounds from light calibre rifles." Ray snorted with contempt. "It's no wonder the buffalo are cranky. These cases probably came from an illegal AK47 owned by some city Sunday shooter," he joked.

Nelson settled back in uneasy silence and watched the country break into sandy woollybutt and turpentine covered ridges that made so much of the area virtually inaccessible. The newly dozed track Ray was putting in so the station could truck cattle skirted the rocky ridges. They turned onto it and bumped along the broken rock exposed beneath the grey gritty clay.

Chapter 5

THE OLD BULLDOZER WAS SLEWED ACROSS the newly cleared track when they reached it. Bleached dull yellow, the machine sat beneath a thick layer of dust smothering every exposed part of the machine. It was covered with a matting of twigs and branches that showered the dozer, its open cab and Ray every time they pushed through the bush.

The overhanging heavy steel canopy was dented where countless tree limbs had fallen across the machine. The dark overflow stains from the fuel and hydraulic tanks seemed to seep further into the fresh dust on the machine as they looked. Only the shiny hydraulic rams and the front of the blade looked clean and new.

One long caterpillar track had peeled off and lay slewed in the dust at an angle to the machine.

"Hope it's not as bad as it looks," Nelson commented as he gratefully climbed out of the pickup, pleased to get away from Wendy and to have room to move once more. "What do we have to do?" He walked around the machine, examining it carelessly, his riding boots kicking up puffs of dust, as Ray explained how the upper track had to be pulled up over the two track rollers leaving the upper and lower sections running parallel to each other.

Wendy stared at the squat machine. So much depended on it and she realised she knew so little. What am I doing here? she wondered. She shrugged the thought away, not wanting to test her newly formed conviction too closely. I have to learn about these things, she decided. She listened carefully as Ray answered Nelson's casual questions.

"Is it serious?" Wendy asked anxiously.

"We have to split this track to get it back on. I tried to jump it back on myself, but it didn't work," Ray explained.

"Is there anything I can do?" she asked.

"You could get a fire going for the billy later on," Ray suggested. "If you don't mind, boss," he added, taking the sting from his rejection. She nodded unhappily, and stayed near the machine.

Nelson had the tool box from the back of the Toyota by the time Ray had decided where to split the track. "Split him here, I reckon," Ray directed as they sat down in the dust and worked on the bolts holding the track links together. Nelson held one large spanner while Ray heaved on the nut.

The nut suddenly let go and Ray sprawled on his back, narrowly missing Wendy as she jumped quickly to one side. He looked around. No words were spoken, and that was reprimand enough. She moved out of the way.

Ignoring everything except the job, neither man spoke as they worked. Wendy realised they were self-sufficient, so she found shade under one of the spindly quinine bushes and watched them from a distance. They sweated, dust clinging to them as they wrestled with hot metal.

She brushed at her own clothes and skin, annoyed with the dust and the old unwelcome feeling of grime and squalor it brought with it. Some days she didn't mind, but today, sitting alone while the men worked oblivious of her, the dust irritated all her senses. She stood up and angrily brushed the leaves and twigs from her jeans in several hurried slashes, pausing briefly to appreciate the feel of her figure which she knew was becoming leaner.

He is too busy to notice anyway, she decided. Only partly shocked by her thoughts she watched them again, heads together, muscles straining and skin shiny in the sunlight with rivulets of sweat despite the difference in colour. Her loneliness was suddenly tangible and she longed for words of friendship. I like them both, but Nelson...

She left the thought unfinished as she concentrated on the head stockman for a minute.

She watched his bony arms strain against the pressure of a seized bolthead, his strong dark hands bunched against the bright steel of the spanner. His battered tall-crown hat had fallen from his head exposing his jet black hair. His wide nose seemed to emphasise his strong jaw and broad lips surrounded by coarse dark stubble. His dark brown, almost black, skin gave hidden depths to his deep-set eyes, hidden in the perpetual squint of the bushman.

He's as strong and bold as this country. He's a good head stockman, and he's not bad-looking either, Wendy acknowledged. The memory of the touch of his body against hers on the rough trip out returned unbidden and catlike, caressed her warmly. He looked up from his work and she felt embarrassed under his gaze. It was as if he had read her half-formed thoughts. She looked away at the surrounding bush.

The country grew more fascinating for her each day. She stood and walked into the bush, her arms clasped around her chest. The sharp scent of the hot leaves mixed with the pungent dustiness of the light soil. Forgetting the men and her worries for a moment, she let the bush embrace her as she wandered.

Nelson watched her go, casually admiring the swing of her hips. Ray, his back to the disappearing woman, straightened up.

Together they laid the track out flat and worked the dozer into position. Nelson stood to one side and rolled a smoke while Morgan slowly backed the machine down the unrolled track plates. Morgan used a load binder to lift the tracks over the drive sprocket. Accustomed to working alone, he suddenly remembered Nelson.

"Hey," he shouted. "You reckon you can spare the time to give us a hand here?"

"Don't know? You paying better than station wages?" Nelson asked, an open smile backing the question.

"I give you fella plenty tea, sugar and flour," Ray joked in return.

"Throw in some tobacco and I'm yours for a week."

"You're on," Nelson bantered.

"You know," Nelson said seriously after he had butted his cigarette in the dust with the toe of his boot, "it's still true. There are still stations employing blackfellas under those sorts of conditions. It's not right. The ringers ought to turn around and blow the bastards out. Just shoot them like the mongrels they are," he finished harshly, momentarily forgetting his usual caution around white fellas.

He looked challengingly at Ray who was standing by the dozer. "We both know land rights hasn't really changed things much since the invaders arrived … "

"Don't call me an 'invader'," Ray snapped with unexpected vigour.

"Why not? Your people came here and stole this land from us."

"I was born here, mate. This land belongs to all Australians, black, white or brindle. You were born here too. You belong to this land, but I belong to this land too," Ray replied, his voice a low growl.

"You only been in this country a few years. I was born right here, and I'll fight for the right to stay here. This is my traditional country."

"Argh, bullshit, Shortjack. You and I both been in this country for a long time. I know you were sent to Darwin as a kid under the old Welfare Ordinance Laws. I reckon that should never have happened. There should never have been a Chief Protector with those powers. Kids should never have been separated from their families and sent to mission schools, but we can't change the past. How long you been back in this country of yours, this traditional country?" he challenged.

"I've been back here for over four years. I'm a proper blackfella," he said bitterly. "I was sold with the station when this other mob took over."

Ray stared out at the dry scrub and fished for his tobacco tin as he formed an explanation.

"I knocked around the back of New South Wales and the top end of South Australia for years before I came up here. I've knocked around this Gulf country for over four years now. I feel I belong to this country," he observed with simple sincerity. "This pungkuthuyi country, it's not part of my dreaming, but it is part of my singing."

"But chilpu," Nelson said respectfully, "you're different from most whitefellas. Maybe you got a bit of colour in you somewhere back in your history. This is my traditional country, but don't worry," he laughed, "I'll let you live here when the revolution comes."

"You might be right," Ray shrugged and smiled, any rancour in the discussion dismissed as quickly as it had come. He went on seriously. "But hey, you want to be careful. That sort of talk will get you into trouble in town. They don't like you educated blackfellas."

"Education," Nelson sneered. "They say: You get educated, you go to him fella school every day, and you be sure to get a job. That's the biggest whitefella lie of all," he spat.

Both men sat moodily considering the truth in what they had said. Ray rolled a cigarette and they let the sounds of the bush creep around them. They watched a small goanna with a yellow tail dart in and out of the tumbled rocks near the new track. Carefully Ray pinched the butt of his cigarette when he had finished and put it back into his tobacco tin.

"Why you always do that? You smoke them again?" Nelson asked.

"When I've got a tin full, I bury them," Ray explained and a forgotten memory stirred.

"What for you do that?"

Ray shrugged his shoulders and remembered the old lessons. The enemy can track you by following the trail of Hershey bar wrappers and discarded cigarette butts. When he is close enough he can smell the beef sweat and the peppermint toothpaste. Or so they told us. He snorted and didn't give voice to the memory.

"Hey, I got you for a week," he chuckled, changing the subject. "I'm not paying you a fortune in rations to sit around. What I want you to do is guide the first link up over the drive sprocket."

It was a full hour before they finished and it was only then they realised Wendy hadn't lit the fire for the billy. She was nowhere to be seen. Snatching his rifle, Ray and Nelson headed into the bush to find her. Both tracked her meandering course easily.

Chapter 6

THEY'LL SURELY MISS ME NOW, WENDY pleaded silently. Please, let them miss me. She heard the strangled roar of the bulldozer idle down and then stop. Silence and her racing heartbeat replaced the distant noise. Despite the heat, cold sweat doused her trembling body.

The old bull buffalo ten metres away flicked its left ear as he too acknowledged the oppressive silence. Standing higher than her shoulder, the hulking grey buffalo peered at her with piggy eyes, the great curved ribbed black horns cutting off escape. He stretched his head a little further to investigate the trembling figure in front of him. His massive curved horns moved closer to the ground.

Clearly he is undecided what to do, Wendy thought in a moment of ridiculous clarity. It gave her no comfort. She remained rigid but trembling with fear, her eyes fixed on the beast alone. Time disappeared.

Her aimless wandering had confirmed her fascination with the station and the country. The bush was enchanting until the giant grey buffalo materialised from the scrub. A deep sickness in her stomach replaced her relaxed happiness of only a few minutes before.

The spindly quinine and thin paperbark offered no protection or refuge. The buffalo stood between her and the small sandstone outcrop. Her first impulse had been to run, but fear crippled her muscles.

Stand still and then back off slowly, screamed her memory. She grasped at the snippets of advice she remembered from casual conversation with Ray. Mean, unpredictable and dangerous sprang unbidden to the forefront of her fear.

She willed her feet to move but they resolutely disobeyed. Mesmerised, she watched the buffalo's slow moving bovine eyes. Compelled by a rigid fascination to observe, she saw the spittle dribble from its blue-grey lips.

"God, let them come," she half whispered, the sound unreasonably loud in her ears.

The dark grey, almost black beast with pale mud-caked bristles on its shoulders filled the world. The once appealing untidy scrub was suddenly unseen. I want to be sick. I'm going to be sick. Don't be sick, she screeched soundlessly. She felt the childhood fear of darkness return and claw her body. Ice-cold sweat clamped her T-shirt to her shoulders. The fear was worse than the gnawing cell of loneliness and poverty that had threatened to engulf her as a child, and which, now her husband was dead, closeted with her at night to become an unwelcome and unresponsive partner in her bed.

The explosion shattered the world. Her stomach turned and heaved as the bullet thunked into flesh with a sickening finality.

The buffalo suddenly folded its legs. Still staring she saw the massive body apparently shake the ground as it fell. She imagined she saw the dust billow as it gracefully rolled onto one side. One raked thick black horn grotesquely held its head above the white grass. Blood bubbled in foam flecked froth from its mouth. She closed her eyes, relief mixed with horror as a bright red stream ran from its rubbery nostrils.

The sweat clung even colder as she turned gratefully into Nelson's strong black shoulders and his secure dark chest was suddenly there instead of fear.

"Hey," he soothed, his bubbling accent soft.

"I was so scared," she sobbed. She huddled gratefully into Nelson's protective embrace. She clapped her hands to her ears and fought back the gagging in her throat when Ray, standing beside the beast, fired a second shot. Still trembling, and somehow getting worse now she could move, she nestled into the curve of Nelson's shoulder and threw her hands around his neck. She felt greasy hair against her arms and her mind constructed a delusion of the strong comforting embrace she had often sought from her husband.

Certain the beast was dead, she turned fully towards Nelson, her fear melting into uncontrollable spasms as the aftermath engulfed her.

"Thank you. Thank you. My God, thank you ..." she blurted.

The head stockman held her gently for a while as he watched Ray warily prod the fallen buffalo with his boot, rifle at ready. Both of them had too often seen an apparently dead buffalo lumber to its feet and make a final dash for vengeance so they knew not to take this one's death for granted.

Carefully Nelson lowered Wendy to the ground and sat beside her. She clasped him for support. She curled, legs splayed ungainly beneath her, sobbing in fits and starts. Her short hair rubbed against the side of his face as her body heaved against his and her breasts, naked beneath her T-shirt, rubbed against his chest.

"Proper dead?" Nelson asked, already knowing the answer. Wendy looked up, eyes swollen and sniffled back a head full of tears as Ray answered.

"Yair. He's dead. Bit of a pity, but then you can't always tell with these old bulls. They might be dangerous, and he probably was," Ray said regretfully. He pointed at the horns with the muzzle of his rifle. "Good set."

"Proper good set. Good shot though."

Ray shrugged, and from habit bent down and collected the second shell case. Working the bolt he cleared the rifle and pocketed the spare rounds. "You alright?" he asked Wendy as he walked over, rifle held low with the muzzle pointing to the ground.

He stood over her, rifle held confidently. The sweat on his shirt and trousers had turned the white dust to grey mud. Fresh from changing the dozer track, his dirty hands and arms seemed indistinguishable from the grease and oil on his khaki clothes. Only his broad-brimmed light tan stetson and calm sun-creased eyes separated him from the surrounding bush. The rest of him faded into the spindly drabness of the untidy quinine bushes. She was humbled by his matter-of-fact approach and his apparent lack of real concern.

Taking a deep gulp, she struggled to master the remnants of the blinding panic that had assailed her. She breathed deeply, but it ended in a sob.

"I'll be right in a minute," she mumbled.

She managed to sit gamely in Nelson's arms for a few moments before succumbing to uncontrollable shaking.

Satisfied she was safe, Ray turned before she collapsed again and walked back to the dozer. He easily followed the track they had made in their search for Wendy. He had finished one smoke and was rolling another when the others arrived back, walking apart like a newly estranged couple.

He jumped down from where he had been sitting on the broad metal track. Wendy was agitated. Her lips twitched momentarily before she could speak. She lashed him from the depths of her fear and anger.

"That wasn't necessary," she scolded with an edge of hysteria induced by never to be forgotten fear. "You could've just frightened him away with a shot."

Ray shrugged off any reply, reminding himself she was new to the bush.

"That magnificent beast had every right to live," she shouted at him. He started back as she continued. "I was just watching him. He wouldn't have done anything at all. He has a right to be here, just like the trees and the rocks. Just like we have a right to be here. You just shot him for the fun of it!" she accused.

Behind her Nelson rolled his eyes at her shame. She was his boss, and it was unnerving to see her lose her dignity. As a newcomer she had much to learn. Her shame reflected on him so he carefully avoided Ray's eyes. Ray leant casually on the track of the dozer, and, careful to make no sudden movement, lifted his smoke to his mouth, worried she would charge him like a wounded animal.

Hysteria snaked across her features, eyes wide as she punctuated her accusations with a semaphore of hand signals.

"Didn't you read the new signs on the boundary gate?" she shrieked. "It says Punkatoy station is a flora and fauna sanctuary. Guns are prohibited. You know why it says that? To stop trigger happy bastards like you who want to shoot anything that moves in the bush. People like you don't care what they kill. You're sick in the head."

He had seen fear turn to aggression before and knew matching it with aggression was no solution. He waited for her to draw breath, not prepared to match her anger so it could burn out just as quickly as it flared.

"If you want me to work here, I carry a rifle. I shoot what I think is necessary for food or safety. If you don't like it, then I'll pull out now," he stated calmly.

"That's right. Take the easy way out. Killers like you are just cowards," she screeched and then fell silent.

It was a random, unthinking barb which sliced cleanly through Ray's reserve and intentions. He turned his back on her and walked to the front of the dozer. Gripping the top of the thick blade he controlled his shaking anger. Her silence challenged him for an explanation.

"I nearly killed a man once for doing that sort of thing," he growled quietly, looking away from her and speaking into the bush. "But then, he was just a nasty little warrant officer sweating in the jungle and you're just a frightened little lady," he muttered, remembering with some bitterness it had been enough to earn him a dishonourable discharge. No regrets then, and none now. The softly spoken words cut through her venom, coming as a sharp verbal slap and breaking her mounting hysteria.

Wendy felt Nelson pulling her towards Ray's Toyota. "Come on, Missus," he urged, and reluctantly she followed.

"I'm sorry. I never realised," she mumbled in unheard apology as Nelson started the Landcruiser.

"I'll drop the Toyota back tomorrow," Nelson shouted, turning the vehicle around. Ray waved them away and Nelson drove off toward the station with Wendy sobbing silently beside him.

Ray watched them go, sardonically evaluating the change in Wendy in a few short hours. She was lucky the buffalo didn't charge at her this time, but she'll learn, he thought. He listened to the silence of the bush as he carefully pinched the butt of his cigarette and placed it in his tobacco tin.

Foolish woman, he decided without malice. He climbed onto the dozer and turned back to his camp, the steel tracks screeching across the disturbed rock.

Chapter 7

WENDY LOOKED UP FROM THE TABLE where she was writing, the brittle faded plastic laminex table top chipped and broken at the corners. The clock told her it was nearly four in the afternoon. On most days, time meant very little, but once a week it was important. The mail plane kept to a schedule and she was forced to keep an eye on the time every Thursday if she wanted to mail her letters. One elbow on the table, she sucked the blunt end of the pen meditatively. The dirty louvre windows refracted the bright outside light dully, making the age-stained walls even darker.

The ceiling fan, fly-specked and greasy, circled doggedly above, fooling neither the flies nor Wendy. The distant throb of the generator shed beyond the Big House yard was a constant background to the imaginary cool swish of the fan. The island bench with two dirty plates on it was a playground for flies. Several other plates dried in the heat of the day, waiting to be put away in a cupboard or used again.

I must get and clean up this room, she thought. She knew she wouldn't. I hardly ever seem to get the time now with all the station jobs. I've barely got time to keep in contact with my old friends, she acknowledged.

Carefully she folded and sealed the letter she had just written. She put it on the pile of letters she had already written and glanced at the clock again. Time for one brief letter to her American friend, Kathy, she calculated.

Proudly she wrote 'Wendy Lindon, Punkatoy Station, via Katherine, Northern Territory,' in the upper righthand corner of the paper.

"Dearest Kathy," she began and her handwriting looped and twirled across the page, some words dotted with little flower petals and other flourishes. "Life is so wonderful here. As I write I can see the birds playing in the trees just outside the windows. Their twittering playfulness is a constant background to work on the station. I'm living so close to nature. It is wonderful after being locked away in the city for so long. The bush is such a welcome change from city life." She shied away from continuing the written lie.

"I suppose it is still cold down where you are. We have the most glorious weather. Every day the sun is shining and there is only a gentle breeze. The days are warm, but not too hot. If I'm out and around the station I often rest for a few hours in the afternoon. I seem to get so tired. There is so much to learn, but I'm sure I can do it."

"I've been driving around the station (we don't call it a ranch), inspecting cattle and fences and yards. I have a contractor and ringers (you call them cowboys) to supervise. Sometimes we camp out in swags." She paused, and decided she needed to explain. "Not sure if you know what a swag is. It's a really thin mattress with sheets and blankets all rolled up in a canvas cover. It's a bed roll, not a tent, so we sleep on the ground with absolutely nothing between you and the stars. By golly its fabulous."

"It's still hard to believe. The station is 4,000 square kilometres. That's about 1,500 square miles to you – bigger than Rhode Island." And she drew a small smiley face before continuing. "It is all so exciting. It is a wonderful life, even though it is sometimes hard work, and I'm so glad Andrew talked me into making the change."

"He talked about it so often, but it seems almost unreal now I'm actually here. My only regret is Andrew was killed before we could really start to enjoy the change. Now the station is all I have. Sometimes it gets a bit lonely, but there are so many things to do so I am not very often lonely."

She contemplated adding a sad face but decided not to, her anger at his betrayal more persistent than mourning.

"I do miss all the people around me. Every day here it's the same faces. You see them when you wake up, and you look at them all day. There are no strangers here, no new faces, and in some way it makes it lonelier," she admitted.

She paused in her task and listened for the drone of the mail plane. Only the fan and the generator answered her. Most of the ringers were out at Buffalo Yard mustering camp so the station was unusually silent.

"I'm writing this in a bit of a hurry because the mail plane is due in shortly. We only get the mail plane here once a week. I do miss the letters every day, but when they do come it makes me feel much less isolated. I suppose it is a small loss because there are so many other compensations for living here in the bush."

She wondered if it would ever be really true. It was too soon to be able to make an accurate judgement and she did not want to examine her commitment too closely just yet. She knew she would have to give herself more time if everything was going to work.

"I wonder if you could send me a copy of the latest *Women's Weekly*? I've tried to order one from Katherine (not you, Dear, but the nearest town.)" She drew a smiley face. "I haven't had much success and I would like to see the new winter fashions. Could you spare a Myer or Roger David catalogue? Not that I buy anything from them, but the catalogues give me an idea of what is happening on the fashion scene. We are so out of touch here. I hope to come down South to visit later in the year and it would be dreadful to be out of date."

"I've had letters from all the people we used to know, and from some of the teachers I worked with. It's so nice to know the people you worked with still remember you. I still think of them."

"I must rush now, I can hear the plane coming."

She signed herself "'With all my love, Wendy," and quickly folded the letter, making sure it was neat. Dashing off the Melbourne address on the envelope she picked up the bundle of letters and raced out to the station Toyota. The sound of the plane disappeared in the hills as the tiny Cessna completed its circuit before coming in to land on the station airstrip two kilometres away. She dropped the letters on the ground as she hastily opened the door of the Toyota pickup.

"Damn," she snapped and hurriedly picked them up. "Damn! Damn! Damn! The mail bag's in the kitchen!" She cursed, more for the frustration of new lessons forgotten than for the inconvenience.

On the last mail day the pilot had testily reminded her the mail was supposed to be delivered to him in the official Australia Post bag. It's not the same as just posting a letter, she had been told. She threw the letters onto the dashboard and raced back for the calico bag.

She was on the edge of the gravel airstrip, busy trying to spot the plane, before she noticed Ray's pickup. He was, as always, leaning against the bull bar with the inevitable cigarette in his mouth.

Look at him, she thought as she coasted to a stop. He never seems to change, clean shaven when everyone else has untidy stubble. It is always the same old khaki work trousers and low-crown hat. He either wears a khaki shirt or sometimes a blue singlet, but they are the only changes. Yes, she noted, he's even got his work boots on. I wonder if he sleeps in his hat and boots. The image of him tucked up in a swag on the ground with his boots and hat on was amusing, so she was smiling when she went over to him.

"Got any mail coming in?" she asked, barely suppressing an unexpected giggle.

"Yair. A couple of hydraulic seals are supposed to be in this mail drop," he said casually.

"This means you'll be able to finish the dozer work soon?"

"It depends. The country is starting to change. I was going to come up and see you after the mail plane. It might take a bit longer than I first thought."

"It can't take longer," she insisted. "I'll be ready to shift cattle from there next week." She crossed her fingers behind her back and hoped the plan would come true.

"Don't panic. I didn't say I wouldn't be finished in time. I just said it might take a bit longer than I thought. I reckoned I would be cut-out by Tuesday, but there's another couple of days work left. Thing is, it's going to cost you a bit more."

Wendy's need to reply was forestalled as she watched the plane land. She held her breath until the plane landed and the pilot switched off the engine. He was long and thin, and when he got out of the plane he uncurled like a spider crab emerging from its hole in the sand.

"By cripes, Greg, I never know how you fit into the cabin," Ray remarked as he walked over. The pilot smiled thinly at the well-worn joke and tersely pointed to Ray's cigarette. "We would've gone up by now if there were any problems," Ray observed, ignoring the unspoken request to butt his cigarette. "Any mail for me?"

"No mail. Could be in the station bag."

From behind the seat the pilot took one sealed calico bag with a Punkatoy tag attached.

"See you remembered this week," he said as he exchanged the mail bag with Wendy.

"Yes, I remembered but I nearly forgot. Oh, I get so excited when I hear the plane come in. I just raced out. I'm not into the routine. I was so worried

I would miss you. I won't forget next week either," she promised in a spray of enthusiasm.

The pilot dourly accepted the outgoing bag without further comment and folded himself back into the cabin of the plane. Instrument checks completed, he looked quickly to see if they were clear, started the engine and gunned the plane to his take-off position. Wasting neither time nor a wave, he took off and banked quickly towards the next stop on the mail run.

"He must be a wonderful person to do this job," Wendy enthused.

"He gets paid just like the rest of us," Ray commented.

"But think of all the happiness he brings. Every week he delivers letters to people who have been waiting days to get them. He brings the outside world close again. It must be such a happy, wonderful job."

"He brings the bills as well."

You often spoil things, don't you, she thought as she watched in silence as the plane disappeared over the harsh white rocky hills.

"Do you want to open the mail bag here, or wait until you get up to the station?" Ray asked, wondering if his spare parts were in with the station mail. She hugged the mail bag. The bulge of the letters was enticing and she was suddenly happy with the prospect of his company despite his cynicism.

"Come up to the station. I'll put the kettle on and we'll have a cup of tea." She almost told him it would be nice to have his company, but she caught herself in time. She drove ahead nursing a growing flutter not entirely confined to the pleasures of opening the mail.

Chapter 8

"COME IN," SHE YELLED. "NO NEED to be formal here. Sit down. You have black tea with lots of sugar." He nodded. "Oh gosh! Here I'm deliberately teasing myself," she confessed to him. "I really want to rip the mail bag open now. It's just like getting a present every week. The suspense of waiting is half the fun," she giggled.

Ray had rolled one smoke and finished it before the tea was poured. Then Wendy opened the mailbag with a flourish and tipped the contents onto the kitchen table. Ray studied the handful of letters from a distance, waiting for Wendy to sort through them. The vast majority were bills, he noted, their clear windows a dead giveaway.

"No parcel for you," she said anxiously.

"Doesn't look like it, but it won't stop me working."

She noted his lack of concern, and so, reluctantly dismissing her own worries, surrendered herself to an orgy of letter reading. It was the one day of the week when the thousands of kilometres between friends disappeared.

He waited for her to finish. He drank his tea slowly from the tacky, unclean metal pannikin. Somehow tea from the teapot never tastes the same as tea from a billy on the campfire. I suppose it hasn't got the same smoky flavour, he mused and let his eyes wander over the kitchen with its dirty dishes and dusty surfaces. This place has gone downhill since I was last here. She must be pretty busy trying to get the station back on its feet. It's always dusty in the bush, but you can't afford to live in filth. Anne always keeps her quarters and schoolroom clean at Clara Valley and she's busy teaching and looking after the camp kids. I must catch up with her again, he reflected. It's been a while.

The pleasant memories of Anne receded as, mildly repulsed, he watched a cockroach crawl from under the loose lid of the metal flour drum by the fridge. Not in my camp you wouldn't, he declared silently. There are a few girls down at the ringers' camp. If she can't keep the house clean by herself, or if she hasn't got the time to do it, then she can always get one of the girls to do the job for her. Perhaps she doesn't know. He looked at the unclean pannikin more closely and winced.

Wendy finished reading two letters and was in the process of opening another. "No other letters for you, Ray?"

"No mail," he agreed, his thoughts interrupted.

"Just hold on a minute. Help yourself to tea. I always get so excited when the new mail is here," she told him distractedly, her attention already turned to opening the next letter.

He nodded, wryly noting how she pushed the window-faced envelopes to one side. I'll talk about the job when she has finished with the mail, he told himself as he rolled another smoke. He slouched in the kitchen chair and rubbed his sweat-stained hat against his forehead for a moment.

He mustered the patience of the silent bush and the rocky ridges. He waited, as he had waited so many times before, beside broken-down vehicles, in solitary bush camps, by airstrips, for people who were often late, or, as now, for spare parts which failed to arrive. At first he had chafed against the delay, but the bush had forced him to accept its own pace and now he was content with the slower rhythm.

He drew on his cigarette and let his mind wander back to Clara Valley and to Anne, the new school teacher there. She was a pretty woman in her own way, and her approach to the isolated outback life was quite a contrast to Wendy. They had talked a few times, and despite their infrequent contact, it was becoming more than just passing friendship.

It seemed ages before Wendy had finished with her letters. Some she re-read several times, savouring the words of distant friendship, while others she glanced through, putting them to one side so she could come back to them for further reading in her leisure time. Finally she opened the numerous bills and added them up. The figures were impressive and daunting.

The letter from the bank she left to last. It was a terse reminder another ten thousand dollars were due as minimum payment on the station loan by the end of the month. It also listed the required capital improvements to the property and demanded an interim report. She put it to one side, ignoring it as she had with their previous letters.

She glanced at the clock on the wall. "Oh my goodness! Ray, I'm so sorry. I got so involved in the mail. I hope you don't think I'm rude."

"Mail day is always the same no matter where you go. Every station stops when the mail comes in. Same on base too," he added involuntarily, but she didn't notice.

"Have some more tea."

She got up quickly before he could answer and put the kettle on. Sitting down, she put her elbows on the table and cupped her chin as she leaned forward.

"Do you ever miss the city, Ray?" she asked brashly.

He bridled at the direct question, resenting the casual probe into his past. It was not the bush way to ask personal questions. Too many had their own private reasons for living and working in remote parts of the Northern Territory. At twice the size of Texas and with less than 150,000 people it was a perfect escape. Foolish woman. She should know better. But then, she has only been here a few months. She will learn, but if she's not careful, she'll learn the hard way, he decided.

She misunderstood his silence.

"You do miss the city," she declared. "I miss the city a lot," she admitted. "Life is so out of touch here. I never get to see what they are wearing in the city. It's so hard to keep up. When I go back on holiday I don't want to look months out of date."

"I suppose you're right."

She missed the cold contempt in his voice. She smoothed her short light brown hair away from her exposed ear and let her fingers run down the nape of her neck. Despite the gritty station dust, the touch pleased her and she gently smiled.

Gosh, I wish I could get my hair trimmed and have a good shampoo and rinse, she thought. It's so hard to get really clean and stay clean now. For a moment she smelt the perfume of the hair salon and remembered the light-hearted chatter. The smell was so clean and fresh. She ran her other hand over her straight hair, preening in the memory of a life disintegrated.

The bubbling kettle intruded and she carried the tea pot to the table. Standing beside Ray as she poured more tea into his pannikin she noticed his suntanned neck and the strong set of his shoulders. I wonder where the suntan stops? Unexpectedly warmed by the image, it drove the ghosts of loneliness away. She sat down on the chair beside him and reached across the table to retrieve her own cup.

"Do you miss the city?" she asked again, hoping to draw him out.

"Never!"

She recoiled from the curt answer.

"What's wrong? I'm sorry if I've said anything wrong." She leaned forward and touched his strong forearm. She felt him tense and start to move away. Reluctantly she let him go. "Please tell me. It's important to me. I often think I make mistakes, but nobody will ever tell me," she implored.

They all just stop talking, she lamented silently as she waited for Ray's answer. Ray... Nelson... the bastard manager George before he left... the ringers...they're all the same. One moment they're alright, and then, they just shut up. Then it doesn't matter what you say, they only answer in grunts. It always seems to be my fault. I don't understand these people. It's as if they can't speak at all. Unbidden and unwelcome, she felt a lump form at the base of her throat and she swallowed deliberately to get rid of it.

Ray looked straight ahead through the dirty louvres. He spoke gently, hiding the effort the explanation cost him.

"You don't make many mistakes. You've been doing very well by yourself since the crash. It's just ... how do you bloody explain it? In this country you don't act like a policeman."

"I don't understand?" I never seem to understand, she despaired. I wish I was in Melbourne, at home with Kathy and John, or Sandra and Ross. Perhaps even the kids could come home. And no bills. God, I wish he would stay, she added.

"Stop being a copper," he suggested.

"What? Stop talking in riddles. I need your help. Please," she whispered as sudden tears began to form. Her throat choked and she couldn't swallow. She reached for the cup of tea to hide her distress, but gave up. Tears were hot beneath her eyes and his face blurred. He did not move and she reached out for his strength.

She groped for a tissue, but she rarely carried any because they spoilt the cut of her jeans. She pulled the bottom of her shirt from her jeans and wiped her eyes dry, not caring how much of her body he saw. She snuffled, and then tentatively reached for his shoulder.

"I' m sorry. I don't know what happened."

"Yair... well." He left his thoughts unspoken and his embarrassment was a revelation to her. "As I said, only policemen ask personal questions in this country and it is their right by law alone. A man's business is his own ... or a woman's for that matter," he added as an after thought. "If a bloke wants to tell you something, then he will. You don't ask."

Wendy nodded politely even though she didn't understand. What a stupid idea, she thought. How can you ever get to know people if you don't ask questions? Kathy and I ask a thousand questions every time we met. I wouldn't know anything about her if I hadn't asked. Men don't always want to talk, but they always do if you encourage them. It's ridiculous, she concluded, but smiled invitingly, encouraging him to continue.

"Well, can you tell me something about other people?" she asked demurely.

"No. It's not my place and it's just gossip. You'll find out in time. Just listen. You can learn a lot in this country by listening."

She cupped her hand to her ear comically. "Hey?"

Ray laughed lightly with relief and she joined in. He reached for his tobacco tin and papers. Wendy stood up quickly and returned with a large bottle of rum, unscrewing the top before she reached the table.

"You want a rum?"

"Reckon I could keep one down."

"I 've got some coke. Hang on."

"Just water, thanks. Doesn't have to be cold," he assured her.

"I've got Coke," she insisted as she went to the fridge.

"Only ever break rum down with water. Now you've opened the bottle you may as well throw the top away," he told her with mock seriousness, relieved to end the previous line of conversation.

"What do you mean'?"

He didn't answer and she returned with a can of Coke and two glasses. He refused a glass, and poured some rum into his empty pannikin. She poured herself a hefty rum, mixing it with coke.

"Come on," she prompted. "Tell me what you mean." She theatrically clapped her hand over her mouth. "Sorry. I'm acting like a policeman."

Ray took a solid drink of rum and felt its rough embrace. "I could drink a bit at the moment," he admitted. He drank again.

"Throw the top away," he explained. "It means once the bottle is open it hardly seems worthwhile to stop drinking until it's empty."

He smiled wryly at her and she found it oddly attractive. She lifted her glass to him and drank deeply. Despite his jest, he did not want to encourage her into excessive drinking.

Together they drank, each in their own quiet desperation, the level of the bottle dropping as the sun slid behind the giant tamarind tree.

Chapter 9

SURROUNDED BY THE DARKNESS AND DEEP into the bottle, Ray started. "I was born down south in Victoria," he told her as he played with the nearly empty bottle on the table. It was almost an apology. His softly spoken words stumbled against the dull pale paint, cracked and flaking off the walls of the narrow kitchen. He stared past the lazy frazzle of insects clustered around the weak light globe, some stuck fast to the sticky curl of flypaper.

I think I know what this must be costing you, Wendy realised as she listened to him. You look at me, but never at my eyes. Perhaps you will before the night is out, she mused to herself.

"After a stint in jungle greens I came back to Australia and then I spent most of my time in the bush." He knew it wasn't the full story and for some reason he didn't want to cheat her. Compelled, he continued, looking past her into the darkness outside. "Knocked around chasing opals for a while and then went mustering cattle."

"Why a ringer and not cowboy?" she asked, giving him an excuse to take a side track.

"In a muster and at night time, you ride in a circle – a ring – around the mob to stop the cattle from rushing – stampeding, as the Americans call it. Out here a cowboy is just an odd-job man working around the station looking after farm animals."

He drank again, and she waited expectantly.

"Worked cattle up this way for a while, and now I'm working my own dozer for a stint."

"How long have you been working in the bush?" she asked, suddenly confident he would tell her without taking offence at the personal question.

"About ten or twelve years." He paused as pictures from those years formed in his mind, each a perfectly formed flashcard from his life.

"Good years," he concluded finally, attention focussed on the wide-eyed window-sill gecko snatching insects with casual ease.

Wendy saw the pause. And some bad years, she thought, and let it rest. She relaxed, sifting the information he had given her and resisting the urge to keep on questioning.

"Tell you something," he started diffidently, choosing to take another side track. "Bit of unrest in the ringers' camp," he observed. "Reckon they seen the kaditcha man. Old feather foot," he explained, realising she wouldn't understand. "You might call him a witch doctor and laugh at the superstition, but for the ringers he is as real as you or me. They reckon he is singing someone so they are all frightened."

"I really don't understand."

He sighed, pausing for a moment to consider how best to explain and then continued in the same soft murmur.

"It's complicated, but it's better if you have some idea so you know what's going on. It starts with a person's singing. His song is his life story and the history of his ancestors. That gives him a song line which is like the tracks through his country. It's marked by rocks and trees and waterholes and shelters where important events took place. He has an obligation to look after these places. We call them sacred places, but that's not quite right. The obligation to look after these places means they go walkabout, particularly at ceremony time. You won't get work out of the ringers' camp when this happens. But you got to let them go because you'll never hold them here."

Unconsciously drawing a pattern of circles and lines with his finger on the tabletop, he continued. "Song lines are what binds a man to his country and the country to him. Do the wrong thing by your country, or someone else's country, and the kaditcha man steps in. Mind you, he's not just about punishment. He is like a professor and he holds knowledge of all the song lines in this pungkuthuyi country. When people break the lore he is the one who delivers the punishment."

"They call him feather-foot because he wears emu feather shoes bound with blood so he can't be tracked. He takes something belonging to his victim. It might be a hair, a pannikin, a boot, anything. Then he sings his victim. People who don't understand this talk about pointing the bone, but that's not true. The kaditcha man's song steals his victim's singing... his connection to country. Break the connection, and a fella dies."

He wiped clear the dust-drawn pattern in the same way as the Old People wiped clean the initiation ceremony patterns in the sand so the un-initiated could not see them.

"The kaditcha man has his own powerful song so he can break the link between his victim and his personal singing. It's not the same as casting a spell because when he steals his victim's singing it sucks out his soul. I've seen healthy men suddenly sicken for no reason and then die. The victim knows he has been sung, and he just accepts it. And when he dies he becomes unknown to the rest of the camp. They can't use his name so they call him kumanjayi."

Ray paused, deep in thought. The shattered rocky landscape with its steep stone escarpments, gigantic boulders, and hidden spring-fed pandanas palm pools had become more than just a work place and refuge.

"Just reckon you should know," he concluded and took another sip of rum.

It was the longest talk she had ever heard from him. Rather than consider it in silence, she felt the urge to talk to show her appreciation, although she had nothing she could add to his explanation of song lines. She decided to tell him more about herself. It's insane, she though wildly. He doesn't want to know. He doesn't care. But tonight I care about him knowing. She stared at the dark liquid in the glass and took a sip, picking up the earlier thread in the conversation.

"I came from down South too," she blurted before she could change her mind. "But you know this already. I spent all my life near Melbourne. I lived in..." Staring into the rum, she paused and gathered her courage. "I grew up in city slums. I won a school scholarship and became a student counsellor. I wanted to help those inner city kids, and I did, until I met Andrew at a charity function. He took me away. He was in business, but now things have gone to shit." She looked up. "I love the city and its life, but I hate the slums. And now I'm up here where there are more trees and cattle than people."

She paused, the enormity of the change striking home once put into words.

"I always wanted to live close to nature. In the city as a kid I always believed it was important to save the trees," she said, almost convincing herself. "Well, recently I've come to see that," she conceded.

"You want to help to save the whales," he observed with apparent sincerity.

"Yes. It's so important," she agreed. "They are such magnificent creatures. They're free and kind. Man is so cruel. We always want to kill or imprison. We were lucky to be able to save the seals. Now we have to stop the slaughter of our kangaroos. I'll never allow anyone to shoot a kangaroo while I'm at Punkatoy," she declared.

"We got'ta keep the whales in the ground," he chuckled laconically.

"Yes," Wendy agreed before she saw the jest and the drink softened the fall.

"Oh goodness! You're such a tease, "she bantered. She finished her rum quickly and poured another as a torrent of feelings coursed through her. She looked at him less covertly. His eyes twinkled in the light, hands gripping the table with rock-like solidarity, and he slouched comfortably in the chair.

I bet you ride a horse in the same way. You've got the build to slouch your way through life and take anything you want. She thought boldly, I wonder if you want to take me? She smirked, playing with the top button of her shirt. He turned to her, and mistaking her reaction, smiled laconically at his own sly joke about the whales. She undid the top shirt button, her heart suddenly racing, and she gulped more rum to still it.

She deliberately tried to spoil her reckless momentum with her husband's name. "We used to go out a lot, Andrew and I." It didn't work, but she persevered. "Every weekend we would either go to a friend's place or they would come to ours. We never had big parties, only two or three other couples, but," she embellished, "as they say, we always danced the night away. They were usually clients of Andrew's, or people he met through his work."

"I bet you had lots of fun," Ray said blandly, looking at her without judgement, and then looked away again. He concentrated on the pannikin and the rum bottle, uncomfortable with her story. It's only the grog talking, he assured himself. She needs to talk it out, but that is as far as I'll go.

"We always had fun," Wendy struggled on. "With lots of friends it is hard not to have fun. If I ever felt depressed I would buy some new clothes or go out to dinner, or to a movie, or to a show. There were always so many things to do. Andrew always used to say he would have to take on an extra job if the Government stopped him claiming me as an entertainment deduction on his tax." She laughed fiercely. "Most of my old clothes are no good up here because there is nowhere to go," she finished savagely. "I've got work clothes on order, but they seem to take forever to arrive."

"You must be lonely now, living here virtually by yourself."

"I'm not lonely," she tautly denied. "I get letters and I can ring up on the radio and talk to people."

"Trouble is…" he paused, feeling the rum begin to talk for him. "Trouble is so many of our friendships rely on the little bits of life. Without the little things to bind us then so many friendships disappear."

You often spoil things, don't you? she repeated silently as she heard herself lie to him and herself. "I'm still very good friends with all the people I used to know down South," she pouted with defiance to cover the loss.

Embarrassed, he paused, unsure of how to retreat. He hoped she hadn't misinterpreted his concern and they let the silence linger.

At sixteen, she reflected, I was a pretty young girl, looking older than my years. God knows it gave me an easy way out of the backstreets, but I wasn't prepared to go down that path. Some of my friends did and after their initial charms were exhausted, they were literally cast on the kerbside in the back lanes of the city.

She was too smart and determined for that life. Instead she learned to add some flirting charm, inveigling and deftly managing a small parade of older men and tutors who indulged her whims, enabling her to complete her studies. She then cast a wider lure designed to permanently drag her away from the squalid stench of poverty.

Andrew was a good and calculated catch, and in time she grew to genuinely like him, but not enough to turn the facade of love into something real. Nestled in a bed of security only money can buy, she wallowed in the luxury of boredom and ran with the sociable green causes of the day which now, to her surprise, on Punkatoy, somehow seemed more real.

His death had revealed a pit of debt which diluted the impact of grief, leaving only fragile shards of the relationship.

"I've gotta be going soon," he warned, breaking her chain of memory. "I'll finish this rum, then head off down the track."

"Stay the night," she heard herself ask. Committed, she leant forward, heart pounding loud in her temples. Reaching across, she laid her arm along his, searching for his hand to restrain him, tentatively reaching for his clean-shaven cheeks. "Please," she implored. He didn't move.

He's like a frightened animal, she realised. I can see his muscles twitching just like the young colts in the horse yard. I want him to love me.

"Please, Ray." Her voice became a husky whisper. "I'm so lonely. Please, just to have somebody in the house for tonight. There is a spare bed," she ended lamely, knowing full well he knew she never intended he should use it.

He looked at the space between them, trapped and uncomfortable. She leant closer, ready to brush his lips with her own. She felt her nipples harden against the fabric of her shirt and already she imagined him naked in her arms.

Ray turned away. Picking up the pannikin, he drank the remaining rum. He put it down firmly. "Don't take it personally, Wendy, but you don't need me. It's only the grog. You have more than enough guts to make it by yourself," he murmured gently, talking as he would to a frightened horse in the yards.

"You conceited shit," she snarled, turning on him. Her building emotions gave her the strength to match his rejection with her own. She buttoned the top of her shirt. "You've got a cheek. You're welcome to stay if you wish. I only thought it might save you the long drive back to your camp."

"Which reminds me," she snapped, smoothly switching to a cool business-like manner, relieved to be able to change the subject and leave her foolishness behind. "When do you think you'll be finished?"

Unruffled by her outburst he replied, "A couple of days."

He's just ignored me. She was stunned. He hasn't even changed the way he speaks. He's not a bit sorry, and just as she hated him for it, she was drawn to the strength she saw there.

"It's absolutely vital the job is finished on time," she continued coldly. "The ringers are out there now building the yards. I've got the choppers booked for the end of the week,' she smoothly lied. 'We'll be ready to truck cattle in a fortnight. We can't truck them without the road you're putting in. We're relying on you to get the job done on time. Believe me, there'll be hell to pay if it's not," she threatened.

"Why take the wild scrub cattle? Wouldn't it be easier to take some of the cattle closer to the station?" he interrupted, trying to calm her down with the diversion.

"They're breeding stock," she asserted with apparent knowledge.

"I see," he agreed, knowing they were not. "How many cattle do you think you'll get out of the wild country?" he quietly persisted.

"They estimate about a thousand head," she told him crisply, repeating her husband's optimistic prediction.

"I doubt you'll get enough to pay your costs, let alone the bills you got in today," he stated simply.

"You will get paid, don't worry!" she snapped, startled by what she really suspected was an accurate estimate. "Everybody will get paid. The bank, the companies, the fuel distributors, the ringers and the stock agents. Money is not a problem," she asserted, the rum adding to her defiance as she wished it were true.

Ray nodded slowly in apparent agreement but without conviction.

You know I'm lying, she understood dumbfounded. But you don't care, or you don't worry. I wish I knew which. "Actually you're right. Money is a problem," she conceded boldly, wanting to pierce his equability and make him react.

Ray nodded, accepting what he already knew to be true.

He understands. He knew all along, but he doesn't condemn me. Why? she wondered in astonishment. All Andrew's friends have stopped writing. Only my old friends who haven't caught up with the situation keep on writing. All I get is bills and more bills. The bank is screaming for money and I just haven't got it. It's never-ending, just like home when I was a kid. I personally owe you several thousand dollars, and yet you don't say a thing. Why? she agonised silently as the rum's false courage seeped away.

Ray stopped nodding, his decision made. He looked directly at Wendy.

"I'll have the road finished in time."

"But I can't pay you," she insisted.

"Yair, that's true. I guessed it soon after I started the job."

"Well, why keep going?" she asked in disbelief.

"Got no other work on at the moment," he lied, scoffing at her concern. "May as well keep on working. If I start taking 'sit down' money in the Dry season then I might lose the habit of working altogether."

"But I can't pay you," she repeated, trying to make him understand.

"Look, Wendy," he explained kindly, "You're taking a gamble on these cattle. You might win. If you do then you'll probably pay me." She missed his wry smile.

"I'll definitely pay you."

"As I said, you'll probably pay me. But one thing is certain, you can't take the gamble if the road is not finished. You take a risk," he shrugged, "I take a risk. In this country we all take risks and usually people help you out in the long run. I mean, if nothing else, I can always cut the job payment out in killers."

Wendy was perplexed and a frown wrinkled the skin around her eyes.

"Killers." He continued. "You know, shoot a few cattle for beef. It doesn't really cost you anything if they're unbranded clean skins and it saves me money on rations."

"Yes, I understand, but ... why would you do this for me?"

"Why not?" he countered. "You're going through a pretty rough patch at the moment. It would be a mean bastard who wouldn't give a hand."

"But I can't give you anything in return."

He shrugged.

Determined to give him something, she stood up and leaning down, kissed him full on the mouth. He broke away, but she held his neck in her hands.

"Hey! Don't get too carried away," he protested. "I'd better be going, and don't ask me to stay, because I won't. Thanks for the rum."

He upended the bottle and drained the last drops from the bottom. "Told you to throw the cap away," he laughed and walked out the door into the night.

Chapter 10

WENDY WATCHED THE TOYOTA LIGHTS DISAPPEAR, gobbled up by the fantastic shapes of briefly illuminated trees and dark shadows. The rum made the kitchen lights seem harshly bright. She flicked the generator switch on the wall and heard the engine die. Fumbling for the remains of her glass of rum and Coke in the darkness, she walked unsteadily through the door and sank into one of the low chairs that had looked so pretty in Melbourne but were now so incongruous in the lean-to patio with its dusty floor to ceiling louvers and tattered flywire.

Her eyes sorted through the jumbled shapes of the garden in the starlight while her mind assembled a kaleidoscope of memories.

Punkatoy, she snorted. More like purgatory. Coming to this place was an unwelcome obligation. Now Andrew's sudden death had revealed a previously unknown level of debt, there was no way she could go back with head held high.

"How could you?" she snarled softly, fingernails biting into her palms. Unbidden tears threatened to form, whether for his loss, or his deceit, she was uncertain. Teeth clenched and gritted, she shook off the maudlin memory. There was only another hard path, forward.

She drank the last of the rum and Coke, revisiting the final time she had seen her husband. All four of them were standing around the new Landcruiser station wagon. She had decided to stay at the homestead while he took the other two investment partners on an inspection of the four thousand square kilometre property.

She was part of the scene and aloof from it. It was early morning, the remnant skirls of mist sneaking through the treetops. Wendy saw Andrew look briefly over his shoulder as they drove off. Her glimpse of his head and shoulders was the last she had seen of him and the others. She did not stretch to an imagination of the crash.

She remembered overhearing one of the police describing the accident. 'Lost it in the gravel on the bend and rolled. No chance for the poor buggers.'

"Poor bugger," she dully heard again behind her headache. She opened her eyes, squinted, and closed them again. The lounge chair she was slouched in was uncomfortable after the long night. The glass on the floor was sticky with rum and Coke, ants busy around its rim.

"Poor bugger. She be asleep."

Morning had broken and some of the wives and girls from the ringers' camp were outside the screen door looking for the weekly ration handout. They giggled as they debated if they should knock again.

"Hold on," Wendy croaked and felt the nausea hit. "I'm coming," she whispered as she staggered to the bathroom.

Chapter 11

1985, JUNE, MID-DRY SEASON.

"ANY OF YOU BLOKES SEEN CHARLIE around?" Nelson demanded, walking into the workshop.

The two ringers repairing a tyre stopped. Two old battered Toyota pickups were parked-up on jacks on the oil stained concrete. One just needed better tyres. The other they had towed back after Nelson had broken the gear housing. It required more advanced mechanical work. The best of its tyres went to the other Landcruiser. Cannibalising vehicles to keep others in service was an endless task.

"Well, don't just stand there. Have you seen Charlie?"

Douglas, just a few weeks returned from his latest time in jail and still surly, ignored the question.

"No, boss," Victor Giblet answered, his arms as thin as the tyre lever he was leaning on.

"I thought he was here," Nelson accused.

"Yair, he was, but he be go over that way." Victor pointed with his lips and a lift of his head.

"Thanks. Make sure you get those tyres changed over and repaired. I want to use the Toyota later today."

The two ringers made no acknowledgment, but Nelson knew they understood. The vehicle would be ready, but it would be late in the day. He was about to move when he spotted Charlie coming across the broad poorly gravelled yard from the generator shed. As he waited, he unconsciously put his hands on his hips, arms akimbo. He caught the disapproving glance passing between Victor and Douglas. Their mobile faces talked without the need for words.

Bugger them, he thought. I'll stand like a whitefella boss if I want to. I'm the boss now. He concentrated on staring stonily ahead. Next they'll be saying, 'You too good for us, Nelson,' just like the times he had been pulled into line by his own people.

Even when, under the Welfare Ordinance Law, he had been forcibly separated from his mother as a child for his own protection and sent to Darwin, he still mixed with other Aboriginal children. The law of the time could not prevent the attention of relatives and cousins. It tried, but did not break the ancient bonds of kinship and skin.

I was bloody good with a slingshot, he recalled proudly as he watched Charlie's languid progress. I could pick off a bird from a good long distance. I used to boast about it a bit and all the other kids would never believe me, even though they had seen me do it. They always used to say, 'You lie, Nelson.' I showed them one day. I stoned Mister Wilson's pet galah when everybody said I couldn't hit it over the distance.

It had been a delicious way to get back at the white teacher who subjected them all to such daily humiliation. But it had all backfired.

The kids hated me because I had shown I was better than them. 'You too flash for us Nelson.' They only started talking to me again after I deliberately missed a few easy shots. He sighed at the memory. I was still in trouble with the Old People, he recalled.

The Old People's disapproval of the wanton killing of the galah had filtered back to him. Before then he had only ever killed for food. Killing for fun was balanda way, a foreign way. Not for the first time he glimpsed an inkling of the sort of life he had been born into, and taken away from.

Couldn't make it with the whitefellas either, he grumbled as he watched Charlie saunter into the workshop. The kids were still saying, 'You lie, Nelson.' So I let Mister Wilson find out it was me. When he canned me in front of the class they all knew it was me but then they called me 'Flash Nelson.'

Just like a white boss, he beckoned Charlie over with his finger, and instantly regretted it. He relaxed, and met Charlie halfway across the open floor.

"You come out with me today. We have to pick up a bit of gear from those new yards at the top end of Buffalo Yard."

Charlie's eyes widened with fright.

"Yair. That's right," Nelson reminded him harshly. "Remember what I say last time?"

Charlie nodded vigorously, believing Nelson's death threat was no idle talk.

"Could be away a while, so throw in your swag and mine. Get mine from my room here after you come back from the camp," he ordered. "Grab some corn beef from the camp while you're there. We'll take this Toyota when the wheels have been swapped over."

"You take Victor or Douglas, boss. Victor been want to go bush a long time. Take that cheeky fella Douglas. He been in jail many time. He always fighting, so take him bush, settle him down. I don't want to go bush. I stay out of trouble here. I sit down here with my wife."

"If I wanted Victor or Douglas, I would have told them. I want you!" he hissed. "So just make sure you have got all the gear ready by smoko. Grab a tarp as well," he added as an afterthought, wishing to avoid suspicion about the load they would pick up from the plane wreck.

Charlie padded off reluctantly, his bare feet sliding across the ground. The trouser cuffs were frayed from dragging on the ground now he was without his boots, unable to replace the ones he left behind the day he and Nelson walked back from the crashed plane. He anxiously jammed his tall crown hat further onto his head.

"Come on, boys. I want the best tyres off that busted Toyota and onto this one by the time Charlie comes back with the gear," Nelson ordered.

The two ringers squatting flat on their feet with elbows resting on their knees stood up slowly. Later they would talk about Nelson's whitefella way. As they gossiped around the campfire in the ringers' camps away from the station the story would grow as all stories do in the bush. A man's reputation preceded him, and Nelson's was building fast.

"You want me go out with you?" Victor offered.

Nelson knew he couldn't trust anyone else with the secret of the gold. He was hoping he could trust Charlie, but he cautiously backed his trust with frequent reminders of what would happen if Charlie breathed a word to anybody. Charlie had rarely been separated from Nelson since they got back.

"No. Charlie's a good man."

"He be sick, you know, boss. It bite him here," and Victor pointed to his flat stomach. "Maybe someone sing him," he grinned.

"He only gammon sick," Nelson countered. "He's feeling lazy. He don't like walking. He be OK when we get out bush again."

Victor shrugged, accepting Nelson's decision, turned to help Douglas change the tyre.

Chapter 12

CHARLIE SULKED SILENTLY AS THEY DROVE out in the afternoon heat towards the new camp beyond Buffalo Yards, the roughly graded station road soon reduced to well-worn wheel tracks twisting around rocky outcrops and between the ever-present grey woollybutt trees and the low scraggles of quinine bush. Twice he asked Nelson to stop, and he had disappeared into the scrub with a roll of toilet paper taken from under the front seat. He offered no explanation, and Nelson recognised the grip of fear he held over the man. He was pleased.

Later it was hard slow driving, picking a way cautiously over the broken ground and patches of sand grasping at the tyres. By nightfall Nelson was tired from the concentration required to safely negotiate the washouts, the holes filled with bulldust, the sharp flints threatening to slice tyres and the never-ending tussle against the bucking steering wheel. They made it as far as the edge of the rough broken country escarpment which concealed the crashed aircraft.

It was difficult work threading the Toyota through the spindly wattle scrub running along the base of the light grey and white rockface. Cluttered layers of slab-sided boulders rose steeply, concealing half-hidden caves and chasms snaking deep into the mother rock. The uncomfortable sullen silence smothered any echoes of the grinding transmission. Fading daylight and the inevitable lapse in concentration resulted in a puncture from a fire-hardened stake of wattle.

"Bugger it! We camp here. You change the tyre and I get the billy on."

Without a word of protest or acknowledgement, Charlie resigned himself to the job. Moving sluggishly he found the jack and took it to the rear of the pickup. He put it down and walked around to the other side of the tray, making a separate slow trip for each item he needed. The billy boiled well before Charlie had the vehicle lifted off the ground. The job finally finished, he abandoned the tools in the dust.

Nelson, meal finished before Charlie had the wheel nuts undone, half-dozed by the fire. Tyre changed, Charlie shuffled to the camp, wide feet dirty with dust. He lifted his swag from the tray and threw it on the ground some distance from Nelson. Wordlessly he wiped his hands on his trousers, slowly cut wide slices from the chunk of cold corned beef, filled his pannikin with warm black tea and leaned back against his rolled swag. He ate and drank in silence, watching the stars emerge and the pale white rock-face beyond the firelight, grateful Nelson didn't want to talk.

Please be quiet, Charlie pleaded silently. I don't like your talk. Last time we out here, you be go mad. That cheeky talk get us both in jail. He looked nervously towards Nelson, resentful of the disruption he was causing to the comfortable co-existence of the stock camp, the station and obligations to country. I wish I had told Ina. I tell her when I get back, he promised himself, and immediately felt his heart miss a beat as he thought of his wife and children back at the ringers' camp. No I won't, he hastily corrected. If Nelson find out he kill me.

He slowly unrolled his swag by the fire, and risking one glance of hatred and fear at Nelson, he went to sleep on the ground. The once-thick canvas swag wrap was worn thin with age and he struggled to keep his chest warm while the fire warmed his back.

He was nearly asleep when he became vaguely aware of Nelson moving. He tensed in the uncompanionable silence, but Nelson was only getting into his swag on the other side of the fire which was now a bed of glowing coals.

Charlie lay unmoving and watched the stars, bright in the clear black sky, their light ghosting off the pale boulders and casting deep shadows in the fissures. The escarpment hunkered down, drawing shadows around the secret ceremony places deep in the nearby cliffs. He shuddered as a curlew shrieked a desperate wail of the dead. The pale rock walls and cliffs answered back, magnifying his dread and desperation.

Chapter 13

CHARLIE WOKE INSTANTLY WHEN NELSON LIGHTLY kicked his ribs. The billy was boiling and the tangy blue smoke was a familiar camp smell that started every day. The beauty of the dark silhouettes cast by the awakening dawn were lost on him when he remembered the reason for this trip. Sullenly, he got up, wiped the sleep from his eyes and, pinching one nostril, blew snot onto the ground.

A dingo howled softly in the distance, its call echoing along the escarpment. Two other dogs answered, setting the birds twittering through the spindly wattle. He wriggled his toes and decided he still didn't miss his boots. Straightening his sleep-tossed shirt, he put his hat on before silently rolling his swag ready for the morning's work. Nelson pointed soundlessly to the billy and pannikin. Charlie clasped the warm tea gratefully. The flush of dawn turned salmon pink then orange but the sight of the breaking dawn passed them by.

"You walk in front. You remember where to go." Nelson directed after a time, while he sipped his tea. Charlie nodded dumbly. A black and white willy wagtail, always a teller of tales and a harbinger of mischief, darted and chattered over their heads. He looked at it anxiously and knew only trouble would come from this place.

"I'm relying on you to pick the best way in. I want to get the Toyota right up close. It'll save us having to carry the boxes too far."

There was no escape, and Charlie let the information sink leadenly into his already sickening gut. Nelson stood and splashed the dregs of his tea into the fire. Then, strangely, he kicked dirt over the camp fire.

"Can't take any risks," he snapped in reply to Charlie's unspoken question. "It would be great, wouldn't it? This plane has been there ever since it crashed. A bloody great bushfire is just what we need now. You just make sure you put those cigarette butts out every time today. You're living on borrowed time, boy. One mistake like that and you dead man," he threatened needlessly.

Charlie threw his swag onto the tray and without looking back, started his slow walk toward the crash site, pondering on how he might thwart Nelson's plans. Fear and resentment dulled his thinking and for hours all he heard was the white noise of the roaring pickup behind him, grinding along in low gear. Picking his way through the broken rock and needle-pointed spinifex clumps, the country embraced his daze, numbing all thoughts until Nelson smashed him across the shoulders.

"You useless blackfella," he ranted. "I've got a flat tyre a hundred metres back, and all you can do is walk on. Didn't you hear me shouting?"

Charlie looked at the ground, ran his hand across his thick grey stubble and studied his gnarled feet grey with dust. There was no point in getting angry or hitting back. It wouldn't change the future. He knew he wouldn't live to see another Wet season. His fate unfurled with the discovery of the plane crash. It was settled when he had decided to remain silent and stay at the station instead of shifting camp into the tiny settlement two hundred kilometres away on the broad river flats. Pungkuthuyi was his country and he knew he would die in its embrace. Confronted and comforted with this inarticulate wish, he stoically accepted the consequences.

"Go back and start changing it," Nelson instructed brusquely. "We must be close to the crash, so I'll take a look-see ahead."

Charlie did as he was told, and Nelson stalked off into the thickening timber. By the time he returned, Charlie had changed the wheel. With two flats, they had no spare left.

"You go and follow my track," Nelson shouted eagerly as he jumped into the cabin. "You can't miss it, not with eyes like yours. You're one of the best trackers I know."

Charlie didn't acknowledge the easy insincerity. He easily picked up the track and only stopped when he reached the aircraft.

Nelson drove the Toyota as close as he could to the open cargo door. Everything he had hoped for was within reach so Charlie's sullen assistance irritated him.

"I'll tell you something, boy," he growled insultingly, getting out of the Toyota. "I haven't done anything to you yet. You're walking around like some old fella been singing you. Well, you're not going to die just yet, but you will if you let anybody know about this. I don't need a kaditcha man to sing you. I'll do it all by myself!" he threatened. "Until then, you work when I say so."

The threat of a malign spell cast by, what others called a witch doctor, shook Charlie deeper into lethargy. Charlie shifted uneasily, his feet working patterns in the sandy ground. He spoke for the first time since the sunrise.

"I reckon someone be sing me already. I seen men who been die when they be sung. My guts feel that same way."

"That rubbish talk. The only thing going to kill you is a bullet or the grog. Do as I say, and it'll be the grog, unless that missus of yours hits you proper hard one day." Nelson laughed grimly, worried he might have gone too far. Charlie shrugged dejectedly and looked away to the once-flat layers of tan rock now tilted to one side and thrust upwards, great slabs hemming the horizon.

Nelson ignored Charlie. He wanted to surrender to the urge to immediately rip the tops off the boxes to confirm the gold was still there. Last time they had opened them all. Several of the boxes contained once crisp, but now disintegrating banknotes as well as gold. Only the small ingots of gold, stamped with the Netherlands Bank of East Indies seal, had any value. The seven boxes were a wealth beyond dreaming just a few metres away. He wanted to fling the lids back, but he still needed Charlie.

"Listen here, Charlie, this is the opportunity we have always waited for. I've organised to sell the gold. You know what that means?" He didn't wait for Charlie's answer. "It means we can buy this station. We can buy back this country of ours. This is sand goanna dreaming. You belong to pungkuthuyi dreaming. It is your dreaming and my dreaming."

"We can never get it back any other way," he emphasised. "The Land Rights Act won't let us put a claim on here because it is a working station. If it was vacant Crown Land, or if it was unused because the station went broke and no other whitefella wanted it, then we could claim it. Even then it would take years. That claim in Katherine took nearly ten years to go through. With this gold we can buy this country!"

"Just imagine all this country is ours again. No more white bosses. No more whitefellas. Just us. The gold is our freedom. We buy the station outright, then turn it into Aboriginal land forever."

"And Charlie," he dropped his voice enticingly. "There is enough here to keep us for a long time. We can live traditional way. Anything else we need, we have the money to buy it."

He swept his hand toward the boxes. "Here is our freedom. What you think, Charlie? It's the only way, hey?"

Wanting to avoid Nelson's whipping tongue, Charlie agreed. "It good idea, boss," he answered blandly. Decades of subservient co-existence meant his voice gave no hint of his disagreement, but he was terrified, his deepest fears confirmed. This was not their gold and jail was the inevitable outcome no matter what Nelson said.

Nelson breathed a silent sigh of relief because Charlie didn't see the real problem which came from how to dispose of the gold. We can never buy this station because they would ask where the money came from. If they knew, then the Dutch Government would ask for it back. There is only one way we can win. He pushed on with Charlie's deception.

"All we have to do is take these boxes down to the mouth of Corella Creek not far from the crabbers' camp."

A family of Vietnamese had been camped on the creek for several weeks, working the mudflats for the prized large mud crabs. Fleeing from war-torn Vietnam, the older generation had drifted into the thriving mud-crab and fishing trade, working the remote Gulf rivers, far from the reach of law and regulation. It grew into a family business, operating from rough temporary and secretive camps hidden in the mangroves. Nelson had gone to them and reached an agreement for the illegal sale of the gold at what he suspected was a very deep discount to the current price.

"Why give him to Chinese men?" Charlie asked, suddenly perplexed, the thoughts of danger thrust temporarily to one side. "Shouldn't we put him in the bank in Katherine?"

"Too far and too heavy to take to Katherine," Nelson improvised glibly. "Better to take it down to the coast. We send the gold by boat to the bank in Darwin. The important thing is we will get our money," he lied.

You gammon, Charlie thought, recognising the lie. I want to finish with you so I can sit down with my wife and family like we always have. Trouble, he be come, he worried and then fearfully nodded his head in acceptance as he felt Nelson watching him.

"That good, boss," he managed and Nelson knew it was a lie.

"Come on," Nelson snapped. "Load these boxes. It's a long trip to the Corella mouth on the coast. We avoid the station and go through Goose Hole."

Reluctantly and slowly, Charlie reached for the first box oblivious to the imperious sand goanna resting in the darkness of the aluminium carcass.

Chapter 14

THE HEAVILY LADEN TOYOTA PICKUP WAS light on the steering with all the weight over the back axle. The rear tyres, flattened under the bullion, flopped and squelched along the rough track. Nelson was acutely aware of the extra area they presented to stakes and sharp rocks so he carefully picked his way along the barest suggestion of a track. It was a difficult trip from the crash site, but once hidden near the river, it would be easy to transfer the gold in the future.

Charlie was sullenly silent and Nelson saw him flick another cigarette butt carelessly out the window.

"If you can't stop throwing those butts out, then you'll have to stop smoking," he snarled. "Give me your tobacco tin and papers." He held out his hand.

Charlie looked at him absently. "I forget. I promise I not do it again, boss."

"Yair. You bloody forget a lot today. You forget to talk. Before too long I might forget to keep you alive."

Charlie said nothing, slouching a little deeper into the corner between the seat and the door.

"Can't you understand? This gives us freedom," Nelson remonstrated.

The track bent around the base of a rocky escarpment. Wallabies bounded up the steep face and paused to look down on the slow moving Toyota. Nelson veered off the already ill-defined track and carefully followed wallaby tracks on a new path weaving between the trees and towering grey termite mounds.

Trees grew more densely as they approached the river. Tall dark-trunked bloodwoods fought for space alongside mighty paperbarks and thriving white ghost gums. Green mangroves huddled on the river bank beyond. The tracks of wallaby and cattle wound through the scrub and towards watering points on the river's edge.

A sand goanna darted back towards the distant escarpment, running towards them for a moment. It stopped, standing up on its hind legs to get a better view of the disturbance. It waved its head from side to side, then dropped to the ground. Nelson followed its hidden progress through the rippling grass. It is meant to be, he told himself approvingly.

He stopped the vehicle suddenly as the ground dropped away beneath them. High on the bank, the river moved in a slow arc below them. A steep faint wallaby track struggled down to a narrow rocky shelf which plunged into the clear deep water. Scraggly bushes bunched near the base of the pea gravel clay and beside a solitary purple rock jutting onto the shelf. He switched the motor off and, sitting quietly, watched carefully. Charlie cowered in the corner.

The wide river flowed sluggishly in the slack tide. Mosquitoes, attracted to their sweat, began to whine annoyingly. Nelson scanned the deep shadows cast by the mangroves lining the opposite bank. Nothing moved in the water between the smooth plates of pitted rock on one side and the curve of the creek on the far bank. He shifted his search to the opposite bank of the narrow river. In the fringes of the shadow he saw the big old crocodile he was searching for. He tapped Charlie on the shoulder, and felt him jerk away at the contact.

"See that old croc over there?" he asked.

Charlie followed Nelson's gaze and picked out the slumbering reptile, dark slatey grey beneath the shadows. "Him fella a big bugger."

"Him big fella alright. At least we know where he is. Sometimes he camps over this side of the creek. Watch him while we work," he directed, knowing he would sometimes have to rely on Charlie for any warning if the croc moved. Perhaps it was his sand goanna singing, so as a land creature, his fear of the amphibious reptile was instinctive.

"Don't worry, boss. If he move I be gone before he hit the water," Charlie affirmed with newfound vigour.

"Get this stuff unloaded proper quick. I want to camp back on the main track tonight well away from here. Let's get into it."

Charlie jumped out quickly, eager to finish the distasteful job so he could return home. Together they carried and stacked the boxes by the jutting purple rock. It was hot work made hotter as the mangroves trapped the heat and the sounds.

"Whoa back there, Charlie," Nelson gasped as the sixth box was stacked neatly on top of the others. "Take a blow for a minute." He leant back against the boxes and began to roll a cigarette. Charlie sat under a scraggly bush, as far from the water as possible and watched the crocodile on the other bank. Clutching his knees to his chest, the nausea of fear lay bitter in his stomach. Nelson also moved back from the water's edge.

"He must be a grandfather," he suggested to Charlie, who nodded miserably. "I reckon he more than four metres long. You look at the slide mark just over there.' He pointed to the pale mud on the rock shelf, dry and cracked under the sweltering sun. "It's wider than these boxes."

Charlie pulled up his trouser leg and rubbed the roughened skin. He picked absently at an old scab while he looked with no interest at the cut which had turned ulcerous overnight. It was sore, but not painful enough to stop him working. With trepidation he wondered if it was the beginning of his singing sickness.

"I reckon the old bugger comes up here in the morning and sleeps beside this rock," Nelson commented again, determined to keep Charlie bound with fear.

Charlie stopped picking at his leg and his eyes flashed around. The dry mud and broken grass clearly proved Nelson right. He watched the croc again, making sure it had not moved.

"Don't worry, he not come over here now," Nelson smirked, enjoying Charlie's fear. "He is good protection for the gold. He a good watchdog." Nelson laughed harshly.

"We not camp here tonight. Hey?" Charlie pleaded.

"No. I want to camp on the main track tonight."

"But I thought we wait for boat to come?"

"What for?"

"To collect that gold. You say him be go Darwin by boat. We can't just leave him here. Shouldn't we wait for that boat?"

"It's not due for a couple of days. I'll come back when it's due in. Until then nobody is going to take this lot with old grandfather living here." He flicked his cigarette butt carefully into the water.

"Back to work," he commanded.

Charlie didn't move when Nelson walked back to the Toyota. Nelson was lying again, this time more obvious than before. I in biggest mobs of trouble. I a dead man for sure. I must tell Ina when I get back to camp. I must tell her so we can stop this cheeky business, Charlie decided.

"Come on," Nelson shouted angrily, dragging the last box to the edge of the pickup's tray.

"You lie," Charlie said quietly, firm in his conviction.

"What?"

"You lie, boss. I know you sell him gold and keep him all for yourself. When you get caught you be in biggest mobs of trouble. You make one big sorry camp from this. This all wrong way."

Nelson strode over, grabbed Charlie by his shirt front and pulled him to his feet. Pushing him against the rough clay of the river bank, he drew one hand back, his fist already bunched. Charlie twisted but Nelson held him firmly.

Suddenly Nelson shook him with rage, smashing Charlie's head against the yellow pebbled-studded clay and opening a gash.

"You're the one in mobs of trouble," he shouted. "I have sold this gold," he admitted, "but all of us mob are going to benefit. You're right, it isn't going to Darwin, but don't let it worry you."

"You want to be croc tucker?" Nelson swung Charlie around. "Have a look," Nelson yelled wildly. He twisted Charlie's shoulder and pointed to the water. "The croc's gone. He's down there just waiting to take you. He smell your blood already. What should I do? Should I leave you here, or should I let you go back to camp?"

Charlie struggled, frantically searching the still water. He imagined the croc lying on the muddy bottom watching him, its glassy cold brown eyes piercing the dark water. He tried to back away, but Nelson held him.

"Well?" Nelson demanded, his voice low and harsh.

"I be say nothing," Charlie blurted.

"Not good enough," Nelson whispered, fighting the urge to throw Charlie into the water. Too many questions would be asked in the ringers' camp if Charlie suddenly disappeared without explanation. He silently cursed his need to keep Charlie alive to complete his plans. He pulled Charlie closer.

"You tell them in the camp we been chasing scrubbers..." He screwed his eyes until they became ugly slits.

"No." He furiously changed his mind because chasing bush cattle meant bringing fresh meat into the camp and they had none. "Tell them we broke down. That's why it took so long to get back. If I hear a whisper of what has happened here then I will feed you to this crocodile. Understand?" he finished, his voice vicious in its threat.

"Yes, boss."

Charlie staggered to the ground as Nelson shoved him towards the Toyota. He ignored the cut on his head, the bloody matted hair attracting tiny flies and midges as they finished unloading.

He sat miserably beside the pickup while Nelson wrapped the tarp over the six boxes, hiding them from all but close inspection. The old crocodile, which Charlie hoped would rise from the water and take Nelson as he worked, did not appear.

Despite his fear, he was determined to tell his wife. His aching guts rebelled against his complicity in Nelson's lies and told him he had been sung.

Chapter 15

A RIPPLE OF FEAR, AS SUBTLE as the fuzzy feather footprints Victor claimed to have seen, had the ringers sulking in the workshop, pretending to work. Conversation stopped as Nelson stepped into the shed. They know something about the gold, Nelson fumed. None of the ringers seemed to be around when he wanted them. They hid away in the corner of the store room, or tinkered with equipment well out of his sight. They lurked in the most distant corners of the work yard. Preparations for the next muster had slowed to a standstill.

The ringers faded into the gathering darkness instead of standing around joking as they usually did at the end of the workday. In ones and twos, they skulked off as the day drew to a close. Douglas, as always, surly and quick to take offence, seemed coiled for a fight. Victor scuffed through the dust with Charlie following morosely. Conversations muted, they deserted the workshop, leaving a waft of tobacco smoke.

Watching the sun sink rapidly behind the tree line and the sharp escarpments beyond, Nelson irritably kicked at a tyre on one of the Toyotas. The wheel wobbled when he booted it. Kneeling, he wrenched it with his hands, and the wheel shook easily. The wheel nuts were only finger tight.

"Nothing is done properly," he cursed. "Every job over the last few days has been the same. It's either not done, or done so badly that it has to be done again. I'll fix the bastards. They'll learn some respect!" he hissed. He stormed from the now deserted workshop.

Nelson made for his quarters, thinking about what he needed to do. The tiny single room was his alone – a coveted reward and escape from the communal and overcrowded ringers' camp. He took pride in keeping it clean, making sure each day the bed was made, the old brown woollen army blanket straightened and folded. Although roughly repaired, screens kept the flies and mosquitoes at bay and the gas cooker left no smell.

He pulled up the steel-framed chair, leaned back against the tin wall, slowly rolled a cigarette and considered the problem in the camp. No matter how he looked at it, Charlie was at the centre of the discontent. Cut him out just like the stallion they had chased weeks earlier, and the rest will follow. Decision finally taken, he stood up and made for the ringers' camp, built well beyond the boundaries of the work yard.

The ringers welcomed the smoky tang of campfires drifting in the sluggish evening breeze, driving all but the most persistent flies and mosquitoes away. It was too early to start cooking, so the men had gathered round the campfires to talk and whisper urgently amongst themselves. There were good bosses and bad bosses, crooked bosses and incompetent bosses, and bosses you walked away from. What sort of boss was Nelson? The arguments ebbed and flowed in snatched and muffled bursts.

The Aboriginal ringers' camp was well away from the Big House and the workshop, so the men felt easy in their softly heated discussion of Nelson's merits. As head stockman and acting manager, Nelson had recently moved into the white ringers' quarters near the workshop. Their quiet evening discussions never reached Nelson's ears.

Motionless outside the cluster of men, Old Harry sat cross-legged on the ground, looking obliquely into the distance, apparently disinterested in the whispers of discontent and speculation. His scraggy unkempt hair and beard, white with age and his tobacco-stained teeth gap-toothed from tribal initiation, conferred quiet authority. His black bony knobby knees rested like a pair of parliamentary maces. The muscles on his upper arms hung loose below rolled sleeves, the thick cords between shoulder and elbow clearly visible. The uppermost of his ancient initiation scarring was just visible in the neck of his faded blue-checked flannel shirt. His throat was further scarred where steel had chafed agonisingly many, many years before.

"What you say, old man?"

As softly as drifting smoke, the question floated in his direction. Without looking up, he fluttered one hand, dismissing and discarding the thread of discussion. Dismissed, the discussion took another direction, riding uncomfortably on the back of a nervous atmosphere initiated by whispered rumours of the feather-foot kaditcha man haunting the camp.

Built amongst the sweeping white trunks of the ghost gums clinging to a semi-permanent waterhole, the rough framed iron huts of the ringers' camp slumped on the barren ground. The huts were flat roofed with rusty corrugated iron. Wooden louvre slats replaced the original glass louvres, leaving the inside in the perpetual darkness favoured by furry pests and their reptilian predators. Wooden doors, destroyed in Wet Season cyclones, were replaced by bits of hessian salvaged from the mustering camps and cattle yards.

The campfire and black cast-iron camp ovens replaced broken stoves. Smoke blackened sheets of corrugated iron bent around white piles of ashes, sheltering the camp fires from the south-east winds. Grey and red dirt puffed endless dust in the Dry and sticky mud in the Wet. All slept on old wire-frame beds or on the concrete floor on rodent-nibbled foam mattresses with torn and dirty covers. In the Dry season families slept outside, the stars above and the cool breeze fanning the embers of the fire through the night.

Dogs walked about at will, fighting the children for scraps of meat, then barking and snarling amongst themselves for possession of the scraps. The skinny, often naked, children played in the dirt and made their own games around the camp, pushing toys made of twisted wire and circular tobacco tin lids. Their demands were met without question because discipline was the responsibility of grandparents who were mostly not in the camp.

Many of the children were supposed to attend school, but correspondence lessons were hard to teach when they had to compete with the tramp of cattle and the clink of bridles. The older children drifted between staying with relatives in town two hundred kilometres away and the station camp when school and town fighting got too much for them.

Six other ringers worked with Charlie, Victor and Douglas on the station. It was a young man's game, but even so there were enough wives and children and extended family to make the competition for space in the camp a daily battle. The station killed meat for the men and their families, and they in turn shared with their older relatives who stayed with them. They supplemented the station's rations with bush tucker, more by choice than by any need forced by shortage of food. Few preferred beef when the aromatic tang of wallaby cooking on the coals drifted through the camp.

The men sat and smoked and argued quietly while the children played, the dogs fought and the women started preparing the meals. The low murmur of voices stopped when Nelson walked uninvited into the firelight.

"You fellas talking about me," he challenged. "Well, you get those other blokes and bring him all up here. We all talk together."

Making no acknowledgement, Old Harry pursed his lips, silently signalling one of the young boys. The boy ran off and slowly the other men drifted over in answer to Old Harry's summons. Bare feet scuffed the ground while others walked reluctantly in high-heeled riding boots scuffed colourless with years of use. They sat or stood around. The women and children gathered as well, as they were entitled to, sitting outside the circle of men. The dogs sensed the meeting and joined, sometimes tussled by human friends, but never cursed.

"I don't know what Charlie has been telling you," Nelson growled, feet apart and hands on his hips. The fire was between him and the assembled camp. "You tell me first. Hey?" he challenged.

Covert glances were exchanged but most avoided his stare with downcast eyes. Only Old Harry refused to look away, his decision for the camp made days earlier.

"Well, chilpu?" Nelson asked addressing Old Harry by his respectful tribal title. "You tell me."

Old Harry turned his hands up, pale palms outwards and Nelson saw the almost imperceptible shake of his head. It is not the way to ask, he told Nelson without speaking a word. The others waited silently on the clash of wills.

Nelson shrugged, insolent in obedience, and squatted on his haunches. If it had been traditional men's business, the women and children would have been sent away. Their presence told him he had to convince the entire camp.

He waited as tradition told him he was supposed to. When Old Harry pursed his lips and languidly lifted his right hand in benediction, Nelson began, speaking softly and even the dogs quieted.

"We have a chance to buy back this land of ours. This land always been our land. This is pungkuthuyi dreaming. These hills, these waterholes, this country, it is all our country. It my singing and yours. Them whitefellas stole this land from us. We have lost the old ways because the whitefella forced us from our land."

He saw Old Harry nod his head slowly in agreement and thought he was on the right track. He lifted his voice.

"Our grandfathers fought for this land, but we lost the fight. They stole from us and now we can be tossed off it at any time. Tossed off our own land!"

"Until we own our land again this never change. Best way to get this land back is in whitefella way. Traditional way no good. We have to buy it."

"How can we do this?' he asked rhetorically. "I know how. I tell you secret business."

Several of the men shifted uneasily. Secrets meant trouble. Men and women could not have the same secret business. Charlie sat stolidly, confirming his fate was sealed and a life of comfortable compromise destroyed by what Nelson was about to reveal.

"Charlie and I found a plane crash from the war. There was gold in it. I have sold the gold, and soon we buy the station. Imagine that!" He gave them no time to think as he painted his own picture of success. "We will own the station. This country will be ours again forever. No whitefella could take it away from us. The gold is our freedom."

Old Harry continued to nod. Nelson took it to mean the old man agreed but he felt a wave of fear from the others.

"Why sell him fella gold to Chinese men?" The question came amongst the murmur of apprehension. Victor repeated what he had heard from Charlie, confirming Nelson's distrust.

"Because it is the best way."

"Why not put him in the bank in Katherine?"

"Because they'll want to know where the gold come from," Nelson answered brutally.

"It be no good," Victor suggested, quietly gesticulating with his bony hands and scrunching his heavy eyebrows. "That fella gold, he be stolen. When they find out, we all be in trouble. No more sit-down here. Nelson be go to jail and we'll have to find another camp and new jobs."

As soft as a midday breeze, a murmur of agreement rippled through the group. Nobody stirred or looked directly at Nelson.

"It our only chance!"

The drink-scarred voice was loudly rude, startling the conventions of quiet, serious discussion and respect.

Douglas stood up, looking at the group, insolently daring them to disagree. Rolled-up shirt sleeves wrapped tightly against his upper arms. His tall-crown pale-sandstone hat, which rarely left his head unless dislodged in a fight, was angled back, the turned down brim hiding his eyebrows. His short dark wiry beard jutted from his jaw. One hand rested lightly on the large hard metal rodeo buckle of his wide leather belt, ever a threat and a weapon when needed. As always, he was ready to fight, and Nelson was encouraged by his support.

"He be right. Buy this station then we be free. No more hand-out, no more work for white boss. We be like that Wattle Downs mob, like that Reedy River mob. They own their own stations. On this station we got cattle, and without whitefella, we got plenty bush tucker. I say Nelson right."

"You wrong," Victor challenged firmly from where he sat on the ground, his voice a quiet languid rebuke. "You been in jail already many times for fighting in Borroloola. You ugly cheeky one. What for you listen to him?" he asked, turning to the others.

"You been in jail too," Douglas reminded him, sullenly insulted to be singled out. "You all been in jail sometime because policeman don't like blackfellas."

"I been jail because I be drunk," Victor protested, his wiry body quivering with indignation. "You been go jail because you always cheeky fella. You been go jail because you spear that kumanjayi long time ago."

The others murmured, fierce in their agreement. Interrupting, Old Harry spoke quietly, the old scars on and beneath his throat rippling. Douglas sat sulkily and they all listened.

"I agree with Nelson. This our land. We can't get him back fighting like the Old People. But, like Victor say, we can't buy him back with stolen money because whitefella stop us. I think you tell the Missus at the station what you find and let Government mob make him mind up. Perhaps they reward us then."

Most of the men and women muttered their agreement guessing this was the old people's decision made long before Nelson burst into the camp with his demands. In previous days, the old people and Old Harry had sat cross-legged around the campfires and considered what Charlie had already told the camp. There was right way and wrong way. There was yolgnu way and white fella balanda way. There was Old Harry's way and young men's way.

Harry had listened patiently, and then shaking his head slightly, made a binding decision for all in the camp. Now the low babble of conversation supported Old Harry.

Defeated by decisions taken long before he arrived this evening, Nelson sat down in the dust. Only a show of force would cower the camp and then, however reluctantly, they would follow. Fear was the lever but it needed more than just Douglas and his ability with his fists. In the expectant silence, one of the scruffy dingo-yellow pups ambled over to lick his hand. He fondled its ears, the pup giving him an idea for cementing his authority.

The dogs held an important place in the camp. They were treated as people and were expected to find their own food and look after themselves. The bond between man and dog was not one of affection, but of respect for their place in the scheme of life.

Decision made, Nelson spoke crisply, playing quietly with the pup.

"You could be right. Perhaps the Government will take the gold away from us," he conceded, speaking to the group without acknowledging Old Harry.

"But perhaps it is time for us to fight for this country of ours again. The gold gives us an opportunity. Without our country, without the gold, we are nothing."

He glared at the others, daring them to look back but all chose to avert their eyes.

"I sick of being nothing!" he spat. "I say sell the gold and buy our country back. Douglas will support me and I want no opposition. It is our only chance! You must support me!"

The pup playfully tugged at his fingers and growled in mock anger. None of the assembled camp looked at him, all eyes avoiding a confrontation. Only Old Harry held his gaze until Nelson looked away.

"This your pup, Donovan?" he asked gently but with deep menace. Charlie's young son nodded his head, proud but frightened at being spoken to.

Nelson looked at the men in their worn dusty clothes, at the women in dresses faded by the sun and at the children covered in camp dirt. He found and held Charlie's reluctant gaze as he casually snapped the pup's neck. He threw the twitching pup between the fire and the ringers.

"Oooaaww!" They cried as one, recoiling, horror etched on their faces. It was as if Nelson had killed a child. Tears of absolute defeat shone on Charlie's face.

"This be our way now! My way! Nobody talks! This is secret business!"

His threat clear to all, he stood and strode from the camp. Douglas followed him into the darkness.

Surrounded by the babble of discontent, Old Harry sat unmoving, a song building behind his lips.

Chapter 16

1985, JULY, MID-DRY SEASON.

"THIS IS AS FAR AS WE can go, Missus." Nelson stopped the Toyota pickup on the edge of the steeply eroded dry creek. "The fence ends on the jump-up."

Beyond the creek was a vertical wall of brittle grey and purple stone flecked with white, rising a hundred metres into the bright cobalt-blue sky. She loved the term 'jump-up' because it perfectly described the way the ridges punched up from the flat plain, overpowering the landscape. Above were several terraces, all backed by ragged rock faces. Smooth-barked white snappy gums straggled amongst the huge broken blocks of stone and all were protected by hardy needle-pointed spinifex. The terraces stretched as far as she could see on either side, the land all-embracing.

To their right the rocky steps continued closing in, making a secluded cleft where the creek was born from a spring-fed pool. A raging cataract in the Wet, it was now just a slowly trickling waterfall slipping over the rockface into a semi-permanent pool only to disappear into the sandy creek bed where they now stood. Part of his song line, Nelson knew about a rock pool higher up the escarpment, but kept it secret.

"The fence only goes over this creek?" Wendy asked, getting out of the pickup. The fences were the key to her financial future and they had been inspecting and repairing them for a week. It was impossible to get even a four-wheel drive across the gully. White sand was washed high against the leaning wattles and heavy paperbarks. Several salmon gums with trunks of delicate pink grew in the middle of the stream bed.

"We'll have to get over to check the fence," she instructed Nelson with the confidence of work routines now mastered.

Nelson shrugged his shoulders in acknowledgement and started clambering down the embankment. He traversed the steep sides, working his way diagonally to the bottom. Not for the first time, Wendy watched his backside, tight in his jeans, as he scrambled along the eroded wall, looking for an easy way down. His black body moved with fluid grace and supple hands danced easily as he kept his balance. Unshaven for days, his dark stubble had turned wiry.

He is part of the country, strong and hard. He belongs here, she mused, resting against the bulbar, finding herself more at home than she had ever imagined. Any grief at Andrew's death had quickly evaporated on the discovery of his debts and been replaced with the grinding labour required to escape. After a week of long, rough rides checking and repairing fence lines, she understood why so many ringers naturally leaned on the bull bar. It was a relief to get away from the constant spine-rattling ride over rough unformed tracks running for kilometres along-side the fence lines.

No time to rest, she reminded herself crossly, remembering the written list of items the bank demanded as evidence of her ability to run the station and as preconditions for extending her loan.

The fences have to be checked and repaired. How else can I convince the bank I can run the station if the fences aren't in order?

She moved quickly away from the Toyota, shrugging off the fatigue that followed days of constant hard physical work. She envied Nelson, always so awake and energetic. She clambered as best she could down the slight track he had made. She felt his eyes upon her and she was pleased with the attention. Reaching the sandy bottom, she brushed her hair back from her ears before walking to where he rested against a dry log.

"Let's go," she commanded, and walked off through the deep soft sand. The sand forced her to swing her hips and she knew Nelson watched from behind. Temporarily out of breath she halted at the other side of the creek bed and when Nelson joined her, she let him find a way up the steep bank. She admired his lithe body as he easily climbed up the bank and she made no secret of following his movements. At the top, he turned, caught her eyes and smiled knowingly at the game they were both playing.

The unavoidable intimacy of weeks of physical work had drawn them together. She saw him everyday and the growing familiarity had created an easy working relationship. Now I can do the same as you Nelson Shortjack, she acknowledged. She heaved herself to her feet as he reached the top, and followed him. He was already walking slowly along the fence, checking for broken wires.

"This fence looks alright," he said as she fell in beside him. "It's only a short section between the top of the creek and the base of the jump-up. The cattle can't climb the jump-up, so no need to fence any higher."

It was an endless unforgiving task maintaining the fence lines inside the nearly 300 kilometres of boundary fence. Some fence lines ran for 30 kilometres or more. Cattle enclosed behind the wire were the mainstay of the station and comparatively easier to muster.

"Remind me why we are doing this?" she teased, looking for an excuse to take a break.

Nelson welcomed the break. He sat on a rock, pulled his tobacco tin from his sweat sodden shirt and rolled a cigarette before slipping into his relaxed explanation. Although they had discussed this before, she was content to listen, his words tumbling gently in the shade amongst the fallen boulders of the jump-up.

"There are feral cattle and poddy calves out on the other side of the fence that have never seen a man. They come from the stations all about. Some of them are Punkatoy mob, some are Open Valley cattle and others are off Coolibah Downs. They're all unbranded cleanskins. If we can muster them on the flat country and brand them, they are ours. We brand the poddy calves and let their mothers go if they're already branded."

"We need good fences to keep our quiet cattle on the inside country. If the wild cattle mix him up then they get too hard to muster. Later we can muster the wild ones from outside the wire when they come down from the stone country for the water. Later in the year we set up some spear traps on the waterholes."

"Spear traps?"

"We fence the water hole and leave just one gate with rails angled inwards like spears. The cattle need water so they push aside the rails when they go in, but they can't get out because the gate rails fall back and close up like spears."

"Oh, I see … I didn't know," Wendy conceded meekly, the weeks of hard work sapping her initial misplaced optimism. Oh golly and gosh had all but disappeared beneath the relentless demands of dust and grit. "There is so much I still don't know. I rely on you to help me. I'm so lucky to have you around the station."

She reached out to hold his hand but she found his muscular forearm instead. She felt the strength beneath the coarse dark hair and sweat. "I've got to save this station." To herself she silently added, I have to make a go of it. That's why I've been doing the fences with you. I can't tolerate the thought of this country being taken over by someone who doesn't care for it. You understand? Once only a convenient half truth used to motivate Nelson, it had surprisingly taken on more resonance with each workday in the bush.

Nelson nodded solemnly, her ownership of the station essential for his plans, although she could not know that. She let go of his arm and sat down on a black sandstone block in the shade of a wattle. She hugged her knees. Nelson squatted opposite her and began to roll a fresh cigarette.

"This is ancient country," she whispered, awe catching her voice. "I've really noticed it over the last weeks. I didn't realise just how old this country is. It has a spirit all of its own and it challenges you to adjust. Often in places like this I look up and expect to see some of the Old People just standing nearby."

She looked up and made a show of glancing around the towering rocks. "You ever think that?"

"Sometimes, Missus, if they haven't all been killed," he replied sourly.

"Are the Old People still out there? I do so wish I could meet them one day," she gushed. "Someone in Borroloola said there were still Old People living the old ways out here who had never seen a white man. It must be so wonderful to live close to nature."

Nelson drew heavily on his cigarette. "That time, he be finish," he muttered thickly, and she missed the bitterness in his voice. "New time now."

"You must love this country," she told him, oblivious to his reaction.

"Yair, Missus."

"Do you ever miss the old life? Isn't it hard living and working on the station after the freedom of living in the bush?"

"Yair, Missus."

"You don't want to talk about it, do you?" she murmured, embarrassed her blunder had fractured the easy relationship developed over previous weeks.

"No, Missus."

Nelson flicked his cigarette away and stood up. "We got work to do on the fence across the creek."

He stalked off and Wendy watched him moving confidently over the rough ground, moving without effort. She liked the ripple of his body under the thin Western style shirt. She imagined him naked, spears gripped in the pale dark-lined palms of his hand and master of the land. He's just part of the land, she decided. Take away the hat and boots, and those clothes, and he could be one of the Old People. He's strong and fit. He could survive in this country. I would die within a day unless I had someone like him to help me.

She sighed and watched several mischievous willy wagtails flitter amongst the leaves. As gracefully as she could, she went down to help Nelson with the fence.

Chapter 17

"BLOODY STUPID IGNORANT WHITEFELLA BITCH," Nelson fumed and muttered quietly as he angrily tossed the last of the fencing tools down into the sandy creek bed. "She doesn't have a clue about my country, but she's white, and that's all that matters. Just because she is white she can own the land. Because I'm black, they expect me to bow and scrape. Yes Missus, no Missus, please Missus," he spat.

"And all the time she flaunts herself, teasing the ringers. Look at her." He grunted with forced contempt, watching her climb down the creek bank. His gaze lingered, admiring her awkwardly attractive descent. "She is a pretty one," he conceded, "and she can work too," he admitted reluctantly. "But she's still a white bitch," he reminded himself, admonishing his desire.

Her voice floated up and she waved for him to come down.

"I suppose it's not all wasted," he whispered under his breath, clambering down the creek bank. "All this work is really for when we get the station." The prospect cheered him up, and when he reached the bottom he happily took charge of the job. The fence was strung high in the air, stranded above the creek bed. The bottom wire was broken, carried away by Wet season floods. There was a clear gap the cattle could walk under.

"We re-hang the bottom wire right across," he indicated brusquely with a wave of his hand. "Then tie some wooden poles to the bottom wire so the cattle can't walk under the fence. You remember how to tie a figure eight join?"

"That's the one where you make two loops that interlock, "she ventured uncertainly.

"Not bad, Missus. That's him. You string the bottom wire and I'll find some fallen timber for the poles underneath."

While Wendy tied off the old wire, Nelson wandered downstream. She worked hard, slipping constantly on the small pea gravel of the dry clay bank. She tied one end of the new wire around the post. The sand dragged at her feet while she struggled to run the wire to the fence post on the other side of the creek. The wire snapped back, stinging the side of her face. She stifled tears. Throwing the fencing pliers to the ground, she stamped her foot.

"Bugger it," she cursed. "Damn, damn, damn, oh bloody damn!" Her frustration burned with shame as Nelson laughed richly behind her.

"You look like an emu trying to stamp out a fire," he chortled. He mimicked her action, lifting one foot high and stamping up and down. "Just like emu," he chortled again.

"Well, you look like you at a corroboree," she countered tersely.

Nelson laughed, miming a few hand movements that looked like they could belong to a ceremonial dance. Sweat-sodden shirt flapping, boots stamping the sand and waving his battered hat, Wendy found herself laughing.

"Alright, alright," Nelson sobbed at last. They both stood, hands on their hips, breathing heavily. Wendy recovered first, and picked the pliers from the sand. "Show me how to tie the knot again," she requested.

"Look," he said, "hold it here." He stood facing her, his pink fingernails pointing the way as he instructed her. "Now with this hand," and he guided her thin and now roughened fingers, "make a loop. Bring the wire back over the top."

Her hands felt warm in his. He felt the cuts and abrasions on her trembling fingers and he forced himself to concentrate on the job.

"Put this piece through the loop. Now you can do the rest."

She looked at him in confusion, her short hair falling back from her face. He watched her small hands form the second loop. Her hair fell forward as she bent her head in concentration. She's so useless, he marvelled. She doesn't belong in this country and yet she is trying so hard. She looked up as she finished, and he quickly looked away, avoiding her eyes.

She handed him the joined wire and he went to fasten one end to the other fence post. He looped the wire around the post but could not get enough strain on it as he pulled back, his footing uncertain on the red clay bank.

"See if you can pull the wire towards the post," he suggested.

Back to back they strained until she suddenly slipped on the rounded pea gravel and cannoned into him. Together they tumbled in a heap, slipping and sliding down the crumbling creek bank. She fell on top of him, and, exhausted, lay there for a moment, the curves of her body impossible to ignore.

"I'm sorry," she giggled, and he knew she didn't mean it. His skin prickled at her touch, and he drew back in surprise at his reaction and desire.

"Hey missus, get off please," he pleaded without conviction.

"No rush," she whispered, prolonging the contact. Finally she stood up, slowly and deliberately brushing her breasts and hips.

"Get me a screwdriver so I can tension this wire," he told her thickly. She went off, hips swinging as she struggled in the thick sand. She's not bad-looking at all he thought. I wouldn't mind giving her a poke. He shook his head in disgust at the unbidden thought. She's just a whitefella slut, he savagely reminded himself, desire refusing to retreat.

When she returned, he faced her with a steely bitterness he needed but which she didn't deserve. They worked together, the silence only interrupted by his unnecessarily curt demands and a pair of flittering willy wagtails. She followed, matching his pace and determination, toiling and sweating together. The thin gritty dust clung to them both. Neither would give in and they looked at each other with relief when the last rail dropped to the ground.

She stood beside the log, hands on her hips, head thrown back and chest heaving with fatigue. Her face flushed with exertion and sweat, trickling thick on her skin, plastered hair across her forehead. Beneath the dust and grime of the day's work, the T-shirt clung to her, damp with perspiration. She heaved her chest up and down in slow exaggeration as she breathed deeply and left him struggling with his composure.

Chapter 18

"YOU KNOW WHY WE'RE DOING ALL this fencing'?" Wendy asked, breathing returned to normal. Nelson glanced over his shoulder, surprised at such a stupid question. She was sitting demurely, her legs drawn up in a strangely attractive way. She didn't wait for his answer, so he went back to work, grateful for the distraction.

"I've got to show the bank I can work the station. It's not just a matter of mustering some cattle quickly and selling them. I understand that now," she admitted, acknowledging her debt to Nelson. "It's more complicated. I have to show the bank I can do it properly and then they'll give me more time."

Nelson reached back to get some more wire. "I don't understand," he said and started to tie the new wire into place.

"I'm sorry. It's simple really. There is no money now. I've got a bit," she corrected and rushed on, "and I have some money Andrew left me, but it's not enough. The bank wants to call in the loan. If they do then I will have to sell Punkatoy. I could never do that. I belong here. I know it. I feel it in my heart," she protested.

Nelson worked slowly, letting the familiar fencing tasks mask his consternation. He listened carefully and with growing concern as she blithely picked away at his plans.

"The only way I can save Punkatoy is to renegotiate the loan with the bank. Until then all I have to do is meet the next repayment. Even if I get the cattle trucked, by the time I actually get the money from the stock agents the date for the bank payment will have passed."

"So you see, I have to show the bank I can run the station. If I can do that then they'll let me have enough extra cash to pay for the muster."

"I have to make them believe I can pay them. Keeping the fences repaired is one of their conditions. If they can see I am making improvements then they might give me extra time on the loan payment."

She continued coldly, voice devoid of the desperation that gnawed at her everyday.

"At the moment they want to sell the station as soon as possible so they can get their money back. Unless I can meet the next payment within the next ten days, then they want to put it on the market. They say they have interested buyers already. If I can't convince them or pay them, then I will lose Punkatoy. I'll lose everything."

"Oh Nelson," she sobbed, "what can I do?"

Nelson shook his head with alarm, his desire for her temporarily forgotten. You can't sell now, his mind screamed frantically. If you sell now, the new owners might not want me here. If I'm not here, then I can't take this land back. I only need a few more weeks and then the station will be mine.

"Are you sure they are going to sell the station soon?" he asked as calmly as he could, head down and focussed on hitching the branch to the lower edge of the fence.

"They won't sell if I can meet the repayments and convince them I can run the station as a profitable concern in the near future. They're only interested in their money. They don't know this country. They don't love it like I do!" she declared, sudden tears splattering the dry sand where they were quickly absorbed.

"What about me, Missus?" Nelson asked, trying to keep his voice unconcerned. He already suspected the answer, but wanted to hear it confirmed before he made any decision.

"It would depend on the new owners. They might not want to keep you on. While I'm running the station you'll always have a job, Nelson," she assured him. "I need you so much. Without your knowledge and advice I wouldn't be able to make a success of the station," she conceded.

"How much money do they want?" he asked, the possible solution jiggling amongst the confusion of thoughts and objectives in his mind.

"I have to pay about ten thousand dollars each month. That's all I have to make." She made it sound easy. "Of course I need some extra to run the station, pay the wages and hire the contractors," she claimed confidently, lightly dismissing the costly extras that dwarfed the repayment requirements.

"That's why I've been running the generator only of a night. It's enough to keep the fridges working and the meat frozen. It saves so much fuel only using it of a night. I might have to turn it off earlier though. The fuel company won't supply any more fuel until I pay them some money," she added almost gaily, hoping to push away the spectre of grinding poverty.

"It's a hard way to live. Are you really sure you want to stay here? It'll be a long haul to get on your feet and a lot of hard work. Wouldn't it be easier just to sell up and go back to Melbourne?" Nelson probed.

"Oh no! I couldn't go back. No-one talks to a bankrupt. No-one talks to the poor," she joked, the bitterness hidden and it made the truth seem a little softer. "No. I don't want to go back. I couldn't. This is where I belong," she finished seriously.

Nelson didn't answer. He sat in the sand, deep in thought while Wendy looked around, strangely comforted by the quiet. She's got guts, he decided and his admiration surprised him. I can't let her sell out. I just need a few more weeks for the crabbers to deliver. If she goes soon then the future is too uncertain. Perhaps I should give her a couple of thousand?

Don't be stupid, he told himself sharply.

He started to roll a cigarette to give himself time to consider the idea.

She would want to know where the money came from. She might not, you know, he contradicted himself. She might be too happy to ask any questions. By the time she got suspicious it would be too late. He lit his cigarette and watched the dead match twirling in his fingers for a few moments before tossing it into the sand. I don't know, he groaned silently. I need more time to think. He stood up, cigarette jammed in the corner of his mouth.

"Come on. Cheer up. This is strange country and anything can happen. Give us a hand to hang these rails." He paused and spoke more diffidently, unsure and unsettled by his intentions. "When we finish we can go upstream a bit. There is a permanent pool amongst the rocks." He turned back to his work to cover the confusion of the new situation.

Chapter 19

PALE PINK AND WHITE SANDSTONE GLISTENED darkly under a steady lacework sheen of water dribbling down the broad cliff face at the rear of the cleft in the rocks. Towering ancient grey near vertical slabs of stone hemmed the pool on three sides, soaring above the glassy water. A constant stream of bubbles burst from the sandy floor. In the clear water, tiny fish darted for cover under the furry bearded moss overhangs at the foot of two large paperbarks. Curled in deep shade, the cool water delivered respite from the burning pea gravel further downstream where Nelson and Wendy had just finished repairing the fence.

Wendy watched birds flash and dart as she sat in the water, arms stretched out and the cool liquid lapping her chin. The little willy wagtails, skittering balls of black and white fluff, gossiped amongst themselves before dipping to drink the cool water.

She let the water soak the grit and dust from her clothes, watching the circle of discoloured water spread around her. She shifted from the dirty patch she had created and let the slow current wash the dirt away. In the now clear water, she watched little spotted perch dart up to her feet and giggled as they nibbled at her toes.

She began to wash herself, massaging her armpits under her T-shirt, longing to take it off and feel the cool bite of the water directly on her skin. "What a bath!" she murmured to herself. "Nothing but blue sky above and fish below. Genuine rock slate walls," she told herself, describing it as if it was an advertisement in a luxury resort brochure. "You'd pay a fortune for a bathroom like this in Melbourne but they could never build one to match it," she sighed.

She rubbed her stomach and then unbuttoned the top of her jeans. She sluiced clear the sweaty grit from under the waist band and washed between her legs, lingering for a moment to let the water wash around her. Reluctantly, she refastened her jeans, the ghost of intention almost dismissed. Stretching her arms again, she floated contentedly in the cool water.

His shirt drying on the lower limb of a paperbark, Nelson lay on the mossy bank, watching her with side-long glances. Deep in thought, strategy competing with distracting desire, he quietly smoked in the soft light filtering through the tree tops, his wet skin glistening dully in the dappled shade.

Wendy turned slowly in the water, evaluating him through half-closed eyes. Your body is lean from work and your shoulders are so strong. You've got funny bony elbows and knees, but it's all muscle in between. You look so funny with your dark brown skin and pale soles. I've never seen you without boots, she realised with a start.

She closed her eyes, feeling the caress of the water, surrendering to the returning ghost of intention. She imagined Nelson holding her and she felt a lump of self-pity block her throat. "It's been so long since anyone held me," she reflected silently. "Ray said I have to work it out for myself, but I don't think I can." She dipped further into her fantasy, the water wrapping enticingly around her as the willy wagtail chatter increased.

Dissatisfied, she stood up quickly, water streaming from her shoulders. She squelched across to Nelson, stood over him, then shook like a wet dog, splattering him with water. He rolled away quickly and sat up.

"Hey! Tobacco costs money. You can't make him wet," he protested too strongly, his discordant thoughts disrupted.

"Who cares? I'll be broke tomorrow," she answered gaily, and for the moment she didn't care. She sat beside him, drawing up her knees. "It's beautiful here. These trees and rocks are timeless. Who knows what they have seen? What do they care? Who knows if I'll ever see them again? "she finished, self-pity distorting her voice.

Nelson glanced away, still unsure of what he would do. To remain on the station was vital but he didn't know how he could trust and control her. For a moment he was grateful for the distraction.

"This is an old place," Nelson agreed. "It's a secret part of the dreaming of this country. You can call it Wagtail Springs."

"Is it the proper name?"

"No."

"But what do you call it?" she queried, tilting her head and looking intently at him.

He paused for a moment, then lied. "Some people call it Wuulnpila Springs. They're all wrong. The name is only known by some of the old people in our mob."

"That's terrible," she cried indignantly. "The knowledge should be preserved. You must try to find out, Nelson, so you can tell your children and they can tell their children. It's unforgiveable to lose that knowledge."

Embarrassed he did not really know the traditional name for the waterhole, he nodded in bitter agreement. "You want to save these places?" he asked, groping for more information to help him make his decision. She nodded seriously, giving him her full attention.

"I want to save these places too," he agreed. "It is my history. I think we could save these places together, you and I. If you lose the station, then we'll lose this knowledge. Perhaps the next white man to own Pungkuthuyi country will not be interested in these things," he suggested, waiting expectantly for her response.

"Own what?" she asked, not recognising the language name. "Oh, you mean Punkatoy," she guessed. "Yes, it takes a special kind of person to love this country the way it needs to be loved. You must have feeling..."

"Do you think we could work together?" he interrupted.

"Why yes, of course. While I'm here, you'll always be here as manager," she reaffirmed. "You know this country so well and there is so much you can teach me about it. I know there are so many wonderful places here just waiting for us to discover them."

"There are many places," he began, now more certain of his strategy for control. "We could keep them ... "

"I hope there are," she interrupted without thinking. "Tell me a story!" she demanded. "I'm sure this place has many stories."

Nelson shook his head in refusal, determined to continue with his proposal.

"Please, Nelson. It seems so right to listen to an old story while we're sitting here. There is only us, the trees, the willy wagtails and the history of this place. You can feel it," she shivered and clutched at his arm. Leaning on his shoulder, she felt him relax. He shrugged easily, time no longer important now he knew what else he had to do.

A traditional tale of lust uncoiled from the back of his mind, summoned by the black and white willy wagtails flashing across the water. Always gossiping about wrong side love, they listened as he started down the path they knew so well.

"Unchi was a good hunter and he loved a beautiful woman from his own tribe. She had been given to another man," he started, dredging his memory for the half-forgotten fragments of the children's story.

"Whenever he went hunting he plotted how he could take this woman for himself. The elders were angry because he would not give up this wrong side love, and they banished him from the tribe. He went off by himself, and he no longer hunted with the tribe."

Nelson paused, remembering the story book one of his cousin's children had left behind in the camp. All he had to tell was children's tales culled and written down by uninformed whitefellas. He clutched at remembered details.

"In time he decided on a plan to get the woman. He made a nulla nulla and disguised it by covering it with small white feathers. Soon he came upon the woman he loved alone at the waterhole."

"Was it this waterhole?" Wendy gasped, hand over her mouth.

Nelson nodded, not prepared to say the lie out loud and spoil the mood. "They argued about wrong side love but she wouldn't leave her husband, so he killed her. Then he dropped the nulla nulla and ran away into the hills. The elders found it when they came looking for the woman. The willy wagtails, who since the dreamtime, have always gossiped about wrong side love, told the elders what had happened."

"The elders sung him and turned him into a paperbark tree. Now the tree has little white flowers like the feathers he used to disguise his nulla nulla. As a tree he must carry his deception forever for everybody to see and he cannot leave the waterhole," Nelson improvised.

"That's wonderful," she sighed. Putting her arm around his shoulder, she nestled her head against his neck. "There are many wonderful places here. If only we could keep them."

He lay on his back to still his growing tension and looked at the sky through the skein of paperbark leaves and blossoms. She shrugged and he avoided looking at her. The tingle of her touch was fresh upon his skin. His loins stirred and he wondered how she would react if he embraced her. The clean smell of her damp hair lingered and his heart raced, slipping down the path of total commitment.

"You said you needed ten thousand dollars to keep the station going," he probed softly.

"Yes. Why, do you have it?" she joked.

"Yes."

She pulled back and looked at him, lips parted and eyes wide. "You're kidding," she blurted.

"I got some money I saved," he lied easily now there was no going back. "I can lend it to you but only if I was sure you would keep the station and I stay on," he admitted.

"Of course you can stay," she shrilled in delight throwing her arms around his neck. Both fell to the mossy ground and she kissed his open mouth. He rolled over and lay across her, heart racing to match the beat of hers. Her touch, cool and soothing on his skin, did little to dampen his desire.

She looked up at his proud face, liquid brown pupils holding her gaze. Savouring the tobacco taste of his lips, she cried childishly, "I love you! This is a Place of Starting Again," she trilled, and exhilarated, she squashed her lips against his soft moist mouth.

His breathing quickened and his urgent touch rippled down her spine. She felt him harden and lowering one hand, she caressed him gently. He was tight beneath his jeans and her hardening nipples scraped against her damp T-shirt.

"Hold me," she pleaded and she felt him respond, shuddering as he stroked her hair. "Love me, please … now … I need you," she whispered. She unfastened his belt and jeans while he excitedly caressed her breasts with powerful hands. Tearing at her T-shirt, he squeezed and kneaded, pinching her nipples with one hand. With the other, he pulled her jeans below her hips. He pushed her legs apart before she had time to do it for him and thrust strongly past her panties.

He finished long before she wanted him to. Unsatisfied, she contented herself with holding him tight, her head deep against his chest. A small breeze played across the water and cooled her back. She listened to the willy wagtails chattering amongst themselves and she was fully content for the first time in months.

Nelson lay beside her as his breathing slowly subsided. His desire satisfied, he returned her embrace, kissing her gently, his lips exploring her pale body. She nuzzled him, content to hold and be held. The sun warmed their backs until the afternoon shadows thickened.

He examined his weakness, seeking justification. If this is what it takes...
he scolded himself. He left the thought unexamined, his body responding of
its own accord to the gentle curves of the woman lying across his chest.

"Come on, Mawu, we must go," he whispered gently.

"Why Mawu?" she murmured thickly, running her fingers through the
tight black curls on his chest. His body was cool to her touch.

"It is my special language word for you."

"Thank you. It sounds just right," she whispered, dragging her nails
lightly across his stomach. She felt him shiver and harden.

His eyes wandered over her white body, his dark skin making her very
pale by contrast. Mawu is the right word, he agreed silently, needing the
reminder of his reality. Mawu, he repeated, for a maggot is what you are.

Chapter 20

1985, AUGUST, MID-DRY SEASON.

RAY SLOWED THE TOYOTA AS HE scanned the faint dusty track, no more than a pair of tyre marks weaving through trees and red clay termite mounds poking above the bonnet-high grass. The day-old cattle tracks meandered down the lefthand side. He scanned the thick scrub on either side, looking for a 'killer.' As part of his work contract, Wendy let him kill a cow for his rations, but like all station owners, she preferred if it was an un-branded clean-skin.

He reached automatically for his tobacco tin and then left it in his pocket. Despite hours searching for 'killers', he never smoked while he hunted, a discipline still acknowledged. Tobacco smoke alerted the hunted, something few of his American colleagues learned in Vietnam.

From the corner of his eye, he spotted a small mob of cattle hidden amongst the low scrub and stunted grey woollybutts. He slowed to a crawl even though the gentle breeze was blowing towards the vehicle and away from the cattle. For most of the daylight hours the cattle lay in the deep shade of ghost gum and dark-trunked bloodwood trees, and when called by the evening breeze, they wandered down to drink at the scattered waterholes. The best time to kill for meat was in the cool of the late afternoon.

"Whoa back," he murmured to the Toyota.

He recognised the unbranded clean-skin roan cow he had seen a few days previously.

"You beauty," he whispered. "You're just the girl I've been looking for. You're tucker-box brand now," he chuckled. He stopped, and left the motor running, its noise masking his own as he grabbed the rifle and carefully opened the door.

He squatted, hidden by the front of the pickup. Using his knees as elbow rests, he carefully sighted on the nervous beast seventy metres away. Perturbed by the grey vehicle, the cow flicked an ear and looked directly into the rifle scope. No earmarks, he confirmed with satisfaction, taking up the pressure on the trigger. Through the scope he saw the beast lift her head and turn to bolt just as he fired. He heard the bullet smack into the near side leg and saw her stumble.

He was up and running before the two red cows with her had time to make a start for the heavy scrub themselves. He ejected the spent cartridge, the still warm brass casing slipping from his grasp. "Bugger!" he snapped, and turned back to collect the empty.

It was a poacher's habit, or so they told him now. Station rations were best replenished with meat taken from cleanskins, or from the neighbours' cattle – but only if you cut off the ear and tag. Once he had been told picking up brass was a basic survival in the jungles where men hunted men. The old drills died hard. He found the empty shell case and stuffed it into his top pocket, one eye on the roan cow lumbering through the wattles dragging her injured foreleg.

"That'll be tough meat, but easy to track," he conceded.

He turned back to the pickup and reaching it, switched off the engine. Noise was no longer needed to mask his activities. He pocketed another five bullets from the box behind the front seat. He picked up the two butchering knives and set off into the wattle.

"She'll not die in any more pain than I can help. I just hope the day some bastard decides to shoot me it is quick and clean," he commented to himself.

The hoof marks were easy to find in the sand amongst the black trunked wattles. The cattle had bunched up and run together. Within ten metres the old cow had started to bleed and he followed the dull red spots.

"Poor girl. You're the first I've missed for a bloody long time," he apologised. Two red cows galloped along the edge of the slope but the roan cow turned towards the rough broken rocky country higher up the steepening slope of the escarpment.

Ray walked quickly, the occasional small spots of blood and trampled grass enough to guide him. The cow's broken foreleg left intermittent drag marks, first in the sand and then over the small broken blocks of sandstone. Carrying the rifle angled high across his chest, he followed the tracks into the thickening timber.

White snappy gums and untidy quinine bush struggled between odd-sized jumbled rocks. He walked as quickly as he dared, worried about twisting an ankle on the uneven ground. Occasional nutwood trees grew amongst the ghost gums, their dark tessellated bark a contrast to the smooth grey rocks. The heat of the day was still trapped beneath the heavy vegetation.

He spotted the roan cow sheltering under a white gum. He quickly sighted and fired. She collapsed as birds shouted, leaping into the air. He walked to where the cow lay and cut its throat to let it bleed out. More blood in country already stained with blood. The whispers of massacres, old and more recent, came unbidden, ghosting down the escarpment.

"What a stuff-up," he growled. "The country is too bloody rough to get a vehicle in here easily. What a waste!" He spat in disgust before lighting his cigarette. He looked around with exasperation.

"Well, I'll be blowed!"

A faint residue of tyre tracks were caught in the lowering sunlight. "If they can get in here, then I can too."

Chapter 21

RAY PARKED THE PICKUP BESIDE THE dead cow and lowered the tail gate. A bed of freshly picked green eucalyptus leaves covered the bottom of the dusty tray. The aromatic cushion would keep the meat clean and the flies at bay.

He checked his two knives for sharpness, and then from force of habit, cut off the ears, throwing them into the back of the Toyota. "No ears means no brand, which means it must be a clean skin," he chortled. "And that is almost legal."

Deftly he quartered the beast, throwing each leg onto the bed of leaves in the Toyota. The green leaves kept most of the flies away from the fresh warm meat. Butchering finished, he needed another layer of broad leaves to cover the pale red flesh to keep the dust from the meat. The meat would set overnight and the next morning he would bone out the quarters. Starting the pickup, he followed the lightly sketched wheel tracks, the sun flashing low across the tree tops as he scanned past the wattle and quinine looking for isolated eucalyptus trees and their broad leaves.

He drove slowly into a small valley between vertical plates of rock all canted to the left and pushing up towards a shadow-hidden saddle in the escarpment. Unwelcoming broken stone tugged at the wheels.

He saw the broken tail of the plane before he saw the rest of the aircraft. He stopped, the dismembered beast in the back forgotten. For a short time he stared, hat brim pushed back and hunched over the steering wheel. It's a Gooney bird he realised, remembering they called the armed versions of the C47 "puff the magic dragon" when they floated over enemy positions spitting mini-gun fire. Absently he let out the clutch and the vehicle lurched forward before stalling. Opening the door, he left the Toyota where it was, and assessed the wreckage.

She's an old one from the last war, he thought, not from Vietnam. Still got some of the camouflage paint and a faded once-orange inverted triangle symbol instead of an Australian rondel or US markings. Unarmed, he noted as he walked along the starboard side. She's come down pretty hard and suddenly by the look of her. The undercarriage is not even down. She's ploughed in at a fair speed. Poor bastards, I bet they didn't know what hit them.

It wasn't the first downed aircraft he had seen, and crash features tugged at the edge of his memory. Interested and intrigued, he carefully searched for bullet holes and damage. What started the fire? he wondered. Burst fuel tank ... a bullet in the wrong place ... perhaps sabotage? Guess we'll never know, he conceded.

Peering beneath the wing roots, he saw the top of a metal box. The box, breaking the cargo restraints, had skidded forward and then fallen through the metal where it was weakened in the fire. Ray noted it with interest, and continued prowling. He peered inside into the open cargo door near the rear of the plane.

"Fuck!"

The large sand goanna hissed at him. Rearing on its back legs, it flicked its long tongue at him, aiming to intimidate the intruder. Ray stood his ground and watched the reptile. Hearing and feeling no movement, the goanna relaxed, dropping slowly to all fours. Majestically it turned, stalking into the dark body of the plane.

"You're an old one. I can almost hear your bones creaking as you walk away," he chuckled with relief.

Stepping back he noticed a scuffle of footprints around the cargo door. He stood to one side, reading the message in the tracks. One man wore boots, and the other had none, his broad footprints flat in the dust. The tracks told him two men had unloaded something from the plane. The broad drag marks were still clear. He followed them to where they intersected the tyre tracks he had followed.

"A Toyota," he concluded, "but then, so is just about every vehicle in this country. Tracks aren't too old," he reckoned as the tyre tread was not scuffed by the wind.

He rolled a cigarette and worked through the possibilities. It's a long way for souvenir hunters to come, or tourists, but it is still possible, he supposed, although it's really out of the way. The ringers didn't find it, that is for sure. They could never keep quiet about it. The whole camp would know within a day.

No, he decided, it had to be souvenir hunters, although the barefoot impressions left room for doubt. Might be worth having more of a look around, he concluded, putting his cigarette butt back into his tobacco tin.

He skirted the left side of the plane, and checking for the goanna again, he pulled the box out from under the wing, very surprised by its weight. With mounting curiosity he retrieved the axe from the Toyota. He split the locked metal tabs and lifted the lid.

"Bloody hell!" he whispered. "Here's an end to all our troubles."

Gold ingots filled one half of the box. Disintegrating paper notes filled the other half. A coat of arms with three rampart lions was deeply impressed on each bar, the letters N.E.I clearly visible.

He closed the lid and sat back on his heels. Rolling a smoke, he recalled a campfire yarn, it seemed tall at the time, but perhaps now not so tall after all. The tale was told by an old fella well known for his eclectic collection of yarns. They had found an old .50 calibre shell fallen from an ancient dog-fight and he was recalling his escape from the Japanese attacks on Darwin in February 1943.

He painted a picture of an airfield in bedlam, with damaged aircraft, fighters and bombers, lining the edges of the airstrip. The hangers were just a skeleton of bearers and trusses above blackened engines and the twisted remnants of another sixteen aircraft amongst white aluminium ash. The pitiful remains of a P40 Kittyhawk, strafed as it tried to take off, had one intact wing canted to the air above an intact engine, the rest of the aircraft destroyed.

Bombs exploding behind, a Dakota headed for the US base at Townsville, struggled to get off the ground before the attack intensified. With no fighter escorts available, the only safety came from the nearby towering Wet season thunderheads.

It was, the old raconteur recalled, carrying the last of the gold reserves of the Netherlands East Indies from Java. The plane was never seen again and despite his tendency to embellish a story, he made no suggestion about where it might be found.

Ray studied the drag marks in the sand. If those other boxes were full of gold like this one ... Suddenly uneasy, he left the thought unfinished. He pushed the box back under the wing.

We might just wait a while. There is something not right here, he decided.

Chapter 22

RAY COASTED TO A STOP IN the station yard and switched off the Toyota. It was weeks since he had come into the station. The Big House squatted underneath the trees, listless in the heat. The lazy slap of the sprinkler setting the pace for the day. The slow saddle-sore monotony of a Slim Dusty country and western song drifted from the other side of the workshop over the murmur of the men on smoko break. Not sure how he was going to tell Wendy about the wrecked plane, he let the mid-morning sun warm him, ignoring the unusual silence.

The dogs, suddenly aware they had been caught napping, raced out snarling and barking from their shady hiding places. Ray ignored them. Disappointed by his lack of reaction, they returned to their shade and he walked to the workshop where the ringers were sitting around a table. Nelson was not with them.

"Gidday there."

"Cup of tea?" someone asked. Ray nodded his agreement.

"Looking for the Missus," he said, sitting down and accepting the thick black tea in a chipped pannikin. He threw the ears from the old roan cow on the table. Nobody commented, accepting he had the right to a killer and appreciative of the ears to add to the station tally. Victor pushed the battered sugar tin along the table.

"She up the big house today. She be away most days," Victor told him, his long thin hands gracefully indicating the direction.

"Fair enough. I'll go and have a yarn to her later. Where's Nelson?"

"Probably up the Big House," Victor suggested flatly, his narrow face struggling to give nothing away. Ray caught the glances passing between the men.

"He been living here?" he asked, pointing to the white ringers' quarters behind him.

"Some of the time," Victor replied, a gleeful smirk sneaking across his lips.

Ray nodded sagely, accepting the fact without comment, and drank his tea. "That something belong them," he commented evenly. The others laughed openly, relieved to share the open secret. Only Douglas sneered derisively.

Ray looked at Douglas over the rim of his pannikin. You bastard. I don't like you, he thought grimly. You're always full of resentment and always use your fist before you use your brain. If anyone is going to stir up trouble on this station, it will be you. If Wendy has any sense, she'll make up your pay quickly.

"Every day he be away all day with the Missus, so he not need his swag now," 'Victor suggested with a chuckle. He pointed to Nelson's faded green canvas swag roll in the corner of the room. "Perhaps I take him back to the camp."

The others laughed, faces easily breaking into broad, good humoured grins. "Hey! He be pretty flash now. He only be a ringer from the camp a few weeks ago, but now he nearly station owner," Victor added, eyes twinkling with youthful amusement. A fresh fit of laughter rippled through the men. Ray smiled, chuckling with them.

"She still be the Missus?" he suggested.

"Oh yair, boss," several replied to a chorus of chuckling, and Ray knew then she had lost their respect. Tea finished, he stood to go.

"What's wrong with the gen set?" he queried, suddenly aware the usual thumping of the noisy generator was absent.

"Nothing wrong," Victor chuckled, still trying to contain his mirth.

"It's bloody nice and quiet and peaceful without it, but it should be running."

Douglas sneered again. "She only runs it at night."

"Fair enough," Ray replied easily, disguising his concern. Once you start cutting the electricity, then things went downhill quickly. He paused at the edge of the workshop.

"Where's Charlie?"

"Him be plenty sick. The Missus want to put him on the flying doc plane, but he won't go," Victor replied. Ray waved in easy acknowledgement and went over to the Big House.

It was Nelson who shouted, 'Come in,' when he knocked on the screen door. Both freshly showered and Nelson clean shaven, they slumped in low chairs, empty cups on the low table between them. Nelson's hat was on the floor. Beyond the broken flyscreens and dirty louvres, the withered garden looked as hot as the room. The immobile ceiling fan left the cobwebs dangling listlessly in the breezeless room. Grit scrunched beneath his boots as a cockroach scuttled under the matting covering the unswept concrete floor.

"Sit down," Wendy invited. "Have a cup of tea." Not waiting for an answer, she immediately got up and went to the kitchen. He didn't need another cup, but it was an invitation to stay and talk. He lifted the brim of his hat in puzzlement and let it fall again before sitting. He watched Nelson at ease in the chair.

"Hear Charlie's been crook," he commented.

"Yair. That's right. Nothing to worry about. Just imagination," Nelson assured him off-handedly.

"That's not like Charlie. He is pretty tough."

Nelson nodded in agreement. "Tribal business, chilpu," he said in a confidential whisper. He smirked and put his hat on. "I better be going. Got to keep those lazy boys working, or we'll never make a go of the station." Full of confidence he strode arrogantly through the door without a backward glance.

"Has Nelson gone?" Wendy asked, returning with the teapot. "He didn't have to go."

"Wanted to get the ringers working again," Ray said, abstractedly accepting the tea poured into a stained and chipped pannikin.

"Great. They have been a bit slow lately. They don't seem to work as hard as they used to."

"Could be because of Nelson," Ray suggested.

"No. Nelson's alright. He's terrific, in fact. I never realised how much he knew until we were out repairing fences. He knows this country and he loves it. It is his country after all," she challenged with uncalled-for aggression.

He paused, taken aback at her response and increasingly disturbed by Nelson's newfound arrogance and the disrespect amongst the ringers.

He thought as the silence lingered, instinctively reaching for the all-purpose bush excuse. It's something belong them, he decided but now it seemed an inadequate response. He readjusted his sweat-stained hat and pushed forward boldly, reticence be damned.

"Yair ... Well that could be part of the problem."

"How so?" she bridled.

Ray sipped his tea. Committed to unaccustomed interference, he wondered how he could warn her without hurting. She waited for his reply. At length, he started.

"Look, as I've said before, good luck to you, but remember one thing. As head stockman the boys will take Nelson's orders because he can always blame the boss. To the ringers he is still really one of them."

She looked away, no longer hungry for information if it challenged her personal commitment.

"Before he could always say, 'Look, I don't want to do this, but this is what the boss wants.' They would all grumble about the boss, and do the work. Nelson was better than the rest of them, but because he had to take orders from the Missus, he was still one of them."

"Now he's not one of them. They see him as boss, and they blame him when things go wrong. Do you see what I mean?" he asked, desperately hoping she would understand.

"I think you're making it up," she responded primly. "I'll do what I think is right."

"Whoa back there," he said quickly. "I don't care what you do. That is something belong you. But once the boys start jacking up on Nelson, then the station will start to go downhill. When you want to muster, you won't be able to because the boys won't be interested. You have to show them Nelson is boss, or else they will just try him on. At the moment he is a gammon boss – a make-believe boss. They want him to prove he is a proper boss. He can't do it because you have shamed him."

"I have not! There is nothing to be ashamed of at all. He's great – in bed and out," she added in spite. "I'm not ashamed of our relationship," she snapped defiantly.

Ray shook his head in exasperation, regretting his involvement. He leaned forward. "That's not what I meant," he explained gently. "Nelson's idea of shame is not the same as yours. You have shamed him before his people because he comes when you beckon. They feel ashamed for him, not because of him. You have shamed him because you have belittled him, so you have insulted him before his people."

He struggled for the words and Wendy glared, giving him no quarter.

"Look," he pleaded, hands outspread. "If you're going to sleep with him, then give him respect. Don't just send for him when the sun goes down and you feel like it. Take away his shame and the boys will work much better for him."

He looked at Wendy and her answering gaze was steely.

"I don't know," he surrendered in frustration. "It's none of my business ... " He tugged at his hat and increasingly uncomfortable, he changed the discussion. "But it would be good if you could make a go of the station. It seems a pity if you muck it up by mistake."

Sitting back in her chair, she looked out the window at the birds playing under the sprinkler.

"Thank you, Ray," she whispered, watching the birds. "I think I understand what you mean."

"I'm a clumsy sort of bastard," he apologised.

"No," she turned and leaned forward, touching his arm. "No, you're not clumsy. I'm the one who is stupid ..." Leaving the rest unexplored, she rapidly changed the subject.

"I only realised in the last week I really don't know anything about station work. Nelson showed me that. I didn't have a clue how to repair a fence until he showed me."

"You been out doing fences yourself?" he interrupted.

"Yes. Nelson and I spent the last ten days repairing the fences," she beamed with pride. "He's the one who kept the station going these last weeks, but I am learning more every day. I haven't got the time to feel lonely now. I'm so busy. I have to keep the fences looking good so the bank will let me keep the station."

He could not keep the concern from his voice.

"Are they going to sell?"

"If I can't keep up payments, they will sell. They say they have a buyer. I've got to show them I can run the station and meet the payments."

"I think you can do it," he agreed encouragingly. "If you're prepared to help yourself then you'll find in this country there are a lot of others who will give you a hand."

She smiled in acknowledgement. "It's funny you should say that. Max over on Open Valley said he would be happy to lend me some of his stock camp boys later in the year if I needed them."

"Do you think I can trust him?" she asked suddenly concerned and seriously. "I know he used to muster the top corner and steal Punkatoy cattle."

"Of course you can trust him. He didn't steal your cattle. He just picked up the cleanskins. Ok, maybe he did a bit of poddy dodging." He saw her querulous look. "You know, taking the unbranded weaners and hitting them with your own brand. You'll probably do the same thing when you muster out there. He just genuinely wants to help you out."

"Nelson said the same. I just hope you're both right," she concluded uncertainly.

Ray made no reply, and the conversation lapsed. He wondered how he could steer the conversation around to the real reason for his visit. Rolling a cigarette, he waited patiently for an opportunity.

Chapter 23

"I ONLY USE THE GEN SET of a night," Wendy explained eventually, desperate to break the uneasy quiet following their discussion of Nelson's changing relationship.

"It happens when the money gets tight," Ray ventured, sensing an opening to raise the true purpose of his visit.

She nodded slowly, reluctant to fully acknowledge her plight.

"Look," he stuttered, suddenly plunging in, "I can lend you ... no ... that's not right ..." He started again, overcome by the desire to do something rather than continue to stand aside and observe.

"Look, I can give you some money to keep you going. I have some gold. Sell it, and you get enough to keep you going for a while until the station gets on its feet," he blurted.

"I couldn't do that! I couldn't take your money. I won't take charity!" she snapped instinctively.

"Well, it's not exactly my money," he drawled, surprised he was more comfortable now the process had started.

"I certainly won't take any stolen money!" she snapped again.

"Yairs... well, it's not stolen either," he hinted enigmatically.

Wendy glared at him, expecting an explanation. Ray leant back and looking at the ceiling, started to explain, telling her just enough for her to understand.

"There is an old plane crash from the war over near the Koolatang boundary. It's hidden in some very rough country." He looked at Wendy and answered her questioning scowl. "I was out there getting a killer yesterday."

She nodded curtly, listening with her head cocked slightly to one side.

"There's a box of gold bars in the plane." He hesitated, deciding not to tell her about the tyre tracks and foot print activity at the crash site until he was more certain of an explanation. "Being an old crash from the war it's a fair chance the gold was stolen anyway. A couple of gold bars would help you out. Melt them down, and while the mixture is hot, pour it into a bucket of water. The gold explodes into little puffed nuggets like popcorn," he explained knowing she wouldn't understand. "It's impossible to trace the source so it's easy to sell. Could you live with that?"

Wendy's mouth was open, struggling to form words. "You mean there's gold on Punkatoy?" she managed eagerly. Ray nodded. "It would be all I need," she squealed, hugging herself. She rolled back into the chair, her open optimistic smile unstoppable.

"It's fate, Ray. It's just fate. It's just meant to be!"

Suddenly she leant forward, euphoria temporarily at bay. "What about you?" she demanded. "Why give it to me? I can't possibly repay you for a long time."

He paused in contemplation, the question forcing him to examine his instinct. For most people, gold was a means of escape from a life disliked, he thought. But, he now acknowledged, I escaped years ago after Vietnam.

"Look on it as a soft loan," he said carefully. "I could use a bit of extra money, but as long as I can do a few repairs on the dozer, I'm happy enough. If I had any more I would probably drink it, or just keep on working until it all disappeared," he joked, ignoring a niggle of doubt suggesting this might no longer be completely true.

"I won't take it," she said firmly. "I will not take charity. I will only take it as a loan. I'll repay you as soon as we start trucking cattle. OK?" she asked aggressively.

"No problems. Suits me," he answered easily.

"Oh Ray!" she squealed again. Leaping onto his lap, knocking his hat from his head, she kissed him quickly. "It's so wonderful. I would never have believed it could happen. This country is so incredible."

Embarrassed, Ray pushed her away and she returned to her chair.

"I'd love to see it. Will you take me out? Today, please take me out," she cajoled, leaning towards him.

"No."

"Oh, why not?" she asked with a pout.

"The pilots' remains are out there. I'll bring the gold into the station. Then you can call in the police so they can take care of things."

She silently nodded in agreement. "At least I'll be able to tell Nelson I don't need to borrow his hard earned money," she informed him brightly.

"I didn't think Nelson would have any," he blurted, surprised and unsure if she was joking.

"Oh yes he has. He offered to lend me some so I could keep up the payments on the station. He's absolutely wonderful. You're both wonderful."

More disturbed than he cared to admit, he abruptly stood, grabbed his hat and started for the door before she could assault him again.

"That's good then," he acknowledged over his shoulder. "I'll be back in a few days time," he promised, no longer certain he was doing the right thing. Nelson's unexpected access to money and its implications dogged his thoughts all the way back to his camp and on the last afternoon shift on the dozer. Boots and bare feet became a repeated litany. The swirl of dust, the squeak of metal tracks over tough, unyielding rock and the undulating engine roar barely enough to pause his thoughts – boots and bare feet. He continued turning over possibilities as he smoked the last cigarette of the day under a canopy of crisp stars.

Chapter 24

SLIGHTLY BEWILDERED AT RAY'S SUDDEN DEPARTURE, Wendy watched him drive off, the dogs chasing the Toyota as far as the first gate before turning back to flop into shady resting holes. She stood by the window for a few moments, dirty mugs in one hand, enthralled by the prospect of enough money to keep the station going, and perhaps, some money for luxuries. Pirouetting, she imagined the room as it might be if she could afford to redecorate.

"Those louvres will go," she gestured grandly. "A couple of nice picture windows would be much better. A nice tawny carpet would go well on the floor. Get rid of these useless fans, and put an air conditioner over on the long veranda ... and perhaps another one in the kitchen."

She walked across the room, touching the back of the chairs, imagining the rich feel of leather instead of the greasy stickiness of dirty vinyl. Only money could ever banish the smell of poverty. She drifted to the bathroom, wrinkling her nose in disgust at the ancient bath and cracked tiles. The dark green pitted concrete floor was cold and squalid. White limestone encrusted water stains hung beneath the taps. She shuddered, the image too close to her childhood for comfort, and closed the door.

She continued to the main bedroom and ignored the unmade bed. She caught sight of herself in the mirror. "God, I look awful," she lamented. Slowly, for the first time in months, she picked through her wardrobe. The clothes were faded, all losing the daily battle with constant grit and dust and the unrelenting sunlight of everyday station work. She selected the best of the T-shirts and the smartly cut, high waisted jeans she had last worn to Stephanie's Restaurant in Hawthorn. It seemed, no, it was, a lifetime ago.

"I'll have no financial worries now, and if I can't celebrate, then it's a pretty poor show," she fantasied to her image reflected in the spotty disfigured remnants of the dresser-top mirror.

She changed quickly out of the work clothes she wore every day. She pirouetted in front of the mirror, pleased with her figure, leaner now from station work. Satisfied the new jeans and T-shirt matched, she combed her hair. She checked the mirror again. Satisfied with her reflected image, she went to find Nelson to bring him home.

She paused at the Big House yard gate and took in the layout of the station grounds. The workshop was the largest building in this domain. Enclosed at both ends, the wide work bays were crowded with equipment and vehicles, many of them under repair or waiting for parts. To the left was the cannibals' graveyard. Trucks, pickups, loaders and rusting machinery were abandoned, offering up their innards for makeshift repairs on other vehicles. Beyond were stacks of oil and fuel drums, some full and others empty, waiting for reassignment as track markers, impromptu supports for stock crates or broken equipment.

To the right, the generator shed teetered against a large ghost gum, the white trunk stained with diesel soot. Beyond towards the backwater lagoon was the ringers' camp, campfire smoke drifting through the corrugated tin shacks and disappearing into the thickening bush. Tin window shutters, red ironstone stained concrete floors, tumbling dogs and small children delivered a different life. Standing stoic in the distance, Old Harry gave a languid wave, but of greeting or dismissal she was not sure.

She turned away to the scattered assortment of tin sheds, some standing, some leaning and some, which had given up the fight with white ants and gravity, were in total collapse. Yellow dust clung to all, and all retreated beneath the brutal Dry season sun and pounding Wet season rain.

Not exactly kings in grass castles, she admitted, but gold makes a difference to all our dreams. With a satisfied smile, she opened the rusty iron gate, and set out in pursuit of Nelson. She found him in the workshop standing over Victor. He glanced at her, and turned back to Victor who was nervously fiddling with an old sealed bearing. "You keep at it, boy," he snarled quietly. "I'll talk to you later."

Avoiding dirty discarded tyres, walking carefully around tools and broken car parts abandoned on the gritty floor, she waited by the workbench, careful not to touch any of the filthy tools or parts. Her clothes, fresh and new, made a startling contrast with the ringers' work-stained shirts and jeans.

"All dressed up and nowhere to go," Nelson quipped. "What's the occasion?"

She smiled brightly at him, struggling to contain her excitement. "Ray found some gold on Punkatoy," she enthused, unaware the ringers had stopped work to listen so they could gossip later.

"Yair... well......right. Yair," Nelson spluttered. "Come over here," he finally managed. He took her arm and led her outside, stopping when they reached the far side of the front end loader away from the open-sided workshop. He rested his boot on the perished flat front tyre. He knew the men were eager to listen in, so he kept his voice low.

"Tell me again," he hissed.

"It's simple," she repeated, not understanding his concern or the need for secrecy. "Ray found an old crashed plane yesterday when he was looking for a killer. He found a box of gold bars in the crash and he has offered some of it to me as a loan. Isn't it wonderful? You'll be able to keep your savings and the station will still be ours."

"That's true," he demurred, desperately trying to work out how it would affect his plans.

"He's bringing the gold back to the station in a few days and then he wants to let the police know about the crash – "

"Why?" Nelson interrupted, thoroughly alarmed.

"He said there are some bodies. They have to be buried. It's wonderful isn't – "

"Shut up!" Nelson snapped. He turned away from her suddenly frightened gaze.

If anybody else finds out then everything is lost. Ray Morgan, you're dead, he swore silently to himself, the decision sudden and final. I've no choice because I just need a bit more time. He turned suddenly on Wendy, who was still stunned and a little scared by his show of temper.

Fighting to keep his voice smooth and pleasant, he asked, "Has he told anyone?"

"Not as far as I know."

"Good."

"What do you mean? What is the matter?" she asked apprehensively.

Nelson put his hands on her shoulders and held her tightly an arm's length away. "Listen, Mawu, things aren't quite as I told you the other day," he said gently. She shook her head in confusion, suddenly worried he would abandon her.

"I've got the money alright. That is no problem, but you need to know how I got it."

He pulled her into his arms and hugged her close, knowing it was what she needed if he wanted her continued co-operation. Relieved, she melted into his embrace, clean clothes forgotten. The closeness of her body softened his voice. He whispered close to her ear, her hair gentle against his lips.

"I found the plane a while ago. Remember when Charlie and I broke down in the mustering Toyota?" She nodded, delighting at the touch of lips on her ear. "We found the crash. We found one box," he lied easily. "I arranged with the Vietnamese crabbers camped down near the mouth of Corella Creek to sell it for me. You understand ... I have the money, but it's not... it's still a bit warm," he finished.

She nodded her understanding and he held her closer, wrapping his arms around her back ready for embrace or restraint. She accepted his explanation with relief, willingly surrendering to his mastery. She buried the illegality of the gold in the warm embrace of his arms.

"I'll see Ray tomorrow," Nelson suggested firmly. "As long as he keeps quiet there is no problem. We have to sell the gold and the Vietnamese are the best people to do it. It is important nobody knows about it. If anybody ever finds out there will be questions asked. We don't want to answer those questions, do we?" he asked quietly, successfully keeping any hint of menace from his voice.

She looked into his limpid eyes. "I understand," she whispered huskily, "and I'm sure Ray will understand."

Nelson grinned down at her, his face genial, but eyes hard. "Thank you, Mawu." He kissed her savagely and she responded with fierce desperation, while he thought of how he would kill Ray Morgan.

Chapter 25

NELSON CRADLED THE AK47 AS HE worked his way slowly through the scrub towards the metallic squeak and screech of the bulldozer and its shrouding cloud of dust. The engine roar rose and fell as the machine pushed material over the rocky saddle and then backed off again to gather another blade full of gravel and dirt. The stubby wooden-stocked assault rifle was tauntingly unfamiliar in his hands. He stopped, hidden in a stand of wattle, and practised raising the assault rifle to his shoulder. The comfortable pistol grip gave him good control of the weapon but not of nagging disquiet. Shooting a beast or a wallaby was an everyday callousness. Killing a friend was more difficult than an instant promise made in anger.

He was now very pleased he had insisted on a sample rifle before closing the deal with the crabbers, even though Ray had stumbled across the empty brass shells from his practice shoot. He squinted, aiming at a tall termite mound. With imaginary precision he shot two phantom cows and several imaginary kangaroos. Not satisfied, he practised twice more, throwing the rifle to his shoulder. Each time he felt the power and saw thirty bullets strike home in one conclusive burst.

Striking a bold revolutionary pose remembered from posters in his university days, he rested the butt on his hip, muzzle high, and hand firm on the pistol grip. Pivoting slowly, he inspected the country around him and a smirk of satisfaction spread across his broad face. The thin scrub offered little protection, but plenty of concealment. Once he entered the thickets of wattle they would hide him as easily as they hid the cattle from the ringers during each muster. Ahead was a low stony rise, and beyond, the cloud of dust from Morgan's machine cast a constant shadow against the sky. He walked confidently towards the noise of the bulldozer, knowing Ray was unsuspecting and concentrating on his work.

It's time you paid the rent, he muttered, struggling to persuade himself his intentions were justified while he carefully made his way up through the jumbled rocks and boulders. I'm sorry it's you first but you leave me no choice, he reasoned with his reluctance. You can wreck everything if you tell anybody about the plane crash. You're white, just like the rest of the invaders, he spat with forced contempt.

Chilpu, he remembered, and snorted with disgust. Ha! You don't deserve to be called Old Man. You're just a shit whitefella who reckons he knows a bit about the bush. You don't know a thing about my country. You have to die, you bastard whitefella. He flailed his doubts to one side, picking at old scabs of resentment and injustice while anger banished reluctance and burned his skin. Muttering to feed his courage, he kept low, working his way towards the sharp-edged rock slab on the crest of the rise. He mustered every past insult, real and imagined, until bitterness cloyed his mouth, mixing with the dust of his land. He wriggled into place between two grey boulders, careful to avoid the spiked spinifex.

The banana-shaped magazine bumped around the jutting rocks as he struggled to get a good shooting position. Frustrated, he knelt, threw the rifle to his shoulder and sighted on the cloud of dust seventy metres away.

The dozer moved backward and forward as Ray pushed a sheet of loose dirt over the rocks sticking up from the saddle between two low crests. Each push took him a little further over the rough ground, leaving a level finished track behind him. Dust hovered thickly as he worked and reworked the small area. With automatic movements he alternated between forward and reverse with monotonous regularity. His ears were attuned to the squeak and clatter of the tracks and undercarriage. He listened to the healthy roar of the motor. He knew the machine, the sounds it made when it was happy and the groans and scrunches of serious trouble.

Nelson aimed through the heavy dust and pulled the trigger tight. The recoil caught him unawares and the first twenty rounds spewed high as the barrel kicked upwards.

The explosive dzzzzzzzzztt whine of the first bullets took Ray by surprise. Long-gone days of military training threw him to one side and he cleared the clattering tracks, earmuffs torn from his head as he rolled on the ground.

Nelson saw Ray fall, and he quickly resighted, holding the trigger down, the distinctive sound of metal on metal rattling loud as the last ten rounds punched through the dust until the bolt slammed home empty. Above the ringing in his ears he heard the dozer change note, the decelerator springing back to full throttle. The machine forged ahead, dirt and rocks tumbling in front of the blade. He peered through the dust, his incoherent elated shouting unheard above the noise of the machine.

"What if I missed?" he suddenly asked. "How could I?" he answered in jubilation, but caution ruled so he flopped low against the rocks, waiting for the dust to clear so he could confirm the kill. It would be a simple matter to mash the body under the steel tracks – a stumble, a fall, an accident gone wrong in the loneliness of the bush.

Driverless, the dozer rooted into the rocky ground. The blade snagged on a deeply buried boulder, the machine slowly pivoting, before stalling in one final grunt.

Hydraulic oil streamed from a line of holes in the tank beside the driver's seat. "I hit him!" Nelson exclaimed jubilantly, not knowing the bullets had spent their force on the oil. As the dust dispersed he glimpsed Ray's fallen shape on the ground behind the machine and then the prone figure looked up cautiously. Wounded, not dead. "Shit!" He spat into the powdery dust. He snapped the magazine from the rifle to reload then angrily slapped it back into place in disgust. "No bloody ammo left," he cursed quietly. "A few seconds for thirty rounds," he swore, intently searching the ground around the now silent dozer.

Laying low against the warm rocks, a knot of fear shafted ice cold through his guts when Ray dashed from the low rock to the protection of the dozer. His crouching run was low and fast and unhindered.

"Shit! I missed him."

Nelson scrabbled back down the slope, heedless of the prickly spinifex. He stooped and ran away, the blood pounding in his ears blocking out any pursuing shout. Reaching a wattle thicket, he slipped inside, his breath a raging gasp. He waited, the now useless rifle held tight in shaking hands.

Chapter 26

CROUCHED BEHIND THE DOZER, RAY LISTENED to the steady piddle of oil falling on the steel tracks. The manifold cooled and cracked as he strained to hear any sounds beyond the machine.

Blood welled slowly from his shoulder and the thick coating of dust on his arm soaked it up. A bullet had broken the skin, a biting sear of heat as it passed. The first burst had spent itself on the hydraulic oil tank while the last of the bullets had plucked the stuffing from the arms and back of the seat. The second, more accurate burst scythed through the dust directly into the open cabin, but by then he was over the side, slipping on the hot steel tracks and then scrabbling on the ground.

He waited, wondering only where his assailant was. The long forgotten copper taste of fear and action flooded his mouth.

"Come on, mate," he hissed. The electric shock of fear was cold on his skin and chilled sweat trickled beneath his ears but refused to roll down his spine. He listened over his racing heart and concentrated on sounds beyond the machine.

Nothing.

The distinctive heavy chtud-chtud rang in his ears, an instantly recognisable memory – the sound of the enemy with an AK47. From memory too came the instinctive crouch and calculations of combat.

"Come on, mate, you've used one magazine, let's slap the other one into place," he softly chanted by rote as he had been drilled, imagining the movements he would make if he held the assault rifle. "The best shooters tape two magazines together, end to end. Slip the empty out, reverse it, and slap the new magazine in."

No movement, no noise.

"You're no professional, mate. Only a fool fires on full automatic. You haven't used an AK47 too often, I'll bet." He grimaced, about to bet his life on this judgement.

Dusting his hat and pulling the brim low against the sunlight, he cautiously lifted himself onto the steel track, and keeping low, scrabbled under the seat for the short steel pry-bar he carried. It was a poor weapon of defence but better than nothing. Blistering hot from the sun, it slipped from his fingers and clattered on the tracks, the sound of metal on metal shouting 'shoot now' across the rocky ridge but there was no answering blast of gunfire.

Picking it up gingerly, he carefully scanned the rock ridge, peering through the gap between the track and the drive sprocket teeth. Methodically he quartered the ridge, looking for tell tale vertical movement or the gleam of an eye to give all he needed to expose an otherwise hidden animal or sniper.

"Used all your ammo, have you?" he whispered. "Let's see what you're made of."

He darted to the other side of the dozer, glancing at the gaggle of bullet holes in the tank, linking the arc of fire to a point directly opposite on the rocky rise. As he expected, no more bullets splattered the ground, but he walked carefully up the low ridge searching for the gunman's position.

He found the thirty bright stubby brass shells quickly. Same as the other brass I picked up, he noted angrily, wondering if this was a shooter copycat of the German tourist who had recently gone on a random killing spree across northern Australia before being killed by police across the West Australia border near Kununurra.

"It'll be the last time this tourist uses this rifle. That's if it is a tourist," he finished doubtfully.

He cast around and found the tracks leading away from the rise. He followed them through the torn spinifex clumps, angry eyes focused on the country around him, probing for his hidden enemy. Further on, rocks gave way to scree and then to sand covered with a layer of thin fallen leaves in wattle thickets. The imprint of smooth heeled riding boots was occasionally clear in the sand, but often only the scruff of newly disturbed leaves guided him. Carefully he scanned the low bushes, searching for a crouched shape or unexpected movement.

Wiping sweat from beneath his hat, he shuffled cautiously through the oven of heat trapped below the canopy of wattle leaves. He crouched for some time in the wattle thicket where Nelson had sheltered, the narrow-leafed trees offering only a thin screen of protection from prying eyes. The tracks told him his quarry was long gone and no longer a immediate threat.

"Fuck me!" he gasped, the inevitable adrenaline departure leaving hands suddenly shaking in a cold sweat. He deflated in the meagre shade, rage supplanting fear.

"What right have you got? What right now...?" He spat viciously into the scrabble of footprints where Nelson had cowered, stabbing the steel pry-bar into the hot sand. "What right do you have to make me feel like this? I don't want to die, and I don't want to kill you either. That time is gone. Now I have things I want to live for." And in that moment he unconsciously resolved his commitment to the pretty school teacher.

"I've done nothing," he reasoned coldly. "Why should I have to walk and sleep in fear just because you – whoever you are – decided to have a bit of fun?" he snarled.

Squatting, he took his tobacco tin from his pocket and with unsteady hands, rolled a cigarette. He imagined a pure fantasy of revenge and it was a balm for his fear. He remembered the seductive caress of the trigger and the cringing warrant officer bully on the wrong side of the rules of engagement. Back then he had thrown the SLR assault rifle to one side, but the memory of 'what if' never went away.

He lit the cigarette, his need for calming nicotine greater than the danger of discovery and concentrated completely on the drifting smoke. Fear sat beside him, and he reluctantly acknowledged its unwelcome return.

I'll find you, he decided, and when I know who and where you are, I'll hand the matter over to the Law. This isn't the Mekong Delta or the Wild West. "No, this isn't the Wild West," he repeated to himself with a determined whisper. "But if the Law won't come to you then I'll make sure you go to the Law," he vowed.

Resolved, he flicked the cigarette to one side. He stood, and then retrieved the butt, pinched it out, and returned it to the tin. He tracked Nelson to where the station Toyota had been hidden. He bent down and inspected the riding boot imprints clear in the grey dust.

"You've got trouble with one boot, old mate," he said. "It's been half-soled, and now it's lifting."

"Big deal!" he scoffed, kicking the ground. "I'm looking for someone who drives a Toyota pickup, wears a half-soled boot and is probably about my size. That should narrow it down to about eighty per cent of the ringers in this country."

Returning to his Toyota at day's end, the smashed HF radio behind the front seat came as no surprise.

Chapter 27

'TUESDAY, AUGUST 8,' WENDY WROTE NEATLY in the yellow exercise book, scoring two lines under the date. Sucking on the top of her pen, she leant her elbows on the narrow kitchen table, by now heedless of the grit covering all. Mind made up, she started writing.

'I still can't get over the excitement of the last week,' she wrote in still fanciful script, but with fewer hearts and flower petals in place of full stops. 'It hardly seems twenty-four hours since Ray was here offering me enough money to buy the station. And then to have Nelson tell me more about the gold. It's fantastic. I have to tell someone, even though I am not supposed to. Dear Diary, can you keep the secret safe?'

"Last night Nelson came across when I asked him. I asked him to stay in the house permanently, but he was very nervous.

He said he would think about it. I admit I am a bit peeved – as if he should have to think about it at all. It is so nice having someone beside me when I wake up in the middle of the night. He was going out to talk to Ray about the gold from the plane crash and then go out to the coast. I do hope Ray agrees, but then, he is such a kind person he is sure to."

She heard a vehicle pull up and the dogs barked. Peering between the dusty louvres she saw it was Ray. She guiltily closed the diary, and quickly hid it at the back of the kitchen drawer.

"Come in," she shouted before he had time to knock. "Would you like a cup of tea?"

He opened the door with his left hand and she noticed his right arm was stiff. He winced as he lifted his hat a fraction before settling it on his head again. His trousers and blue singlet were pale with dust and his skin carried the dark grime of work. He shook his head in refusal.

"Could I use your radio?" he asked.

"Certainly. What's wrong? Isn't your radio working?"

"It got smashed up yesterday afternoon."

"Was there an accident? Oh! Are you alright?" she gasped, hands going to her cheeks. "Let me see," she demanded, rushing to him. "It's your arm, isn't it? I can see you're hurt."

He shrugged his shoulders, but the raw slash across his bare brown arm was a magnet for her. Giving in, he sat down. "It's only a scratch," he protested.

"It could get ulcerous," she said, suddenly knowledgeable about tropical medicine.

"No. It's more of burn. Some bastard took a shot at me."

"Oh my God!"

She recovered, hands over her eyes. "It's terrible, terrible, terrible. What happened? When did it happen? Who shot at you?" she blurted.

"Blowed if I know, but I aim to pull him up short. He smashed my radio as well. I'd like to get the copper from Borroloola out here so I need to use your radio."

"Now, I don't like coppers, but they have a job to do, and if things turn ugly, I would prefer to be on the right side of the Law. I don't mind taking a few killers, but when people start shooting I'd prefer to have the Law behind me."

"Use the radio quickly. You might be able to stop them before they have gone too far," she urged.

"No point. This happened yesterday afternoon. I tracked him for a bit, but he took off. Didn't seem much point in rushing off to the police. I wanted time to give it a bit of thought."

"Yesterday? It happened yesterday? What a pity Nelson didn't go out to you yesterday. He was going to but then he went to the coast instead."

Ray didn't move and he hoped his face did not reveal his surprise. Wendy looked at him, eyes wide and ran her fingers through her hair. He absently noted her wedding band had been removed since his last visit.

"What did he want to see me about?" he asked with as much casualness as he could muster.

"About the gold you found." She looked at him, her eyes trusting. "He wants to talk to you. It's very important. I'll get him."

She stood up quickly, and before he could stop her, she was out the door and heading towards the workshop. Ray waited quietly, a multitude of strange thoughts colliding in his mind and driving out his intention to use the radio. He needed to fish for information before firming his growing suspicion this attack was from no wayward tourist well off the beaten track.

Expecting Wendy to return, he was surprised when Nelson walked through the door as if he owned the station. Wendy followed in his wake.

"Gooday, chilpu," he said cheerfully. Ray nodded, not trusting himself to answer. Nelson sat at one end of the table. "Get some tea, will you?" he commanded, and Wendy started filling the kettle. "What's the problem?" he asked.

"You tell me," Ray answered blandly, the bait disguised with studied disinterest. "According to Wendy, you wanted to see me yesterday."

Nelson forced a broad smile that never made it to his eyes.

"Yair, I wanted to catch up with you, but I got tied up out at the coast," he lied.

"Didn't realise you were going to muster out there," Ray probed, setting the hook to catch a bigger lie.

"Just went out to check on the yards," he said, confident of his right as boss to make the decisions on the station and laying groundwork for a cover story if he needed the ringers near the coast to help with his future plans.

Ray leant back on his chair. "Go on."

Nelson, confident in his cover story, missed the hint of menace. "I was on my way out tomorrow to see you but no need now. Anyways, you told Wendy about some gold you found the other day at the plane crash site."

Nelson leant forward, hands on the table. The clean shirt sleeves were rolled up tight around his biceps. He drummed his fingers on the table as he continued crisply, defying Ray to contradict him.

"I found the same crash a few weeks ago. There was more gold there, but I took it away. I must have missed the box you found."

He pinned Ray with a threatening stare. "I've arranged for the gold to be sold, and I'm lending some of the money to Wendy so she can buy Punkatoy. A blackfella like me, he can't go selling gold on the open market. Poor bugger me, I would go to jail for taking gold that's been lying around for years. Same could happen to you," he threatened casually.

Ray stayed where he was, arms folded across his chest, apparently unmoved by Nelson's threat.

"You want us all to put a bullet in the body," he observed laconically, gently setting the hook.

Nelson snapped back in his chair, worried Ray knew who had shot at him. "What do you mean?" he asked defensively, hands gripping the edge of the table.

"Years ago if one of the boys got too out of hand in a stock camp they sometimes got shot. Every whitefella in the camp had to put a bullet into the body so they were all guilty of murder. None of them could ever tell the Law because they would be ratting on themselves as well."

"So are you suggesting we do the same? Are you trying to make me equally guilty so you can be certain I won't go to the Law?" He considered adding his own threat, but refrained, more interested in understanding Nelson's intentions.

Relieved to be free of suspicion, Nelson turned to Wendy. "Come sit down here and listen," he directed. Wendy pulled her chair closer to Nelson and he held her hand.

"We both want to help Wendy. The gold is no good as it is, so it has to be changed into cash. The Vietnamese crabbers down on Corella Creek have the contacts for this. They already swap my gold for cash, and they can do the same for you. It's no great problem, and all of us will benefit. But if the police find out, then we can kiss our money goodbye ... and the station too. We end up with nothing and in jail."

Ray watched them both, Nelson confident in his argument and Wendy trailing in the web of deceit. Wendy sought Ray's fingers to unite the two men in their conspiracy. He didn't move and her hand fell short on the table.

"Sounds fair enough. How much gold did you find?"

"About as much as you," Nelson answered, the evasion quick as a cardsharp cheat.

Ray nodded, his face relaxed. You always were a terrible liar, he decided. The tracks say there were more than two boxes in the plane. You're cooking up something else, Nelson Shortjack. Your pockets will be well lined by the time this is all finished. I wish I knew what for? Let's just see how far you'll go.

He slouched, arms crossed and feet stretched out beneath the table.

"I'm happy to keep the lid on it if we split the money three ways. No loans. Just a straight split. I'll go with you to the crabber's camp and they can tell us how much cash they'll give us. I bet it won't be anywhere near the market price, but as you said, the gold is still warm. A three-way split of our two boxes of gold. Sound fair enough?"

"No problems," Nelson agreed so rapidly that Ray knew he was lying again. He manufactured a smile of gratitude and waited for the objections and counter proposal.

"You'll have to trust me," Nelson explained, his expression genial. "The Vietnamese are very suspicious people. They trust me because they know me already. If you suddenly appeared, they might pull out of the deal completely."

Ray looked noncommittal, hoping to draw Nelson deeper onto his hook, but Wendy set the barbs.

"I trust you," Wendy offered, looking at each in turn, her eyes bright with greed and hope. "I trust you both. You are such wonderful men."

Now certain the lovers were going to split the bulk of the money between them, he agreed, satisfied he knew what was happening.

"Yair, it's alright by me. It's no skin off my nose either way," he said truthfully. "As long as I get my share I'll have all the money I need." He leant on the table, and Wendy seized his hand, squeezed it, and then held Nelson's arm.

"Thanks," she confirmed with simple sincerity, convinced of only good outcomes.

"What happened to your arm, chilpu?" Nelson asked. Emboldened with success, he knew it would be unnatural if he didn't ask.

"Someone took a shot at me. That's what I came in for. I just wanted to let the boys at Borroloola know. Can't use my radio, so I want to use the station radio," Ray explained as if he was still perplexed by the random shooting.

"Wouldn't worry about it," Nelson dismissed police involvement with a dissolute wave. "It was only a mob of gun happy tourists. They took a shot at me yesterday." He grinned, lying smoothly to Ray and ignoring the look of horror on Wendy's face.

"How can you be so sure they have gone?"

"They were headed back down the road towards Borroloola. I chased them for a while, but they were too fast."

The story rang as true as the false smile glued to his face but Wendy took it at face value.

"Oh! The tea!" Wendy cried, jumping to her feet. Both men rolled a cigarette in a silence that had once been companionable, while she made the tea. Satisfied his story was accepted, Nelson turned his chair, stretched his legs and crossed his feet. Ray quietly noted Nelson's half-soled boot coming away at the join.

"Must have been pig shooting," Ray suggested. "What sort of rifles were they using?"

"Sounded like a .303," Nelson lied effortlessly.

"That would be right," Ray agreed, bait taken and the lie well-hooked and landed.

Why? Ray wondered. I don't care if you knock off most of the gold you found. I've got enough to keep me happy without having to be greedy into the bargain. Why are you worried about me? What else are you hiding?

He drank his tea calmly.

Chapter 28

THE GREY KANGAROO BOUNCED OFF THE heavy bulbar with a sickening thud. Brakes full on, Wendy slewed the Landcruiser pickup to the left across the gravel road, stones rattling along the bodywork. The Toyota shuddered to a stop in a cloud of yellow dust.

"What did you stop for?" Nelson demanded, but Wendy was out of the door before she heard his question. The grey doe was dust-covered and bloody where white leg bones poked through broken skin. Grunting, she kicked one hind leg feebly, no strength left to prick her ears in fright as Wendy approached.

"Come here quick!" she yelled to Nelson.

"I'm coming," he answered grumpily, grabbing a tyre iron. "Out of the way," he directed, brandishing the iron bar, ready to kill the doe.

"No! No! She's still alive," Wendy cried. She held the grey furry face with its bloody nose close to her dusty T-shirt, rocking back and forth as the animal struggled.

"Get out of the way! It's nearly bloody dead anyway. Shift so I can give it a belt across the head."

Tears welled and she shook her head violently as soft shudders of death wracked its body. Wendy hung her head and wept quietly while Nelson stood nonchalantly by the tailgate.

The joey squiggled in the still warm pouch. With a life of its own, a pink, almost hairless tail, wriggled free of the soft furry pouch. The joey clawed at the cooling walls of his refuge with outsized feet. Wendy felt the movement between her tears and, reaching carefully into the soft pouch, grabbed the struggling mass.

She pulled him gently from his hiding place and clasped him quickly to her chest. Bulging dark eyes darted around the bright world. Large ears twitched, the sunlight picking out the red veins on his hairless skin.

"He's alive," she crooned, looking over her shoulder at Nelson, stick still held loosely in his hand. "Isn't it wonderful?" Turning back to the joey, she hugged him fiercely and felt the tiny heart beating against hers.

"Give me your shirt," she demanded. Scowling, he reluctantly complied, throwing her a bundle of cloth, leaving his strong shoulders dull black in the bright sun.

"That's no good," she snapped. "Button up the front to make a sort of pouch. Come on! Quickly!"

"It's a waste of time, Mawu."

"It's not. I can save this baby," she insisted.

"It'll die anyway," he growled with matter-of-fact certainty, absently scratching the thickening stubble of his beard.

"Just shut up and button your shirt to make a pouch. That's all I'm asking you to do."

Shaking his head in resignation, he slowly buttoned the shirt. You stupid bitch, he sighed. Dead is dead. You'll learn. If I didn't need you for a few more weeks, sometimes I wouldn't even bother to talk to you. You make me sick, and knew his desire for her made him sick as well.

"Here you are. Let the joey feel his way into the opening so he'll feel comfortable and warm, Mawu. He won't struggle as much," he instructed handing her his shirt.

She stood, holding the tiny bundle close to her body. "You drive, please," she asked.

He shrugged and checked the front of the pickup for any obvious damage. Taking the driver's seat he drove forward, the gravel road snaking along the lower edges of steep cliffs, shades of grey on grey in the sunlight.

"Where are you going? Turn around. I've got to get..." she searched for a name for the smooth-skinned joey, "Bunty back to the station so I can look after him. He looks just like a Bunty, doesn't he?" she crooned. Limpid eyes searched her face while the bulbous nose twitched with fear.

"It looks like a dead joey to me," he responded dryly. "It'll die of shock within half an hour no matter what you do. We have to keep working on the fences if we're going to convince the bank you can run this place. Don't waste your time on something that is going to die anyway."

A dry creek wound its way beside the road, only tall white ghost gums indicating its course. A few kangaroos peered through the listless tea trees, ignoring the pickup trailing a slow curling cloud of boiling dust.

"Turn around!" Wendy demanded. "If you don't turn around this baby Bunty is going to die. The fences can wait but this baby can't."

"So what?" Nelson asked cruelly.

"I can save Bunty. We have to save him. I'll never forgive you if Bunty dies!"

Nelson angrily stomped the brakes in frustration, the Toyota lurching to the left, stopping angled across the road. Pale yellow dust swept over them, smothering the cab. Wendy glared furiously, about to berate him again, but he cut off her protests.

"It's too small to eat, and it's too young to survive," he explained through gritted teeth. "You've got to learn this," Nelson snapped brutally, patience exhausted.

"You of all people," she accused. "I thought you would have understood. The Old People cared for the animals in their country."

"It dead already!" Nelson pointed out roughly. The tiny head flopped in her arms, sightless eyes staring at the unforgiving dry scrub beyond the windscreen. Wendy sobbed loudly, holding the small warm body closer. Nelson shook his head, contempt difficult to conceal.

"You bastard!" she spat. "I thought you were different."

"You listen here," he growled, finger jabbing the air. "This country is my country and we have our own rules. In this country you're either alive, or you're dead and eaten. The dingoes would have taken it within an hour." Contemptuous of her concern he waved his hand dismissively to take in the tottering escarpment and the washed-out grey green scraggle of scrub on the flat stretching towards the rise on the other side of the valley.

"It was dingo bait from the time you hit the 'roo. It's no good wailing, because it doesn't change the way things are. Dead is dead, and weak is dead. If you can't eat it or use it, then it is useless. You reckon you really want to learn about this country, then this is the first thing you learn. Your soft-hearted greenie rules don't apply in my world."

He sat back, angrily rolling another cigarette. The tumbled rocks, the rearing termite mounds, the listless leaves all waited indifferently, the outcome inevitable. Eyes red-rimmed, she looked at him sullenly.

"Will you help me bury him?" she asked in a small voice.

"Give it here," he snapped, knowing she still didn't understand. Reluctantly she handed the warm bundle to him. He roughly pulled the dead joey from the makeshift pouch, and before she had time to move, threw it out the open window onto the dusty windrow.

"You bastard!" she screeched and threw herself at him. He fended her off, easily holding her flailing fists. He let her go when she dropped her arms in frustration. She cringed on the far side of the vehicle, weeping weakly. "I thought you would know better. I thought you would care," she lamented over and over again.

"Mawu," he whispered quietly, more to himself than to her. "What do you know? You take my land and then tell me I do not know how to live on it. Mawu, do not tell me what to do on my own country!" he hissed.

"At least I'm not cruel," she accused, huddling in the corner.

Nelson bit back an angry reply. A few more weeks, he seethed wordlessly. Just a few more weeks and then you and your stupidity will be gone. Maggot!

He smashed into first gear and for a while only the rumbling of tyres on the gravel road cut the silence. Reason supplanting anger, he put his hand her thigh, smiling through gritted teeth. He felt shamed at what he was about to do, and was relieved there was no-one else to listen.

"I'm sorry," he started, his throat choked with self-contempt. He swallowed several times before he could bring himself to continue and she took it for contrition.

"I'm sorry I've upset you," and that much at least is true he thought. "Let me try to explain. This is my country and my dreaming. It is the country my ancestors lived on for thousands of years."

"Doesn't give you the right to be cruel," she hissed.

"What is cruelty? It is a whitefella word. Cruelty is the luxury of an overfed world. You use a hot branding iron on the cattle. But that's not cruel, is it? It helps you to make a dollar it's OK." He breathed deeply, his words clipped.

She did not pull away when his strong calloused hand stroked her thigh gently. He marshalled his thoughts away from bitterness, for he wanted her to understand even though he knew she never really could.

"Cruelty is something belong to fat people with plenty of food. When you struggle everyday to find food then cruelty is a luxury you can't afford. It won't fill an empty belly. Our people lived off the country but we only killed for food. Your mob kill for sport, just for the fun of it. Isn't that the cruellest of all?"

She bowed her head, nodding agreement. She took his hand. "I think we should ban all guns and make shooting illegal," she said seriously.

He snorted, loathing the need for his gentle explanation and her simplistic views. A dead kangaroo is more important to her than the cruelty of generations of suffering, he realised. She doesn't see the real human cruelty around her, so he told her.

"You know Old Harry?" he asked, and saw only ignorance in her eyes. "He's the old bloke in the camp with white hair and long beard. He doesn't actually work on the station, but he has always been in this country. You have a close look at him next time you go down to the camp. You look at his ankles, and around his neck. Look carefully, because they look like his other tribal scars at first."

"What am I looking for?"

"They're whitefella scars from when he was chained like a dog for days. You whitefellas give a dog a leather collar, but they made his out of iron. It heated in the sun and burned him. The chains on his ankles cut his flesh to the bone."

"Stop it," she moaned, using his shirt to cover her ears in denial.

"Cut his flesh to the bone when they took him to Borroloola. They made him walk in front of the policeman's horse tied by the rope to the saddle. They started here at the station, at Pungkuthuyi, and they didn't stop until they reached the lock-up at Borroloola. More than two hundred kilometres over bloody rough country."

She shook her head slowly in disbelief and horror. Nelson gleefully twisted the knife.

"But it wasn't cruel because he was only a blackfella," he spat.

They drove on in silence, Wendy absorbing the indifference of the wide-spread flat between the hills skirting the shallow valley, pale-trunked sentinels of snappy gum and dark bauhinia trees shimmering in the heat.

You hate us. You hate me. Is it any wonder? she admitted to herself. We raped your country and destroyed your people and your language. She turned, breaking the silence. "I'm so sorry, Nelson," apologising humbly for herself and her race. She ran her fingers down his bare brown shoulders.

"It's not you personally," Nelson conceded, hating the necessary lie as he spoke it. "We have to tell the rest of the whitefellas what has happened.

We have to make them understand we own the land and the land owns us.
I think you see now."

"I do," she cried, eager to please him and placate a world full of past sins.
"Let me help you," she implored. "Please tell me how I can help."

"I will, Mawu," he affirmed, a satisfied smile lifting the corners of his
mouth and creeping across his face.

Chapter 29

WENDY SAT AT THE KITCHEN TABLE, pen poised over a new blank page of her diary and listened to Nelson in the shower. Distracted, she imagined his naked body shiny with water. She fondly remembered the sour musty tang he left in the bed and the texture of his calloused hands gliding smoothly across her body. She shivered in anticipation before returning to write in her secret diary.

"Nelson told me today how this country was stolen from his people. Now I feel like a thief and a rapist. I can't understand why he is not bitter. If I was him I would probably want to kill every white person in the area, but Nelson is not like that," she wrote.

"He is kind and gentle, even though I thought he was cruel today. Perhaps I was wrong. Cruelty is for fat people, he said, and now I think I can see what he means. Perhaps he is right, but it was so sad to see the beautiful little joey die."

She heard the shower stop, so quickly closing the diary, she hid it at the back of the kitchen drawer. Her breasts were tender against the gritty T-shirt, and she rubbed them lightly, her nipples springing up. Effortlessly surrendering to desire, she slipped out of the T-shirt and wriggled free of her dusty jeans, discarding them on the floor before she opened the bathroom door.

Chapter 30

"THEY HAVE GOT TO PAY FOR living on blackfella land," Nelson repeated to Douglas as the old Toyota crept down the rough path towards Corella Creek, moving too slowly to raise dust despite the parching August sun. Nothing moved, the country dozing in the heat. After weeks of waiting, the guns supplied by the crabbers were within reach. He suppressed his excitement and continued to goad Douglas in preparation for the pick up.

"You right there, Nelson. Them whitefellas rape, and murder our people and our land. I want to smash 'em!" Douglas snarled, willingly taking his aggressive cue from Nelson. Weeks off the grog had not improved his temper, and the growing itch for a fight and to hurt remained unscratched. He ran his fingers across the hard edge of the wide plate buckle on his leather trouser belt.

Taken off and swung wildly, the belt and buckle were a brutal escalation in any fight. At a pinch, the short-bladed castrating knife could be pulled from its belt pouch. He grinned fondly with the memory of a single wild brawl, berserk with grog and bloodlust, belt and buckle swinging wild streaks of blood, whooping with sheer joy at unleashed violence. It was only once, but reputations were made by this.

"Payback is right. They call us Aboriginals and deny us proper recognition. For them, we are non-existent people. We are not Aboriginal. We are warriors!" Nelson gripped the steering wheel tightly, his face distorted with contempt. The language was beyond Douglas, but he understood the feeling.

"I be proper blackfella and I be proud of it," Douglas said at last.

"That's right," Nelson acknowledged. "Sorry. I sound like one of those city kooris I used to know. But you know what I mean. It's one law for the whites and one law for the blacks," he railed.

"It be mainly jail for blackfella," Douglas stated as a bland accepted truth.

"True one," Nelson agreed bitterly.

Douglas laughed, narrow eyes twinkling with sudden good humour above his tangled sharp-bladed beard.

"I only be out here at the station because of that policeman in Borroloola," Douglas confessed as their laughter subsided.

"He run you out of town?"

"Yair. I was just sitting down there for a few weeks having a few drinks with my mates. Every night that policeman, he be lock me up. Reckon I fight too much, but most of the time it only a friendly fight."

Douglas looked away, a sullen slant coming to his shoulders and watched the thick tea tree and flaky tufted trunk paperbarks drift by. His right hand curling and unclenching against his left, the memory of rage unsatisfied.

"I really want to kill that Eddie from Five Emu, but some other fella, he hit me from behind," he added seriously. "I tell you, Eddie dead next time I see him. He too cheeky fella. He lucky man because that policeman lock me up. He tell me he lock me up for longest time if I stay in town, so I come bush for a while. I been sit down here now."

"What for you want to kill Eddie?"

"He shame me, I think," the simple explanation excuse enough.

Nelson smiled, satisfied he made the right choice in selecting Douglas for this meeting. Douglas had a natural insolent urge to fight and he needed the visible threat of violence for the meeting with the crabbers. But he needed more from Douglas and with the crabbers' camp drawing closer, he had no choice but to take the inevitable next step. Turning his attention back to driving, he slowed, and began to run down the side of a creekbank.

"We gotta fight the whitefellas," he said seriously, introducing Douglas for the first time to his true plans. Despite confidence in his choice, a sliver of doubt remained about his ability to turn Douglas's sullen aggression into something more purposeful.

"The whitefellas say, 'Look at them blackfellas. They always fighting amongst themselves.' We have show them how strong we really are. I want you to help me."

"Hey! What that!"

Nelson slowed almost to a halt, arms crossed over the steering wheel. "I want your help to throw the whitefellas off Pungkuthuyi. I want you to be number one offsider."

"You don't need my help. You be go buy the station. You said so yourself," Douglas reminded him.

Nelson snorted with contempt. "You really think the whitefella would let us use stolen gold to buy one of their stations? No way! They won't give us anything without a fight. The only way we're going to take this station back is the same way they took it off us."

"How that be?" Douglas asked, incredulous.

"Simple. We blow the bastards out just like we shoot scrub bulls."

"Eh! They'll lock us fella up forever."

"Not if we're strong enough to win. A few well-armed men in this wild country can hold off an army. It's guerrilla warfare. They did it in Zimbabwe and they're doing it now in South Africa. We can do it here easily."

Douglas took off his hat and ran his fingers through his lank hair. He pursed his lips and frowned. He studied the inside of his dirty tall crown hat, turned the front of the brim down a bit more, then put it back on his head. "I think you been drinking, hey? Who help us? We need guns, biggest mobs of guns."

Nelson reached over, grabbing the shoulder beneath the checked flannel shirt. "Listen," he hissed urgently, glancing at the twisting track. "I've got the guns. Once we start, others will join us. The mob back at the station will join us, even if we have to force one or two. This land is our land, and our brothers know it. With good guns we win easy because we know our country."

"You got guns?" Douglas's eyes gleamed at the possibilities. This was better than endless fights in squalid drinking camps, rolling in the dust, fuelled by grog and a never satisfied rage.

"Yair. AK47's. That's what I traded the gold for... guns and ammunition." And cash, he added silently.

"What be an AK47?" Douglas interrupted.

For Nelson it was the iconic weapon of revolution, featured on every liberation poster he had seen but for Douglas the appeal would be more basic.

"It's a fully automatic rifle like Rambo use. They're simple to use. I've got one already, and I tell you ..." Taking his hands off the wheel for a moment, he sprayed the bush with an imaginary burst of fire. "Beats a spear," he laughed.

"We pick them up later today and then we do some training. Once we're ready, then we'll make our demands. I know we will have to fight, but we have the advantage because Punkatoy is so isolated so we can pick our own time and place."

Sitting in silence, they both, for different reasons, savoured the prospect. Douglas, happier thinking with his fists, ventured a question.

"What we want?"

He half turned to Nelson, who stopped the Toyota, draping his arms over the steering wheel. Avoiding confrontation, Nelson looked straight ahead and spoke quietly into the distance.

"First we take over the station. I'll force Wendy to leave and we'll run the place. No more whitefellas on the station. No white owners, no white managers, no whitefellas at all. This my sand goanna singing and whitefellas has no part of it."

Nelson grinned to himself, imagining the country fat with cattle and alive with game. Good food whenever he wanted, the freedom to give his own orders and enough money to meet his needs. It was worth fighting for.

"Two," he continued boldly. "We take over the Yellowbank Mining Lease on Coolibah Downs. They really on Pungkuthuyi dreaming country. The uranium is ours, not theirs. They should pay us for the right to mine there, and we should get the money."

"There are only a few caretakers looking after the mine at the moment, so it'll be easy to take it. We'll have to fight because the mining company and the Government won't want us to have it."

Douglas smirked in anticipation of playing out his favourite Rambo action sequences. Imagining the kick of the assault rifle in his hands, bodies falling, he smiled broadly. He could feel the money from the mine royalties in his hands already and he broke into a wide satisfied grin.

"Thirdly," Nelson continued seriously "Ray Morgan has to go. We need his machine but we can do that sort of work ourselves. We don't need bastards like him working here, taking our money. We get rid of him early," he instructed, not voicing his real reasons.

"I blow the bastards out, no worries," Douglas promised enthusiastically. "Come on boss, let's go."

Satisfied, Nelson moved off, slowly picking the way along the faint yellow pea gravel path winding between the thick scrub, swerving suddenly, to avoid a large sand goanna arrogantly stalking across the track. Collect the gold first, then the guns. He drove on at a crawl, the bush apparently oblivious to their passing and planning. Thinking ahead about how to best handle the coming handover of gold for weapons and cash, he turned his thoughts back to his first encounter with the crabbers and what he had learned.

Chapter 31

1985, JUNE, MID-DRY SEASON.

THE WARM JUNE MID-DRY SEASON sun battled the south easterly winds but failed to warm anything beneath the deep shadows concealing the bush camp on the edge of the mangroves. Nelson knew how he handled the first contact with the Vietnamese crabbers was important if the gold proposal was to succeed, so he waited patiently and watched the little woman fuss about the crabbers' bush camp.

Arriving by boat in Darwin as refugees fleeing the communist regime, some chose, or were forced, to live on the edges of the European community and they slipped easily into the grey world of semi-legitimate activity. For those who knew nothing but a life of fishing amongst Mekong mazes, the lure of plundering remote coastlines for crab and illegally netted fish was too great to resist. They supplied lazy and less scrupulous local licence holders in a well-established illicit trade. Some who knew little other than fishing also knew smuggling and they retained their contacts. It was a conduit for drugs and other contraband.

An old faded blue plastic tarp was strung between two trees, sloping away gently from the ridge pole. A red Honda generator clattered away in the mangrove thicket, its noise rippling clearly across the open water. Petrol drums were stacked near the camp. Bleached red and blue plastic trays rested in unstable piles at several points around the camp. A jumble of metal mesh crab pots lay scattered under the trees. The entire camp and its equipment skulked warily under the dense cover of the mangrove canopy, discovered only by the midges and mosquitoes.

The woman was short with a thinness only relentless hard work can bring. Her straight black hair tied back under a faded nylon American-style tractor cap matched the loose black peasant fishing pants. She worked repairing the white nylon nets used to fish illegally in the river. Nelson quietly angled around the camp so he could walk towards her front on, but in her concentration, she did not see him.

"Gidday, Missus," he shouted over the noisy petrol generator.

She jumped, dropping the bamboo needle she was using to repair the net. She backed away slowly towards the open tent, eyes not leaving him.

"What do you want?" she asked defiantly, assessing the threat.

"I want to talk," Nelson replied, standing still and holding his hands out and open in front of him.

"Yes," she acknowledged, backing into the tent to lean against the edge of the table. He saw her right hand move slowly behind her. Finding the long bladed filleting knife, she stopped fidgeting and leant back casually on the table, armed and ready to move quickly.

"What do you want to talk about?" she asked, more confident now a knife was within reach.

Anxious not to frighten her, Nelson squatted on the ground, hoping he appeared less threatening. "I want to talk some business with you. When are the men due back?"

"They'll be back very soon," she assured him. She darted a few steps to the generator, flicked the switch and the motor died. She was back at the table in one quick movement and again standing close by the knife. "They'll be back very soon. They aren't far away," she said, confident the silenced generator has sent a distress signal.

"Good. I wait." He sat on the ground, legs crossed in front of him. The mid-morning sun beat on his back and warmed his hat. He guessed the silent generator was a signal for the men to return. Slowly he rolled a cigarette while they both waited in an uneasy stand-off for the sound of the returning outboard. Together they listened to the flies buzzing around the fish scales and discarded crab claws and then to the buzz of an outboard motor.

An aluminium dinghy, piled high with empty crab pots, skidded around the corner and edged quickly into shore. The young man standing on the bow was searching the shore for trouble before the boat touched the muddy bank. As soon as the boat stopped, he jumped off, knife held openly in his right hand, the cutting edge uppermost. His stance, learned in the back streets and bars of Saigon, was professional and experienced.

"What do you want, buddy?" he demanded in perfect American GI English, stalking towards Nelson. "Get out! Scram."

Nelson remained sitting on the ground. "I want to talk business with you," he ventured more confidently than he felt.

The young man stopped, knife held ready by his side. His jeans and T-shirt were wet from pulling crab pots. He shifted the open-meshed baseball cap on his head and rubbed the sweat into his lank black hair. Hard, dark expressionless eyes watched Nelson. "Don't move," he instructed, and Nelson gleaned nothing from his face.

The older man, confident of his son's ability, climbed slowly up the river bank. His deeply lined face told Nelson nothing more than a story of long and patient suffering, different only in detail from the stories enfolded in Old Harry's face back at Punkatoy camp. His sea-bleached clothes were damp from sweat and water spray. He stood to one side, effectively hemming Nelson in.

"I am Tran. What you want?" he asked simply, his accent pronounced.

"I need some help, and I think you might be the people I can do business with," Nelson proposed, gambling on the lure of money to attract initial interest.

Tran considered the request and its implications. No stranger to working just outside the law he quickly decided the proposal was no threat.

"We do not have many visitors here. Business visitors are always welcome. Come, stand up and sit at the table."

Nelson stood slowly and followed the old man into the shade beneath the tarp. The son followed and Nelson felt a slight ripple of fear tumble down his spine. Next time, if there was a next time, he would bring back-up. They all sat clear of the roughly hewn wooden table, each tense and ready to spring into action if necessary.

"Your business?" Tran asked without preamble.

Now the moment had come, Nelson was unsure how he would broach the subject. The old man's directness had reduced his planned indirect approach to shambles. They don't waste anytime getting to the point, he thought. I would prefer to talk a bit, sound them out and get the feel of them before I asked them to help me. He looked at each of the men. Their hard faces and brittle eyes told him nothing. Where to start? He looked at them again, searching their expressionless faces for a clue.

"Well?" Tran asked impatiently.

"You do a lot of crabbing here. You do some fishing as well with the square hooks." He inclined his head towards the illegal nets, hoping to indicate his tolerance and kinship in illegal activities. "You know these waters well."

"You came to tell us your business, not to find out about ours," Tran interrupted briskly.

Nelson nodded eagerly in agreement, not wanting to lose this chance because his entire plan hinged on their co-operation. Sitting straighter, he matched their directness.

"I want to buy some rifles and ammunition." He paused and saw no reaction in their immobile faces. He continued carefully. "I want to buy AK47's or American surplus weapons. I can pay." He stopped, trying to force the men opposite into some reaction.

Tran's cold gaze sliced through him and he averted his eyes to look at the clear estuary water beyond Tran's shoulder. The short silence seemed to stretch for minutes.

"Cannot help," Tran replied flatly.

"Perhaps you know someone who can," Nelson blurted too quickly and they immediately understood his desperation and vulnerability.

The old man considered the question again calculating the value of Nelson's weakness. No-one moved while he thought, flies crawling undisturbed over his leathery face.

"Perhaps I know someone," he conceded. "But they would need a lot of money. Do you have a lot of money, Mister Aboriginal from the bush?"

"I have money ... but not with me," he added, suddenly more frightened as he understood the danger he was in without support. He held his breath and Tran's gaze.

"Perhaps we can talk some business, my friend," Tran said, and shuffled his chair closer to the table. Nelson stiffened, thinking it was a signal, but the son did the same. Nelson noticed the knives had disappeared and, breathing a silent sigh of relief and hope, he also shuffled to the uneven table.

"This is my son Paul. He has a Western name because now we must work in a Western country. My other sons are in Darwin now with a load of crabs. We sell them through a cousin of mine. Your name is?"

Nelson told him, aware the old man had listed his sons and cousins so he would understand the threat. Mistakes would be dangerous.

"This is my country," Nelson countered, although it made no difference to the barely tolerated homeless refugees. "I need seventy rifles, preferably AK47's and ammunition to go with them. And cash," he added.

Tran grunted. His son sat silently at the table, while the woman looked up from where she was working over the small gas stove.

"You wish to start a revolution, Mister Aboriginal. If you had so much money you could buy this country." He laughed dismissively, tears of amusement slipping down the lines of his face. Stung by his contempt, Nelson played his major card.

"I've enough gold to buy..." He didn't finish before the old man suddenly stopped laughing and slapped his hands on the table.

"Gold! This is good. Gold is very good in Vietnam now the Communists have destroyed our lives. Tell me more please."

"I have bars and I can deliver them here, but only when the guns arrive."

"It is not your gold," Tran stated with blunt certainty but without any hint of condemnation.

"True, but no-one is looking for it either. It was lost forty, nearly fifty, years ago."

Tran raised an eyebrow of interest. Nelson gave a brief background, careful not to reveal too much detail and giving away nothing about the location.

"I see," Tran grunted when Nelson ended his tale. Trust was not easily given, but a single "sample" weapon could always come in handy for other tasks. Gnarled fingers absently explored the smoothed table slats while sunlight dappled from the estuary waters. Risk, and trust and opportunity had carried him this far, but survival was not without obligation. During the pause, the woman served red plastic bowls of spicy steamed fish and boiled rice. She gave chopsticks to the men and a fork to Nelson.

Tran nodded. "I have cousins who might be willing to help you. Gold can help them get more of our family out of the 'new' Vietnam," a term he spat with contempt. "They would need to see the gold before they agreed to help."

"I would need to see the rifles before I hand over any gold," Nelson countered, encouraged and emboldened by the concession.

"Very wise," Tran agreed. "You bring a sample of your gold next week and I will have a sample of the rifles we can supply."

"With ammunition," Nelson insisted.

"Yes, with some ammunition, for one is not good without the other. No? This is good."

Tran offered a short grin before lifting the bowl to his lips. "We'll talk of price then," he added after a few mouthfuls. Nelson nodded agreement, head low over his bowl to hide his jubilation. He would need stronger protection than Charlie could provide when it came to collecting the shipment of rifles. Douglas was the brawler in the ringers' camp and the best bet for insurance.

Chapter 32

1985, AUGUST, MID-DRY SEASON.

"I DON'T TRUST THIS MOB," NELSON warned Douglas as they drove slowly towards the crabbers' camp to collect the rifles he had bargained for. Three boxes of gold bars weighed heavily on the tray so Nelson drove carefully along the indistinct tyre tracks. They left behind four boxes as insurance for future use, still carefully covered with the dirty green tarp. The big old crocodile had watched them silently from the other side of the river.

"They drove a hard bargain," he explained.

"They rip you off," Douglas muttered darkly sullen. "It always the same. If it not them, then it be those whitefellas who own the pub, or run the store. They rip you off. You should wait until you got full price."

Nelson protested. "I tried when I went back with the first sample. Best I could get was three hundred and fifty thousand dollars."

Douglas snorted. "That not even enough to buy a station straight out," he spat. "They be rob you. They rob you blind, the dirty bastards. You going to let them do that?"

"Until we have the guns we have no choice, but then ..." Nelson left the rest hanging, hinting at a plan of revenge more to placate Douglas's goading than with any tinge of reality.

"And how many guns they let the ignorant black boy buy?" Douglas sneered, quickly ducking to avoid the wild punch Nelson threw across the cab.

"Watch the road," he suggested as they veered off the track, two slim saplings slapping under the bull bar. "Settle down and tell me what they give you."

"I get seventy AK47s and a thousand rounds of ammunition for each rifle," Nelson said proudly, daring Douglas to scoff again.

"How much each?" Douglas asked, trying to work out the price surreptitiously on his fingers.

"All up, rifles and a thousand rounds of ammunition each is about three hundred fifty thousand."

"Hey! Look out! You been rip off big time!" Douglas scolded. "My cousin in Alice Springs, he buy .308 Winchester rifle for seven hundred dollar!"

"Listen, arsehole! These aren't bolt action rifles. These are illegal automatic assault rifles. The only way we can get these is through the crabbers," Nelson sighed in exasperation. With forced patience, he explained again, repeating what Tran had also just as patiently explained.

"These are more expensive because they come from the black market in Vietnam. Then someone get paid to smuggle them across the sea. Police, and custom inspectors all have to get paid. They really good rifles, but so expensive because everyone want them. Sure we pay a lot extra, but I think it's worth it."

Nelson nursed the pickup over broken rocks, following the winding pathway through the scraggly paperbarks and ti-tree. Heat lay across the ground, too lazy to lift for any breeze or give way to their slow progress, unbidden sweat the wages of their task. He was not ready to let Douglas know the best he could get was one dollar in three for the estimated value of the gold. As the only way to convert gold into arms, Tran held them in a position of weakness and he could only hope there came an opportunity to extract some revenge. Meanwhile Douglas didn't need to know all the details, particularly to $70,000 in cash included in the deal because cash so easily converted into grog. He needed his anger focussed on Tran.

Douglas skulked under Nelson's patient onslaught and spent ages scowling at his calloused knuckles, forming fist after fist. "You could be right," he grudgingly admitted.

"As I said, I don't trust these blokes, but I have to trust them until we get the rifles in our hands," he rationalised. "Let me do the talking when we get to the camp. Stand behind me and to one side and watch them, particularly the young fella. They all look very handy with the knife but I reckon he really know how to fight," he warned, remembering the boy's casual proficiency with a knife.

"Want me belt the bastards if they move?" Douglas asked eagerly, punching Nelson playfully on the arm.

"Nah. Just take it easy. If there's going to be a blue, then just make sure we're the only ones still walking when it stops." He shuddered at the thought of what could happen if they lost such a fight.

"No problems," Douglas assured him with cheerful confidence and anticipation. He flexed his muscles and bunched his fists, jabbing at the windscreen.

<h1 align="center">Chapter 33</h1>

THE ALUMINIUM BOAT WAS PULLED UP on the shore, dappled grey by the overhanging mangroves. White nets were securely hidden under blue plastic tarps deep in dark shade. They drove slowly into the camp, parking the pickup carefully so it was also hidden under the mangroves. Tran, his son Paul, and the small woman sat easily around the table. They did not rise as the ringers walked towards them.

"Morning, there," Nelson announced, stooping to enter the lean-to tent. Douglas stopped outside, one hand dangling on the ridge pole rope, the other resting on the wide flat belt buckle. Tran nodded his greeting, gesturing Nelson to sit. He ignored the strong ringer standing outside the tent.

"You have the gold?" he asked without preamble, already knowing the answer after one glance at the heavily laden Toyota.

"You have the guns and ammunition?" Nelson countered quickly, comfortable with Tran's directness and using his own direct questions to mask an uneasy fear of further deceit.

"No."

Nelson saw both Douglas and the crabber's son, Paul, tense, ready for action.

"Why not?" he growled, wishing he was armed with more than his fists and a single ringer.

"Tides. The boat comes tonight and we unload in the morning," he explained simply and shrugged his shoulders at nature's intransience. He smiled broadly and Nelson could not tell if he were lying or laughing at their expense. He scowled coldly at Tran, hoping Douglas was watching Paul who sat behind his left shoulder. Tran's smile remained guileless, his hard eyes dark stones buried in his face.

"We wait, and together we meet the boat when it comes in," Nelson countered, mustering as much unflustered firmness as he could.

"I think not."

"If we do not wait together then the deal is off," he bluffed boldly, sweat instantly between his shoulder blades. Silence took possession of the tent, magnifying the smallest sounds. He heard flies buzzing and water quietly lapping along the muddy bank, rippling along the sides of the aluminium dinghy. The generator noise seemed muted and he almost heard Tran's eyes slide smoothly to catch Paul's attention.

"OK. We wait together," Tran agreed. "Later we move down river to a better landing place. I will go ahead with the boat and Paul will show you where to follow. You leave my part of the payment here before we go."

The sweat between Nelson's shoulder blades turned cold. Nelson shook his head slowly in disagreement, but the older man pretended he did not understand.

"No," Nelson insisted at last. "You get paid after I've seen the guns."

"You go now," Tran said simply, crossing his arms in a covert signal.

Paul jumped to his feet before Douglas had time to move, and was in position as Douglas bunched his fists ready to smash into the lithe youth. He stood loosely and easily, watching the wiry ringer and waiting for his father's instructions. His right hand dropped low over the hilt of his knife.

Nelson glanced rapidly between the older man and his son, trying to watch them both at once. The woman rose and stood innocently by the end of the table, a long filleting knife on the chopping board within easy reach. She watched her husband and the family waited for Nelson's reply.

"Some now and the rest after delivery of the guns," Nelson suggested, knowing he was trapped at a disadvantage, but not willing to surrender without a protest. He weighed the odds. Douglas and he against three knives was not the same as a staggering brawl between drunks.

Tran shook his head slowly, confident Nelson would capitulate, the shipment of arms too important to jeopardise.

"Alright. I leave your share here, but," he insisted, "we all go to meet the boat."

"This is good," Tran agreed quietly, leaving it unclear if he referred to gold or the gun collection.

Paul spun lightly on his toes and sat on his chair in one fluid movement. Nelson had a fleeting glimpse of a smirk. Douglas kept his fists ready and stood feet askance, every inch a frustrated brawler.

"Why tonight?" Nelson asked.

"We avoid the Coastwatch," Tran explained, suddenly relaxed and affable. "They fly regular flights during the day. We can set our watches by them," he smiled, and Paul laughed briefly. "We always have time to pull our nets. It is not them we have to worry about. The policeman from Borroloola sometimes comes along the creeks. He has taken our nets twice, but he has never taken us."

"The day he does, he dies," Paul interjected calmly, simply stating a fact.

"It is not the way," the old man reprimanded sternly.

"Yes, father," he answered respectfully, dipping his head a fraction.

Nelson watched the whipcord-thin young man and wondered about the relationship between father and son. You'll kill me if your father even so much as hints it, he decided and shivered despite the security of Douglas standing nearby.

"Coastwatch rarely fly at night so it is easy for me to guide my cousin up the river in the moonlight. Paul will stay with you until I return," Tran politely explained. His son showed no surprise at being offered as a potential hostage. "We unload quickly. It is a long way from Irian Jaya and it would be foolish to be seen by Coastwatch because we too slow."

Nelson nodded agreement, then his face puckered as he thought. "Irian Jaya?" he asked. "I thought the guns were coming from Vietnam, which is why they were so expensive." He stopped, remembering the way the family moved together with catlike swiftness when threatened.

"Our cousins spread across the oceans of Asia when the North took over our country. Many good men now live in many places. Some work as merchants, some smuggle along the coasts, while others help our people escape the communist oppressors in my homeland. Their paper money is worthless, so we only accept gold. Some can't pay in gold, so they pay in kind, or in arms stolen from the bastard soldiers who trample my country."

Battles won, Tran was at ease beside the rough table, comfortable in his faded white singlet and wide cotton trousers, feet cool in open sandals cut from old rubber tyres. One leg drawn up, he rested easily, an American cigarette dangling from the corner of his mouth, fingers twirling an old metal American lighter.

He was unusually talkative, and Nelson wondered if they were being told because they would never have the chance to tell anyone else. Once the gold is delivered there is nothing to prevent these bastards from murdering both of us. He shuddered, glad he had brought Douglas along for protection, although his value was untested. Sighing, he pulled the tobacco tin from his shirt pocket, and distractedly rolled a thin cigarette, lighting it with a match.

"These rifles are no good to us, but many rebels in the region have found a use for them. The rebels in Irian Jaya pay for them with a little gold and with other," he paused with a ghost of a smile, "home grown commodities so many young Westerners need to feed their habits. From there to here is only a short run for an innocent fishing vessel struggling to catch enough fish to keep a family alive. Coastwatch do not trouble my cousin unless he comes within Australian fishing limits. They think his boat is too old to be used for smuggling."

Tran looked uncomfortable for a moment, embarrassed by his detailed explanation. "Your guns come from Vietnam; yes, but it was a long time ago."

"But come, unload your payment before the day finishes." He gestured for Nelson to leave while father and son remained seated watching the two ringers unload the vehicle.

"Them bastards," Douglas hissed, loosening the ropes holding the boxes in position.

"I know," Nelson agreed.

"You should blow them out after we get the guns," Douglas snarled. Nelson considered the idea again as Douglas angrily speared the tie-down ropes over the tray. He expected, and received, treachery. He wanted Douglas prepared to act, but only when he thought it was the right time.

"If they try to back out of the deal, then I might consider it, but until then we stand by my word." Douglas grunted in deep dismissive disgust and jerked the first box to the edge of the tray, ready to lug it to the camp. All the boxes unloaded and inspected, they sat uncomfortably in the shade of the pickup, clearly no longer welcome in the camp. They glared covertly at the family eating a meal of rice and fish in the afternoon shade under the tarp while they sat against the pick-up tyres and used the short-bladed castrating knife to pick at a warm tin of bully beef.

Waiting in silence made sullen by Douglas, they saw the golden sun slip quickly into the flame red sunset. They watched the dark muslin shapes of the flying foxes swoop silently above, silhouetted against the early yellow moonrise. When the old man went down to the dinghy they stretched and stood up, waiting for the Vietnamese youth to come to them.

Chapter 34

PAUL GUIDED THEM THROUGH THE LIGHT scrub along the top of the river bank until they reached a tiny backwater protected by thick mangroves blocking out the moonlight. The mangrove trees clung to the edge of the bank which had been washed out after the last cyclone. It was a good deep mooring point.

They all waited, the acrid bite of cigarette smoke driving away the mosquitoes. The rough barking cough of a crocodile, the bubble of the rising tide amongst the mangroves and crab holes and the gentle plop of barramundi feeding delivered a gentle wave of background noise. Then the phosphorescent bow wave of the small fishing boat trailed the steady beat of its motors across the dark silky water. Tran's dinghy bobbed in the glowing wake.

The wooden boat moved slowly, Tran standing confidently on the bow guiding the skipper. The boat looked large against the dark bank of the river. Despite the run-down appearance of the boat, Nelson realised the motor was well-maintained and was running sweetly. Paul slipped out of the pickup and took a small torch from his pocket.

The thin beam slashed across the moonlit water capturing the golden glow of a crocodile's eyes before the skipper swung the boat alongside the shore. Paul moved expertly, tying the mooring ropes securely to the trees. He shouted in Vietnamese to the crew on board and a short walkway was pushed from amidships. Tran reached the shore first, and the captain of the vessel followed him. Wordlessly, Tran handed Paul four small, soft waterproof sachets to stow in the dinghy.

The captain wore loose ragged cotton trousers and an old pair of Adidas shoes. His strong bare torso looked dark and powerful in the moonlight.

Nelson studied him carefully and saw only the same short grey hair and uncompromising ancient face that he also found on Tran. He searched for weapons, but the dull silvery moonlight made it difficult. The motor was turned off and the sounds of the night dived into the silence.

"This is Pham," Tran said. The Captain bowed a fraction. Nelson looked at him carefully, trying to judge him as an opponent. "He has come a long way. He says if you are quick he will be able to leave before dawn. He has no desire to remain here during daylight," Tran informed Nelson, not expecting to discuss the schedule.

Pham gave no sign he heard the conversation. Nor did he look around as two of the crew members came off the boat and formed a loose semi-circle behind him.

"If everything is in order then we should be able to unload the rifles quickly," Nelson replied, standing his ground.

He fought the temptation to look behind to check on Douglas. He peeped carefully from the corner of his eye at the two deckhands. They were much younger than either Tran or Pham.

Tran turned to the captain and spoke to him in his own language. The deckhands were calm, but Nelson felt uncertainty grow in his stomach. He stole an apprehensive glance at the two fit sailors again.

"Pham says there is no problem. Your sixty rifles – "

"My seventy rifles," corrected Nelson.

"So sorry. Your sixty rifles – "

"I ordered seventy rifles. Now you tell me you only have sixty. It's a bloody rip-off!" he stormed indignantly. The two Vietnamese stood motionless against his tirade. Nelson's fists began to form a punch, and then he breathed deeply instead, forcing his fingers to stretch. It was another fight he couldn't win and they knew it. He shook his finger at them, rocking slightly on the balls of his feet and struggled to keep control of himself.

"You have sixty. Alright, but I only pay for sixty."

"Same money," Pham grunted firmly, hands defiant on his hips.

"Never," Nelson snarled impulsively.

"We go," Pham countered confidently and turned on his heel.

From the corner of his eye, Nelson saw Douglas jab a sharp punch at the nearest deckhand's jaw. Shoulder dropping, Nelson started toward Pham but stopped when he saw the weedy deckhand sidestep Douglas and somehow smash him to the ground. Douglas collapsed in an untidy and final heap. The deckhand spun on one foot and aimed a kick at Douglas's face.

Pham sharply snapped a few Vietnamese words and the sailor stopped his kick in mid air. "No need," he translated for Nelson. Douglas did not move and Nelson heard his tortured breathing. Paul and the other deckhand had circled quickly behind Nelson and he knew they would defeat him more easily than the other sailor had thrashed Douglas.

He straightened up slowly and faced the two older men. You're dead, he thought, trying to smile pleasantly at both of them.

"Perhaps we can talk," he suggested. Neither man moved, so he continued, swallowing his pride and anger. "I would take these rifles and five thousand dollars cash for the same amount of gold as you wanted for seventy rifles."

Tran and Pham conferred quickly in Vietnamese. Tran turned to Nelson. "My cousin said he would be happy to deal with you on such terms. He will give you five thousand dollars because he understands how disappointed you must be because of this mistake."

"Thank you," Nelson responded, loathing the need to be polite but pleased and relieved he could show Wendy some cash as he had promised.

"OK," Pham agreed easily. He waved to the deckhands and they walked up the boardwalk to start unloading.

"You have the one thousand rounds of ammunition for each rifle and the rest?" Nelson asked before Pham could follow the sailors.

"We have one thousand hundred rounds per rifle as you ordered for sixty rifles," he replied smoothly.

"But we should have more because there is supposed to be one thousand rounds per rifle for seventy rifles." Nelson struggled to keep a plaintive whine from his voice.

"We give you one thousand rounds per rifle as you ordered," Pham repeated blandly, confident he would not be challenged. Two deckhands leapt lightly to the ground and stood poised by the boat.

Nelson calculated quickly, tapping a finger on his thumb as he multiplied. Pham waited patiently while Nelson struggled with the calculations.

"You have sixty thousand rounds?" he asked.

"Yes. There is no problem?" Pham queried, a picture of innocence, hands held out by his side, palms up.

Douglas groaned and sat up, rubbing the back of his neck and cursing foully. He searched for his hat and jammed it on his head. The Vietnamese ignored him and Nelson willed him to stay where he was rather than come up fighting. Douglas struggled to his feet and groggily leant against a tree.

"There is no problem," he agreed, his voice rough with shame at the loss of thousands of rounds. Pham nodded slightly and the deckhands jumped back on the boat.

Nelson and Douglas sulkily watched the crew unloading the long rifle boxes. The dull green ammunition boxes followed, including a box marked with a white slash. Pham surreptitiously confirmed it was the cash box.

"How do I know each box is full?" Nelson asked.

"You could check each one, but need such a long time. Look at the seals; they're all intact. Look at the boat; see how much higher she rides in the water now she is unloaded. There is your proof."

Nelson looked at the fishing boat and even to his inexperienced eye he had to agree it sat higher out of the water than when they had started. He still couldn't shake the feeling something was wrong. Suspecting more treachery, he searched for another proof to allay his fears.

"I want to see the guns and ammunition," he demanded, still unsure about the boat.

"You may open them all if you wish."

Pham nodded his approval and deckhands began to break the seals on the first of the ammunition boxes. Two sealed dully galvanised tins nestled inside, Chinese writing and numbers atop each tin and turnkeys flush on the ends like so many tins of bully beef. Nelson nodded approval confirming there was no need to open the other ammunition boxes. Keeping Douglas in the dark, he had no choice but to trust the specially marked cash box held the correct amount.

The deckhands moved to the stubby rifle boxes. Nelson walked over, rolling a cigarette to quell his excitement. Douglas followed unsteadily at his heels, eager to see the weapons. Ten assault rifles lay side by side, banana shaped magazines in a separate compartment at the end of each box. The last box was one rifle short and Nelson looked up suddenly when he came to it.

"There are fifty nine there," Pham assured him calmly, his voice reasonable. "You already have one we sent you some time ago. I hope you did not think it was free." He and Tran exchanged amused glances and chuckled contemptuously.

Nelson drew deeply on his cigarette to cover his anger and put a restraining hand on Douglas's rigid body. Your time is near, he seethed silently. He drew back the last of the pungent smoke and flicked the butt away. Taking his time, he rolled another, lighting it before he could trust himself to speak.

"Your blokes can unload the gold. No need to count it, because it is all there. You have my word."

Neither of the older men reacted to his carefully calculated insult, but a taut hand feinted, slashing past Nelson's ear, as a deckhand moved by to unload the Toyota. Nelson watched hatred smoulder in Douglas's eyes and, eyes narrowed, he matched it with his own anger making a tinder ready for spark.

Chapter 35

PHAM SCREECHED IN HIGH-PITCHED VIETNAMESE and a deckhand smashed his feet into the small of Nelson's back, sending him sprawling to the ground.

He tried to roll to one side, but the little man was an astoundingly persistent heavy weight on his shoulders. The man's small hand ground Nelson's smouldering cigarette into his lips and he stifled a shout. The thin hand let no sound escape and Nelson floundered for breath. Tossing his head, he glimpsed Douglas pinned beneath the other deckhand. He swung his bunched fist back over his shoulder and gloried in the smack of flesh. His satisfaction was short-lived when his free arm was swiftly pinioned painfully and twisted in its socket. Nelson spat out his cigarette and roared defiance.

"Shut up!" Pham hissed. "Listen."

"Get fucked!"

Nelson tried to free his other arm but was hit again across the side of his head, then both arms were pinioned before he had time to gain any advantage.

"Listen," Pham hissed urgently again.

The dull throb of the aeroplane engines came louder in the night. He looked towards the boat, heart pounding in his jagged retching chest. Everybody cowered immobile behind any available cover. He nodded his understanding, and the deckhand released the pressure on his arms. Douglas also lay quietly, face down in the clay and gravel, more forcefully subdued than Nelson.

The high-winged twin engine silhouette was clear against the stars as it passed overhead, the pale moonlight running dully across its body. They all remained still and listened until it droned into the night and disappeared.

Slowly the Vietnamese got up and went back to work. Nelson flexed his shoulder as his assailant moved off without a word. Nelson stood and walked over to the two older men who were talking rapidly, faces animated with concern. He felt a surge of pleasure at their discomfort followed by a flash of fear deep in his bowels, wondering if they had been seen by the Coastwatch.

The two men ignored him until they finished their own discussion, listening for a change in engine noise signalling a quick return sweep to investigate the area. Nelson stood beside Tran and rolled another cigarette, tobacco spilling from the paper.

"We have not been seen," Tran told him. "But it is best to be sure. We must not use any lights until they return later tonight on their way back to Darwin. Do not smoke."

Reluctantly Nelson dropped his half-rolled cigarette and squashed it beneath his boot.

"We can't leave until tomorrow night because they may still fly their scheduled daylight patrols tomorrow. My cousin would not have time to get out past the fishing zone tonight. He is not happy, but it can't be changed."

Nelson nodded, very happy with the disruption to their plans, but frowning a pretence of concern. It gives me time to shift all this gear, he calculated. I didn't realise there would be so much. It'll take several trips. While they're stuck here because of Coastwatch, they can't disappear when we're away on each trip. Once I've got the guns away from here it is a whole new game. Perhaps Douglas has the right idea.

With a friendly open smile, he mimicked Tran's previous curt observations, chuckling quietly at their discomfort.

"This is good."

Chapter 36

NELSON GRATEFULLY TOOK ONE HANDLE OF the last of the wooden ammunition boxes and balanced it on the edge of the pickup tray. It was their second fully loaded trip. Douglas jumped tiredly to the ground and took the other rope handle. Lighter than the rest, and unbeknown to Douglas, it contained the last of the ammunition and the cash. Together they carried the box across the spinifex slope to the large stack already under the overhang and plunked it down. Nelson sat on top of a boulder near the mouth of the cave while Douglas slouched on the ground with his back to the pile of boxes.

The rock overhang, halfway up the gentle slope at the foot of the rock face, was well concealed by a screen of stubby trees and quinine bushes. Thick, horizontal layers of rock stacked atop each other provided cover for the cave, leaving it indistinguishable from other overhangs in the rock wall dotting one side of the gulley snaking into this fissure in the escarpment.

Sitting above tree top height, they gazed across the rough ground stretching several kilometres before rising quickly to another pale white stony ridge in the chain of rocky ranges submitting to the unwavering sun. Not so far below, the roughly graded station track weaved through ti tree scrub dotted with white-trunked snappy gums and occasional larger ghost gums. Access to the concealed overhang was easy but difficult to find unless you knew where to look. The land embraced the heat, refusing to shimmer with a mirage, indifferent to the travails of man and beast.

Douglas picked an old abandoned stone axe from the scree on the cave floor, turning it idly in his hands, the cutting edge rounded and worn smooth. He pitched it outside, arcing over a distant glint in the cobalt sky before tumbling soundlessly into the crushed spinifex.

"What we do now?" Douglas asked, not catching the tiny flash of silver above the drab olive carpet beyond the cave entrance.

"We go soon. The Coastal Surveillance plane won't be back this way for a few more hours, so we can be long gone by then. Anyway, we're well back from the coast here."

The plane had flown back early in the morning before the first twinges of the dawn lightened the sky. All activity unloading the boat had long stopped by the time it returned. Pham had refused to let them take the guns and ammunition away during the night, claiming their headlights might be seen. Too frightened and alert to sleep, Douglas and Nelson had struggled to keep awake until daylight.

Everybody had frozen when the Coastwatch plane returned unexpectedly early on the outward leg of a new daylight run. Tran reckoned it was a new flight schedule and Pham had agreed, now unable to depart until the Coastwatch passed over them again. They allowed the ringers to leave while they waited under the mangrove cover.

Douglas stretched back, yawned and idly picked at the rough paint slapped over the white stencil letters on the side of an ammunition box.

"I need longest sleep."

"Don't we all," Nelson agreed. "Cover these so nobody can see them and then we can knock off for the day. We head back toward the station and camp on Three Mile waterhole. Sound fair enough?"

Douglas yawned again, continuing to chip at the cheap peeling paint. "I reckon them bastards be sitting down on the river too frightened to move until tonight. I hope they really sweat. We should blow them out, Nelson," he muttered without any real enthusiasm.

"No point. I might need to use them again," Nelson scowled. "But if I do use them, it'll be under different conditions from this time. They robbed me. Try it again and there'll be big trouble," he boasted.

"Hey! Look out!"

"Don't take the piss," Nelson snapped, thinking he was being mocked.

"No, boss. I not mean that. Have a look at this. I think they been rob us proper this time."

Nelson vaulted down from his seat on the boulder near the mouth of the cave. Douglas picked furiously at the green paint and more white letters were exposed. Nelson didn't need a second glance to see the number 1100 clearly.

"Fuck me!" he spat angrily. "That's one thousand one hundred, not fifteen hundred bullets, in each box." He did the maths quickly. "We're about forty thousand rounds short."

He hit the top of the box with his open hand. "The thieving bastards," he shouted. He hit the box again and again, the spreading sting a welcome outlet for his exploding temper and rage. Douglas jumped to his feet, revitalised by the prospect of a fight. "Let's blow them out, boss" he shouted with exhilaration.

Nelson heard him, but continued cursing with monotonous repetition. "You fucking mongrel bastards! You fucking mongrel bastards!" he seethed. His fists bunched tightly, he shook them at shoulder height and bowed his head in rage and frustration.

"Come on, boss. They can't beat us now," Douglas urged, excitement lending persuasion to his voice. "Grab a rifle and we go teach them a lesson."

Nelson ignored him with a frenzy of anger, smashed his open hand repeatedly against a box. It jarred his wrist and the hurt was a welcome vent for his fury.

"They been make a fool of you, Nelson. They been shame you. I shamed of you," Douglas taunted. Nelson glared at him over his shoulder, looking for a way to satisfy his temper.

"This always the way. They all be bastards. They steal everything from us and now it payback time. What you waiting for? Let's do it!" Douglas urged, spoiling for a fight.

"We get our gold back," Nelson agreed, breathing heavily, struggling to think in the haze of temper. "But nothing else. I might need to use them again. No shooting unless we have to. Understand?"

Douglas nodded furiously, already tearing the top from one of the long rifle boxes. He lifted an ugly weapon high above his head with one hand.

"Yakai!" he whooped, grabbing a magazine with his left hand. Reluctant to let go of the assault rifle, he rested it on top of the ammunition boxes. He fumbled with the ten round stripper clips as he filled the curved magazine. Completed, magazine rammed into place, he ran his hands over the smooth deadly shape of wood and metal. Deep brown eyes sparkling, he broke into an unpleasant grimace, instantly loving the comfortable solid weight of the weapon.

Nelson stalked determinedly down the spinifex slope to the Toyota and took his AK47 from behind the front seat. Residual fury now coldly under control, he methodically used three stripper clips to fill the magazine. Douglas looked at the rifle quizzically.

"It has been behind the front seat since we loaded up the gold," Nelson explained quietly. "I didn't tell you because I didn't want you blasting away last night. You were quick enough with your fists," he laughed appreciatively, "but if you had known there was rifle in the Toyota you might have killed someone."

"You not wrong there," Douglas agreed with deep conviction. He slapped the full magazine for emphasis and then held the Kalashnikov low on his hips. Scything an arc across the scrub and swinging away from Nelson, he braced for the recoil and pulled the trigger. The concentrated snarl of wild anticipation disappeared when nothing happened.

"Hey! What wrong with this one?" he demanded savagely.

Nelson kept the amused smile off his face. "Let me show you." He pointed to the rate of fire selector on his own rifle.

"Down is fully automatic. Midway is semi-automatic single shot so the rifle only fires each time you pull the trigger. Up is safety. Make sure you keep it on semi-auto." he explained rapidly before Douglas had a chance to protest. "You have about three seconds a magazine on full automatic, so keep it on semi-auto."

Douglas nodded his agreement, flicking the selector tab up and down experimentally.

"Aim a bit low for a start. The rifle rides up as you fire until you get used to it. Cock the rifle like this." He pulled the cocking handle back and let it go. The breech block slid forward, smacking home with a solid mechanical ring.

"Try it."

Douglas worked the mechanism a couple of times, ejected brass rounds bouncing from the boulders. Smiling gleefully, he removed the magazine and reloaded. Slapping the magazine back into the rifle he pulled the cocking handle again and another live round spat out. He looked at Nelson in frustration.

"Whenever you take the magazine out you must work the action with the cocking handle to clear the breech," Nelson demonstrated with his own rifle.

"How you know all this?" Douglas asked, admiration and new respect clear in his voice.

"How I know all this?" Nelson sighed. "I be hedgjumuckated," he mocked, dropping into a patois parody of pidgin English. "I been go to university."

"Yair, but tell him true," Douglas insisted, the rifle propped on his hip, muzzle pointing to the sky. He took his weight on one leg and put his hand on his hip. He held the pistol grip easily, face bursting with pride.

"You look just like the mujahideen, those Afghanistan guerrilla fighters, or those African freedom fighters," Nelson proudly observed. He picked up his rifle and cradled it in his arms comfortably across his midriff. He imagined how he looked and his chest swelled with suffocating pride.

"I spent twelve months in a dirty stinking city. A year where they jammed their history, their whitefella culture down my throat," he grumbled, his camp accent becoming more pronounced as the bitter memories were retold. "A year where I was honorary blackfella so no-one ever said a bad word about me because I was black. The only difference between there and here is around here no-one ever says a good word about you because you're black."

"Twelve months I took shit. That's all I could take before I pulled the pin. But I learned ... I learn alright ... I learn things they didn't want me to know. Those city kooris showed me things I never understand before. I reckon they live worse than we do. Imagine living without dirt beneath your feet; breathing foul air everyday and never see the bush? It's worse than jail, and I been there too."

For some reason, the image of the orange book cover of *The Wretched of the Earth* remained intact in his memory. "Without our country for ourselves, we are nothing. Talk, talk, bloody talk, that's all them city kooris do. I didn't want to waste time talking."

"Some of the whitefella university students support the Zimbabwe African Peoples Union and they loved me because I was black. They were always talking about Che Guevara, Mao, Robert Mugabe, Malcolm X and Ho Chi Minh."

Obviously the names meant nothing to Douglas, so Nelson explained.

"They be revolution freedom fighters. They send money to Zimbabwe so they could buy rifles like this. The white bastards just laughed when I told them I wanted money to buy rifles for us. Blackfellas never as good as black Africans." He spat into the dust.

Memories revived, he sneered. "They were just little boys playing games pretending they would join ZAPU in Zimbabwe. They just pretend because they never have the guts to go. But they had an AK47. Someone's brother who was conscripted and sent to Vietnam had smuggled it home. A few of us practised using it. They were only playing games," he scoffed with contempt.

"I wasn't."

"I not know," Douglas acknowledged, not entirely understanding but still holding his pose, weapon balanced on his hip, fuel for his aggression.

"We've stopped playing games now, so get in," Nelson snarled, the first flares of temper replaced and revitalised with cool simmering hatred and determination.

Douglas jumped on the tray and leant forward over the top of the cabin, assault rifle ready, as Nelson crashed the vehicle along the crude bush track, heedless of the boiling plume of pale dust. Douglas crouched, branches ripping angrily at his face and slashing at the Toyota. Anger transferred to his driving, the motor roared as Nelson wove through tea tree and ghost gums. Speed, not stealth, was the solution.

Chapter 37

STONES RATTLING LOUDLY UNDER THE CHASSIS, engine roaring, the pickup burst into the small landing clearing by the river, but it was already too late. The pirate smuggler had weighed the risks and left soon after the Coastwatch plane had first disappeared from sight. Nelson slammed on the brakes, pounding the steering wheel with his fists. The Toyota pitched forward on worn springs, smothering them in a wave of choking dust.

Douglas stood in the back, feet splayed. He cocked the rifle viciously in one short angry movement, and sprayed a burst on full automatic across the clearing. In fearful wonder he watched dust puffs stitch across the flattened grass and he kept his finger hard on the trigger. The weapon bucked in his hands and across the river the water boiled along his arc of fire.

Brass shell cases spat in a flashing stream from the rifle, metal on metal rattling mechanically loud, as the relentless heavy chtud-chutd hammering was absorbed by the thick mangroves and drowned by screeching birds. The empty breech block thumped home. Shocked in awe, even the silence rung in his ears.

"Fuuuuck!" he gasped a drawn-out cry, staggered with surprise and awe.

He remained rooted to the spot, gazing across the water in wonderment, ecstasy painting his broad features. His white teeth bared between parted lips as he panted in short gasps.

Nelson remembered the thrill of the first time he had fired the AK47 so he could not condemn Douglas for feeling the same. He leant on the side of the Toyota and rolled a smoke.

Elation slowly abating, Douglas eventually slid down and squatted on the tray, rifle upright between his legs.

"They should be dead," he snarled with quiet vehemence.

"Three seconds on full automatic," Nelson chided gently. "We can't afford to waste ammunition."

Douglas bowed his head, reluctant to let his blazing eyes meet Nelson's gentle admonishment.

"They knew they had cheated us and they weren't game to hang around until we found out. I bet the crabbers have gone as well," Nelson surmised, resigned in bitterness.

"We go and see!" Douglas demanded as calmly as he could, adrenaline still fizzing and he felt the thrill of anticipation. He stroked the warm rifle with rough tenderness. Nelson didn't answer, but reached into the Toyota and pulled the magazine from his rifle. He handed it to Douglas. "Semi-automatic only," he reminded.

"Yairs." Douglas pushed the selector into position with deliberate and exaggerated movement.

"Make sure it doesn't vibrate back to automatic on these rough roads," Nelson teased, the good-natured tone belying his intent. Douglas smirked, then laughed cruelly, a shiver of anticipation rippling across his shoulders.

Nelson carefully drove towards the crabbers' camp, hoping to catch them unawares but, as he expected, it was abandoned. They had departed in haste, and the unwanted detritus of bush camps was littered under the trees but still in deep cover.

Cheated, Douglas slashed bursts of badly aimed shots at empty petrol drums and with little satisfaction, watched them leap and tumble.

Chapter 38

CHARLIE PEERED CAUTIOUSLY THROUGH THE TANGLE of leaves and branches, searching the mangroves on the opposite bank for the big old crocodile. All he saw were the wide slide marks in the black mud where the reptile liked to bask in the sun. Nervously, he scanned the creek bank in front of him, but spotted nothing lurking beneath the overhanging mangroves. Only four of the original seven green boxes remained stashed under the tarp beside the rock and he knew he was too late to get completely rid of the source of the problem.

Mosquitoes buzzed around his head and settled on exposed skin. Bone weary, he absently watched their thin bodies bloat with his blood, their pinpricks of pain nothing beside the ache in his guts. Accompanied by constant stabbing pain, it had taken him four long, hot, exhausting days to walk from the station ringers' camp to the bank of Corella Creek.

He foraged on the way, happy to feel the clean bite of the sun, a balm on his bare back after gratefully discarding his threadbare pale blue shirt. His gaunt body pleased to accept the soft caress of the dry earth when he slept beneath the stars. It was good to be in his country, but the pleasure had not taken away the crippling pain in his stomach or the bouts of nausea reeling behind his eyes.

Apprehension and fear twisted his guts into painful knots as it had so many times over the past weeks. He rubbed his bare belly and ignored the biting bursts of pain. Squatting in the shade, he waited patiently for his head to clear and gathered his strength for the task ahead.

Five days earlier he summoned his wife, Ina, and Old Harry. They sat in the grey dust by the cold camp fire and he had spoken softly without rancour. Under the shallow shade of the bauhinia tree he gave words to his fear.

Ina sat with her back to the two men, grateful to be included in what was really men's business.

"Nelson drag us all into biggest mobs of trouble," he concluded. "I think I be already dead. This life be finish," he confessed, right arm waved languidly to encompass the camp and station. He paused, unable and unwilling to name his dreaded belief that Nelson had sung him. "I can stop Nelson. I sure Nelson not want to buy the station. I think he steal all the gold for himself," he guessed incorrectly.

Old Harry, deeply lined face immobile beneath his unruly beard, gave no appearance of listening, his attention apparently fixed on a distant point beyond the camp. He idly fondled the ears of the brindle dog beside him. Other dogs, hoping for a handout, loped into the group, and Charlie gently brushed them away. Ina sat cross-legged, large breasts bulging in the shapeless faded print dress. A dog chewed at one of her discarded, unmatched dirty thongs.

"Get out, you cheeky dog," she snapped irritably and sent the dog yelping with a slap from her open hand. She brushed her dusty hair back, disturbing the flies and they rose from the corners of her eyes only to settle back in moments. She ignored them, concentrating on the far rocky outcrop and waited for Old Harry to speak.

"Perhaps you right," Old Harry concurred, the scars on his neck moving as he spoke. His bony fingers twined around each other and then separated. "But how you know?" he pouted, lips pointing to Charlie.

"I be sick ever since we find that plane. That gold be no good to me. I think he keep it all for himself, but we all be in mobs of trouble," Charlie lamented with depressing fatalism.

Unseen, Ina nodded her agreement and mumbled to the earth at her feet, not looking at the men. "That right, Harry. He been proper sick since that time. It bite him all around the belly all the time,' she explained emphatically. "I reckon he be sick because of Nelson and what he do. Nelson sing him! Charlie good husband and I not want him die."

Keeping her dark eyes to the ground, she picked the ragged hem of her dress with diligent distraction. She stole a glance sideways at Charlie as they waited for Old Harry to give his judgement. Charlie rolled a cigarette with nervous fingers and recrossed his legs to ease the pain in his stomach. The dogs crept back and he envied their ability to sleep long and undisturbed on the hard ground as he, until recently, had done himself.

"This our country, Charlie. We fight for it and we lost it many years ago. We always be here because, this country, him die if we not here. Yolngu ways will not beat balanda ways. My father tried. I tried and now only a few of us left. Nelson wants to try a new foreigner way, a balanda way. Maybe, his singing is our singing too. What for we try to stop him?"

Harry sat easily in the dust, his outstretched pale palms resting on each knee, tough feet and broken nails grey with dust beneath frayed jeans. "Nelson work for our people and he wants to use peaceful balanda ways to win this land back for all of us," Harry concluded, his low liquid voice travelling no further than the ears of the nearby dogs.

"Why my Charlie sick then? Hey? If that Nelson only be do good things, then what for my Charlie sick?" Ina demanded, speaking out of place. "That Nelson, him be sing my Charlie because Nelson, he be trouble. Him and that cheeky fella, Douglas," she finished stridently, hooded eyes cast to the ground.

She stopped waving her arms and pulled one hard broad foot onto the top of her knee. She picked at the old scab of a partly healed ulcer above her skinny ankle. Charlie scrubbed his tan high crown hat across his brow, both embarrassed by her outburst and ashamed he had not the courage to say it. He waved his hands, palms down, across his front, silently apologising for his wife.

Old Harry ignored Charlie's apology and stared beyond Ina's back and bowed shoulders. The flat ground beyond the ringers' camp gave way to a pot-holed black soil plain dotted with rich green bauhinia trees and dull grey woollybutts. Cattle ambled lazily back from their morning water, seeking the thicker shade around the base of the sharp rocky rise on the far side of the airstrip.

Two grey brolgas, heads bent and wings clasped seriously behind their backs, peered hopefully for a meal amongst the dried-up claypan, stalking towards the bend in the waterhole where the hunting would be better. Harry studied the land, absorbing the details of life and the daily struggle to avoid death and let it engulf him. His country was never an innocent bystander.

As a young man he had not the patience to wait as a guest in his own country, reliant on the whims of whitefella intruders who laid claim to the ridges, escarpments and the sheltered plains. He carried the penalty for impatience, his whitefella scars coming before his deeply incised tribal initiation cicatrices, each telling a story and another step in education.

He worried about losing an already slender hold on the land because of one greedy person. His people worked together in yolngu way. Charlie was wrong. Nelson barely knew his singing and he certainly didn't know enough to steal away a man's singing. Charlie's sickness came from plain fear and Old Harry wondered what threat Nelson had used. Perhaps, he considered, there may be a need to restrain Nelson. Face immobile in thought, his hands unconsciously begin an idle design in the dirt, the sinewy grace of a sand goanna emerging from the dust. He glanced down, and quickly scrubbed away the beginnings of the drawing, reserving it for another time and sacred place.

"Perhaps this balanda way will not work if he takes all the gold for himself. If he be sing you, then he say a lie to us. You only been eat good tucker?" he asked diffidently.

"Yes," Charlie confirmed, knowing full well his diet had nothing to do with his sickness.

"Of course he been eat good tucker," Ina retorted indignantly, her prowess as a cook questioned. "He be sick because some fella singing him."

"What you want do?" Old Harry asked, ignoring Ina and his eyes avoiding Charlie, not wanting to pass judgement yet on Nelson who belonged, however incompletely, to his own singing.

"If we tell the Missus, then the Government mob will take the gold. Then Nelson kill me for sure." Charlie shuddered, remembering Nelson's threat and the dead pup. He looked around anxiously for his children. They were playing with their friends, teasing some of the dogs. Old Harry saw the nub of the problem and with it Charlie's fear.

"He dead fella if he touch my kids," Ina declared. Old Harry again ignored women's talk, and looked to Charlie.

"Whitefella gold be the problem," Charlie offered. "If no gold, there be no problem. You think I should get rid of the gold?" Charlie asked, looking for old Harry to guide him.

He nodded faintly, a hunter's skill where the movement was not enough to alert the quarry. "Perhaps you get rid of some of the gold," Harry murmured tentatively, hedging his bets. "If only little bit gold left then you only be little bit sick. Hey? If Nelson not greedy then he stop sing you."

The old man smiled gently, pleased at his solution. Ina cried quietly to herself, better at recognising Nelson's greed.

Chapter 39

"BUT NELSON IS GREEDY," CHARLIE TOLD the mangroves, their listening leaves hanging close to the ground. "He already take most of the boxes and we not see any money and I still sick."

He picked indifferently at an inflamed cut on his leg, dismissing the pain. He ignored his hunger and the growing, sickening bites gnawing beneath his ribs. Scratching the coarse stubble on his cheeks and, squinting through tired half-closed eyes, he scanned the silent creek banks cowering in the thick shade. He concentrated on the water, languid and oily green at the turn of the tide, but nothing broke the surface. He waited with patience born of generations.

Nothing moved.

Exhausted from his long trek, he reluctantly stood, knees aching in protest, and cautiously hobbled to the stockpile of boxes beneath the tarp. Terrified by the crocodile, he worked facing the water so he could not be taken by surprise.

Limbs and strength wasted, he pushed and dragged the first box to the edge of the river bank, eyes rivetted on the calm silky surface, looking for any smoothly gliding shadow. Grunting, he pushed the heavy box towards the rocky lip. The green metal box slid over the edge in a solid splash, disappearing quickly.

Taking no chances, he staggered to the boxes set well back from the river edge. Strength drained and gasping, he rested in the shallow shade, pale rocks blistering in the sun. It took all his remaining strength to drag and push the last box to the edge of the rocky bank, but, balance tipped, it finally fell just as easily as the first three, the sluggish tidal water quickly hiding all trace.

Task completed, he stood still, head muzzy with fatigue and watched the silent creek and slumbering bush, his gut stabbing waves of pain. Too late the stench of rotting fish penetrated his exhausted senses.

The crocodile rushed him from behind, the great dark body twisting so the scything tail knocked him into the water. A gentle, smooth splash followed the startled splash and jaws clamped around his chest, crushing away his pain.

In the settling dusk and flowing into the night, the curlews wailed spitefully at each other, conclusion clear but uncertain of who bore responsibility.

Chapter 40

1985, AUGUST, MID-DRY SEASON.

ANNE, THE SCHOOL TEACHER FROM CLARA Valley, sat beside Ray as they drove into Borroloola. She was nearly thirty and he wondered again what she saw in him. Her deep-set dark brown eyes had danced with merriment when he suggested a trip to town. There was no question her short dark hair, slight build and small breasts made her attractively impish. He was pleased he had taken the trouble to put on clean clothes, although he could not shake the dust from the crown of his broad brimmed hat.

"I'm glad you could come," he said, the pleasure of her company softening his voice, drawing him further out of his self-imposed bush isolation. The invitation was a decision made easier after the gunshot attack rudely re-ordered his priorities.

"I just declared tomorrow a holiday," she laughed easily. "The kids don't mind and I told Donny, he's the real boss out there now, that I had a holiday up my sleeve anyway, so there is no problem with the station management. It's nice to go into town with you. I haven't seen you for a while. I'm glad you asked."

Ray drove towards the tiny settlement in silence. Fumbling for words, he concentrated on the road. The narrow bitumen surface made a welcome change from the gravel roads and rough bush tracks he drove on most of the time. The road curved to the right and suddenly the ground dropped away in front of them, the steep descent down the jump-up straight as a rifle barrel.

On the far horizon the distant hills wavered blue in the hazy smoke-filled sky. The purple rocky hillside tumbled swiftly to the clay and black soil flats of the floodplain below. The mighty Macarthur River snaked unseen to their right. Ghost gums and bloodwood mixed with dark leaf bauhina trees on the open country. A small mob of feral horses – brumbies – wheeled on the flat and galloped across the rough and broken ground.

"See the frog," Ray pointed as they sped past the lonely upturned saucer of dark purple rock, twice the size of the Toyota, squatting on the plain below the flat-topped escarpment. "There is a traditional story about the rock," he ventured.

"I know. You told me last time," she reminded him gently.

He felt a flush rise from his neck and redden his ears. His big work boots seemed clumsy on the accelerator and he twitched his fingers on the steering wheel.

"Sorry," he apologised, staring a long way down the road, always alert for wandering stock and kangaroos on these unfenced roads.

"Don't worry. I've heard the story so many times from the children, but I like your version best."

He felt foolish again, and struggled to find an appropriate question to continue the conversation. "How many kids have you got?"

"None," she teased and laughed gaily, amused at his discomfort. His embarrassment melted beneath her easy smile, and relaxing, he grinned. The laughter still dancing in her voice, she continued. "I have fifteen on the roll at school, but the attendance varies depending on who is out mustering. It is very difficult competing with the excitement of the stock camp. I often wish I could go out bush for a while, just to see what it is really like. I've got two weeks' holiday coming up and Donny said I could go out with them if they are mustering."

Ray stored the information, hoping Donny wouldn't be mustering at that time. Glancing from the road, he studied her as she talked. She was so different from other women who had come up from the southern States.

He first met her in the bar of the Borroloola Inn. He had been drinking with Fast Eddy, the grader driver from Clara Valley station who was notorious for his slow rate of work. She joined them because she recognised Fast Eddy and was bored talking school. It turned into a fair drinking session filled with mostly-true rambling yarns. Reluctantly they had gone their separate ways when the bar closed early in the morning.

"What are you going into the 'Loo for'?" she asked, bring him back from the brief reverie. "You didn't actually tell me. Just roll a swag for a couple of days, you said. It's so easy here," she observed enviously. "I would never have dreamt of doing this when I was down South."

"I've got a bit of a problem with the dozer," he explained, comfortable talking about his work, and glossing over the reason for the bullet holes in the hydraulic tank and the tightness across his arm where the bullet had seared his skin. He pushed aside the misgivings he had begun to harbour about Wendy and Nelson.

"Had a bit of an accident with the radio as well, so I need to use one of the radios in town. Doubt if the radio can be repaired in the 'Loo, but I might be able to borrow one from Sid. Also I need some oil for the hydraulics."

"Who's Sid?" she asked, intrigued he had not asked to use the radio when he picked her up at Clara Valley.

"He's another earthmoving contractor. He works out of Borroloola. He's got the camp up the other side of the hill on the edge of the escarpment. We'll probably camp up there tonight."

"Does he have plenty of spare room?" she asked.

"Yair. Anyway, I can always sleep beside the Toyota."

"I suppose you could," she agreed ambiguously and left him wondering about her feelings.

He felt a thrill of nervousness race by. His heart told him he was making the right decision after years content with his own company and holding others at arm's length. He slowed at the intersection before the river crossing and turned left into the small settlement, slumbering on the black soil plain as it baked in the heat. He drove on to the earthmoving yard.

A Cat 130G grader was parked in front of the portacabin transportable accommodation units, the ATCO branding giving them their universally recognised name although they were more commonly called dongas in the bush. Designed to be loaded onto a semi-trailer, the units were a light construction of thin sheet steel and insubstantial wooden panels lining the inside of each room. A giant step-up from a canvas wrapped swag bed-roll spread on the ground, the long white boxes were an increasingly common feature of remote work camps. The first unit of small dogbox bedrooms faced the kitchen and toilet block. A heavy canvas tarp stretched between the two units, casting shade and trapping windless heat.

A Wabco scraper was pulled up in front of the quarters, one elevator motor removed for repairs. A nuggety man with steel grey hair worked on the gearbox at the workbench, clean light blue overalls bright against his tanned skin. He dropped his tools when Ray pulled up.

"Gidday there," Sid greeted them, wiping his hands on a clean rag. "How are you, Anne?" he asked with easy friendliness, and she immediately felt welcome. "Come and grab a beer," he continued before either of them could reply. He stepped instinctively to one side and politely waved to Anne to go first.

"Thank you," she demurred and Ray loved her gracious acceptance.

Two cold blue cans of Fosters in well-used foam stubby coolers and a chair for Anne were in front of them before Ray had found his seat. Sid lifted his can. "Cheers," and they all took a welcome pull on the cold beer.

"Would you like a glass?" Sid asked, concerned he had forgotten to inquire. Anne shook her head and sat back in the chair, leaving the can on the table.

"How's that mad Missus going out on Punkatoy?" Sid inquired, relaxing in a faded orange plastic office chair. The camp was roughly carved from the bush and was a bower-bird collection of equipment, parts, spare tyres and odd items picked up at Government auctions. With no apparent order, they roasted in the sun, cluttered in the narrow shade of trees, or simply gathered in untidy piles in much the same way as Sid collected information.

"She's struggling, but I think she might make a go of it," Ray answered.

"I hear she has come into some money," Sid suggested, gently probing for information by implying he knew more. Grog and gossip fuelled every small isolated settlement.

"If she has I hope she has enough to pay me," Ray joked and took another drink to cover his surprise.

You have a way of asking all the leading questions, he reflected. It's hard to tell just how much you know and how much you are guessing. It's your talent and it's no wonder you always have work around the region. You're a trap for the unwary, he reminded himself.

Sid folded his hands in his lap, unconscious of his broad chest under the open front of his overalls. "And how's Clara Valley?" he asked.

"It's hard work, but the kids are good," Anne answered.

"You teachers never work."

"Not enough work and overpaid," Anne replied deadpan, the oft-repeated joke wearing so thin it didn't warrant a rebuttal.

"That's right," Sid acknowledged gravely, his seriousness belied as his face grew into a broad grin, eyes twinkling with another tease. "I reckon you work harder than this bludger here."

"I still work dawn to dusk," Ray answered quickly before catching the jest. "And it's seven days a week," he added knowing he had been set up.

Ray took another drink, pulling his hat brim further down to hide his face with mock offence. With increasing fondness he watched Anne as she answered Sid's questions about the various people on the station. It was a gentle conversation where Sid stitched together a complete picture of the recent movements in the area. Ray marvelled at his easy natural ability to gather information. He looked up from beneath his turned down brim as Sid spoke to him again.

"I hear Nelson Shortjack gave Wendy some money and they were going partners in Punkatoy. Could be a good thing. I hear she is serious about keeping the place even though the bank would be asking for their money back by now. The fuel mob were asking for a few dollars from her the other day. She must be well into them on credit, but she promised to pay them out within a week." Sid stopped and waited pleasantly for Ray to add another trinket to his bower-bird collection of gossip.

"Who's putting that one about?" Ray asked and again wondered just how much Sid really knew, and how much was guesswork.

"Bit on the radio here and there. Nothing is private on VJY, you know that. I was standing by waiting to make a call to Darwin when she came on ahead of me. You can tell the new people. They think VJY is just like a private telephone instead of an open radio network where everybody can hear." He laughed deeply. "Yet I bet she listens in during the day to the radio traffic just like everybody else."

"I'll remind her again," Ray promised. "If she is serious then she'll have to get used to the lack of privacy on VJY," he continued, giving away as little as possible.

Sid ignored Ray's reluctance to add a new morsel to his gossip collection. He switched his attention to Anne. "Have you been caught out on VJY yet?" he asked affably.

"Not that I know of, but if I have, I'm sure you would be able to tell me," she laughed and finished her beer.

"Haven't heard a thing, but if I do I'll let you know," he assured her happily, enjoying the bantered rejoinder. "Another beer." It was a statement, not a question.

There was temporary silence as they opened the new cans and took the first sip. A breeze rustled the tree tops, providing a moment of relief from the heat and bringing with it a waft of diesel and oil.

"Blackfella told me about the partnership," Sid ventured, putting his beer on the table. "But you know how they are, they often only get half the story ... and then they get that half wrong," he grinned tolerantly, always amused at the foibles of human nature.

"That's not true, Sid," Anne remonstrated.

"No," Sid agreed. "Truth be known the blackfellas know more about what is happening in this country than the rest of us. Isn't that right, Ray?"

"Sometimes." Ray was non-committal, avoiding the trap set to confirm the story.

Sid let his answer pass unchallenged and the conversation drifted onto other things. Somehow a meal was cooked and over a leisurely steak they talked, swinging easily between good natured banter, serious discussion, idle gossip and speculation and drank some more. Ray settled into the comfort of relaxed conversation and for a while the pleasures of a solitary campfire under the open stars were forgotten. It was edging towards midnight when they began to call an end to the drinking.

"What's your problem anyway?" Sid asked, opening what was supposed to be the last beer.

"Split hydraulic tank," Ray replied, the drink beginning to pull at his words.

"That's strange. How did you get a split in the tank? I've never heard of it happening before." Sid was genuinely interested in the mechanical problem.

"Not a hole, just a crack opening up. It's been weeping for a while, and the other day it just opened up. I was working a bit of rocky country, and the next thing I knew I started to lose the hydraulics."

Ray knew he was giving unnecessary detail, but the need to cover the lie made the story more complicated. The drink didn't help him to keep his explanation concise. "Thought I had done a hose, but then I saw oil pissing over the track. No damage to the hydraulic pump, thank Christ."

"No cavitation at all?" Sid quizzed.

"No," and it was a conscious effort to resist the temptation to bury the bullet holes beneath more detail. He held the rest of a rambling answer back.

"You want some oil then?"

"Yair. About two hundred litres if you have it to spare. I'll pay you for it, no problems."

Sid waved his hand in easy dismissal. "Replace it when you have got some spare."

"Yair, I know what that means," Ray chided his friend. "You won't ever remind me, and if I don't remember then it ends up as a gift."

Sid was unconcerned. Shrugging his shoulders, he drank some more. "What's it matter?" he asked. "It will all even out in the long run. I'm not so desperate for a dollar that I have to charge everybody. I'll remind you if I am."

"Thanks anyway, but I'll order more oil tomorrow. They'll drop it off here and it's yours. Which reminds me, can I use your radio? Mine is on the blink," he lied again, and wondered briefly if he should confide in Sid and tell him the full story. He decided against it. His livelihood depended on his word and his reputation and he had agreed to keep quiet. Besides he wanted to know a lot more before he decided what he would do.

"Go for your life. I would lend you another one, but all my spares are out with the main camp at Bucklin Hills. I might be able to round up one for you tomorrow," he offered. He stood up. "Catch you in the morning. Spare beds in the end room." Dropping his empty can in the bin, he waved as he went to his room.

Ray and Anne lingered in companionable silence. Their few brief chance meetings had been more than pleasant and thoughts of her crossed his mind as he worked during the day. The dozer attack forced a closer examination of his feelings and to this direct invitation rather than a chance meeting.

He made his decision and finished his beer. "I'll roll my swag beside the Toyota."

"Thanks," she said softly, and kissed him strongly before going to her room.

Ray sat until the tingling on his lips had disappeared. The stars twinkled brightly above, cold and clear in the warm night air. He breathed the clean breeze floating over the immensity of ancient land before easing up the escarpment. I could get used to the idea of having her around, he thought, and having confirmed the prospect, went to the Toyota and unrolled his swag beneath the universe.

Chapter 41

RAY WATCHED THE SUNDAY MORNING SUNRISE from his swag. The cold sky turned pink and then a brassy green which reached out into the beginnings of the blue daylight. The dark silhouettes of rosewood trees gained colour and form slowly as the sun burst over the distant escarpment. In the river valley below, the morning mist curled amongst the treetops licking the ghost gums and paperbarks. The avian cacophony of screeches, squawks like tearing metal, whistles and drawn-out bubbling whoops prohibited sleep.

Suddenly the day was warm, and rolling out of his swag, Ray reached for his sweat-stained stetson. He pulled his bunched socks from the top of his boots, tipping them upside down. Satisfied nothing had crawled into them during the night, he pulled them on and laced up.

He shook his head and two days' drinking sloshed a little uncomfortably behind his eyes. He felt tired, but fit. He straightened the clothes he had slept in, closed the canvas covers of the swag and rolling it, hoisted it into the back of the pickup.

He cleaned his teeth in a little water from his pannikin and washed his face from the water drum on the back of the pickup, using the water sparingly. He shaved quickly in tepid water, combed his hair, and replaced his hat. It was a swift, routine, disciplined preparation followed every day. Refreshed, he faced the day and breakfast, the sun no more than two horizontal fingers high above the horizon.

Sid emerged from the bathroom still wet from his hot shower. "Morning, there," he called with a cheer. "Help yourself to breakfast."

Ray thanked him and knocked gently on the door to Anne's room. He heard her muffled sleepy reply, and knocked again until he got a petulant "Alright, alright!"

The three of them ate in silence, each coping with the morning in their own way. Anne, struggling to wake up after the run of late nights, hugged a coffee cup with silent addiction. Sid and Anne engaged in desultory conversation while Ray loaded the pickup. It was a slow and gentle start to the day and they all moved like sleepy lizards garnering their strength from the sun. It was nearly nine by the time they got away from Borroloola.

"How's your overhang?" he asked as they crested the jump-up.

"No problems," she laughed. "The grog doesn't worry me a lot. I'm just not real keen on early mornings after late nights," she explained. "What about yours? I'm sure you had more to drink than me. I had a camp on Saturday afternoon while you and Sid wandered off with another cold can in hand."

"I gave him a hand with the scraper motor. We hardly had any grog at all," he protested innocently and shared her warm laughter.

"You ever been to Ryan Pool?" he asked suddenly. He waited with cautious anticipation for her reply.

"No. Are you going to take me there?" she asked boldly and grinned invitingly. She slid across the seat and leaned against him. He didn't shy away.

"Why not? We have time," an easy confidence now in his voice.

He drove, comfortable with her body close to his. Reaching over he put his arm around her, steering the heavy vehicle with one hand, elbow resting easily on the window sill. Turning onto the rutted side track, he reluctantly returned both hands to the wheel. Anne slid to the far side of the seat to give him more room and he wryly smiled his appreciation.

He picked his way along the cattle pads meandering through untidy leafy wattle growing in the sand. The dense growth obscured the rock slabs tumbling out of the ground, so when they came to the edge of the pool, the wall of pink and white rock was a surprise. The base of the wall sloped gently, leaving a shelf of rock by the water's edge. Pandanus palms leant across the pool, long thin leaves spiralling into tight spiky crowns. The pool was deep silky green, perfectly hiding shy freshwater crocodiles diving away from the intruders. Anne watched birds dart from the deep shade and dive into the smooth water, each time scooping a beak full to drink. A pair of plovers, caught unusually silent, stood with yellow knees in the shallows on the opposite shore, apparently embarrassed by their lack of karking vigilance. The rich tang of cattle lingered in the air.

"It's beautiful, Ray," she said at last. "Are there crocs here?" she asked anxiously, searching the placid water.

Ray sat down, his back against a paperbark and rolled a cigarette before he answered. She joined him, shoulders resting comfortably against his and waited for him to answer, happy to adjust to his pace.

"A few, but don't worry, they're only freshwater ones. They won't hurt you. If you sit quietly you might spot one over by the clump of pandanus. I often see one there. He is about a metre long."

He smoked in silence, powerfully aware of her beside him.

"I can't swim anyway," she admitted, remaining seated, content to absorb the feel of the bush, for once placid and welcoming, rather than harshly possessive of its isolation.

"Have you got any family?" she asked after a while, and to his surprise, Ray felt no resentment at the question.

"Down South," he answered easily and looked at Anne. The graceful curves of her body relaxed against his, her small feet, dainty beside his heavy soled work boots, made for a strangely matched pairing.

Why do I want to tell you? he asked himself. Perhaps you have a right to know before we go any further. There was a pleasure in talking because he knew she would make no unnecessary demands.

"Down South," he repeated softly. "I haven't seen them for yonks. I sometimes think ... I've been thinking lately," he corrected, "perhaps I might look them up during the Wet."

He looked across at Anne. Her eyes were closed. She didn't acknowledge, nor deny, nor condemn and he was grateful for her understanding and tolerance. He did not ask the same question in return even though he knew he had the right.

He felt the anger of the past return, now muted by time, but still unwelcome. Recently he thought of his parents more with regret than with the old bitterness. They had never understood the reason for his dishonourable discharge and despite the later American scandal of My Lai, they, and Army command, simply refused to believe Australian soldiers could be involved in anything similar. The Army had closed ranks around the warrant officer's crime, choosing instead to condemn Ray's intervention.

In some perverse way his parents' shame had become his. The remote bush became his refuge which offered no judgement and little solace.

I wonder if they understand even now? Just because he had command authority doesn't mean he had the right to...

He left the train of thought unfinished on a path long since abandoned. Anne's soft interruption of his brooding reminiscence was welcome.

"My family still writes, but I don't often reply. We have grown apart, they and I. They live in a suburban fortress behind locked doors. They don't talk to strangers but they give donations to the hungry and poor in other lands," she murmured softly, her words unusually stilted.

"I can't live like that. It's grinding my family down, but they don't see it. If you can't help those around you, then what is the point? That's what I like about the Territory," she declared. "Talking with Sid reminded me just how important it is to help others. It's not about charity. It's help where help is needed and where you can."

"I guess I'm just running away," she concluded with the merest hint of regret. She shook her head slightly, dismissing the seriousness.

"Give me starlight over neon lights anytime." She laughed, clear enjoyment echoing across the pool.

"We all are," Ray agreed truthfully, and then hastily watered it down. "A lot of people say people in the Territory are running away from something, often the Law," he finished hoping to sidetrack the conversation away from the unpicked scabs of his reflection.

"The Law is only to protect the rich and their property," she snapped with unexpected vehemence. She pointed a friendly finger at him and continued in softer tones. "You work hard, and I bet they hound you for every last dollar of your tax money. But if you were a Big Shot with millions, then you can get away with millions in tax evasion. There is one law for the rich and jail for the poor."

He was surprised at the strength of her conviction. "But what can you do?" he asked, quite pleased her thinking was similar to his own.

"Nothing," she sighed. "The best you can do is try to make a better world for people despite stupid laws. Education helps. Authority has to earn respect just like everybody else."

"I agree. That's one of the reasons why I'm still working on Punkatoy even though I've a feeling I'll be lucky to cover my costs, let alone make wages. If you can't give someone a hand, then you can't hold your head up. Sid was right ..."

He let the sentence hang, his tongue twisting around the words he wanted to say. He held back, afraid to implicate her in what was really stolen gold.

"Let's say Sid was right," he amended, thinking out loud. "The only way Nelson could get money would be to steal it from somewhere. So if he and Wendy were to buy the station as partners, it would be with stolen money."

"As long as it wasn't actually stolen from somebody, then there wouldn't be any problem," Anne suggested enigmatically.

"How do you mean not stolen from anybody?"

She thought for a moment, her face serious with concentration.

"The banks rip off thousands of people every day just by borrowing their depositors' money at low rates and lending it out at excessively high interest and with hidden fees. And if some little thing goes wrong, they foreclose, just like they're doing on Punkatoy. The Government rips us off all the time. Look at the tax on diesel for your dozer. It's supposed to go to build roads but it all ends up in the city suburbs."

She trailed off lamely, not sure if she could fully explain her support for the battler.

"Who are you? Red Robin Hood?" Ray gently jested.

"Maid Anne actually," fluttering her eyelids theatrically.

"So say Nelson got his money from selling stolen cattle," she continued. "They say Sidney Kidman did the same thing and he was respected as Australia's biggest landowner."

"A lot of Territory stations built their herds with a fair amount of poddy dodging and they're still doing it in this region," Ray commented, probing to see just how far she was prepared to go down this path. "But it would be a criminal conspiracy between Nelson and Wendy if it is true."

"So what?" Anne shrugged. "If it means they can keep the land, then what is wrong? At least Nelson belongs to this country. The next bloke who comes along to buy Punkatoy might well be a Japanese investor only interested in ripping the guts out of the country so he can make a profit. That would be legal," she added with contempt.

"Wendy is down on her luck, and they want to kick her in the guts. She's fighting back, and good on her, I say," she finished defiantly.

Ray found comfort in her agreement and his heart grew with affection. He half-smiled with inner pleasure, appreciating unasked for support and justification from another person. He was surprised at the warmth of his feeling. Wanting to protect her, he put his arm around her shoulder and pulled her closer. He picked at the beginning again.

"Sid was right," he repeated. "I probably won't get paid for the work I'm doing on Punkatoy, but she needs a hand. So why not? As long as I can cover my costs and take a few killers, then what does it matter?" he ended lamely, still wanting to protect Anne from the full truth about the gold.

"That's one of the reasons why I love you," she commented as if it were an accepted fact and he also accepted it, no longer frightened of the tentative beginnings of his own commitment to her. The picture of this moment at Ryan Pool instantly etched itself into his memory, every detail scribed with happiness. She filled a place in his life he was reluctant to acknowledge was empty. His throat closed up and he waited for the unexpected rush of emotion to pass.

"What do you want to do?" he asked at length.

"Let's sit here for a while," she replied, comfortable on the soft sand and the warmth of his shoulder. Guessing his thoughts, she chuckled warmly and hugged his arm.

"The ringers ..." she laughed with amusement. "Don't get me wrong; they are good blokes; but their approach to women is comical. They believe in 'wham, bam, and maybe a thank you ma'am.' I guess I'm too sentimental or romantic, but they think I'm just playing hard to get."

She looked at Ray, slightly scowling into the middle distance.

"You look like a jealous husband," she joked.

"Perhaps I am," he laughed and hugged her tightly. She returned his embrace and then broke away.

"Come on, let's go back to the station," she suggested.

A flash of disappointment arced across his happiness, but he accepted her wish. "No worries," he replied, hoping she wouldn't hear the slight catch in his voice.

"Oh, don't be disappointed," she scolded gently. "Why do men always assume women are on the pill? Besides, it doesn't suit this week," she bantered. "Perhaps I'll be better prepared when I see you during my September holidays," she suggested.

"Holidays? How about a fortnight in a dozer camp?" he asked, making it a sudden joke, not daring to expect she would agree.

"You'll have to invite me properly first."

"Miss, would you care to visit my bush camp during your next holiday break?" he imitated the false brightness of a television advertisement. "We offer most facilities at the starlight motel and there is no charge for your room. All meals provided free and served in front of magnificent views of the Territory bush."

"Do I need to bring my swag?" she asked.

"Please yourself," and suddenly bold, continued, "You don't have to unroll it."

Chapter 42

"HOW THEY KNOW CHARLIE IS DEAD?" Nelson cursed, savagely flinging the pickup into the quiet ringers' camp and stopping in a cloud of dust. No ringers, no women and children playing, just Old Harry alone in the camp. "I don't understand it," Nelson fumed. "How do they know already?"

Douglas held tight to the grab bar on the dashboard. Nelson had driven in a wild rage since discovering the four boxes of gold were missing from the creek bank. The bare footprints and the crocodile slide made the story easy to follow. Tearing back to the camp, Nelson had not spared the Toyota and its rattles seemed even louder. Douglas flexed his hands which were sore after holding the dashboard bar tight for the past hours.

The two Kalashnikovs slid to one side and hit the gearstick. He angrily pushed them back to Douglas, who grabbed the muzzles with one hand, pitching forward when Nelson slammed on the brakes. Nelson cut the motor and throwing the door open in one explosive movement, stormed towards Old Harry. Douglas followed, leaving the rifles leaning against the front seat.

"You sent Charlie back," Nelson jabbed his fingers, accusing Old Harry. "You sent him back to dump the gold into the river. Well, you're too late! He only got two boxes," he lied, "and then the croc eat him!" he shouted triumphantly, confirming what the camp had only guessed.

Old Harry stood comfortably alone outside the corrugated iron huts, calm in the storm face of Nelson's rage. The women, usually outside gossiping and playing cards, were absent. The children sulked in the stifling huts aware only something was wrong.

Old Harry looked at Nelson blandly, but alert to a curlew screeching far away. His dark eyes hung back under the shadow of his tattered broad-brimmed hat with its broken crown while he calmly watched greed work amongst the folds of anger on Nelson's face. With a snort of disgust, Nelson looked away from the old man's unflinching eyes.

Charlie's wife Ina burst from the doorless hut, grief writhing across her features. Skinny legs carried her towards Nelson until the dogs and children at her heels slowed her down. One small girl held Ina's faded print dress tightly, pulling it from her mother's shoulder. Ina pulled at her dress distractedly, wrenching the bunched material from the child's hand. Wailing, she hit her head and pulled at her hair.

Another child suddenly burst into tears, understanding the connection between her mother's anger and Nelson's torrent of abuse. She looked up at her mother and she too began to hit her head and pull at her tangled hair with one hand while clinging to Ina's knee with a skinny arm. Her greasy spiky hair hurt when she pulled, and she cried more for pain than sadness.

"Kumanjayi dead," she cried and began to wail, understanding the curlews' shrieking cry for the dead during the night was meant for her ears.

"Of course he's dead," Nelson spat, his voice coarse with rage and clenched fists held fiercely by his side. Only the women gathered around him, children clinging to their ragged dresses. "He's dead because he try to stop us," he shouted at their grief-stricken faces.

Children drew back and hid behind each other, jostling brothers and sisters in their fear. Old Harry stood mutely in front of them as Nelson fumed.

"Charlie died..." he started.

'Oooaaaw!"

The women drew back in horror at the forbidden use of the dead man's name. Betty put her skinny arms around Ina's shoulders in comfort and sympathy. They sobbed together.

Harry's face clouded and he stepped forward, tall and proud, his duty clear.

"He kumanjayi," he hissed, disgust deeply-seated in his quiet scold. "You know that."

Nelson gritted his teeth with frustration, not yet finding a way to turn this to his advantage.

"Yair. I know that," he snarled.

"You respect him. Hey!" Harry growled with unexpected ferocity.

Nelson turned away angrily, stalking to join Douglas who was leaning against a smoothly worn ghost gum tree. He saw the ringers returning to the camp, wondering if they were angry and how he would deal with it.

The ringers slouched and shuffled towards the camp, in no hurry because they all knew of Charlie's death. Much to Wendy's frustration, they had been recalcitrant workers ever since Nelson and Douglas had disappeared days earlier.

Curlews had been wailing from the depths of the bush all night, their mournful shrieking 'weer-loo, weer-loo' a cry for the lost spirits of the dead. The men heard the birds and prepared for an uncomfortable sorry camp where the spectre of the dead dominated events.

"At least he died a long way from here," Nelson commented to Douglas. "If he die here, we would have to shift camp. Can you imagine? Here we are, just about ready to start on the most important thing we have done in a hundred years of white occupation, and we would have had to shift camp and rebuild it somewhere else just because some mongrel bastard decided to die here instead of down at the river. Won't we ever learn?" He shook his head in anger at the restrictions of tradition, gouging a hole in the dirt with the toe of his boot. "Now Harry says Charlie is kumanjayi ..."

"Hey! Look out!" Douglas muttered.

"Not you too," Nelson groaned. "He's dead. It doesn't make any difference if we use his name or just call him kumanjayi or ... deadfella. It was alright for the Old People. They could afford to shift camp every time somebody die. But this is not the old times. We have to change some of the old ways. The old ways have not worked. If they had, we wouldn't be living like this." He slashed his arm angrily at the camp around them.

"Old ways not always the best ways!"

A knobby kneed stone curlew shrieked in disagreement.

The women crowded around Ina who sat immobile on the ground between the huts and dead campfires while the others prepared to shift to the women's sorry camp. She wailed quietly as the women worked around her, preparing a slurry of cold white ashes to daub across her body. The children cowered in the background, baggy print dresses and dirty torn T-shirts hanging loosely from skinny frames. Frightened by the mourning activity, they were sullen and quiet.

Old Harry stood aloof to one side of the wailing women, one arm behind his back holding his other elbow. His white hair, discoloured with dust, poked out from beneath his stained tall-crown hat. His yellow strained grey beard was roughly cut, jagged edges not enough to cover the thick scars on his neck. He watched the preparations for the sorry camp, satisfied to see they observed the old traditions. He turned his attention to the men walking from the workshop and he wondered what would happen when they reached camp.

"Look at them," Nelson sneered in disgust, eager to deflect blame and pointing to the dusty women in their tattered dresses. "Imagine waking up in the morning with one of them beside you in your swag. They either skin and bones or blobs of rolling fat. The whitefellas take all our beautiful woman and when they finish with them then they get fat eating whitefella tucker and drinking grog. They make us like this," he accused, "and we help them by letting them run over us without fighting back. That time be finish."

"Charlie –," he corrected himself rapidly, "kumanjayi die because he didn't do as he was told." He stopped, the idea and solution coming to him fully formed and tempered in the fire of his anger.

"Come on," he snapped and walked out boldly to intercept the ringers before they reached the camp. Douglas followed warily, uncertain of the reception, but happy to take on any challenger. He untucked and unbuttoned his shirt in preparation, sending a clear fighting message to any challenger.

The ringers stopped in an untidy group. Most looked at the ground, broad brimmed hats hiding their eyes and faces from Nelson's hard stare. Only Victor Giblet, now the senior man in the group, looked straight ahead, his stare diverted by neither Nelson nor Douglas. Others glanced at the group of women who had their arms entwined in a big protective circle around Ina.

They were slowly moving her out of the camp towards the bush to make their own sorry camp. They would cover her body with a white paste of ashes and clay to ward off the spirits of the dead so she could fill her mourning time sitting in the bush, her grief private. At night she would hear the curlews' wail and know from the eerie shriek that Charlie's spirit wandered lost amongst the trees and rocks of his country.

Chapter 43

"IT BE A SORRY CAMP," VICTOR instructed, his bony hands fluttering by his side, not trusting Nelson to respect the ceremony. Oldest of the ringers, thin in build, clothes hanging from his narrow shoulders and almost clean shaven, he was a reluctant leader.

"It's a proper sorry camp," Nelson answered lightly. "Charlie's dead," he said deliberately, drawing a line of control. He watched the ringers start back at the mention of the dead man's name. Only Victor looked at him, his narrow face wrinkled with affronted anger. The others scuffed the ground beneath bare feet and battered boots, shamed by Nelson's rudeness.

"That kumanjayi," Victor insisted, an edge to his voice and fists curling. Douglas edged closer, hands hooked into his metal belt buckle, ready for a fight. Victor wilted, scuffing the dirt.

"Kumanjayi die because he not listen to me," Nelson explained easily, content to have made his message clear that he controlled both worlds. "That big old crocodile down on Corella Creek been eat him all up because kumanjayi disobey me."

"Hey!" several men grunted in surprise, looking up to study Nelson again. He stood easily, shoulders thrown back, confident of meeting any challenge. Douglas stood taller, bunched his fists, sniffing the whiff of a brawl.

Old Harry diffidently sidled over, his eyes searching the ringers, looking for hostility. He stood to one side of the two groups and spoke into the space between them.

"You been sing him?" Harry accused, his voice low but every man heard the question clearly. The Lore demanded respect so he waited for Nelson to condemn himself with a lie.

"I sing him," Nelson agreed lightly, not frightened by the lie and happy to use it to bind the camp with hobbles of fear. "I know kumanjayi not listen. I warn him. Remember kumanjayi's pup?" he reminded them, his voice dropping low with menace, the threat explicit.

All the men looked at him, some pushing their hat nervously across a brow. Several nodded at the memory, a low murmur passing amongst them with shuffled dust. Victor flicked his eyes towards Harry, who stared at Nelson, his face crumpled in a benign frown. Harry betrayed no other response although the fraudulent claim was a deep insult to the lore of the country and its song lines.

"I warned him, and I warned you. Kumanjayi didn't listen, so I sing him and now he dead. You listen to the curlews tonight," he predicted, confident the nocturnal birds would continue crying because they were nesting. "Kumanjayi can't finish up proper because he did the wrong thing. That's why I sing him."

"You lie," Harry whispered quietly, throwing his words softly into the surrounding bush and avoiding the eyes of men. "Only the Old People can sing a man. You not know how. I think you kill him yourself."

"I see Old People a long time ago, old man," Nelson countered boldly with contempt, giving confidence to the fabrication. "That's why I came back here from down south. They been teach me how. I'll sing anybody who doesn't believe me," he challenged, the threat sufficient to avoid answering Harry's accusation and exposing the lie.

Old Harry was silent. This was not a fight won with idle debate or fists. Nelson carried no tribal initiation scars. He had missed the boy's business camps when he was taken away to the mission school, and later when he was sent down South. Only those who had passed through the many necessary levels of initiation knew how to sing an enemy. Their bodies all carried the hard-ridged cicatrice scars to prove it.

Only the Kaditcha men with the power and knowledge of tribal lore could take the responsibility to steal away a man's song. When a man lost his singing, he lost all connection with his country. It was a connection which nourished man and country alike. With nobody to look after the country and visit the important singing sites to perform the ceremonies, the country would wither and die. When a man's singing was taken away, he too withered and died. A man and his country were indivisible, their fates tied together with bonds created by Dreamtime ancestors and ancestral beings since time began.

Harry shielded the contempt from his deep-set eyes, listening and framing the appropriate punishment as Nelson continued on his chosen path.

"I haven't seen kumanjayi since I left here three days ago. Isn't that right, Douglas?" he appealed, needing only this confirmation to finish tying the knot of fear to bind the men.

Douglas pushed his shoulders back, jagged beard pointed like a shovel-nosed spear and put his hands on his hips. "That right," he agreed wishing he had one of the rifles from the Toyota in his hand.

"Kumanjayi died without me touching him. I could do the same to all you mob, but you are going to help me win back this country of ours." He glanced back at the now silent and deserted camp. "The women are gone. Is there any man here who wants to go with the women?" he challenged insultingly. No-one moved.

He smirked with satisfaction, all amongst friends now.

"Let us sit by the fire as the Old People did, and talk about how we going to win."

He turned his back on them, confident they would follow and walked to the unlit cooking fires. Douglas led the way, and the others straggled along, deceived and bound by ancient ties.

Nelson sat in the dust and waited for the ringers to assemble on the ground around him.

Old Harry sat outside the semi-circle, back turned to Nelson in apparent defeat. He crossed his legs and draped his thin arms across his bony knees so he could listen while deciding what and how much to sing. Picking up a twig, in dots and crosshatched lines, he sketched the outlines of the punishment.

Chapter 44

NELSON SURVEYED THE SHUFFLING NERVOUS MEN as they sat or squatted on the bare ground. Some rolled cigarettes while others picked at scabby sores. Old Harry sat, aloof from the activity around him and apparently irrelevant.

They were ringers, not revolutionaries. He needed their support, not their commitment, so he sent Douglas to the Toyota, returning with two AK47s. The shuffling stopped and jaundiced eyes opened wide. A Kalashnikov cradled in his arms, Douglas sat inside the semi-circle. They watched the rifle, mesmerised, as Nelson talked, his voice low and sure. Douglas relaxed, watching the weapon exert its power.

"Our brothers in South Africa and Zimbabwe have learnt what we have to learn. Whitefellas will not give our land back to us. We must take it from them with force as they took it from us. It is a time for action; it is a time for struggle. We have waited one hundred years for this day. The waiting is over." He took a weapon from Douglas, and waved the AK47, pushing it towards the men, muzzle held high. "Now we make them pay for living on blackfella land."

Fascinated, none of the assembled men moved, their eyes on the short ugly assault weapon as Nelson shook it above his head.

Only Harry concentrated on the distant bush and beyond sight, the towering escarpments with their battlements and hidden caves.

You're all still just ringers, Nelson thought assessing the men, foreign struggles mean nothing. You have no pride. You're too beaten to think of breaking out of the system. They have squashed you into the ground. The threat of singing can push you so far but I need more.

"Look at you," he sneered in disgust, switching his approach from the thirst for revenge to fear and insults to cajole their support. "You don't eat, you don't drink, you don't piss unless a whitefella lets you. We live in shit because they won't let us live the way we want to. They take our women and our land, they destroy our lives and the animals we always hunted … and you let them."

He felt the shallow waves of discontent in the covert glances, the resetting of haunches and above all, in the silence sliding under drooped eyes.

"You mob shame me. You shame me proper. This country, him fella all buggered up. You mob bugger him up. Victor, you been bugger him up. Andrew, you bugger him. I bugger him up. We all be shamed!" he finished stridently and bowed his head aiming for collective guilt to lead to collective action.

His eyes flashed beneath the downturned brim of his hat, watching the men. Not one of them had been spared the kicks of ignorance, the sleights of racism, the casual contempt or the desperation of destitution. It could all be suppressed, but never forgotten. He thrilled to the ripple of anger his abuse had created. He let them think and grow angry.

"Whitefella, him proper bugger up this country," he hissed malevolently. "Punkatoy not much change, but Yellowbank destroy this pungkuthuyi country." He looked up again at the ringers and watched a few heads nod in agreement. "Yellowbank is part of pungkuthuyi dreaming. True one, chilpu?" he asked, knowing Old Harry could not deny his dreaming and the bonds of skin.

Old Harry glared into the distance. "It be true," he muttered, reluctant to assist Nelson in any way.

"They bulldoze the tjurunga stones. True one, chuilpu?" Nelson goaded.

Harry nodded silently, not wishing to be entrapped by Nelson's cause. The tjurunga stones marked the path of the dreamtime sand goanna. Their destruction disrupted pungkuthuyi dreaming and song lines.

"Yellowbank is on Coolabah Downs, but because it is part of pungkuthuyi dreaming we will take it back. It'll be the first step in returning this country to us. Douglas and I will take the men and the mine site hostage. Then we make our demands."

This new strategy caught the ringers unaware and the ripple of anger turned to waves of unease. Boots shuffled and eyes were downcast.

"We put in land claim, hey? They probably give him to us," Victor suggested quietly. Nelson couldn't let attention wander away from him, so he struck back quickly.

"One hundred years is too long to wait already. By the time they consider our land claim most of us be dead. The whitefella live longer than we do. They can afford to wait. We can't wait. We will lodge this land claim the same way they lodged theirs when they first arrived in our country... with a gun. Then they will quickly recognise Punkatoy as our land."

A quiet murmur of discontent passed around the men. Eyes still down, they fidgeted, scribbling in the dust and shuffling uncomfortably on the ground. They needed more than words because that is all they got from Government and with empty words were promises unfilled.

"Hey!" he called and when young Andy looked up, he threw the rifle to him. Despite his surprise, the sullen ringer caught it in his skinny hands. A strapping 18-year-old, it was his third season in the ringers' camp and the few falls from bucking horses had not been enough to dampen his bravado nor satisfy his need for excitement beyond the boredom of the camp.

"Better than a handful of flour and sugar. Hey!" Nelson asked. "You can make any whitefella boss listen now. Government mob move quickest way when you talk with that one. Hey!"

Andy beamed and stood up, gravel scuffed Cuban heeled riding boots uncomfortable on his feet and his single spur dragged in the dust. Holding the assault rifle low, he swung the barrel experimentally, and then fired a long imaginary burst. He lifted the rifle and held it aggressively angled across his chest, his fine young features breaking into a broad grin.

"Rambo, hey mate," he laughed, then tipping his hat low over his eyes Clint Eastwood style, he leant forward dangerously, rifle at ready. The balance felt good, and he flicked the selector switch up and down, the solid metallic click somehow reassuring.

Sitting beside him, Freddy reached up for the rifle.

"Get your own," Andy growled defiantly at the older man, wrenching it away and they all laughed, the tension broken with excited anticipation. He handed the rifle to Freddy and the weapon, along with excited comments, was passed around the assembled men. Douglas cradled the second weapon, standing straight and tall. Nelson took the rifle from the ringers and squatted, rifle butt resting on the ground and the barrel vertical before his eyes. He waited patiently for the joking horseplay to subside.

Outside the circle, Old Harry remained aloof, refusing to touch the weapon. Dark eyes hid his distrust and the ancient scars on his chest quivered as he sat immobile, storing information and weighing it against the old ways. He felt Nelson look in his direction and knew he was dismissed. Satisfied there was no other way, he began to sing silently to his country.

Chapter 45

"THIS IS MEN'S BUSINESS," NELSON WARNED when the crowd settled. "Fighting has always been men's business." The assembled ringers nodded their agreement and listened attentively as Nelson continued. He did not tell them all the details, not yet trusting their loyalty or commitment. His rough voice invited no opposition. The men lazed around, some smiling in anticipation. Andy sat forward at the front, eager, thin hands gripping the rifle stock.

"First we take over the Yellowbank mine. We hold the men hostage and force the Government to speak direct to us. We threaten to kill the hostages if they don't listen to us. Douglas and I do this."

He searched the faces around him and saw relief etched on a few. Gently, gently, he told himself, and smiled a benediction and absolution on them all so they knew he was not asking them to put themselves in danger by breaking the law.

"There no work on the station until we finish," he instructed. "We not work for whitefella wages no more. He proper finish. I want you all make sure nobody else works on the station. We take the station from the bank. All you have to do is sit down – go on strike. Can you do that?" he asked, sure of the answer to such minimal commitment.

"No worries, mate!" Andy answered proudly, emboldened by the weapon in his hands. A mumble of assent followed.

"We not shoot anybody?" Victor asked, voicing the more sober concerns of the ringers who, while not stepping back from a fight, felt uncomfortable with the thought of deliberate killing.

"There is no need," Nelson assured him. "All you have to do is sit down here. We do the rest."

"What for you need rifles?" Victor asked quietly. Several men looked at him, their hands flashing in their laps in silent signalled agreement. They waited for Nelson to answer and he knew he couldn't make a mistake.

"The whitefella has never taken us seriously before. He only understands force. The whitefella took our land with a gun and he'll not let us have it back unless we hold a gun at his head. For too long we walked in the enemy camp without our spears." Holding his rifle by the pistol grip, he waved the AK47 in the air. "Now these our spears!" he shouted triumphantly.

Andy copied him immediately, leaping to his feet, rifle held high and whooping. Two other ringers threw their arms up, fists clenched in agreement. Douglas shot his arm into the air, shaking his fist with excitement. Frustrated with the physical need for action, he bent down and punched the yellow dog beside him in the hindquarters. It yelped and slunk away. As always, it felt good to hurt someone or something and he smirked with satisfaction.

"Fighting men's business," Victor countered softly. "There only be the Missus at the station. What for we need rifles here?"

The men were too involved in the excitement of the moment to pay full attention to the thin, narrow-faced ringer. Nelson replied with confident authority, knowing Victor would pass his explanation through the camp later.

"We don't need rifles to get rid of the Missus. I'll see her later and ask her to leave. I think she'll join us, and if she does, it is OK. We need rifles to keep away other whitefellas who'll want to fight us. I don't want to fight," he claimed, his left hand open in submission, right hand on the AK47 pistol grip. "Whitefellas not believe us if we not have weapons. The Missus is no problem, but all whitefellas must leave the station." He raised his voice so the others could hear.

"There will be no more whitefellas on pungkuthuyi country ever again once we have captured Yellowbank mine. I give you all a rifle so every whitefella know you not gammon. This is dinkum. Will you do this to keep the whitefella out?"

Raised arms, whoops of excitement and stamping feet gave him his answer. His heart grew inside his chest and pride choked his breathing. The ringers were all on their feet. Only Old Harry remained sitting, his back turned to the noisy horde. He heard Old Harry softly whisper, his question strangely able to break through the ringers' loud excited babble.

"When you win, what happen to the mine at Yellowbank?" Harry asked simply, his immobile face sad and weary, already guessing the answer.

"We lease it back to the company so they can mine it for us. There is money in the ground, and we should have it," Nelson answered happily, concentrating on the euphoric ringers.

"It be sacred place. The tjurunga stones should be made complete again so the pungkuthuyi dreaming path is fixed," Harry muttered softly in response, without particular emphasis, as though it was an insignificant observation that belied the importance of Nelson's answer.

"We need the money from the mine to make us masters of our lives," Nelson replied contemptuously, confident now he didn't need the old man's support. Harry didn't respond, and perturbed by plans that changed nothing, he continued the silent singing in his head.

"What happen to anybody who not support us?" Douglas challenged loudly and the group quieted for the reply.

Nelson looked at him and scowling, slowly looked around the ringers, letting his gaze rest heavily on each man. He let them wait in uncomfortable tension.

"I been sing kumanjayi," he lied, voice low with menace. He shot the rifle in the air. "This one, he sing proper loud and proper quick," binding them with fear both ancient and modern. He continued speaking to the subdued men, his voice friendly with confident authority, satisfied he was in command.

"I bring the rest of the rifles tomorrow. I go see the Missus now. The women are away at women's camp. Let them worry about women's business. This is men's business. You make sure they not hear our business. Secrecy is number one."

He studied the ringers again and saw the suppressed excitement lighting their eyes.

"We are pungkuthuyi. Like the sand goanna we are silent until we attack and then we swallow him fella all up."

The ringers laughed, slapping each other on the back, reaffirming their confidence, high with excitement and heedless of consequences. Douglas held the second rifle fondly in the crook of his arm watching the camp and the ringers, contemplating a world without whitefellas. He smirked with deep satisfaction.

Nelson turned and walked towards the big house.

Chapter 46

DISTRACTED BY WHITTERING WILLY WAGTAILS OUTSIDE the window, Wendy turned from the letter she was writing when Nelson strode insolently through the door. Uninvited, he sat at the end of the table, throwing his dusty hat onto the kitchen bench. He breathed heavily, still excited from his victory at the ringers' camp. Impatient, he watched her sign the letter with a flourish and put it with the other two she had written.

"Well, lover?" she asked.

"We're taking over the station," he stated bluntly, waiting smugly for her shocked reaction.

"Oh, how wonderful!" she cried, misunderstanding his message. "The money has come through. I didn't think it would be so quick! You are so wonderful."

She got up and threw her arms around his neck, seeking a cuddle, but he pushed her away roughly.

"You don't understand," he snarled, aggression left unchecked. "Us blackfellas are taking over the station. Not you! Us!" He pointed to his chest.

Momentarily stunned by his snarling response, she sat down to think. This aggressive bark was new, a Nelson previously unseen, but the tone portending violence was universal. She pulled the chair up beside him and leaning forward, put her elbows on her knees, hands clasped in front. Her hair fell forward over her ear and she instinctively brushed it away.

"Let me get this clear," she asked softly, long forgotten experience teaching quietness was the best response to attack. "You're taking over the station. You say you own the station now."

"That's right!" he snapped and watched lines of concentration destroy her face. Triumphant and certain of success, he waited, relishing the moment when she, proxy for all his white adversaries, would collapse in defeat.

She rocked slowly back and forth, absorbing the information and its implications. Without Nelson and Punkatoy, there was only a return to endless poverty and lonely financial disgrace. Her life was built on her earlier escape and she would never allow a recapture. Her decision was quick and irrevocable – move forward together. She stopped rocking and reached out for his arm. Reluctantly, he let her touch him, suppressing a shiver.

"I still think it is wonderful," she agreed with simple sincerity knowing there was no choice.

"Hey what?" he gasped, drawing back from her.

She continued in the same low calm voice. "This is your country. I learnt this over the last few months. We're all guests in this country. I would never own this land because it just allows us to live here temporarily. Remember the Place of Starting Again?"

She looked at him. He had not moved in his chair and his eyes were wide with surprise and confusion. He ran his fingers distractedly through his grizzled hair.

"You must remember. It was where we started ... You know the place with the waterhole. You said some people called it Wuulnpila Springs." She struggled with the pronunciation. "It's my special place too, so I always think of it as the Place of Starting Again. I told you then we're just visitors in this country."

She paused and continued with earnest conviction. "It doesn't make any difference who owns the country, as long as you and your people are able to live here the way you want to. I wanted to do it with my share of the money but I wanted to talk to you about it first. I was saving it as a surprise."

"Is that so?" he sneered, contempt overcoming surprise.

"Oh, Nelson," she took his unresponsive hand between her own. "I love you and I love this country. I wish ..." She faltered, not sure her dream could be rushed. She felt the rigid strength in his hand and mistaking it for agreement, imagined her wedding ring on his finger.

She had planned it all so carefully. First she would accept the money he offered as her share of the gold. She imagined the pleasure of paying the bills and saw the surprised faces of the bank manager and other businessmen. Debt free. The words had a wonderful ring.

She had not decided how she would tell Nelson about her gift of handover when the time came, but in her favourite dream she would be lying beside him, head nestled against his face, his arm under her shoulder, and hand resting lightly on her chest. When his breathing had grown steady and his beating heart returned to normal, she would tell him the handover of the station was her wedding gift to him. In her imagination, he rolled onto his side and folded her in his strong grateful embrace.

"I want to be on this land forever," she finished, the unfulfilled dream lurking behind her words.

"Impossible," he protested weakly, his voice softened in response to her faith in his country.

"But you don't understand," she pleaded, massaging his hand. The gentle warmth tingled on his skin, and he tried to ignore the creeping desire dissolving his resolve.

"I don't want to own Punkatoy. I want you and your people to have this country. It is yours and we have stolen it and kept it from you ever since we arrived. I want to give this land to you," she soothed, picking up the threads of her dream. "Take it for yourselves but don't forget I love you and I love this country too. I'm part of it ... it speaks to me ... you can't exclude me, please," she begged with soft sincerity and desperation.

Crossing her hands across her breasts, she dropped her head protectively as if sheltering a small animal. Nelson missed the soft touch of her hands and her warm embrace. A pang of intimate remembrance shafted through him.

"Listen," she huskily whispered and cocked her head to one side. "Hear the curlews. Hear the willy wagtails. Listen to the dingoes howling out there. They are all talking to me ... to us," she implored, almost trancelike, clutching his arm, a sudden spasm of desire. "This has become my country too. I want to stay here and be part of it with you."

"You can't," he replied more softly than he intended, his resolve weakening. He covered her roughened hands, small against his own and his skin tingled at the contact while he felt himself stir. He took his hands away quickly before his body could betray him further.

"You can't," he repeated more severely with a certainty he didn't feel. "This is blackfella country now and you have to go. We don't want any whitefellas here."

She shook her head slowly, abandoned hands draped uselessly on the edge of the table. Hot tears stung her eyes and she fought them back. "I can be anything you want me to be," she pleaded, her voice coming thickly across shattered dreams.

"You can't be black!" Nelson angrily snapped, his body further betraying his resolve.

Surrendering to her tears, she laid her head on outstretched arms, crying soundlessly and ashamed of her lightly tanned skin. She sobbed because he wouldn't take her in his arms and give the comfort she needed. She wept for the security she had lost. She looked up at his strong proud face and tears blurred the harsh edges of his features, melting them into longed for kindness.

Not moving, he watched her submission, pleased to see the impact of truth striking home and wary of his unwelcome passion.

At least she isn't wailing unbearably like Ina and the camp women, he thought with satisfaction and relief, watching her clean shoulders shudder. Her shiny hair rested lightly on the nape of her pale neck. He looked away from temptation and glanced at her shapely legs, clearly defined in her smooth tight jeans.

Unbidden he saw Ina's thin legs jutting like broken sticks beneath the shapeless folds of her dirty print dress. He shook his head angrily to dismiss the unflattering comparison, and saw only Wendy's soft shapely body when he stopped. He cursed his growing weakness with diminishing conviction.

"Perhaps you can think black," he whispered, confident of her complete submission and using it as an excuse for his desires.

"I already do," she sobbed. "You taught me that."

"You said you would do anything. Did you mean it?" he asked, looking to excuse his weakness.

"Yes," she whispered huskily and, head cocked to one side, looked up at him through bleary moist eyes.

"I need your total support," he demanded. "If you can't give it, then you'll have to leave Punkatoy forever."

Wendy nodded her agreement. Rubbing her eyes with her shirt, she sniffled loudly and through crowded, jostling fears, dared to hope, despite apprehension sitting uneasily in her bowels.

"What do you want me to do?" she asked, giving shape to her submission and hoping she was equal to his demands.

"I am going to take over Yellowbank mine," he stated calmly.

She suppressed a gasp.

"This is all pungkuthuyi dreaming and my people want it back. We can't buy it so we'll take it. Will you help?"

"Yes," she answered quickly, her dream reassembling around her shattered world. "You only have to ask and I'll be there," she offered and her heart begged him to accept, the alternative too terrifying to contemplate.

"When it is all over, you and I will still be here," he concluded simply, his betrayal and lie complete.

She rushed to him and mounted his lap, legs spread wide on either side of his hips. She put her arms behind his neck and stared into his dark eyes for a moment before crushing his lips beneath hers, the taste of tobacco pleasantly acrid on her tongue.

Nelson felt his body respond and he surrendered willingly. He broke away from her tight embrace and buried his face between her breasts, kissing the soft clean pale skin while she ruffled his hair. He pulled at her shirt, working it loose from her jeans, then stroking the smooth sides of her belly while she shuddered with pleasure.

He loathed his weakness in surrendering to his lust.

"Not here. Let's go to bed," she whispered, nibbling his ear, her breath warm and quick.

"Here, Mawu," he insisted, and he felt her body tense momentarily before surrendering.

"Alright." Her hands pulled at his shirt slowly. He let passion ripple as she kissed his chest and then his neck with moist lips, her hands sliding across his back in a smooth cool frenzy.

He rested his arms loosely on her shoulders, waiting until her quickened breathing pulsed rapidly and matched his own.

"To bed, Mawu," he urged, a catch in his voice.

She stopped her frenzied caress, leaning back to look at him quizzically. He said nothing so she stood up and took his hand. He followed, satisfied with her obedience and his control.

Chapter 47

SHE LAY ON HER SIDE AND looked at him in the soft moonlight. He slept languidly, one leg stretched out and the other curled forward, knee bent, supporting his naked body, his back to her. Silver moonlight flowed gently over him, dappling the planes of his body and moulding the tight curves of his buttocks. Strong shoulders, now relaxed, moved gently in time with his slow breathing. His strong face, mellow with sleep, shrugged off any doubts of betrayal. Leaning carefully over him, she kissed him lightly on the cheek. He slept on, so she rolled onto her back beside him.

She listened to the curlews screeching at each other, their wailing splitting the silence. Not understanding their meaning, she ignored their mournful cries as she sorted through the jumble of her thoughts.

I know I should be glad to still have the station, she told herself. Nelson's people have been homeless on Punkatoy for one hundred years. We stole their homes from them just like the landlord took away my father's home. She looked at the patterns of the moonlight sliding ghostly in the room. The sun and the stars, the trees and the rocks, we destroyed them all and replaced them with slums and suburbs until only a few wild places remain on this continent. It is only right to give it back, she decided, firm in her conviction.

But I wish I could have been the one to give it back, and she felt the pull of generosity unfilled and the hollowness of what might have been. She swallowed the regret and watched the bright moonlight touch her breasts, slipping across her stomach to gleam dully on her toenails. I love this country, and it loves me, but why does it have to be so cruel? It is so like Nelson she realised, shuddering as a twinge of apprehension tickled her mind. She refused to think further about Nelson's plans for Yellowbank mine.

His snarling outburst, his first display of unbridled temper, a side of him she had not seen before, was more unsettling than she would like to admit. His tone of voice rekindling unwelcome childhood memories of vicious arguments and dulled slaps beyond thin walls.

Sleepless, she rolled onto her side and drew her legs up tight, nestling into the pillow. Thoughts chased each other while worry nibbled lightly in her gut. She wanted to talk, unsure of herself in the silent lonely hours before sunrise.

She rolled on her back and ran her finger lightly along his shoulders and down to his hips. He shivered, muscles rippling beneath her finger, but he didn't stir. Quietly she slipped out of bed and put on her light dressing gown. She walked softly to the kitchen and eased the drawer open. Taking the yellow covered diary from it, she sat in the fading brightness of the moon.

She chewed the top of the pen, resting it wetly against the side of her nose for a while. A gecko darted across the wall above her, ghostly in the pale light. She chewed abstractedly again, and then wrote carefully, straining to see in the moonlight.

'I love Nelson and I know he loves me.'

She paused and considered the complications buried in the words.

'Punkatoy is ours, but now he wants Yellowbank as well. I can only stay with him if I agree to help. I want to help him, but...''

She paused again, and tried to marshal her thoughts accurately, before committing her doubts and dreams to the uncritical pages.

Chapter 48

OLD HARRY PAUSED TO LISTEN TO the screaming curlews fighting with the light mist in the early pre-dawn light. They were the spirits of the dead not yet laid properly to rest. He shivered involuntarily, the eerie long drawn out 'weer-loo, weer-loo' wail echoing in the light morning mist. There was little protection against the wandering homeless spirits. He shivered again, watching the pink, then orange, dawn paint the black sky, hoping the curlews would allow him easy passage.

A song lurking behind his lips, he picked his way through the sleeping ringers' camp, glancing inside the corrugated iron hut that had been Charlie's home, its squalor a departure point for his journey.

The foam mattress lay on the concrete floor and the dirty brown ironstone stains from children's hands and dogs' bodies reached up the wall from the floor. Once brightly coloured clothes were thrown untidily in the corner, but no dog had slept on them overnight. The chipped white pannikins squatted abandoned on the rickety table and in the gloom, the flies left everything alone.

Around the camp cold ashes lay damply around the edges of the still warm fires concealed beneath white ash. Fingers of smoke drifted low over the barren ground as the sun began to break up the mist. Old Harry stooped and picked up his blackened billy from the edge of a dead fire, absently testing the wire handle twitched to the old milk tin to make sure it would survive his journey. A little further on he picked up his battered pannikin, slapping it hollowly against his trouser leg to get rid of the dust.

He shucked off his old and beyond repair broken-backed riding boots, leaving them for others. With the silent sliding gait of a kaditcha man he passed a sleeping ringer and collected his dusty fighting boomerang from beneath his swag. Shaped like a number 7, the cruel hook was a deadly weapon.

The ringers – his people – mostly slept outside where they could appreciate fully the coolness of the night breezes. Wire-frame beds were pulled up near the fires and the dew sparkled heavily on canvas swag covers. Yellow cheap cotton-waste blankets were scrunched around shoulders.

Victor had thrown his old grey woollen ex-army blankets to one side and he slept with one arm outstretched. His blue checked shirt had pulled from his trousers and was rucked up behind his shoulder blades. His riding boots, also broken-backed, lay untidily on the ground beside his swag, spurs dulled by grit and dust.

On the edges of his dusty swag cover, a long-legged dull-haired blue heeler snored, twitching in doggy dreams. Victor's pale bare feet were soft from wearing boots, Harry noticed, and he felt a pang of remorse for the passing of the old days. They were gone but the Lore was still strong. He paused a moment longer, and, turning his back on the camp, walked quietly into the bush.

The first rays of tropical sunlight fought the blackness above him, extinguishing the stars one by one. The tall ghost gum and bauhinia trees turned from stark black profiles to ghostly softness as the rising sun breathed light and colour into the land.

The rough and broken ground clawed at Harry's feet and he fought back, toes curling around the clods of dirt. Dry grass smoothly tickled between his toes and twigs pricked the bottom of his feet, but he barely felt them in the timeless glory of the sunrise. He let the ground massage his soles and the sun warm his old body as he walked on.

The mist drifted high above the trees against the rocky lips of the jump-up, running in long thin skeins, airborne snakes seeking the shadows. The metallic clink of his pannikin inside the tin billy clashed discordantly in the morning stillness, so he stuffed the billy full of damp grass and put the pannikin on top.

Boomerang and billy comfortable in his left hand he walked proudly into the dawn, humming a song of permission. The sun won battle with the night, and the short, false dawn slunk off leaving deep, solid black shadows lurking against the tumbled boulders and slabs of the escarpment.

The birds welcomed the strong light as they began to feed around him. The cockatoos quarrelled on their flight back from the waterhole, wheeling white against the rock walls while he walked ever closer to the sacred country. Two dingoes paused, uncertain, until they caught the scent of man. They fled to watch him cautiously from behind bushes and clumps of grass.

He paused, a sand goanna moving slowly across the dust, the sunlight not strong enough to warm its blood. Linked by a common Dreaming, he shivered in sympathy, longing for the direct warmth of the sun on his skin. Unbuttoning his faded blue-checked shirt, he abandoned it on an untidy quinine bush. The sun rapidly warmed his body and it felt good against his skin.

The raised cicatrices on his chest glistened with a little sweat. He wore his tribal scars with pride as he walked and watched the land come alive. He stroked the vertical welts on his upper arm, pleased with their familiar shape. He ignored the ridges on his neck and the scars disfiguring his ankles. The whitefella scarring had no role to play in this journey.

Cattle eyed him nervously as he approached them across a small claypan. They flicked their yellow-tagged ears and walked off, making room for him to pass. Harry smiled quietly with satisfaction. Even though he was not a hunter today, he remained a force in his country.

He stopped on the far side of the claypan beside a fallen woollybutt. The pale green branches were cool from the night and he licked the dew from beneath the leaves. Confidently he continued towards the small waterhole at the base of the distant jump-up.

The pool was marked with sharp leafed pandanus and the harsh land suddenly gave way to green grass growing thickly on the sandy bank. The water was stained dark by the leaves from the flaky white paperbarks growing on the far side of the small pool. Harry stooped to cup a mouthful of water in his hand. It was cold and refreshingly brackish.

He took off his grimy jeans and slid into the shallow pool, washing the rank camp smell from his body with relief. He got out, his body shivering from cold but warming quickly in the sun pushing through the leaves. He pulled his belt free of his dirty jeans and buckling it loosely around his waist, he stuck the boomerang through it. Filling the billy, he walked away from the deep shade of the waterhole into the sunlight, jeans and broken crowned hat happily discarded on the ground behind him.

Squatting, he pulled long strips from some dead pandanus leaves and plaited them quickly into a length of cord. He wiped his grey hair back and tied the cord around his forehead. His stiff hair, once matted with sweat and dust, was wet from the waterhole so it spiked back, sticking up in solid points. His white beard frizzed, harsh against his chest.

The sun warmed his entirely naked body and he strode confidently through the sand and then over the shattered tumbled rocks with revitalised confidence, embracing and embraced by the unforgiving, unrelenting landscape, so foreign to so many.

Billy in one hand, he picked his way along the base of the escarpment towards a rocky spur. Hidden from casual observation, faded painted handprints, obscured in overhangs or behind tumbled boulders, pointed the way to the faint unused trail passing through the jump-up and up into the hidden sanctuary beyond. He followed the faint trail easily, the indistinct hum ever-present on his lips.

It took three days, and thousands of years, before he reached the wide-mouthed cave sulking beneath a mottled smooth grey limestone overhang behind the rocky spur. He had eaten a handful of bush apples and killed three lizards which he had cooked on the coals of a small fire. The proud, sinuous sand goannas he let walk imperious, and unmolested, across his path.

Large horizontal slabs of grey and pale pink limestone were squashed between red and orange sandstone. Chipped face fissures and overhangs created a mosaic of hidden possibilities. Giant boulders, cracked and splintered from the sharp angles of the rock faces, littered the escarpment base as if malevolently pushed over the lip from higher up. Their broken disorder resembling the broken limbs of those who had been cornered there and driven over the cliff tops by early white settlers.

The sandstone overhang reared above him, protected by layer after layer of broken slabbed limestone, great curving edges giving way to sharp ledges and unforgiving vertical rock faces. Heavy ghost gum and bloodwoods shielded the low wide entrance which faced away from the south easterly winds and the Wet season cyclonic rains.

The roof of the cave was fire blackened with ancient smoke at the entrance. A small natural rock shelf created a stage halfway back and then disappeared into two dark low narrow caves. Harry sniffed the air and confirmed the wallabies rested elsewhere.

Claw and dragging tail marks were clear in the blown sand on the floor. Harry searched nonchalantly for the old goanna. In time he saw the two-metre reptile curled in the entrance of the first cave.

"Kangku pungkuthuyi," he murmured respectfully and the goanna flicked a lazy tongue in acknowledgement of the ancient wisdom of the kaditcha man.

He searched the walls of the ancient gallery and studied the old paintings. The red ochre and white daubed clay was faded, but the sacred designs were still clear. A giant painted sand goanna arched his way along one wall flanked by the stories of his dreaming.

White knobs of neatly bundled human bones peeked out from narrow clefts in the rock wall. Harry counted the individual burial places, pleased none had been disturbed. In the older crevices the paperbark wrapping had rotted away, leaving only a cushion of dust beneath the bundles of bones. The more recent dead, those murdered in his father's time, remained wrapped in paperbark, only the knobby joints of elbows and long leg bones visible.

Their skulls were placed in a separate niche away from the pungkuthuyi cave so he did not look for them. The low wooden platform in front of the rock shelf had rotted away, the cross members learning to one side so only short uprights remained.

Taking the boomerang from his belt he walked further into the cave, stooping to pick an old, short, carefully pointed hardwood stick on his way, shaking the dust from it nostalgically.

For three days he had committed to his task, and now he did not waver. He chose his seat carefully, goanna behind him, and beyond the mouth of the overhang, the endless unforgiving embrace of his country.

He clapped the stick against the boomerang and the clicking echoed within the confines of the overhang and caves. The heavy trees just outside the overhang trapped the sound, preventing the uninitiated from eavesdropping.

Old Harry clapped the stick and boomerang together rhythmically. He softly sang aloud in language, the liquid vowels droning into air. The goanna flicked his tongue in recognition.

He sang of his own personal singing, of the land, and its dreaming. He sang of the man who wanted it. He sang a yolngu curse on balanda ways, and then, slowly and thoroughly he took away another man's singing.

Chapter 49

WILLY WAGTAILS CHITTERED ABOUT WRONG-SIDE love in the first light of dawn, flitting past the window above Nelson's head. Wendy lay beside him sleeping soundly, her head pillowed on her hands. Nelson propped himself on one elbow and pulling back the sheet, studied her.

Without the tight, form-fitting jeans her hips were soft and yielding. Her pale breasts sagged and her white belly was loose over her dark pubic hair. He shuddered at her pallid form.

Mawu is a maggot. You're a maggot, he reminded himself, getting out of bed before his body betrayed him again. The freshness of the morning and urgency of his mission put an edge on his appetite. He strode out to the kitchen, proud of his dark nakedness. He opened the fridge door and scowled at the meagre contents. Without continuous power, it was more an ant-proof larder than a fridge.

He mixed a flour batter and cut slices from the chunk of cold corned beef while the heavy cast-iron frypan heated on the stove. He dipped corned beef into the batter and placed the pieces in the sizzling fat. "Dogs-in-blankets, dogs-in-blankets," he chanted happily as each piece hit the pan. He checked the kettle, topped it up and watched the batter turn golden.

"Egg flip, you stupid blackfella," he bantered and scrabbled in the kitchen drawers. His rummage uncovered Wendy's yellow covered diary, and out of curiosity he put it on the bench to read later.

Breakfast cooked and thick black tea made, he sat down and started to read Wendy's diary while he ate.

'I still can't get over the excitement of yesterday,' he read. 'It hardly seems twenty-four hours since Ray was here offering me enough money to buy the station ...' He skipped a few lines until he saw his own name written in the careful script. 'Last night Nelson came across when I asked him.'

The meat, covered with batter and tomato sauce, balanced on the end of his fork while he read on, fascinated by her descriptions and flattered. He turned the pages, pausing only when he saw his name until he reached the last entry. He looked at the date and realised she must have written it during the night while he slept. He dropped his fork, and pushed his plate to one side, reading the diary entry with growing rage.

'Punkatoy is ours, but now he wants Yellowbank as well," he read in horror and raced on as she exposed the full details of the plan he had explained. His secrets were betrayed. He snapped the exercise book closed, the unsatisfying sound goading his temper. He threw the book down on the table, anger multiplying as he considered the consequences of her treachery.

Frustrated, he ripped the diary in half and tried to tear the combined pieces again, but couldn't. Shaking with impotent rage, he threw the bits across the table where they skittered to the floor.

"The bloody bitch," he seethed. "I knew I couldn't trust her. She's destroyed everything." Her betrayal fed his anger. "Trouble is, if she leaves she might tell people what she knows. She'll have to stay until the Government gives into our demands," he whispered fiercely, increasingly angry at the position she had forced him into.

He thumped the table with his fist, the sting a welcome accompaniment to his temper. "Bitch, bitch," he cursed, the repetition reminders of his folly.

He slumped back heavily in the chair and through scowling, narrowed eyes, he noticed the pile of envelopes on the far corner of the table.

"I bet she wrote those letters last night," he fumed. He threw tense muscles into welcome action and lunged across the table. Pulling the letters to him, he savagely tore the top off the first envelope. He skipped her stylish address, the words 'Punkatoy Station' written in large letters of possession.

With mounting fury he read the broad details of his plans, revealed to complete strangers. He snatched another envelope, ripping it open. The torn contents confirmed his betrayal. He screwed the paper into a ball, then, not satisfied, he flattened it out and ripped all the letters and envelopes in half in an orgy of destruction. Beyond swearing, he growled and threw the papers across the room.

"That treacherous maggot has betrayed me. The white bitch! I knew I couldn't trust her!" he snarled savagely at the walls, furious at the potential enormity of the disaster. His taut muscles ached dully, crying for release that ripping paper did not provide.

"She can't do this to me," he cursed through clenched teeth. "What am I going to do now?"

He smashed his fist into the table top and the jumping flour tin tipped over, spilling flour across the table.

"The fucking bitch," he repeated monotonously in time to his punches but it didn't drive away the weakness which had lured him to her bed. He shoved the plates away in savage disgust and they smashed to the floor. The wonderful noise gave him no answer to his dilemma.

"God rot the bitch in hell," he sneered the forbidden oath from his mission childhood, the satisfaction of breaking plates not enough to placate his rage.

"What's wrong?" Wendy asked, the noise waking her. Still bewildered with sleep, she stood naked at the kitchen door. She stared uncomprehendingly at the broken plates, white flour dusting the table and scattered paper on the floor.

Still naked, he glared stupidly, consumed by the frenzy of his rage, in that moment hating her completely. Lurching from the table to the stove, he grabbed the heavy cast-iron frying pan in both hands and bashed it across her head before she had time to clear her eyes of sleep.

A scream struggled from deep in her throat, rasping past her broken jaw as she fell to the floor, shocked by the onslaught, spitting blood and broken teeth. Manically, he swung the heavy pan again and again, blood spattering his legs until she stopped twitching.

Panting heavily, he stood over her, now ugly in death, legs sprawled and bloody hands crabbed protectively over her head.

"Mawu!" he snorted, locked in a rictus of rage.

Stomach heaving, he turned away and vomited on the kitchen floor. He crouched on elbows and knees, head bowed and gut churning. He remained doubled over long after the bile had disappeared and the retching stopped.

He stood weakly, torn feathers of white paper and blood stuck to his shins. Using the kitchen bench for support and keeping his back to the corpse, he sluiced bitter vomit from his mouth with water. He washed his face, the tepid water refreshingly clearing his numbed mind. Staggering unsteadily to the table chair, he slumped, damp hands falling across the tabletop sprinkled with flour. He avoided more than a quick peep at her white body. His hands shook, the aftershock of panic swirling around him, blocking coherent thought.

He sighed heavily, agitatedly wiping his brow, leaving white streaks of flour across his forehead and along his arms, completing a grotesque parody of a corroboree dancer.

"What have I done?" The question screamed pointlessly in his head. "She loved me," he groaned. "What have I done?"

No answer came from the pooling blood.

"It's her fault. She asked for it," he reminded himself, swinging wildly between guilt and vindication. "She just a whitefella and they're all the same. They all ask for it. It's no worse than what they did to hundreds of our people," he rationalised, desperate self-justification not a soothing antidote to panic.

"It's only payback." He liked the ring of the words. "It's only payback," he repeated, not yet comfortable with looking at the battered body.

"Why isn't it easy like it was when the Old People killed whitefellas?" he pleaded.

Chapter 50

WHITE BODY, TANGLED LIFELESS ON THE floor at his feet, Nelson stared out the dirty window panes and considered his options.

"If the camp finds out she is dead they'll all bolt into the bush. I told the camp she would be alright, because fighting is only men's business," he pondered, pushing away the panic of discovery threatening to grip him. He dropped his head into his hands and massaged his forehead, smearing the streaked flour to a mourning paste.

Turning past the body, half expecting to see the khaki uniform of the police in the background, he dragged himself back to the table in one rapid movement. Fearing detection, he glanced anxiously around, seeing nothing although he imagined Victor and the ringers glaring accusingly through the windows. They were not there, but it didn't quell his fear.

The urge to run overwhelming, he pushed away from the table, started towards the door, only stopping himself with conscious effort. He slapped the side of his head with an open palm, the dull thunk a sobering relief from the grief of death and indecision.

White flour smeared his face and body from repeated blows. They fed a headache growing to dominate his fears and doubts, taking him down the same path followed by Ina, now besmirched with pale ashes and alone in her sorry camp. The curlews shrieked encouragement.

Pausing for a deep gasping breath, he stopped hitting his head. "Think, think, think!" he snarled at himself. "If they don't know she is dead then they'll stay," he explained carefully to the table top, one fist balled tight and softly thumping over and over again on the table top. "All I have to do is shift her ... dump her in the bush or feed her to the old crocodile on Corella creek.

I'll just tell them she decided to leave in a hurry. They didn't hear her leave because she went north. The boys will believe it."

He put his head in his hands, cautiously turning the makeshift solution over in his mind, examining it from all angles until it sounded convincing.

"There's no turning back now," he concluded, satisfied and rationalising his cowardice. "It's the start of payback. It's the way of the Old People. She was only a whitefella. Payback is yolngu way and we have waited a hundred long years to show the whitefella what yolngu way really means in pungkuthuyi country."

Nelson glanced at the contorted pale body and this time tried to see only a whitefella. He stood up from the table and staggered past the corpse to the bathroom. He scrubbed his hands and face, the water, pink with her blood, swirling down the drain. He washed his nakedness until the blood and white streaks of flour and paper scraps daubing his shins and elbows all disappeared. He smiled half-heartedly, turning away quickly before his resolve disintegrated.

In the bedroom he dressed in freshly laundered jeans and a sleeveless work shirt. Sitting on the rumpled sheets to pull on his riding boots he carefully ignored the familiar bedroom scent. He stood, grabbed his dirt-spotted hat and walked brashly outside to the pickup.

The ringers' camp, lazily silent before the first flush of dawn, carried no smoke, and he grinned happily to himself remembering the women were away. "Let them sleep today," he muttered quietly before throwing the pickup out of gear. Shoulders against the open cabin door, he pushed the Landcruiser silently to the house yard and as near to the kitchen door as possible.

"Maggot! Mawu!" he scoffed again to reassure himself, standing over the buckled body. Forcing his stomach to be still, he took her ankles and tried unsuccessfully to drag the corpse to the pickup. Struggling with her still-warm body, he awkwardly lifted the corpse. Her body flopped over his shoulders, arms brushing his side in an obscene embrace and a repulsive reminder of his desire. Blood stained his clean shirt and smeared his conscience.

Once outside, the station dogs, attracted to the smell of blood, sniffed and growled uneasily beside him. He kicked out savagely and lowered the body onto the pickup tray. Instinctively, he looked around for some fresh leaves to cover the body.

"Don't be stupid. This is not a beast," he muttered guiltily. Ignoring his own advice, he snatched some low-hanging green leafy branches from the white ghost gum in the garden and, without looking, threw them across her mutilated face.

He climbed into the cabin and started the reluctant motor. The noise seemed to scream guilt and he cast a frightened glance over his shoulder in case the ringers, woken by the noise, came across from the camp. Consumed in the lassitude of the sorry camp and Old Harry's absence, not a sleeper stirred.

Forcing himself to go steadily, he drove north from the station. He took the little-used graded track towards Open Valley station. Half an hour later he came to a seldom used turnoff towards Corella Creek and swung the vehicle down the indistinct track. The wheel marks twisted and turned following the natural clearings amongst the trees. Almost halfway to the creek, a pair of dingoes paused as they spotted him.

The dog moved forward, protecting the bitch. Keen ears pricked, he studied the Toyota. Yellow eyes searched for any hostile movement, but he saw none in the approaching vehicle. The smell of fuel and the sound of motors often meant extra easily-scavenged food turned up by a bulldozer blade, or left abandoned around remote work camp sites.

His mate smelt the blood and she circled as the Toyota slowed and the trailing dust cloud disappeared. The dog followed, keeping himself protectively between the landcruiser and his bitch. The two dogs trotted easily behind the crawling vehicle, Nelson watching them in the rear view mirror.

"That croc has just eaten," he reminded himself. "Charlie will be enough tucker for him for a month or so. Perhaps feeding her to the croc is not such a good idea."

Mind made up, he turned off the track and angled deeper into the scrub, pushing his way through small saplings, careful of hard termite mounds and hidden boulders. The dingoes followed the scent of blood, strong in the slight breeze. Nelson stopped deep in the scrub and well away from the little-used track. Satisfied he eased slowly from the cab, and careful not to frighten the dingoes, he pulled the pale naked carcass from the tray. It tumbled grotesquely to the ground, some leaves sticking to the congealed blood.

Feigning disinterest, he gazed over the untidy corpse slumped in the yellow dust. With greater interest, he considered the two dingoes, sitting on their haunches, half hidden amongst the scrubby bushes and staring with curiosity. To their left he spotted the lithe sinews of a sand goanna sidling through the spinifex.

"The dingoes and the goanna can fight over you. It's all you deserve, you traitorous bitch!" he muttered contemptuously. It was a small loss when placed against the gains he hoped to make.

"Mawu!" he spat unconvincingly into the dust, the taste of betrayal unslaked.

He took a lazy roundabout path before heading back to the station, planning his next moves between an unexpected and unwanted haze of tears. Her loss meant more to him than he could ever admit to anyone.

First clean the blood from the kitchen floor, he decided, followed by a change from his blood-smeared clothes. Then we'll start moving on Yellowbank as quick as we can. I don't have much time now she is dead.

Yellowbank ... He shivered in anticipation, encouraging the prospect of action to drive away the memory of her body, softly yielding to the demands of sex and death.

Chapter 51

1985, SEPTEMBER, LATE DRY SEASON.

NELSON LOOKED DOWN AT THE YELLOWBANK mine complex through the binoculars he had taken from the station. His excitement made the image jitter so he rested his elbows on the rock to steady his racing nerves.

Three transportable ATCO donga accommodation and office units were closest to him. The thin white metal sides could not disguise the flimsy construction of the buildings. The NTE logo of the New Territory Exploration company faded on equipment and buildings. The lightweight dongas were designed to be hoisted on trucks and transported to remote work sites.

He identified the single men's accommodation unit. Beyond it on the other side of the gravel hardpan was the site office. The large open-sided workshop and repair bays were on the right of the quadrangle formed by the buildings. A front-end loader, a backhoe, a bulldozer and two trucks were parked under the roof.

The generator room was attached to the end of the workshop and he watched one of the caretakers walk into the building. To the left several ATCO units were joined together to make the communal mess and kitchen.

There, he decided, was where they would strike.

Some trees had been left standing when the camp was constructed, so they grew close to the buildings giving plenty of good cover. He shifted the binoculars and considered the cleared area beyond the complex of buildings. The clearing showed a spattering of regrowth, but the shimmering heat roiled the area making it difficult to distinguish details. Cleared bulldozed cuts extended through the bush, defining the length and width of the long shallow ore deposit.

A fat man in a faded blue singlet and khaki shorts came out of the generator shed and ambled to the site office. Nelson watched him until he disappeared and then rolling over, sat up and leant against a tree.

"Definitely only three of them," he confirmed.

Young Andy fidgeted, shifting the AK47 on his knee. To avoid accidental shots, Nelson had made him take the magazine out, and it lay on a pale rock beside him. Andy nervously picked at his youthful stubble, squinting at the camp indistinct in the shimmering air and wondered what was really waiting for him down there.

"You sure?" he asked, licking his dry lips, the reality of the ambush now more terrifying than the idea.

"Of course I'm sure," Nelson assured him patiently. "The mine is virtually abandoned because the Government won't let them develop the uranium deposits fully. New Territory Exploration only keeps three men on as caretakers at the moment. NTE have fully explored the area and started some preliminary work, but that's all. Other people sometimes come in and out doing more geology surveys. I'm sorry one of their full crews isn't here now, because we would have more hostages to bargain with."

Nelson, absorbed in the details of the attack, was oblivious to Andy's nervousness.

"Why take him over now if not many people there? Why not wait, hey?" Andy asked, shifting his rifle again so the butt was on the ground. He liked its fine balance and security. It had not strayed from his hands since the three of them had left the station in the morning.

They had dropped Douglas off at the Punkatoy boundary with instructions to stop any traffic using the only access road. Nelson and Andy continued towards Yellowbank mine. It had been a long climb on foot to the top of the hill and an even longer wait in the sparse shade sharing the flies with the heat and the tinned spam they ate for lunch.

"We have to move now," Nelson snapped. "The longer we wait, the more chance there is of being discovered."

He rolled a smoke and checked his spare tin of tobacco, tapping it with his finger. Since Wendy's death he smoked almost constantly. The familiar activity calmed his nerves and helped slow the fluttering of regret, or was it excitement? He was not always sure.

Andy said nothing. He rolled his foot to one side so the single broken spur on his riding boot did not dig into the ground. He picked up a stick, flipping the empty spam tin, disturbing the flies and disrupting the line of foraging ants. He tossed the stick away, his thin hands again seeking reassurance in the rough curves of the rifle.

"NTE is supposed be opening the mine for full scale production soon," Nelson explained more calmly. "A big camp is more difficult attack so we have to get them now." He finished his smoke, and fighting the temptation to light another, considered Andy. He saw only a young ringer with a rifle, and in a moment of doubt, wondered if they could do the job.

"I chose you to come with me because you're the best shot in the camp," he lied, but the false flattery succeeded. Andy's thin face broke into a proud grin beneath his high crowned hat and he stopped his incessant fidget. Nelson smiled back reassuringly.

The brief training session in the ringers' camp had been terrible. He had explained the mechanism of the Kalashnikov. He showed them how to shoot in short, controlled bursts to conserve ammunition and protect the barrel.

And then, delirious with excitement and encouraged by the relentless thump of each shot, they ignored everything he instructed. Laughing wildly, they slapped each other on the back, staggering with hilarity, urging others to blast away at the empty oil drums.

"Them kangaroo got no chance now!"

"Hit 'em, Rambo!"

The trees behind the camp took a battering, bark and wood splintering beneath the hail of wildly fired bullets. They fired four glorious magazines each, and by the end of the session the ground was thick with expended stubby brass cartridge cases. The explosion of fun was a long way from the brutal measures needed to capture the camp and control access to Punkatoy.

Douglas was not a good shot, but his loyal enthusiasm and casual brutality compensated for his lack of accuracy. Victor shot carefully and accurately and was by far the best shot in the camp. No kangaroo or beast was safe from Victor, but Nelson suspected he couldn't trust him if it came to shooting a whitefella, so he left him behind in charge of the station. With Wendy gone he did not expect any trouble.

Andy shot well and would equal Victor if they had the time for more practice. His boyish enthusiasm made him a natural choice for the Yellowbank assault party but enthusiasm was not the same as conviction.

Nelson peered at the huddle of dongas through the trees and wondered again about Old Harry's sudden disappearance from the camp. Reluctantly he accepted Victor's explanation Harry had gone walkabout. Old Harry was his own master, and often disappeared on what he called 'business.' Even so, Nelson was not happy with his unexplained absence.

"I know I can trust you," he reassured Andy who still fretting, rolled his foot from side to side, now using the broken spur to grind a hole in the dirt. "All I want you to do is back me up. We don't want to kill anybody. We want to hold them hostage."

Relief washed across Andy's thin face with this confirmation. He was eager and ready for a scuffle, but not for murder.

Nelson picked up his own rifle and laid it against the tree. The spare magazine sat on a rock clear of the dirt and leaves. Andy toyed incessantly with his rifle, shifting it from one position to another.

"Relax," Nelson growled, suppressing his irritation. "We won't move until just before dark. Like the rest of the whitefellas in this country they'll all go to the mess and have a few beers when they knock off. Then we muster them up just like cattle on a waterhole. Hey?"

Andy grinned weakly at the familiar analogy and eagerness flitted across his face, breaking the boredom of the long wait. He lay back against a sloping rock, shivers of anticipation refusing to go away despite his fear. He rested the rifle across his stomach and putting his hands behind his head, tilted his hat forward attempting to relax.

"What you reckon Douglas doing?" he asked.

"He waiting just like us. He has a good spot on the hill beside the cattle grid on the main road so he should be comfortable. He make sure no whitefella comes through the boundary gate."

Nelson was confident Douglas would do his job well. The grid was a natural bottleneck in the steep line of escarpments and ridges and a rifleman could command the ground easily. Surrounded by rough broken country, cut by steep-sided gorges it was difficult to gain access to the station by any other way.

Nelson had to show the Government and NTE he was serious so he instructed Douglas to turn back any tourists and to shoot any police who came through the boundary gate. Douglas, keen to do the job, had taken his rifle and a box of ammunition.

"It be longest way to carry all that ammo," Andy reflected. "You sure he need all them bullets?"

Nelson shrugged. "His choice."

"Yair, but he was a heavy box," Andy complained, still awed by the number of bullets in the long tin cases. He shifted his rifle again, and eased his back against the rock.

"What you do about Ray Morgan?" he asked, unwittingly picking at Nelson's doubts.

"Not much he can do," Nelson replied, confidence hiding doubt. "He's not a bad bloke, and I think he'll leave when we ask him. I didn't have time to see him before we started, but he'll be no problem," he answered glibly. As a threat to his plans he regretted he had been unable to kill Ray as originally planned but the attempt sat uneasily on his conscience. They worked easily together, and although not great friends, he respected his ability and attitude. Events had accelerated after Wendy's murder, so Ray remained unmolested.

Andy accepted his explanation without question and lay silently for a while, the harsh afternoon sun unbroken by the thin cover of leaves. He tilted his battered hat further forward over his nose to avoid the flies. "Wake me when we shift camp."

Nelson nodded, welcoming the stealthy breeze, a sibilant tune rustling over the treetops on wind flowing from distant escarpments. He rolled another cigarette, working on the wording of his demands to the Government and NTE. He again examined the essential elements of his planning.

"It'll take them at least three days to get organised," he muttered to himself. With just three policeman to cover an area larger than all of California it meant the police couldn't mount an attack within the tight deadline he would give them. "There are no special police units in Darwin and the Army only has landrovers for transport so it makes it even more difficult to reach us." He scornfully chuckled at the memory of a slow moving convoy of over-loaded Norforce landrovers picking their way carefully along the rutted gravel road earlier in the year.

He knew time and isolation were on his side and this would force them to agree.

Chapter 52

THE GLOWERING SUN HUNG ON THE horizon escarpment as Nelson hunkered behind the corner of the Yellowbank mine site office, spare magazine cold metal under his shirt. He checked the rate of fire selector on his AK47 for what seemed the hundredth time and the coil of thin cord. He lightly touched Andy's elbow, who shrank back from the contact, arms quivering in time to his rapid heartbeat.

"Let's go. They're all in the mess. You cover the door on this end and I'll take the other one. Keep your head down and run," he hissed and started his crouching run towards the open doors of the mess.

He stopped short of the open door checking to make sure Andy was in position. Taking a deep breath and holding the rifle low on his hips, he burst into the room.

"Nobody move or I'll blow you out!" he bellowed, driving away any lingering doubts.

"What the fucking hell?" growled a thin man in the corner with a beer in his hand. His shirt, sleeves hacked off, and once blue, was stained with oil and grease.

"Shut up!" Nelson yelled. "Stay where you are."

He waved the muzzle across the two men and searched for the fat man in the blue singlet and shorts. The cook was standing by the stove, a beer in one hand and a spoon in the other. "You," he pointed, "come here as well. Climb over the bench."

Nelson darted a glare towards the other end of the mess. Andy stood just inside the door, a stupid grin fixed on his face, arms shaking and the end of the barrel gyrating wildly.

"Get over there so you can cover everyone," Nelson snapped, gesturing to the dividing bench and worried by Andy's jitters. He was relieved when Andy used the edge of the bench as a support, his rifle much steadier.

After surreptitiously dropping his spoon, the cook was poised to throw a long carving knife. Glimpsing movement in the corner of his eye Nelson swung his own weapon viciously, jerking convulsively on the trigger.

The deafening heavy relentless chtud-chtud hammering reverberated in the confined space and he kept his finger on the trigger in blind fury. Bullets smashed through the thin walls, splintering the wood veneer. They thumped solidly into the metal plating above the stove. The knife dropped to the floor and, with an effort, he stopped firing.

The sharp stench of gunpowder lingered in the silent room. He wondered how many shots he had fired. Above the ringing in his ears he heard his own voice.

"Move! Come on. Climb over," he snarled, stepping back from the empty cartridge shells skittering on the floor.

The fat man looked at the serving bench separating the kitchen from the mess with apprehension. He was thickset and carried a well-developed beer gut. Nelson waved his rifle angrily, so he shrugged and clumsily clambered onto the bench. He lay on top like a stranded dugong, then swivelled around on his stomach. He dropped his thick legs to the floor and stood up, puffing and waiting uncertainly for instructions.

"Sit with the others," Nelson directed harshly.

The cook joined the others on the long bench seat, perspiration thick on his face and neck. Andy grinned nervously at the three men, and tried to keep his rifle steady.

Nelson stood alert, legs braced apart, the rifle pointed steadily at the centre of the group. He used the muzzle to indicate the overweight man in shorts and singlet.

"Your name!"

"Cookie," he answered thickly. He wiped his broad hand across his brow and then on his blue singlet. He reached for a beer, but the can in front of him was empty. He played with it, disguising his anxiety and fear.

"And you?"

Nelson shifted the muzzle to the thin man in the corner whose spiky ginger hair stuck out from under a battered pale stetson. His thin hands gripped a beer and a smouldering cigarette. Scabby patches on his hands and arms marred his deeply tanned skin. He looked at Nelson with a challenge in his green eyes and his thin square jaw set tight with a sneer. Suddenly his face cracked with an open smile sending his untidy eyebrows soaring. His yellow teeth were dull in the light.

"Just call me Irish," he scoffed cheekily and Nelson knew he was being mocked.

Nelson fastened him with a stare for a little longer, keeping the rifle trained on him and nodded to the man on the other side of the table. His face was blotched from heavy drinking and his jowls would do a bloodhound proud. The lower part of his face vibrated well in advance of his reply. "Alby," he quavered and, not taking his eyes from Nelson, took a long desperate drink.

He slowly put the foam stubby holder down and removed the empty can with the reverent ceremony of a dedicated drinker. He put it in the middle of the table with four other empties. An alcoholic shudder, exacerbated by terror, sent a spasm of shaking down his shoulders. His deep-set blood-shot eyes pleaded for another beer, but Nelson ignored him.

"I'm Nelson Shortjack," he announced with pride. "You are my hostages until our demands are met. It's payback time. If need be, I will kill you one by one. I will not hesitate to kill anyone who tries to escape. Is that clear?"

"Why us?" Alby asked, voice thick with fear.

"Aaarrrgh, you're joking," Irish scoffed from the corner before Nelson could reply. "Who do you think you're kidding? You need to shut your gob. They'll blow you out of here proper quick smart," he jeered.

Nelson took a step forward, swinging the barrel back to Irish. His finger tightened on the trigger and he dearly wanted to continue the pressure. With an effort, he shifted his finger to outside the steel trigger guard.

"You're the first one I shoot," he promised with cold intent. He savagely kicked empty shells away and stepped back out of reach. The need for a cigarette clawed at his throat, but he ignored it, not able to relax.

"You whitefellas stole this land from us and now am taking it back. We already hold Punkatoy," he boasted. "You are all hostages until NTE and the Government agree to give us control of our traditional land and this mine site. This mine is ours, and this land is our land. We don't want you stinking whitefellas here." He glared at them, almost suffocating with pride.

"Oh shit!" Alby groaned. He groped for a cigarette from the open packet on the table, lit it with unsteady hands and sucked the soothing smoke deeply into his lungs. "What a shit show," he muttered and deep in resignation, leant back against the wall.

"You haven't a hope in hell!" Irish taunted. "Mind if we have a few beers until the cavalry comes?" He made no attempt to move as he drawled his jaunty question.

"Don't move!" Nelson snapped realising too late he had been deliberately belittled. A sly grin creased the other man's mouth, and Nelson felt foolishness burn his cheeks.

Foolishness was quickly replaced with elation knowing with unfamiliar pleasure he could kill Irish in a second if he wished. He laughed, face open with glee with sudden absolute thrilling understanding of his power. Their lives were totally in his hands and the power was his to use when he decided.

He sneered at Irish in the corner. "Until I use the radio they don't even know you are prisoners. Then they'll have to get past my men who are all around us in the bush. We know this country because it is our country. We'll not lose to you invaders this time," he crowed confidently.

He flashed his eyes towards Andy to make sure he didn't expose the lie. Andy, now calm, concentrated on looking dangerous, bending low over his rifle, and scowling.

"You haven't a hope, boy, and you know it," Irish growled dismissively. He pushed away from the table and started to stand up.

Nelson fired.

<h1 style="text-align:center">Chapter 53</h1>

EMPTY BEER CANS JUMPED AS SHOTS tore down the centre of the table, punching through the wood and the floor. Cigarette ashes and table splinters sprayed the three men. Irish was thrown into the corner as Alby fell off the bench and they tumbled together, both cowering beneath the slash of gunfire. Cookie sat frozen rigid on the other side of the table, some beer cans bouncing off his shoulder. Splinters slashed his face leaving flecks of blood.

The breech block slammed home empty bringing the mechanical steel rattle of automatic fire to an end. Nelson stepped back so he could touch the wall even though he knew nobody could get behind him. "Cover them!"

Startled, Andy stepped away from his table and crouched aggressively, rifle held close to his stomach. With a ruffle of shame, he quietly flipped the selector lever from its safe position.

Nelson unclipped his empty magazine, letting it drop to the floor. He tore at the buttons on his shirt with one hand, pulled out the spare magazine and slapped it home. He worked the cocking handle quickly, welcoming the dry rattle of the fresh round sliding into the chamber. He kept the men covered and motioned Andy back to the table.

"Get up!"

Alby lumbered up from his knees, picked up the bench seat and stood it on its feet. Using it for support, he dragged himself up to the table. Seated, he rested his arms on the splintered tabletop, hands shaking desperately for a drink.

Irish rolled to his feet, picked up his hat and dusted it disgustedly against the side of his trousers. He pushed it back onto his head and sat down, insolence in every gesture. As the silence returned they heard the steady drip of liquid on the floor.

"You pissed yourself," Irish snorted with derision. Cookie nodded, uncomfortable in the damp puddle on the seat.

Nelson ignored the exchange, but the smell of urine was intoxicating. His heart fluttered and he chuckled coldly, the pleasure of power melting his tension. He forced them to wait in uneasy silence beneath the barrel of his rifle.

"Next time you die," he commented easily, hoping the very casualness of his statement would cower them more. He watched Irish carefully, hating his nonchalant insolence. He fought back the urge to screech insults into his deliberately calm provocative face that seemed to encapsulate every rebuke, every slight, every slur he had ever endured.

Forcing himself to think, he ignored his craving for a cigarette. He pulled one of the plastic chairs to the end of the table, its steel legs scraping loudly on the dirty floor tiles.

"Irish. You come here."

The ginger-headed man got up cheekily, but he moved cautiously towards Nelson.

"Sit down here and face away from me." Warily, Irish did as he was told. "Hands on the table."

The blotched scabby hands went flat on the table, and Nelson watched the small tremors passing through them with satisfaction. He pushed the red hot rifle muzzle into lank hair, grunting with pleasure when Irish arched his head to escape the burning circle of steel.

Irish shivered and scrunched his shoulders, his fear too primitive to be denied by bravado. Nelson enjoyed the tremors and he smirked grimly at the others who stared back, eyes-wide horror distorting their faces.

"We'll all sleep here tonight," he instructed easily, no need to threaten them again. "We might be here for some time and I want you to be comfortable because comfortable people don't cause trouble. Alby, you go with Andy and bring back some mattresses. One false move, one stupid thing and this bastard dies."

"What do you reckon, Irish?" he finished politely, the question carrying more commanding malevolence than any snarl.

"Do it, Alby. Just do it!" Irish pleaded.

Alby stood up carefully, filthy stubby toes groping for his thongs. They returned within minutes, Alby dragging a single-bed foam mattress behind him. Nelson delighted in keeping the muzzle hard against Irish's neck until all three mattresses were pushed together on the floor.

"Now you white bastard, you lie down in the middle." He took the muzzle away from Irish's neck and pushed it against the side of his face. Irish stood up carefully and with an ember of defiance, dashed his hat to the floor before lying down.

"Cookie, you lie beside Irish. On your back," he growled. "Andy, tie his wrists and wrap the other end tightly around the other bastard's neck."

Andy worked quickly following Nelson's unhurried directions until all three hostages were bound together with unbreakable knots learned the hard way from tethering feral bulls.

"You white bastards chained my mother like this before you killed her when I was a boy," Nelson snarled. It was a lie, but it served his purposes. This pattern of bondage he had learned from his fellow would-be student revolutionaries.

"See how it feels. If anyone moves, you choke everybody else. I hope nobody tosses in his sleep." He laughed harshly.

He pulled up a chair and too excited to sleep, he watched the fatigue of defeat creep over the men on the floor. Determined to get the language correct, he wrote and re-wrote his demands on a piece of paper torn from the exercise book on the mess table.

Whenever he paused, searching for a word, he considered the hostages. Their fear and discomfort always an inspiration.

Chapter 54

NELSON LEANT THE RIFLE ON THE side of the desk in the mine-site office and switched on the VJY outpost radio. It was the only 'telephone' available for remote cattle stations, isolated contractors and mining company camps in the Territory so conversations were clipped to the essentials because the time available on the radio was limited. The radio call was patched through to the normal telephone network but the open channel meant hundreds of people would also hear his demands.

He listened impatiently as the operator went through the morning schedule calls. He toyed distractedly with the microphone and watched the three men in the room next door. The hostages were moved from the canteen to the site office earlier in the morning. Andy stood over them, rifle held loosely with growing confidence. Each hostage sat uncomfortably on the floor, their necks looped together with thin cord.

Nelson clicked the microphone experimentally, suddenly nervous about using the radio as he appreciated the size of his audience. He listened to the everyday chatter as other stations made their telephone calls in their schedule slots. Orders made for spare parts mixed with gossip and mustering plans. He licked his dry lips and putting the microphone on the desk, wiped his hands on his trousers.

He again rehearsed his demands, knowing it was essential he use his best remembered formal university language if he was to get through to white officials. A gap came up in the radio traffic and he grabbed the microphone.

"Eight Sierra Oscar Foxtrot calling VJY," he garbled and released the transmit switch.

"Eight Sierra Oscar Foxtrot, standby please. I have one station ahead of you," the Darwin-based operator replied, her voice calm and efficient.

"Roger roger,' he acknowledged with automatic respect for radio protocol and let the microphone drop to his side, curbing his reckless impatience.

The shame of potential failure flittered and picked at the edge of his mind, walking hand in hand with his failure to silence Ray Morgan. I should have told Douglas to kill him first and then go out to the main gate, but there just wasn't time, he lamented. He regretted the oversight, but it had seemed vital to move immediately after Wendy's death; to leap into action to capture Yellowbank.

Suddenly he was angry to be at the mercy of the distant white operator in Darwin. He listened, determined to disregard protocol and interrupt at the first opportunity.

"Does that leave you all clear, Clara Valley?" the radio operator asked.

"Yes thanks, VJY."

Nelson immediately jammed down the transmit button.

"Calling VJY," he demanded urgently in contrast to the lazy politeness of previous callers.

"Go ahead Yellowbank." The operator acknowledged, recognising his voice.

"I want to make two calls. I want one to 070 551525333 to speak to the General Manager and I want one call to Canberra to speak to the Minister of Aboriginal Affairs. You'll have to find the second number for me. Over," he snapped rudely, glad at last for action.

"Stand by, please. Getting your first number now," the operator replied, her calm professionalism registering neither surprise nor irritation at his instructions.

Nelson waited impatiently, fidgeting with the tightly curled cord and microphone. He imagined ringers in the stock camps, managers on other cattle stations and Aboriginal health clinics all listening to the radio, normal activity arrested because they were interested in why a blackfella would want to speak directly to the Minister of Aboriginal Affairs. He spread the folded sheet of paper and smoothed it on the tabletop, gritty with dust. The words worked over and over the night before, blue ink smudged with sweat and worry. He tapped his fingers on the paper and time stretched as the radio in its green box hissed and crackled, no listener game to break the silence with a comment.

"VJY calling Yellowbank," the green box spat.

"Standing by," Nelson acknowledged automatically.

"I can only get the secretary on the first number. She says the Manager is not taking any calls because he is in a Board meeting."

"I have three hostage here at Yellowbank and I demand to speak to the Manager. This is life or death. I'll shoot the bastards!"

"Say again, Yellowbank," the operator requested, surprise clearly evident in her normally unruffled voice.

Nelson repeated his message with cool satisfaction.

"Is this a joke? There are serious penalties for using the radio to create a hoax."

"This is not a joke," he hissed into the microphone. "You get the Manager on the line or people are going to start dying out here!" he snarled, thumping his fist on the desk, even though he knew they couldn't hear or see it.

He eased his thumb from the transmit button with an effort and listened restlessly, heart thumping with anger and excitement. Seconds dragged slowly and he restrained his urge to hurry the operator by calling her back. Finally she came on, the sudden noise startling him.

"I have the General Manager, a Mister Timms, on the line. Go ahead please," her voice unruffled and professional again.

"Hello. You the Manager of NTE?" Nelson inquired aggressively.

"Yes. I understand you want to talk to me. I hope it is very important," the clipped voice replied, coming disembodied through the front grill of the radio. Nelson wondered what the man looked like and quickly decided it didn't matter.

"I am Nelson Shortjack. I have your three caretakers hostage here at Yellowbank. I will shoot them unless my demands are met. Over."

"How do I know you are not joking, Mister Shortjack?"

Nelson loathed the unruffled modulated tones of public school education, the cool patronising aloofness of the voice on the radio and the suggestion this could be a joke.

"Stand by," he snapped, resisting the urge to grab the rifle and fire a shot past the microphone.

He turned in his chair and shouted through the office door. "Andy, bring Cookie and the rest of them here."

The chain of hostages shuffled into the office. Cookie's arms quivered with the effort of keeping them high behind his back to avoid choking.

Nelson wrinkled his nose in disgust at the smell of stale urine. Cookie shook as he stopped by the table. Nelson, pleased he had made the right selection, depressed the transmit button.

"Listen to this. I know you didn't hire the man, so you probably don't know him, but you have one minute to confirm what he says is correct. His name is Cookie..." he lifted the transmit button. "Cookie who?" he demanded.

"Col Downey," came the stammered reply.

"His name is Col Downey. You listen up."

He let go of the transmit button and turned to the shivering cook. "You tell him you're a hostage." Cookie nodded his head in terror and Nelson held the microphone to his face. "Go on."

"Col Downey here. I've been cook here for seven months. The bastards have three of us! It's no bullshit! Please listen to him! Please, please..." He sobbed pathetically, a dry choke convulsing his face, shaking his jowls, and making the cord bite into his throat. Nelson held the transmit button down a moment longer so Timms could hear.

"You have one minute to confirm his identity. Any longer and he is dead."

He turned to Cookie who was still blubbering, his shoulders bent and wracked by spasms of fear.

"You had better hope your boss knows you."

The fat cook, sobs shaking his body, shuffled back to the room, all three hostages hobbled together like an old-time Aboriginal prison gang. Nelson guessed Cookie would wet himself again and the thought gave him immense satisfaction.

"I have no choice but to believe you, Mister Shortjack. Obviously I cannot prove his identity one way or another. You say you have demands. Please make them known and my Board will consider them." The disembodied voice was smooth even over the hiss and crackle of the radio.

Nelson seethed, wanting to strangle the patronising faceless voice.

"You listen here, arsehole," he grated, mashing the transmit button. "These demands are not negotiable. You will meet them within twenty-four hours. If they are not met then the first man dies. The other two will be dead by the end of the next day. Understand?"

He snapped the microphone off and waited for the reply.

"I understand." The voice finally giving way to unease and he could hear urgent conversation in the background. "What are your demands?"

Nelson took several deep breaths. Time and isolation was on his side, he reminded himself. He wanted to make sure his speech was clear so they knew who was in control and so there was no room for misunderstanding.

"Number one," he carefully read from his sheet and Timms did not interrupt him until he had finished all his demands. Timms agreed to call back before the deadline.

He reminded VJY his call was a matter of life or death so it was essential they connect him with the Minister. His second call took him as far as the Principal Private Secretary to the Minister of Aboriginal Affairs. Now the hurdle of the first call had been jumped, his voice was calmer even though his heart continued to race. Only the threat to hostages and the difficulty of making a fast counter-response bought them to the phone.

"Number one. No whitefellas are allowed in the area known as Punkatoy Station. This area, and the top section of Coolabah Downs containing the Yellowbank mine are part of traditional pungkuthuyi dreaming. It's sacred country. Any whitefellas trespassing on this land will be turned back or shot. We have the weapons and the numbers to enforce our demands. Is this clear?"

He paused for breath, his excitement mounting.

"I have that. Continue, please," the Secretary said with clearly forced calm.

"Number two. We, the traditional owners, the original inhabitants of this land, want total control of this land and its resources from today. We want the same terms and conditions as granted under the Territory Land Rights Act and we want it now, not in ten years' time when some bloody Commission decides," he demanded curtly, straying from his written speech.

"I understand. Are there any more demands?" the faceless voice queried.

"Number three. The proposed uranium mine at Yellowbank is to be allowed to go ahead. We have ..." he searched for the right word, "nationalised it as from today. NTE no longer owns it and we control its future production. The Government is to make sure the mine is given an export licence."

"I have that. Is there any more?" The voice sounded weary through the static of the radio transmission.

"The mine is in our hands and we have hostages. If we do not hear from you within 24 hours then we shoot the first hostage this time tomorrow. The next two will be shot at twelve-hour intervals until we get what we want. Is that clear?"

"Yes." The reply was barely audible as the speaker turned away from the telephone to confer with a background babble of voices. Nelson gleefully guessed others were rushing to the office to listen to what must be an extraordinary call. He continued, carefully enunciating his conditions.

"No police or troops. If you do, the hostages will die. If there is any movement on the road my men will open fire without warning. We have assault rifles and we will use them. It's payback time." He paused, the tight deadline key to his success. "You have 24 hours," he reminded them.

"I understand. We'll get back to you as soon as possible. It is very difficult to reach you." The concern was clear in his voice. Nelson broke into a broad grin of jubilation because they were treating his demands with respect. He left them no choice because they couldn't mount an attack within his deadline.

"I'll be standing by all day.' He did nothing to keep the triumph from his voice. He continued, "VJY, can you please broadcast a message for me? Over," he asked, the politeness unnatural after the hard victory of the last minutes.

"Keep this channel clear. Please inform all stations no whitefellas are to come near Punkatoy or Yellowbank. If they do, they will be shot without warning. Please also make sure the newspapers have a full copy of our demands to NTE and the Government. I'm sure somebody was recording this call," he concluded with smug satisfaction.

"Roger, roger, you bastard," the operator replied venomously, the limits of professionalism broken.

"That leaves me all clear. Thanks, VJY," he responded happily and mockingly polite.

He grinned, deeply satisfied and leaning back on the chair he rolled a welcome cigarette. It was as easy as he had imagined it to be. He listened to VJY put out his warning to all the stations and the contractors who used the outpost radio service. Boots resting on the table, cigarette in hand, he watched the tree tops dancing to the song of the rising breeze.

He smiled condescendingly and listened with an air of comfortable contempt to the chattering stream of pithy, racist and scandalised comments coming over the radio. The Kalashnikov gave him the power to bend them all to his will. The assault rifles, the difficulty in reaching the isolated rugged country and the poor communications were a guarantee of his success. The assault rifles meant he would not fail as his ancestors had failed.

Chapter 55

THE STATION YARD AND BUILDINGS WERE eerily quiet, oppressed under the early morning heat creeping into the shadows. The distant ringers' camp seemed abandoned, no campfire smoke, dogs or children. Ray went to the workshop first and then to the white ringers' quarters, finding only silence.

Surprised, he sauntered to the Big House and knocked on the kitchen screen door. The sound strangely echoed hollowly through the house. Peering through the dirty screen door he saw dirty dishes scattered in the kitchen sink, the HF radio crackling to itself, strangely empty of traffic. He wrinkled his nose in disgust at the horde of blow flies buzzing busily low on the floor. Looking around, he spotted some smashed dishes in the bin outside the kitchen, but he took no particular notice.

The camp dogs had upended the mop bucket on the tired lawn and for unknown reasons, one brindle bitch was licking hungrily inside the dry container. They had torn the mophead to pieces, and like bloated worms, bits were scattered over the scraggly grass.

Perplexed, he returned to his pickup and drove slowly to the ringers' camp by the waterhole. He turned onto the short access track and was surprised when a scattering of empty brass shell cases crackled under the tyres. He squinted curiously at the ripped and torn oil drums further out on the flat, recognising the distinctive jagged edged patterns left when small arms fire punched through steel.

"Fuck! What's going on here?" he muttered to himself, nerves beginning to tingle and alert for trouble. He carefully examined the bush and tumbled boulders along the base of the steep rocky rise, unsure of what to look for, but ready to act quickly. Uneasy, he pulled his rifle from its rest across the dashboard and eased a round into the breech. He scanned the camp as he pulled up, alert for any threat.

Charlie's one-room tin hut was deserted. Dust lay heavy on the bare cement floor and his untidily rolled swag was thrown carelessly on the wire bed frame. Ray guessed it had not been used for some time. A forlorn dog-chewed foam mattress was still on the floor, but the cotton waste blankets had gone. Pots and other utensils balanced on the rickety table with only flies for company.

The women and children are gone, he confirmed, partly explaining the eerie silence. Charlie's gear is still here, so perhaps there is something very wrong with Charlie, he wondered. Curious, he studied the hastily deserted hut again and this time he understood. The totally abandoned and unnaturally silent hut told him Charlie had died.

"It's a sorry camp," he concluded and feeling foolish, took his hand off the rifle. He opened the pickup door and walked carefully, avoiding Charlie's hut which had a look of even greater desolation than the squalor of other huts in the camp. He kept a good distance away and made sure not to step on anything that might have belonged to Charlie.

Victor Giblet emerged slowly from the end hut, shaking sleep from eyes gummed with dust, pale stained trousers hanging loosely from his thin hips.

"Gidday, Victor," he ventured softly. "You got a sorry camp here?" He pursed his lips, pointing towards Charlie's hut.

Victor stopped near the doorway of his hut, one hand behind his back holding his opposite wiry elbow. "That right," he agreed.

"Still woman's business," Ray ventured, trying not to be impolite.

"That right, chilpu," Victor answered, feeling comfortable using the language word of respect because Ray understood what was happening.

Each studied the ground in comfortable silence, lost in their own thoughts, unclear how to ask for help. Other ringers gradually emerged from their single room huts and shanties. They stood quietly, boots and bare feet shuffling in the dust and cold ashes, death and gunfire providing a hangover of remorse.

Why aren't you at work? Ray wondered, sticking a cigarette paper to his lip. Where are Nelson and Douglas? There is something wrong here and it's more than just a sorry camp for Charlie. He nonchalantly rolled tobacco into the paper and put the cigarette in the corner of his mouth, continuing to assess the situation.

The boys are worried. They leaned on veranda posts and bed frames, making a broad ragged half circle confirming Victor was appointed as their unwilling spokesman. Even Victor looks unhappy and Charlie wasn't even a relative of his. He lit the smoke, and puffed gently. Taking out his tobacco tin, he offered it to Victor. Accepting the tin, Victor motioned for Ray to sit down.

Ray sat on the bare grey ground and crossed his legs. The steel caps of his worn safety boots bulbous beneath the soft leather. He sat comfortably, one elbow on the knee of the clean trousers he had put on to meet Anne when she came to the Big House later in the day.

He waited for Victor to speak, knowing he would not start directly into what was worrying him. Victor sat opposite, his narrow face deeply troubled and slowly rolled a cigarette. The other ringers drifted in slowly and sat in a silent semi-circle behind Victor. They gazed into the surrounding bush, or looked at the ground, drawing scribbles in the dust. They picked at old scabs, or worried sand-abraded boots and spurs. They looked everywhere, but not at Victor or Ray. They were content to let him act as their spokesman.

"What for you come here?" Victor asked, an unexpected hint of aggression in his low voice after he lit his cigarette and returned the tobacco tin.

"My friend coming in today and I come to meet her here." Ray was defensive.

Anne had agreed to visit for her holiday so they had arranged to meet at the station before driving out to his remote camp. Despite the increasingly tense camp situation, he felt the warmth of anticipation and he flicked his eyes over his clean shirt and trousers. They were crumpled and beginning to pick up dust, but he was satisfied. He looked up again as Victor spoke.

"No whitefellas allow to come to Punkatoy now," Victor murmured flatly, a sadness lurking behind the words and no challenge in his downcast eyes.

"What you mean, hey?" Ray said quickly.

"Nelson say no more whitefella on Punkatoy." Victor explained, a note of apology in his voice as he looked away from Ray, unable to meet his eyes.

"He cheeky bugger," Ray commented, becoming alarmed and concerned. "What the Missus think?"

Victor looked up and studied at Ray carefully, heavy eyebrows puckered in concentration. He slowly turned his gaze to the ringers behind him. Ray knew they were all communicating silently, but he couldn't understand them. Unease returned, coldly gripping his gut, his mind racing over wild possibilities. He reached for his tobacco tin, rolling a fresh cigarette, a distraction to hide growing turmoil and impassively watched the silent conference.

Too far back to the Toyota, he estimated. I would never get there in time. I couldn't fight them all anyway. One against this many doesn't stand a chance. He rolled his cigarette, casual movements masking growing concern. Come on, speak to me, he silently urged.

"I think kumanjayi go urgently," Victor whispered quietly, pursing his lips to point towards the Big House, confirming the suspicions plaguing the camp.

Nobody had been able to find the Missus after one of the older boys had been sent up to the station for the weekly ration handout. They knew she hadn't taken a vehicle from the station. Nelson's fevered rush when he had returned to the camp had seemed to confirm the curlews' cries but they were too frightened to investigate their deepening suspicions further.

Kumanjayi who? Ray wondered, mind in turmoil as he tried to piece together what Victor hinted at and how it might relate to the empty shells and tattered steel drums.

He glanced quickly towards the heavier distant bush, fearful of a ringer berserk with a rifle. Instead there were only dull green grey trees and white grass motionless under the deep blue sky. His rapid heartbeat seemed louder than his words.

"Did the Missus kill kumanjayi?" he asked, afraid of the possible answer, but wanting to push through the confusion surrounding the sorry camp. He could see no reason why Wendy would need to flee or be involved in Charlie's death.

"Not that kumanjayi," Victor almost snapped, and frustrated, he waved toward the Big House. "That kumanjayi what be live there," he clarified grimly. The ringers fidgeted, adjusting the way they sat, pulling at hat brims and stealing downcast glances.

Ray went cold as if the sun had passed behind a cloud. His arms felt heavy and he tried to speak, but no words would form, his constricted throat blocking their passage. Now he understood why the dogs were so busy around the house. He saw the ringers were frightened and with incredible clarity his mind sorted, selected and rejected possibilities with frightening ease borne of memories and decisions made under fire.

"Who finish that kumanjayi?" he finally asked because it was the question his mind had finally selected and it fitted the picture of flies and dogs and broken plates he had subconsciously observed when he knocked on the flyscreen door.

"I think Nelson," Victor confirmed sadly, shaking his narrow face slowly, smoke wreathing from the cigarette stub.

Ray considered the answer calmly, pushing aside the fury demanding immediate action. Clearly the ringers had been roped into something they felt uncomfortable with but Nelson seemed to hold a whip hand. He needed more information to better assess the situation.

"What for he do that?" Ray asked, the explanation sneaking into his mind before Victor replied.

"Nelson say no more whitefella on Punkatoy," Victor repeated sullenly, aggression replaced with regret.

It gave Ray no satisfaction to know his guess had been correct. Like the clustered ringers, he stared at the dust, hiding his reaction, while Victor spoke softly and he concentrated on the explanation.

"Nelson say it time for payback. He say we take this land back. He tell us no more whitefella run on our country, but he say kumanjayi be OK because fighting is men's business."

There was a pause filled with sadness for old life not disrupted by new paths taken.

"Nelson say he be sing kumanjayi belong this place. He take Toyota and he been go to Yellowbank to kill the blokes there because he say it part of pungkuthuyi dreaming. He got three hostages. He been say on radio he kill any whitefella come to Punkatoy. You hear him, hey?" Victor tumbled words slowed, his question asked, voice low with shame.

"My radio is still broken. How did you hear him?" Ray asked, his mind springing back to life, a screeching squelch of panic built in his ears.

"I be go to Big House," Victor recounted, worry distorting his voice. "I hear radio say Nelson say he shoot any more whitefella come to Punkatoy. Then that brindle dog tell me kumanjayi gone." He meant the dogs foraging in the blood-spattered bucket on the lawn.

"But how is Nelson going to stop anybody if he is out at Yellowbank?" Ray asked anxiously.

"Douglas block the road. He be proper cheeky," Victor concluded simply, concerned because it was Nelson who had brought shame to the camp.

Ray forced himself to sit still. Like all the others, Victor was frightened and worried. He realised he would have to treat him carefully if he wanted any more information. Victor sat immobile, almost resigned to his fate. His bony hands were clasped in his lap, communicating nothing. He refused to look at Ray directly, sliding his eyes away beneath his dark eyebrows and staring at the dust. His shoulders slumped beneath his tattered blue checked shirt, tired and defeated by the growing conviction they were involved in something terrible.

Ray fought down his urge to leave now and race down the rough gravel road heading towards Borroloola. He desperately tried to convince himself Anne had heard the radio message before she left Clara Valley but the wish was unconvincing. Uncertainty gnawed persistently at his doubts. He sorted through the questions he wanted to ask, and then put them all to one side, because Victor would consider them too rude to answer. He needed the ringers onside, his rear secured before he could take further action.

"Nelson been shame you," he stated and Victor nodded sadly in agreement. "Nelson only be work for himself and not yolngu way."

Victor looked up and his eyes slipped across Ray's face to settle somewhere below his chin. Ray concentrated on a dirty stain high on the tall crown of Victor's pale cream hat, not wanting to embarrass him with direct eye contact.

"Nelson say payback time for all the pungkuthuyi people. He want the mine so he get the money in the ground. He want to spend him on this country. He want all this country now," Victor explained unenthusiastically and looked toward Ray for help.

"I agree with him. You belong this country. Nelson wants to belong this country too, but he thinks he can do it by owning this country in balanda way. He doing this thing wrong way," Ray commented sincerely.

"I think you right, chilpu. You belong this country too. You understand him. Old Harry tell me that long time ago," Victor recalled, a blunt statement of fact.

The simple compliment burned on Ray's tanned cheeks, but concern and worry extinguished it quickly.

"Where Douglas go?"

"Him by the boundary gate. Him ugly cheeky fella," Victor offered, satisfied Ray's understanding was good and hoping he might help the camp.

"Will you stay here until I come back?" Ray asked obliquely, testing Victor's sincerity to decide if it was safe to leave.

"We be here. If Nelson or Douglas come back I think we blow them out. That be right way," Victor suggested with thinly disguised relief, and appealed to the ringers for support. They nodded, whispering silent in their agreement. "We still got the guns he gave us," he added.

Ray probed further, eager to confirm his growing suspicions rooted in the brass cases littering the ground.

"How many guns?' he asked directly but with seeming disinterest.

"Biggest mobs. Kill'em kangaroo quick," Victor laughed, relief at returning to safe ground breaking the tension. The laugh was taken up and others looked up, broad smiles displacing scowls of worry. Holding an imaginary rifle low across his stomach by the pistol grip, Victor sprayed shots into the bush. Ray needed no more to confirm Nelson had armed them with AK47's. He briefly wondered what role the Vietnamese crabbers may have played. Poverty and racist exclusion made for unfortunate choices and he bore them no ill-will. His thoughts were quickly thrust aside for later investigation.

"You blow him out! Hey," Freddy instructed in keen anticipation, speaking thoughts left unspoken by the others. Victor glared stonily at him and then turned his attention to Ray.

"Kill him, chilpu," he requested, wanting someone to lift the shame from the camp.

Ray shook his head. "Killing don't solve anything... it doesn't do any good," he reflected, pushing back unwelcome memories of fire patrols and a warrant officer on the wrong side of military conduct

"Killing make you shame, not take him shame away. Payback does not mean killing, it means giving a man a chance. You know that. He stand still while the other man throws his spear. He might be killed, or he might be wounded, but when the spear is thrown he takes his chance, and that finish it," he explained more to himself than to the others.

He stood up and walked to the Toyota, hoping they judged him with understanding and not contempt. 'Kill him,' was easy to say, but who had the right?

Chapter 56

BENDING DOWN, RAY PICKED UP ONE of the empty brass shell cases littering the ground, his guesswork confirmed. Now he understood why Nelson had been prepared to shoot him to keep his secret safe. Heavy with regret, he chided himself for his innocent ignorance and unwillingness to get involved. He flicked the cartridge shell away in disgust and opened the Toyota door.

'What if?' jangled in his ears and drained strength from his bones. Fighting suddenly cold sweat, he leant weakly against the door, crushed by the burden he had created. There was no escaping his responsibility. Neutrality was an illusion sustained by his quest for escape in isolation.

"If I had only guessed at his intentions when I first found those shells then Wendy might be alive now," he accused himself bitterly. "But no! Stupid has to convince himself Wendy and Nelson are in it together just to knock-off some money, even after the bastard takes a shot at me. He even tried to con me into believing he could change my gold into cash. Lucky I never gave it to him."

"Brainless bastard!" he scolded himself.

"What if Anne didn't hear the radio this morning?" he asked himself, terrified she would drive unsuspecting into the ambush set by Douglas. Unbridled alarm flipped his stomach so he could touch his apprehensive fear. A slow burn of electricity snaked across his chest driving all thoughts of Nelson from his mind. The station radio was the quickest way to stop and protect Anne.

He turned the key viciously and backed the Toyota madly along the camp track, swinging the wheel hard over as the pickup rocketed onto the main road. He selected first, grating gears before the Toyota stopped rolling backwards, intending to head for the Big House.

"Don't be stupid," he reconsidered, stamping on the brake and clutch. "By the time I get to the station radio to find out if she has left she'll probably already be on the road. She has no radio in her car. Don't waste time, idiot!" he scolded.

Engine screaming in first gear, he veered up the sloping windrow and swung the wheel hard around. The road was too narrow to complete the turn, so he backed and filled, impatiently swinging the wheel and punishing the gearbox in a three-point turn. He glanced at his watch, time suddenly more important than it had been in months or years. He had to reach Anne before she reached Douglas.

Gravel skidded beneath his tyres and rattled under the chassis, pinging off mudguards and metalwork. One hand on the steering wheel, he laid the loaded rifle across his knees, the muzzle pointing at the passenger door, the cold metal vengeful in his hand. Scrabbling behind the seat for the ammunition box, he fed ten soft nosed rounds into his top pockets while fighting the heavy vehicle and the rough road.

He thought of Anne, with her soft dark brown eyes. She would be driving carefully on the rough and corrugated road, unconcerned and looking at the country around her. He loved her budding understanding of the country and her tenderness. He swallowed against a lump in his throat, acknowledging he would kill again if he had to. Protection or payback could also mean deliberate death. The man who threw the spear usually aimed to kill, but in this case, Douglas would not co-operatively stand still for Ray to take his shot.

"If I don't reach you in time, then you're dead, Douglas," he vowed. Surprised at his vehemence, he shook his head at the way his life was changing.

Chapter 57

NELSON SMOKED WHILE HE WAITED BY the radio, listening with grim satisfaction to the animated conversations and curses that marred the first radio schedule of the morning. After the long night with grumbling hostages, the chatter restored his confidence.

Morning time passed rapidly, but now time dragged slowly into the afternoon giving new meaning to the term 'standing by.' He smoked and waited and smoked and waited, this radio channel kept clear and silent, ready for the reply to his demands.

Staring out the window at the unchanging view he saw the lengthening shadows slowly sliding over the distant pale white escarpments ushering them into darkness. The country patiently endured, oblivious to his momentum for change and uncaring.

He picked up the microphone, pressing the transmit button on and off, wanting to make an inquiring call to VJY, but afraid of the possible answers.

"I will win," he told himself, speaking aloud, but the frequently repeated claim was less convincing than it had been early in the day.

For the hundredth time he pushed the overflowing ashtray angrily to one side, then pulled it back to butt his hundredth cigarette. The radio burst into life and he jumped in alarm and with a frisson of excitement.

"Yellowbank standing by," he blurted, scrabbling with the microphone.

"Roger Roger. I have Mister Timms standing by. Go ahead please."

He ignored the bitterness in the operator's voice.

"Hello Timms. Nelson Shortjack here. Over."

"Shortjack," No pretence of politeness in the curt cold voice. Nelson had expected none.

"I have discussed your demands with my Board. We don't like them, but the Government has told us your tight deadline means we have no choice but to accept them all. We don't like it, but we have to accept their decision. Does it meet with your approval?" he asked in clipped tones and Nelson chortled silently at the effort it must have cost him.

"All OK. Over," he confirmed cheerfully, whooping in triumph once he lifted the microphone button.

"Good. I hope never to hear from you again, until we are in court," Timms snapped with finality.

The VJY operator didn't bother to ask Timms if he was finished.

"All clear, Yellowbank?" contempt staining the edges of her professional voice.

"All clear, thanks VJY. Cheers," Nelson responded happily, polite again now the first step towards victory had been taken.

All he needed now was confirmation from the Government. He knew there would be efforts to develop a rescue mission, but the police force 1000 kilometres away in Darwin was not equipped to handle a hostage situation and at best it was a hard two days' driving to reach Yellowbank. The nearest military base was 1,300 kilometres across the Queensland border in Townsville and although he did not know, it was three times the range of a Huey assault helicopter. He was confident they couldn't reach him before the deadline. His isolated country worked in his favour.

He stayed slouched by the radio, microphone in one hand. Impossible to keep the broad satisfied smiling glee from his face, he chuckled contently and congratulated himself. It had not been a mistake to directly involve NTE. They were able to go straight to the Government in a way that he could not. NTE had forced Government involvement as he had hoped.

Sloughing off the lethargy of the long, curiously exhausting wait, he stretched and, grinning wide in anticipation, wondered how he would release his hostages. It would be as dangerous as unhitching a wild-caught feral bull tethered to a tree. Someone could get hurt and he was determined it wouldn't be him.

Chapter 58

RAY SAW AN UNMISTAKEABLE HAIL OF bullets pepper the road in front of Anne's white Subaru as he fishtailed out of the sharp bend on the wrong side of the road. Bullets kicked up red gravel and stones in front of the car. Anne wrenched at the wheel, spearing into the table drain. He searched for the muzzle flash while part of his mind noted Douglas was firing on full automatic. He searched just a fraction of the steep rocky face before the firing stopped.

Foot hard on the accelerator he tore down the road aiming to get between Anne and the gunman, praying the ringers were correct in saying there was only one shooter and that another burst of fire wouldn't quickly follow.

Steam hissed and billowed from the punctured radiator and the bonnet was a mess of random holes climbing to the shattered windscreen. Anne slumped over the steering wheel, covered with broken glass. Ray calculated the angle as best he could, and relieved, decided the shots might have missed her. He urged the Toyota on, rocking in the driver's seat as if he were spurring a horse.

"A hundred metres," he hissed. "Come on! Come on! Make him fumble his reloading," he urged, appealing to whatever power might be listening. He jammed the brakes, corrected the slide, and stopped level with the Subaru, the higher cabin of the Toyota providing some protection.

Anne shook her head and fragments of glass flashed in the sun. She gazed at him, stunned and unfocused and grimaced weakly, making his heart soar with relief. Rifle in one hand, he jumped out, flinging the door hard against the stoppers. Quickly crouching, he raced around the rear of the tray to the driver's door of the Subaru.

"You OK?" he called frantically, hoping she was and braced to return fire at any moment. He listened for her reply and for the first hammering of incoming rounds. None came. It was as if the gunman was deliberately giving them time to understand how hopeless their position was.

"I think so," she stammered, shoulders shaking against the door, glass glittering as it fell from her hair and shoulders. She managed a small smile amongst the tiny rivers of blood cut by flying glass.

"Get out quick! Move!" he shouted urgently, the roughness hiding his affection and concern. He tugged at the door and it flew open. Seat belt released, she half-fell from the seat, clambered out, then finding her balance, automatically went to stand up.

Ray pulled her roughly into a crouch and continued his rapid assessment of the tactical situation, searching for cover and concealment. The lessons of fire and movement rose to the top of his memory. A deeply-cut V-shaped offlet drain, carved into the pea gravel clay, curved away from the road. The scooped gravel provided a natural mantle and good protection from the gunman. If they were going to be pinned down, it was less dangerous than being next to the vehicles with petrol tanks and jerry cans of fuel.

"Keep low and run to the drain. When you get there, crawl on your belly to the end of it. Go!" he shouted, not waiting for acknowledgement, knowing seconds were vital.

She didn't move. "Go!" he yelled again, and pushed her shoulder. Stunned by the attack and the rough shove, she stumbled and then, trusting Ray completely, crouched and ran as best she could into the shelter of the drain.

The first shots hammered home, the metallic snap of bullets making Ray sweat instantly and persuading Anne to fall flat on her stomach and knees. A quick glance satisfied him she was safe behind the drain's protective bank. He turned his full attention to the shots raining about him. Through the dzzzzzzzzztt whine and burr of ricocheting bullets and the steady deadly chtud-chutd mechanical beat of the AK47, he could just distinguish an inarticulate whoop of enjoyment.

He counted shots as best he could. This time they were fired in short bursts, but were still wildly sprayed.

"Found the selector lever, have you?" he grunted. The side glass in his Toyota shattered. "I wonder if you can shoot?"

He rolled to one side as two rapid shots ploughed through the car roof above his head, spitting off the gravel behind, they burred through the scattered white snappy gums. He hugged the rough gravel scree until the shooting stopped. Another wild whoop of sheer enjoyment echoed down from the ridge, but he could not pinpoint the firing position amongst the sharply angled blocks of broken grey sandstone.

"You're a lousy shot," he concluded, a frail talisman held against fear. All the shots came from one direction confirming it was probably only Douglas shooting. He tried to count up the number of shots fired but he had lost count completely. "Doesn't matter anyway," he reminded himself grimly. "It only takes one to kill you."

Ray sat with his back to the driver's door as Douglas fired random shots, hoping for a lucky hit, or at least, to flush them out. The shots were deliberate and randomly timed, the shooter enjoying his command of the ambush. Each shot a hammer blow followed by the distinctive mechanical slide of metal on metal. The unsophisticated AK47, so suitable for unskilled hands and dusty conditions, was the perfect weapon for Douglas.

"Are you alright?" Anne asked, quavering voice just holding together. She fought the urge to change her position so she could see him.

"Yes. Shut up!" he snapped, concern for her safety overriding any kindness. "Just keep down and out of sight. I don't think he knows you're there," he finished, forcing himself to use the calmest possible soothing voice.

She did not reply and he couldn't see her from where he was. He leant his head back against the door, closed his eyes and concentrated on what he could learn from his attacker.

He breathed heavily and deeply, adrenalin coursing through his body, flinching when another shot spattered broken glass over the roof of the Subaru. Douglas was firing single aimed shots at all the remaining glass, taking delight in the mindless vandalism. A headlight tinkled, and then a bullet burred wildly off the taillight surrounds.

He waited for a shot to crash into his body and he imagined another bullet burn to add to the one lingering after the dozer attack. He gripped the rifle harder and welcomed the pain as his fingers gouged into the wooden stock.

He assessed his position.

The gunman was high amongst the rocks making it difficult to get a clear shot. Much better to get into the protection of the offlet drain and the better field of fire it offered. But first he needed a distraction so he could make the drain safely.

He peeked around the tray at the Subaru's open door.

Two light overnight carry bags lay on the floor and he pulled one out. Duck waddling to the end of the car, careful not to expose himself to the gunman and holding the rifle in his left hand, he threw the bag onto the road, using the momentum to dash in the opposite direction to the safety of the drain.

Four bullets slashed the bag before swinging to kickup dust at his heels. Rifle held tightly parallel to his body and rolling as he had been trained so long ago, he tumbled into the shallow drain. Looking up, he crawled to Anne, curled against the sloping earthworks. A few more shots ploughed into the top of the drain's batter, spraying small stones into clothes and hair. They both flinched and ducked instinctively. Douglas yelled again, his elated words indistinguishable amongst the echoing ricochets and the fading echo of the AK47.

Ray laid the rifle carefully on the earthen bank as Anne uncurled and cautiously crawled to him. She threw her arms around his neck, the broken glass in her hair scratching his cheek. She burst into tears, weeping softly.

He said nothing, but leaned back against the protection of the solid earth and held her tightly. She jerked in his arms when three seconds of hammering fire smashed into snappy gum branches above their heads. Severed leaves fluttered down and he shielded her with his body.

Her jeans were torn at the knee where she had skidded on the rough gravel. Her blouse was smeared red with dust and a long gravel rash ran down her forearm. Flies attacked the congealing dirty red mess. Pale beneath her light tan, she quivered gently in his arms. He hugged her into safety.

"What's happening?" she finally asked, snuffling and wiping her eyes and nose with the back of her dusty hand.

"Nothing we can't handle," he replied calmly and confidently as he could, hoping she would believe him. "It's a long story I'll tell you once we get out of here. Fair enough?"

She nodded, a willing transfer of trust.

"Listen," he whispered quietly in her ear. "I want you to move right down to the end of the drain so you'll be safe. Can you tell me where he is shooting from?"

She nodded, and he waited for her to speak.

"There's a tree about halfway up the hill. It's got yellow flowers and no leaves. He's in the rocks near there," she snuffled, fighting tears. "Are you going to shoot the bastard?"

Ray nodded.

"Good," she agreed crisply and he admired her resolution.

She crawled away to safety, screwing up her courage to resist the urge to look back. She lay flat on her stomach in the bottom of the drain and only then, turning, she watched him, fearful for his safety and dreading the next spray of bullets, praying they missed. She concentrated on doing nothing which might distract him from his task.

Satisfied she was safe, he eased to the top of the parapet of dirt and located the yellow flowers of the kapok tree. Douglas fired another long burst on full automatic, wildly hosing the gravel scree and splintering trees beyond the drain. Before he ducked to the safety of warm gravel he caught a glimpse of the muzzle blast between escarpment cracks.

The firing stopped and she winced as Ray flung the rifle to his shoulder, hoping Douglas had emptied his magazine. The leafless kapok tree panned past the cross hairs in the rifle scope. Douglas jumped into sight, tall crown hat askew, the faded cheap cowboy shirt now flapping open with the exhilaration of every fight he had ever been involved in.

He steadied the crosshairs, watching Douglas hurriedly fix a new magazine, his face slashed with a sneer or a laughing smile above his jutting beard. It was difficult to tell over the distance. No-one else was with him. Ray slowly exhaled, knowing he would only have one shot. The bolt action rifle was no match against the Kalashnikov for speed, but it was far more accurate.

Douglas slapped the magazine home and stood up proudly for a moment, confidently surveying the destruction below and the land beyond. Ray squeezed the trigger gently, keeping both eyes open as the rifle bucked in his hands.

Douglas flew backwards, the bullet taking him in the base of the throat. The AK47 clattered down the rocks. Ray slammed another round into the breech and waited for any movement on the slope. There was none. Panting and heart pounding, he rolled on his back, rifle held to his chest.

"You stay here," he warned Anne before she could move. "I just want to check. I'll be back soon."

Not waiting for her reply, he crabbed warily towards the vehicles, keeping under cover. He rushed to the base of the sharp rocky rise, fear running at his side. No shots came, and although he didn't expect any, he was relieved.

He clambered around the boulders, seeking protection until he reached just below the ridge-line. By the time he reached Douglas's position he was sure his shot had been good. A brief glance at Douglas's shattered upper chest confirmed his estimate. He turned quickly from the corpse, closing his mind to the uncomfortable past even as it intruded and provided Anne's protection. The ammunition box was peeled open, empty magazines resting nearby waiting for a refill. Water bottles, corned beef and damper in an open calico bag, all confirmed Douglas's long term commitment to the blockade.

You had no right, he raged as he surveyed the broken country below from the natural sniper's foxhole. You have no right to resurrect buried memories. No right to force me to shoot. Quivering, he perched on a rock, leaning uncomfortably on his rifle for support. He stared into the distance and the lifeless broken country stared back with defiant neutrality.

Chapter 59

THE JUNGLE WAS A NEUTRAL ENEMY to all and never cared for the causes driving men to kill each other. The thought idled into his mind as he paused to survey the low brooding ranges across the dry country – so unlike the jungles of Vietnam. Carefully, he resumed his clambering descent amongst the slabs of rock, sliced and thrown down from the escarpment. From the escarpment ridge the land dipped to the rough twisting gouge of the stony creek, and then rose slowly but steeply towards another distant ridge. The echo of gunshots was lost amongst the gullies and overhangs, absorbed to nothing by the spindly snappy gum trees and struggling quinine shrubs. All baked and shimmered under the copper sky, passing unremarked judgment. He caught movement and watched the sand goanna threading imperiously through the spinifex on the lower slope.

This country is never neutral, he decided, wiping his brow with his dusty hat. "It shapes what happens to meet its own ends," he muttered, reaching out for the next foothold in the descent.

She met him by the Toyota. He put his rifle on the bonnet before embracing her, happy to comfort and be comforted. Stroking her hair, he smelt the sour tang of fear. She looked up at him, her eyes alive with pleasure and gratitude in a face grimy with dust. He recognised the familiar emotion of death evaded, and knew she, and he, saw the world with new eyes. He hugged her tightly, confirming their escape.

"I love you," he whispered, saying what had flirted at the edges of his mind for some time. He smiled wryly to himself, solitude no longer a suitable companion.

A tightened hug gave him the answer.

"What's going on?" she asked eventually.

"Nelson, the head stockman, is off his head. He's holding three whitefella hostages at Yellowbank. He reckons this land is blackfella country and he aims to kill any whitefella who come on it. He told Douglas to shoot anybody who came across the boundary. Guess you didn't hear the news on the radio? It was on the VJY sched this morning," he finished laconically, chest tight with more than affection.

"I missed the morning sched. I was in too much of a hurry to get here," she confessed, some brightness returning to her voice.

He leant against the bullbar, needing to roll a smoke. The aftermath of action hit him as it always had, his hands shaking too much to hold the tobacco and paper. Anne moved to his side, gently took the tin and papers and attempted to roll a cigarette for him. Grinning at her efforts and then chuckling, he took the makings from her before they scattered on the ground.

"I didn't do any shooting," she explained as he hugged her. He accepted her understanding, but her shaking hands told him she also struggled.

"I've got to talk to Nelson," he said heavily. "I've got to stop him before anybody else gets killed. He is doing it all wrong way. This way will only destroy this pungkuthuyi dreaming and his dream."

"Are you sure he'll listen to you?" Anne asked, voice worried with concern.

"I hope so. I have to try."

"Why?" she asked simply.

He was silent for a while, framing his answer. He squinted across the bonnet at the bush, at the distant ridges and escarpments which had become his home.

"I've stopped hiding," he admitted softly. "You can't let friends take a wrong path."

"Fair enough," she replied and his heart swelled at the simple acceptance and understanding behind her answer.

"I'm coming with you," she added, matter-of-factly.

"No you're not," he snapped, frightened she would be killed or injured and desperately afraid for her. He had seen good mates die in the jungles of a distant land, so for years he had hardened himself against deep friendships. He stuffed life with an endless escape into ever more remote country, travelling too far to now risk another loss so soon.

"No, you're not," he repeated firmly. "I'm not going to take the risk of losing you."

"What else am I going to do?" she challenged, thinking she had him trapped because her car was destroyed.

"I'll leave you at the Borroloola road junction. There's a good spot just off the road on the billabong. You'll be safe there until I get back," he instructed firmly.

"We'll see," she fenced, "but first we have to get there."

Cigarette inexpertly rolled and smoked, he flipped the butt down, grinding it out with the toe of his boot. Escape and evasion no longer driving any need to add pinched butts to the tobacco tin.

He inspected the Toyota pickup. The window glass was gone and bullet holes stitched across the cabin door through the side panels of the engine compartment. Two tyres were shot out, the front one shredded completely. Stooping beneath the vehicle he was relieved to see the fuel tank was intact and the spare tyre undamaged.

He stood up and checked the other spare in the tray. It was flat and although the tray sides were punctured and scarred, the damage was superficial. With trepidation, he lifted the bonnet.

"It's OK," he concluded with a sigh of relief. "I can repair the damage, but it'll be after nightfall by the time we get moving. There's a spare tube behind the passenger seat. Get it out, will you?" he asked, turning to the repair work.

By the time she cleared the broken glass from the seats and found the spare tube, Ray was on the ground jacking up the rear wheel, purposeful activity stilling his shaking hands. She watched him fondly as he lay on his side in the gravel, taut muscles working the short jack handle.

She had glimpsed his fear buried deep beneath his everyday confidence. He had seen her naked fear and their intimate knowledge was a bond between them. She peered at the loose equipment in the tray, not finding his swag.

"Finished by tonight, you reckon?" she reaffirmed.

"Yair. Any problems?" he grunted, pumping the hydraulic jack.

"No. We'll just have to make do with my swag," she grinned offhandedly.

Chapter 60

NELSON SAT BY THE RADIO IGNORING the harsh cigarette smoke clawing his throat, too exhausted from another sleepless night to be annoyed by the rasping dryness. He rubbed his tired eyes with the back of his hand and looked at the wall clock, willing it to move more quickly. Morning light warmed the office room.

"I hope the Government meets the deadline,' he sighed wearily. "They should be back on the air within the next ten minutes. If I don't get the call then, Irish will be the first to go," and the thought triggered an immense feeling of satisfaction. Irish's attitude captured a lifetime of offensive slights and sneering racist comments that built the chip on Nelson's shoulder.

He wondered if he would really be able to take the man out and shoot him in cold blood. Irish was cocky, abusive, insolent, and he had kept Nelson awake for most of the night. Irritated by his constant niggling, Nelson considered the pleasure to be gained by shooting the annoying man. His sort don't belong on pungkuthuyi, he decided, but shooting Irish was a fantasy he also hoped would not become a reality. Shooting Irish meant he had lost his fight to wrest Yellowbank and the station from the Government.

The memory of Wendy's battered body returned and he suppressed a shudder. It had not been difficult to kill in the heat of the moment, but in the cold light of reason, revulsion attacked him when he mopped the blood from the floor. The taste of bile returned with the memory. Angrily, he spat on the office floor, and reached for another cigarette. Killing Irish in cold blood would be more difficult, he decided.

He rechecked the wall clock. Five minutes left. Shedding his lethargy he sat forward, waiting for the radio to burst into life in the last few remaining minutes before the deadline. He re-tuned just to make sure the radio was receiving properly. He turned the volume up to maximum, but only the static hissed and crackled. There was no radio traffic.

Experimentally he pressed the transmit button on the microphone. He wanted to know what was happening but he did not want to reveal any weakness by contacting them first. Reluctantly putting the microphone down, he slouched back in the chair, muscles heavy and his conscience a little worried by the possibility of killing Irish.

*

From his position a hundred metres away, Ray Morgan watched Nelson lean forward and fiddle with the radio before slouching back in the chair. Using the riflescope, he carefully watched Nelson through the office window. Against his better judgment and after a strongly worded protest, Anne was with him.

"He looks pretty relaxed. He's just leaning back in a chair in the office. Looks like he's waiting for a radio call." He lowered the rifle for a moment.

They were hidden under a small stand of bauhinia trees. His battered windowless Toyota pickup was hidden two kilometres from the mine site and they walked the rest of the way through the breaking dawn, stopping when they saw the buildings.

It had taken another twenty minutes for them both to work their way through the uneven rocky ground to where they could get a good look at the site office and the hostages.

Ray shifted the rifle again, careful to avoid any flash from the sun, and studied the prisoners' room. He recognised Andy's thin face. He was sitting on the table top, leaning against the wall with an AK47 cradled across his knees.

Three other men sat curiously upright in chairs although they all looked exhausted. It had taken Ray some time to work out the connection between the rope around their necks and their unusually alert posture.

"The bastard has tied their hands behind their backs and then to a rope going around their necks," he whispered showing a hint of admiration for the professionalism, and wondered where Nelson had learned the Viet Cong method.

Anne crouched beside him, the cuts on her face now only tiny ridges of dry blood. He hadn't wanted to bring her along, but she had brooked no argument when he tried to leave her at the turnoff. He smiled at her, returning the happiness she brought him, the intimacy somehow not out of place as the sun finally rose above the far escarpment. She smiled back, ignoring the early morning flies.

"How many hostages has he got?" she asked.

"The same as we were told. Three. And young Andy is standing over them with an AK47. Nelson must have a lot of rifles and ammunition." He used the rifle to again study the camp.

"I still don't understand how he got all the guns. They cost a fortune, but where did he get them?" Anne asked, not really expecting an answer. While she watched him concentrate, she idly scored the hard ground with a stick, disguising her random fears.

Ray lay the rifle to one side and faced her, sad eyes defeated by guilt.

"He must have got the guns with gold," he explained carefully, trying to separate the facts from his part in their arrangement. "I knew about the gold, but I thought Nelson was using it to purchase Punkatoy ... remember the day at the rock pool? I sort of tried to tell you there, but I had given my word to keep it quiet between Wendy, Nelson and myself. Perhaps if it hadn't been a secret, we wouldn't be here now. It's almost like a payback..." he trailed off, the link uncomfortable.

Remorse crushed his shoulders. I might as well have killed her with my own hands, was his silent self-accusation. He lifted his strong worn hands, eyes scowling with contempt. For years they held only his own life because the jungle proved they were too small to hold the lives of others. Now he wanted to hold two lives tight but one had already slipped away.

"I damn near got you killed," he apologised, accepting the responsibility. He shuddered with fear and hope, wiping his hands on dusty trousers.

"You did what you thought was right," Anne soothed, misunderstanding the full burden of his guilt. "You were happy to see this country go back to the people, black or white, who loved it. You're not responsible for Nelson. You're doing what is right this very minute. There's nothing to regret."

He crossed his arms on his chest, unsure of what to do with his hands. "It was a plane crash from the war," he explained quietly, continuing his explanation. "There was gold on board, and Nelson found it. I found it too.

There is still one box hidden at the crash site, but I'm buggered if I know what to do with it."

"Worry about that after you have talked to Nelson," she suggested practically. "It's more important to decide how you're going to get him to talk," she suggested calmly, mentally adding, 'if he doesn't shoot you first.' Her smile now more a grimace, seeking to hide her fear of losing him.

"You're right."

He turned back to the rifle, peering through the riflescope at Nelson, trying to work out a way to speak to him without endangering the hostages or himself. He saw Nelson pick up the microphone.

Chapter 61

"EIGHT SIERRA OSCAR FOXTROT STANDING BY," Nelson picked up the microphone and acknowledged when the radio finally crackled to life. He sat forward as if being closer to the radio would make the message clearer. Throwing off the lethargy of endless waiting, he stubbed his cigarette excitedly.

"I have the Minister for Aboriginal Affairs on the line. He is speaking on behalf of the Prime Minister. Go ahead please, Yellowbank." The VJY operator was brusque.

"Hello there. Nelson Shortjack here. Over," he answered briskly to hide his nervousness. If the Minister had the power to negotiate, he was satisfied to talk to him.

"Hello, Mister Shortjack. How are you receiving me?" the Minister asked, unfamiliar with the procedures of the outpost radio service.

"All OK. Go ahead, please. Over."

"I have talked with the management of NTE and they will abide by any agreement we, the Government, reach with you," the Minister said pompously, accustomed to getting what he wanted.

Nelson's pulse raced at the word 'agreement' and he listened tensely while the Minister continued to use the radio as if it were a private telephone.

"I understand Punkatoy station is already bankrupt and has little chance of succeeding as a working cattle station under its present owners. Were you aware of that, Mister Shortjack?"

"Yes. I know," Nelson acknowledged impatiently, not seeing how the information was relevant.

The radio gave just the faintest skiffle of atmospheric interference as the day warmed up.

Nelson restrained his urge to call them back, suddenly worried the connection had been broken.

"You electronic bastard. This is all I need! One simple electronic connection between me and victory, and it has to break down!" He snarled at the radio and threw his hands into the air in frustration. He gripped the microphone tightly, willing the radio to speak.

"You must understand the land you are demanding has already been listed for consideration as a Land Claim area because of the inability of the last owners to purchase the land and keep up the necessary improvements," the Minister continued, speaking slowly and at length. "Your hasty action makes it very difficult to consider these Land Claim proposals in their true light..."

What Land Claim? he asked himself. We make no land claim yet.

"Say again. Say again."

"Your hasty action makes it very difficult to consider these Land Claim proposals in their true light," the Minister explained, word perfect and obviously reading from a prepared statement. "If the hostages are released unharmed we'll consider your Land Claim requests as quickly as we can. This Government does not, and will not, give into the demands of terrorists," he finished stridently, anticipating and placating the media reporters.

"We have three demands and unless they are met I'll be forced to start executing the hostages today," Nelson threatened, not understanding the concealed solution on offer.

"Mister Shortjack," and Nelson noted the sigh of patient resignation in his voice, "the Government agrees with your Land Claim in principle but we will not and can not negotiate with terrorists who hold hostages."

Nelson thought carefully, groping for the message and solution the Minister hinted at in his carefully chosen words. He had made no Land Claim but the Minister kept repeating a Land Claim would be granted.

"If I release the hostages, then what happens?" he asked and waited eagerly for the answer to confirm he had correctly understood the Minister's unspoken concealed message and concession.

"If there are no hostages I'll be happy to meet with you and discuss the details of our agreement in principle with your first demand that Punkatoy

Station become a reserved land claim area with access by permit only the same as Arnhem land."

"What about my third demand?"

"I believe we can reach agreement, but you must understand this Government is opposed to the development of any more uranium mines."

"I heard some new export licenses were available and Yellowbank was one of those under consideration," Nelson challenged aggressively.

"You may be right, but it is up to Cabinet to make those decisions. The decision will not be made for sometime yet. You have my word, Yellowbank will be considered very favourably along with other new mines," the Minister replied ambiguously.

"So let me get this clear. You agree to all my demands and you'll set up a meeting if the hostages are released. Correct?" He struggled to keep excitement from his voice.

"Correct."

Nelson grinned broadly.

"We won! We beat the whitefella bastards!" he shouted through the door to Andrew. The young ringer laughed with relief and slid off the table, his rifle still covering the hostages.

"I agree," Nelson replied formally to the Minister. "When we meet?"

"I can be in Darwin tomorrow so I can be at Yellowbank the day after. A helicopter will fly over first to confirm the hostages are free, Mister Shortjack. NTE tells me there is a hardstand in front of the office. Make sure the hostages are all standing out there when the first helicopter goes over at about midday. We'll give you a more exact time later. Do you understand?"

He didn't pause to consider why multiple helicopters were required for a simple meeting. "Roger roger. The hostages will be on the hardstand. That leaves me all clear, thanks VJY. Cheers," he gloated and threw the microphone on the desk in jubilation. Leaping from the chair, he grabbed his rifle and burst into the other room shouting his easy victory.

*

Through the riflescope, Ray watched Nelson smash the microphone to the desk in an apparent burst of fury and frustration. He saw him hoist the rifle and storm shouting into the next room where Andy, rifle held threateningly, stood over the hostages.

"I think we might be too late," he hissed. "He just finished on the radio and raced into the other room shouting."

Ray worked a single round into the breech and kept the rifle sight centred on Nelson.

"I hope he doesn't do anything. There's still time to talk. There has to be a way," he muttered. He concentrated on Nelson's body language to determine what was happening in the room a hundred metres away. He didn't notice Anne nod her agreement.

*

"We've won," Nelson shouted happily, repeatedly jabbing his rifle at the three bound hostages. "You understand, you white bastards?" he snarled jubilantly. "This is our country now. Yellowbank is ours. One hundred years we have put up with you bastards here, and now you're beaten. Even your white Government agrees,' he shouted gleefully, leaping and prodding the hostages with the barrel.

"What happens to us?" Alby asked nervously, sweat dark on the lighter blue of his singlet.

Irish watched Nelson, contempt painted in his green eyes. Cookie slumped towards Irish, tired arms drooping to his side and pulling the knot tighter around his neck. His dry shorts stank of urine and Irish pulled back in disgust.

"I ought to shoot you just for the fun of it," Nelson threatened, admonishing them with a pointed rifle. "Shoot you the same way you whitefellas shot my people over the last one hundred years." Bitter spiteful glee flavoured his words.

"What's the point? You got what you wanted!" Cookie stammered.

"Aaarrgh, don't listen to the jumped-up bastard," Irish scoffed before Nelson could answer. "He's too gutless to shoot us anyway. He only won because the Government is even more gutless than he is," he taunted and spat on the floor with contempt. Having overheard the radio, he eyed Nelson defiantly, challenging him with an open dare he knew could not be taken.

The Government bargain depended on three live hostages being freed. Nelson shook a fist in frustration, hating Irish with fresh fury.

"Come on, you bastard," Irish goaded him. "We heard you on the radio. You won't kill us. If we aren't out there they won't talk to you. You black shit are all the same. You blackfellas, and your make-believe blackfella mates down South," he sneered.

He knew Irish was right. Irish made his victory seem hollow. He loathed the insolent, ginger-haired smiling cocky face and ached to smash it, but fists were not enough.

Infuriated he threw his AK47 to his shoulder ready to fire, but knew he couldn't. Irish laughed until Nelson stepped forward ready to slash the rifle barrel across his head.

*

Tracking Nelson through the rifle scope, Ray saw him lift the rifle and point it at the thin ginger-haired man in the corner.

"He's going to shoot," he murmured, quickly moving the crosshairs to Nelson's chest, firing just as Nelson lunged towards the ginger haired hostage. Nelson's legs buckled and he dropped to the floor as fast as a cleanly shot killer taken in the bush.

"Come on!" he yelled, forgetting his intention to leave Anne behind.

They scrabbled down the rocky scree, heedless of noise and cover. He ran across the hard red clay to the office, reloading as he went, for once ignoring the discarded shell case. He kept an eye on Andy who was standing horrified against the far wall, wide-eyed with shock and staring at Nelson on the floor. Ray slammed against the window sill, rifle barrel slashing the flimsy flywire screen aside.

"Don't move!" he shouted, lungs tearing for breath. "Drop the rifle!" he yelled at Andy and the weapon clattered to the floor.

Andy quickly raised his shaking hands, eyes locked on Nelson bleeding on the floor. Anne stumbled alongside, and he handed her the rifle, confident Andy wasn't going to move. It was an unwelcome memory, but he'd seen the same look of shock and incomprehension freeze people before.

"Keep him covered!"

She handled the rifle awkwardly. It was uncomfortable and unfamiliar in her hands. The barrel wavered as she struggled to keep it pointed at Andy.

"Rest it on the window sill. Don't worry," he whispered reassuringly. "Just make sure you don't shoot me,' he joked feebly and patted her on the shoulder. She grinned weakly and took a tighter grip on the rifle, determined to shoot if Ray was in any danger.

She glared at Andy who was terrified, shaking badly and barely able to stand, let alone fight or run away. He was a ringer, not a revolutionary. She refused to let her eyes wander to Nelson who lay on the floor, breathing heavily.

Ray burst into the room, and kicked the AK47's away from Andy and then Nelson. He knelt beside Nelson who was rasping loudly, his breath coming in great gasps as blood frothed from the gaping hole in his chest. They both knew he would die from the single shot. Ray resisted the temptation to roll him over, not wanting to see the damage from the soft-nosed bullet.

"You left me no choice," he pleaded, unable to look his friend in the eye. Nelson stared back sadly, face contorted with pain.

"It's no good, chilpu. You only take one shot for a killer," he groaned before spitting a mouthful of blood on the floor.

"I wanted to talk with you. I wanted to talk you out of this. It all the wrong way," Ray tried to explain, his voice breaking, but Nelson was not listening to him. His eyes rolled with fear beyond his pain.

"Harry, why you sing?" he asked distractedly, noise ringing in his ears. "Why you sing me?" he despaired.

Chapter 62

RAY STOOD UP SLOWLY, FRIENDSHIP DESTROYED under his own hand. In a trance, he cut the hostages' bonds, reaching Irish last. He didn't hear their thanks as he slumped on the bench, Nelson's last desperate question pummelling his ears. He looked up quickly when Irish lurched across the room and punched Andy to the floor.

Ray grabbed the AK47 and lashed the butt savagely across the ginger-headed man's shoulder.

"What'd you do that for?" Irish demanded, holding his bruised shoulder while Andy cowered on the floor.

"Only arseholes like you think with their fists," Ray hissed in disgust, the rifle ready in his hands. "You don't belong in this country and your kind never will. You and your bosses rape this land and its people and then you wonder why Nelson wants to shoot you! I don't know why I stopped him," he spat, his guilt turning to anger.

"You didn't," Irish jeered. "The gutless Government gave into the black bastard anyway. He couldn't shoot us because our survival was a condition they made before they would agree to his demands."

He jammed his hat on his head and with his thumb, cheekily cocked the brim.

"You shot the bastard anyway and that's good enough for me," he chortled triumphantly and walked out the door towards the canteen and a cold beer. The others followed without a word.

A blind inarticulate roaring hammered his ears and a deep sadness of remorse lodged in his gut, his mistake threatening to drag him into loneliness and retreat. He threw the rifle across the room in disgust and it clattered to the floor. He sat down heavily on the bench, but Nelson's body was too near, so he stumbled into the sunlight, taking dark thoughts with him, and leaned on the bullbar. Rolling a cigarette, he drew it quickly to a stub. He became aware Anne was beside him and was simply glad to be no longer alone.

He squinted across the front of the Toyota, suncreased eyes taking in the silent open bush beyond the camp. He scuffed the ground, thick with the unseen blood and sweat of generations. The creamy dust puffed and billowed as transient as those who walked through it. Anne touched him lightly on the back of his hand reminding him of a different future. He dropped the cigarette butt to the ground and squashed it into the dirt.

A light breeze blew away the acrid smell of gunsmoke and the iron stench of blood. The small-leafed, dark-green bauhinia trees with rough-ridged black trunks huddled amongst the grey drab woollybutts, deep in conference. A pair of white ghost gums stood starkly in the distance, aloof from the minor affairs of those who moved beneath the long streaks of shaggy bark hanging from their limbs. Hills rose at the horizon and beyond, in the shimmer, red jump-up cliffs slashed through the blue haze daring men to take them on.

*

Deep in a distant jump-up, Old Harry fell silent, his work completed. After a time, he sipped tepid water, then stretched his legs and clambered wearily down the escarpment. Lounging unconcerned in the back of the overhang, a sand goanna caught the vibrations of the wind rustling through the trees, an eternal singing whispering across the unbridged gulf.

###

ABOUT THE AUTHOR

Daryl writes with an authentic Australian outback voice, drawing on his experience to take readers to places and lifestyles that are unknown and foreign to many. Although better known for his books on financial markets, and contemporary business analysis and commentary on China, in this novel Daryl draws on decades of work in some of the remotest parts of Australia's Northern Territory.

AUTHOR ACKNOWLEDGEMENT

I am the author of 16 books across multiple genres. Writing is a compulsion, but if it is to move beyond a hobby it must be polished and refined, edited and proofed multiple times before anybody gets to see what is euphemistically called the first draft. Then it ready for assessment by outsiders.

This assessment process starts with friends who are prepared to be true critics. I thank all of my first draft readers, but particularly Clare Robertson and John Glasby. The rewrites they triggered improved the book.

The next step is to put it in front of a disinterested editor. Its not that the editor doesn't care. The editor has no prior interest invested in the work so they approach the task of editing more dispassionately. Every book is better for going through this process of independent validation.

Writing is easy, but getting the result to book publication standard is sheer hard work. Michael Hanrahan and the team at Publish Central are the go-to experts for this.

Digital publishing rests on the authenticity of feedback from readers. Please take a moment to add your thoughts to the relevant web review pages.

First published in 2024 by GTC Publishing

A catalogue entry for this book is available from the National Library of Australia.

Printed book ISBN: 978-1-923007-69-7
Ebook ISBN: 978-1-923225-00-8

Book production, cover and text design by Publish Central
Cover photography from iStockphoto.com and the author

www.ingramcontent.com/pod-product-compliance
Lightning Source LLC
Chambersburg PA
CBHW051254210726
48287CB00002B/499